EARLYFATE

Published in 2024 by Cipher Press

203 Ryan House
12 Smeed Road
London, E3 2PE

Paperback ISBN: 9781917008068

Printed and bound in the UK by TJ Books
Distributed by Turnaround Publisher Services

Cover Design by Wolf Murphy-Merrydew
Edited by Ellis K.
Typeset by Laura Jones-Rivera

www.cipherpress.co.uk

Supported using public funding by
ARTS COUNCIL ENGLAND
LOTTERY FUNDED

EARLYFATE

A NETTLEBLACK NOVEL

Nat Reeve

Cipher press

For CLAUDIA,
beloved and magnificent in equal measure –
the following pages are respectfully dedicated to,
and looking respectfully at,
YOU.

The Orchestrators of My Downfall

(And – admittedly fewer in number –
The Delights of My Existence)

as given by Pip Property

PIP PROPERTY (numerous additional names, accurate and inaccurate, notwithstanding), *myself, a cravat designer under an immense deal of stress, more than qualified to fill both aforementioned categories*

ROSAMOND NETTLEBLACK, *my feral beloved, the darling of the Gower Peninsula, and the only person allowed to tie me to proximate furniture*

EDWINA NETTLEBLACK, *her despotic sister, to whom we do not speak*

HENRY NETTLEBLACK, *her younger sibling, a prodigal of nervous constitution and a member of the Dallyangle Division, to whom I owe an apology*

SEPTIMUS, *sweetheart to the above, also of the Division, possessor of the most superlative hair since* Venus Verticordia, *to whom I also owe an apology*

KETURAH ST. CLARE BALLESTAS, *Director of the Division, notoriously unruffled by the anxieties of lesser mortals, to whom I also (indirectly) owe an apology*

CASSANDRA BALLESTAS, *her daughter, also of the Division, sartorially unhinged, to whom I* might *owe an apology*

MATTHEW ADELSTEIN, *my neighbour, also of the Division, a pernickety detective to whom I very probably owe an apology*

NICHOLAS 'NICK' FITZDEGU, *his lodger, so-called, officially a rat breeder and a Divisioner in all but name, to whom I may also owe an apology*

MORDRED, *a ferret, presently unaffiliated, to whom I – oh, devil take it –*

Persons to Whom I do not *Owe an Apology*

MAGGIE *and* NORMAN SWEETING, *two burglars, with whom I briefly endured a profitable business relationship, who ought to owe an apology to* me

GERTIE SKULL, *also of the Division, beyond hope*

OLIVER SKULL *and* MILLICENT MUSGROVE, *brother and cousin to the above, also of the Division, prone to overreaction when it comes to swordsticks*

MARIGOLD CHANDLER, *secretary of the Dallyangle Town Council, whose fashion choices alone require an apology far broader than just to myself*

GARETH WYN EVANS, *the Nettleblacks' estate manager, self-appointed defender of Rosamond's good name*

ADELAIDE DANADLENDDU, *cousin to the Nettleblacks, nemesis of Cassandra Ballestas, possibly the walking result of some necromantic experiment*

LAWRENCE 'LORRIE' TICKERING, *brother to Septimus, apparently the fiancé-shaped secret of Edwina Nettleblack*

LORD CLEMENT MILTONWATERS, *marquess-to-be, heir to the estate currently owned by his semi-fictional grandfather and managed by his head-hiding cousin, one Lady Elvira Miltonwaters*

And anyone else I can't immediately recall, apologies or otherwise.

CONTENTS

VOLUME THREE

PROLOGUE

The Notebook of Doom
Monday 20th November 1893
For the attention of Henry Nettleblack, at the barest minimum

I have to convince them.

At least, I have to *persuade* them. To assure the wretched Dallyangle Division that I'm not at all the villain they think – the villain they've trapped – but – gracious! How the devil am I to do it? Without a Divisionary soul inclined to listen to me, or humour me, or do anything more encouraging than *lock me in a morgue and blame me for consummately everything?*

I do grant that Dallyangle's indomitable vigilantes do not *lack* either reason or motivation to lock me in a morgue and blame me for consummately everything. But it's distinctly harder to be charitable towards the Division when – once again! – they're flailing three steps behind the disaster at hand! How are these bucolic detectives still funded and functioning enough to kidnap cravat designers in broad darkness? Why are they all – *all!* – so damnably resistant to trusting me? And what part of *Rosamond Nettleblack is in mortal danger* do they not understand?

I can't let them ignore me. Not with Rosamond at stake. Not with the Sweetings (maledizione, and clearly more than just the Sweetings!) still haunting me, and them, and everyone this side of the River Angle. Not when Henry left me a notebook and an ultimatum.

Va bene. I will *write*. You asked for this, you impertinent collective!

THE DALLYANGLE STANDARD

NO. MMCCCXL.

Registered at
the G. P. O.
as a Newspaper.

MONDAY, NOV. 13th, 1893

7s. p. a.

THE HEAD-HIDER UNMASKED!
NETTLEBLACKS ASSIST DIVISION AS
MILTONWATERS AND MAID CAUGHT
IN THEIR OWN CONFESSIONS!

Dallyangle's appendage-juggling menace, popularly known as the *Head-Hider*, has been thoroughly scuppered by our very own Division.

GARDENER DISMEMBERED!

According to Detective Matthew Adelstein, the head belongs to Mr. Paul Gulp, fifty-nine, under-gardener to the Fifth Marquess of Alberstowe. Mr. Gulp was shot whilst working at Alberstowe Hall during the Marquess's annual pheasant-shoot – an accident, so-claimed, but the Marquess's grandson Lord Clement Miltonwaters has declined this editor's request to comment further on the matter. This editor plans to keep asking.

MILTONWATERS DISGRACED!

In a shocking twist, one of the 'Head-Hiders' has been identified as Lady Elvira Miltonwaters, thirty-nine, spinster, niece of the Marquess and former member of the Dallyangle Town Council. Lady Miltonwaters enlisted her lady's maid – Miss Adelaide Danadlenddu, eighteen – to pose as a governess and arrange the movement of Mr. Gulp's remains. 'The head was embalmed,' says Mr. Adelstein, 'at the Gulmere funeral parlour favoured by the Miltonwaters family; Dallyangle's *Fitzdegu & Daughter* knew nothing about it, and readers may rest assured

2

that the Fitzdegus remain a reputable source for their under-taking needs!'

CITIZENS THREATENED!

Dealt the hardest hand was Dallyangle's redoubtable Mrs. Keturah Ballestas, with whose name this editor is sure our readers will be familiar. Mrs. Ballestas, founder and 'Director' of the Division, claims the Miltonwaters head-hiding scheme 'meant to encourage mistrust in our abilities – and to delay our addressing of a truer threat: the violent burglars Maggie and Norman Sweeting.' Mrs. Ballestas showed this editor letters in the hand of Lady Miltonwaters, demanding the disbanding of the Division in terms unfitting for any lady to use, let alone a noblewoman *(please refer to page ten for further particulars)*. But these demands have not been met – the Division are soon to receive a full reinstatement of their funding from the Council.

NETTLEBLACKS LAY MILTONWATERS LOW!

Support came also from an unexpected quarter! Henry Nettleblack (of the *Tincture* Nettleblacks), the Division's newest recruit, whose efforts proved instrumental in the downfall of the Head-Hiders, had this to say when asked to comment: 'I – figs – well – erm – the Division's quite entirely marvellous – and – plums – I'm proud to be part of it – and – I promise we'll – erm – sort out the Sweetings – soon – but everything's fine – yes – quite!'

A PERSONAL NOTICE

Miss Edwina Nettleblack (also of the *Tincture* Nettleblacks, and executrix of the late Mr. Morgan Nettleblack's estate) wishes it to be reiterated on the front page that her younger sister Miss Rosamond is still missing, and has not been seen since November 4th. Miss Rosamond is twenty-three years of age, unmarried, with a pallid complexion, black curling hair, green eyes, and a distinctly Welsh accent. She is of slender build, middling height, and inclined to wear her hair loose, though this should *not* be taken as indicating any looseness in her character. Miss Edwina would be grateful for any information pertaining to her whereabouts - send a line, post paid, to 5 Catfish Crescent, Dallyangle.

A WARNING FROM THE FURIOUS

REPRINTED FROM *THE RODENT'S GAZETTE*

Messrs. Fitzdegu, Vibbrit &c., would be obliged to Pip Property, alleged guardian of a *rambunctious and meddlesome ferret*, if they could curtail the animal's reign of Surrey terror. To the public - if you encounter a white ferret with unusual strength of jaw, you are advised *not to let him in*. This creature has already destroyed innumerable *(continued overleaf)*

VOLUME ONE

CHAPTER ONE

I AM A MESS

The Notebook of Doom, Continued

Concerning Sunday 5th November 1893, and an elopement gone wrong

Despite your insolent detectival overfamiliarity, my dear Divisioners, *I* don't think we're properly acquainted – so I hope you'll accept some preparatory notes. Yes, my name is *Pip* Property (fully Pip Darius Lucrezia Alighieri Participazio, but you can only blame me for the first one), and I don't have a prefix or suffix of any description. Neither do I have time to scrawl an appendix on the concept of *they* as a singular entity – but there they are, and *they* are me. My occupation: cravat designer for the sartorially excellent. My *former* occupation: part-time fence and full-time wits for Dallyangle's burgling siblings Maggie and Norman Sweeting, with whom I trust you're unfortunately familiar. My involvement in that criminality ceased – as Division Sergeant Septimus had better corroborate! – when I tried to lure said Sweetings into a trap for you all, and –

And did not succeed. We shall leave it there, for now.

But what is Rosamond Nettleblack to me? What might I have to do with the scandalous, incorrigible, incorrigibly Welsh heiress to the plummiest medicinal fortune since Holloway sold his Pills?

Let me calligraph and underline it: *I am in love with her. And desirous to extricate her from whatever peril she's in. And not planning to steal her inheritance. Not least because someone else has already done that!*

Where to start? With the greatest respect, sweet Henry, your orders were not specific. But I *have* been with Rosamond – we never made it to the Continent, not after the Sweetings –

Of course. I know where to start, and I don't like it. Two weeks ago, on the fifth of November (how apt!), when I was struck from my very self by the ghoulish force of – to be precise, of fifty loose oranges.

Permit me, if you will, to unleash those oranges now.

*

I scraped off sleep like tar, twisting on a skinny bed that wasn't mine. The papery sheets, the pillow crumpled against my face – all of it stank like a Venice canal, salty enough to crack my throat. I shoved away from it, and gasped, or tried to. The pillow was streaked in my blood, glinting the full sanguinary colour-wheel in the cracks of light: dried brown to stark red and everything between, stamped and smudged in a crooked pattern.

Like a terrible cravat, I thought dazedly – and then, rather more to the point – *where the devil am I?*

Something lurched the bed out from under me. I toppled, pinioned in the sheets, struck horribly damp floorboards. A smash in the gloom ahead – a crate, upending in my direction –

The contents swarmed me, cold and clammy as tiny corpses: oranges, reeling and bouncing over the floorboards. The sight of the gambolling citrus revenants, the smell of the bloody salt, the room roiling under my hands – the whole ghastly collaboration took a corkscrew straight to my stomach.

Absolutely not. I remembered now, and the recollection made it worse. *You grew up in gondolas, damn it, you will not –*

Apparently by way of retort, my throat buckled, and I began to retch.

I scrabbled for my feet. Cracked my head on a splintery ceiling and plummeted back into the oranges. Thrashed through them, grabbing for the steps beyond, scorching my palms on the ankle-thick rope that served as a banister – up into a sharper light, where grey clouds pressed down on grey sea. I flung myself for the boat's railings, flung my head beyond them, and – to the shame of my lineage, and my profound and personal horror – vomited into the waves like a gargoyle.

"Pip! Cariad, I thought you were Venetian!"

Rosamond's walking-boots hammered across the deck. She caught my shoulder, hauled me up like a fishing-net, her arm slipping round my waist – presumably to keep me on the boat, but hardly the most comfortable sensation mid-retch. I wanted to shove her away. She couldn't – *shouldn't* – have been obliged to witness this. Her Pip was nothing but impeccable in the public eye, sharp-tongued and sharp-suited, capable of outmatching any inconvenience.

And I – well, I would be – in mere seconds, surely –

But the vomiting wretch simply slumped in Rosamond's arms. The next I could tell, I was sprawled on the deck, my back cricked to the mast, crisscrossing sailors darting me wary looks. Rosamond settled beside me, knees jutting beneath the panicky pattern of her Morris dress. She slung her greatcoat over my legs, then cupped my chin – she's the only one I let do it, though I wished she could have waited for more privacy. Her face was even paler than usual, white as a fishbone.

Va bene. *She's frightened, and you can fix that. Stop convulsing, sort your suit, and do something worthy of Pip Property!*

"Darling – "

"Breathe," she ordered, voice a startlingly steady mismatch with the fear in her eyes. "Don't give me that look – breathe *properly.*"

I realised I was glaring. I didn't entirely know how to stop. "I'm perfectly fine – "

"You haven't seen yourself." Her grimace twisted my nerves. "With all due kindness, bach: you're a mess."

"I – "

"Pip!" She gripped my chin, taut between the press of sky and sea. "You've been robbed to the gills. You fell off a house. The Sweetings nearly killed you. The Division nearly – I don't know, Divisioned you. I'd be stunned if you weren't a mess."

The match struck in my aching throat, again and again, but there was nothing for it to catch. I hadn't a single retort.

"I'm not saying it's your fault," she murmured, fingers slackening. "But I *am* suggesting – sod suggesting, I'm insisting – that you leave the next part to me."

"But – "

"You were right. I've not been doing enough for our escape. I – I'm sorry for it. It was only – Edwina – "

She swallowed. Studied me a moment, trembling – until something stiffened behind her eyes. "Never mind that. I didn't help like I should have – and look what it's done to you – so no more of it!"

She cupped the horizon, fingernails grazing a distant coastline. "I can get us home. I can keep us safe. You can recover. We can – " – her voice contracted, a sudden spasm of panic – " – we can leave Dallyangle behind."

What?

"We can't just – "

"Hush now," she blurted, touching a finger to my lips. "Don't make your face bleed."

Then she sprang upright, reeling for the prow like a seagull. I tried – but I couldn't follow her. I couldn't do anything more than slump, jaw set against the queasy flick of my throat, and watch the last of our conversation slip from her slender shoulders.

She gasped, curls unravelling in the sea-breeze. And I had to concede: the view would have tugged poetry from a rock. Gower, nurse of her youth, urging her home. Vellum-soft beaches, and a sprawl of fields above them, studded with paisley whorls of forest – but pray don't imagine the Dallyangle fields, retiring and muddy and churned up with crops. *These* fields unrolled down hills, their grass curling in rip-tides; every other hedge had a hem of sheep. The effect was a patchwork quilt draped on sharp bones – or the skin of a strange and sinewy creature.

What the view must have done for Rosamond's equilibrium! Four years in Dallyanglian exile, and now she could return, craning over the waves towards that feral embrace. Towards – astonishing thing! – a childhood home that would welcome her back. Towards all the safety and rest it should have been my prerogative – no, my obligation – to give her.

I groaned. This, apparently, was what twelve terrible hours and one imploded scheme had made of me. A *mess* even to my lover – and now, upstaged by a peninsula.

Helplessness sat in my veins, a sluggish poison, hauling me in and out of yet more wretched sleep. *Leave the next part to me* – and yes, there are matters in which I concede control to Rosamond with giddy delight – but botched elopement practicalities were nothing of *that* sort. I started from another treacherous doze in the back of a homespun gig, jolting awake at its sudden halt, and the clatter of Rosamond's exchange with the driver. The wind blasted their voices away when I struggled down; the breeze was heavy enough to turn land to sea, raking through the gorse-bushes beside the dirt-track. Beyond the bushes, the grass met slate-coloured sky – empty at our level, sucking and plashing below.

A clifftop. We'd arrived.

And then, when I stumbled about: springing from the gorse, the smug incongruous gate of Nettleblack House.

As expected, metal nettles writhed up its bars, sharp enough to snick the skin when I slid my finger over one. Clearly the ostentation was still too new to have softened its edges. Rosamond and this house emerged at a roughly contemporaneous time, according to her, and twenty-three is rather young for a would-be ancestral seat. I had wondered if the family saved all their posturing impracticality for their English residence, but – if anything, the Welsh one was an even worse offender. If this plucky young mansion, preening out of place on a Gower cliff, had anything like a reliable water supply, I would be *stunned*.

I shoved the gate, as my best alternative to loitering uselessly, and staggered up a path gravelled with tiny white shells. The house spread before me, splayed on the mind-spinning funds of the Nettleblack's Tincture fortune, a veritable Eglinton Tournament of bad medievalism. Red bricks, pointlessly exposed beams, every chimney a gangly doppelgänger of Hampton Court. *I* lived in real Venetian Gothic for half my childhood – gracious, Ruskin probably sketched my bedroom windows! Standing before this swaggering imitation was alarmingly akin to being crushed beneath yet more oranges.

"Bore da!"

Good morning? Is it, sirrah?

This tactless greeting was from a bulky man with a beard like buttered toast, striding from the house fit to discombobulate the shell-gravel. His homely suit was unscathed, his age at a guess something mature and half-centuried, his wary frown perturbing. *No* being so much the answer, I confess the pride of Venetian Gothic had very little in their head by way of response.

"I'm afraid Nettleblack House is closed to visitors at the – "

At which, presumably, he noticed the blood.

"Good God! What *happened* to you, boy?"

Exasperation slapped words into my teeth. "I'm not a – I am twenty-seven years old!"

"Gareth!"

Rosamond dived on the man, plaited herself about his neck so fiercely he could barely splutter. "Ga, Gardderchog, beth sy'n bod?"

Gareth. *That* Gareth. Gareth, presently clutching her with a desperate protectiveness that was practically parental. She hadn't exaggerated – mere estate managers didn't receive embraces like that, not unless they'd brought their mistress up by doting hand.

"Miss Rosamond! Pam – ble – sut dest ti yma? Pwy ydy fe?"

Rosamond beamed, dangling from his shoulder like a scarf askew, whilst I scrabbled my paltry Cymraeg into pieces of sense. "Pwy ydy *nhw*, Ga – Pip's my wonder, my delight, my cariad!"

His eyebrows simply sprang. Panic, terror, bafflement, the lot. But no matter – if I woke up, talked as I ought to, and never mind my stinging cheek, or the holes it burned in my throat – it couldn't be too late to salvage a less appalling impression –

"Pip Property, sir." I held out my hand; he kept his mutinously toasting Rosamond's. It wasn't the most convenient moment to notice my palm was also stained with blood. "Delighted to make your acquaintance."

His answering expression was anything but. "So that'd make you – beg pardon – Miss Rosamond's husband, sir? Or – perhaps – her female companion... miss?"

Gracious, they always found time for the question, didn't they?

I flung back my head and laughed – one hopes, keeping to the windy side of hysteria. Rosamond was cackling too. "Maledizione, I should hope not! It's not *sir*, sir, nor *miss* either – it's certainly not *husband* – and no lady would dare make a *female companion* of me. But I am, or so I flatter myself, an influence – a bright influence – the brightest influence! – on my darling's life. I'm a supremely respectable cravat designer – master of my neckwear, captain of my soul – scheming solutions to Rosamond's difficulties even as I speak – !"

"But *first*," – and Rosamond pinched me with a pointed stare – "the supremely respectable cravat designer needs a rest."

I straightened my sodden bow-tie. "Certainly a bath wouldn't go amiss. If Mr. – terribly sorry, I didn't catch it?"

"Wyn Evans," he stammered, not quite of his own volition. "But – "

"Grazie, or indeed diolch! If Mr. Evans has turmeric, Rosamond and I would absolutely murder scrambled eggs – "

"Are you after her money?" Gareth Wyn Evans blurted.

Rosamond stared at him. As did I.

Then I stitched taut every scrap of voice I had left.

"I believe that the only thing I'm *after* is what you're obliged to provide, in your capacity as servant to a mistress who's made her opinion of me beautifully clear in multiple languages."

"Ga, it's fine," Rosamond hissed, as her personal Malvolio flushed. "We've been lovers nearly four years, it's not what you –"

"*Furthermore*, I have my own savings – or will, once I work out how to steal them back from two bucolic fiends by the name of Sweeting. If you met me under ordinary circumstances, you'd be in no doubt regarding my ability to make my way without filching ladies' purses! And if I filch their hearts – I ask you, is *that* a crime, even under this vicious and persecutory state?"

"Pip!" Rosamond was flushed too, a reassuringly carmine hue between *exasperated* and *enraptured*. "Can you stop flabbergasting Gareth before you break your face again?"

I ducked a sardonical bow. It was worth it, even when it flipped my stomach. Stiff at Rosamond's side, the wretched pity had finally drained from Gareth's features.

"Ga – look – Pip's had a terrible day – and evening – and week. And Pip – Eddie didn't even let me write to him, he doesn't know you from suitor! Shall we all start this again?"

Gareth swallowed. With Rosamond's arm cricked round his collar, he hadn't much choice. He still had to chew a formidable breath before he could bring himself to offer me his hand – gracious, it was like trapping one's fingers in a toasting-grille.

"Beg pardon. It's like Miss Rosamond says – I'm only thinking of her."

Obviously. "As am I."

Rosamond slapped down the chivalry with a hand on top of ours, twiddling our uppermost fingers in a ridiculous triskelion clasp. "So! Ga – can we stay here for a bit?"

We both blinked at her. "Miss Rosamond, it is *your* house –"

"Sneakily, then. Don't write to Eddie – Edwina. Don't tell her we're here."

"With respect, miss, I don't know if that's –"

"Just for a bit," she wheedled. More than wheedled. All her persuasive charm – the feral grin, the flick of her fingers under his chin, the velvet trim on her voice. Trimming an edge – too sharp to be softened completely – though I suspect I only noticed it because the persuasion wasn't directly curated for me. "You know chwaer fawr's so difficult with me. You know she loves to ruin my life. Ga, Ga, os gwelwch chi'n dda –"

"Alright!"

For his flustered acquiescence, he received the widest and most wild of my beloved's smiles, which always puts me in mind of Dante's Beatrice after too much coffee. It's an infectious look: he caught it instantly, and even I felt the strain in my face slacken.

Until, that is, he glanced at me. Glanced me over, I should say – it was far more thorough than a glance. His brazen scrutiny wasn't unfamiliar; for Rosamond, I permitted it. Though he was rather taking his time with it – long enough for horrible possibilities to burrow under my eyelids and make me blink – *he can't take her in and lock me out, she wouldn't let him –*

"Starting over, then!" he cried. "A nice warm bath – and tê a bara with scrambled eggs! And you'll be wanting some Nettleblack's for that nasty cut?"

But he didn't mean it. Not sincerely. Not even at Rosamond's behest. Families *tolerate* me; they don't offer me spontaneous generosity, certainly not after any failings on my part. When I skidded into the Grand Canal at the tender age of seven, Mamma had her servants birch me at the water-gate for the ruin of my outfit – and that's one of the more benevolent examples. Thus, when Rosamond's self-appointed parent-steward hoisted up a smile heavy as the sky, and promised me voluntary pleasantries, in the wake of a disaster far worse than tumbling off a traghetto, I – well, I'd very little idea what to make of it.

I only knew I didn't trust it.

"Wyt ti'n rhy ardderchog, Ga," Rosamond managed shakily.

Managed, and *shakily,* because – to my horror – she was suddenly inches from tears. Her eyes glimmered, her throat caught, and the look she flung to me was as desperate as it was beseeching. "See, Pip? I said we'd be safe here!"

Staring out the fissures in her valiant cheeriness, I couldn't even steady her. I could hardly steady myself – my legs were shaking like plucked strings. *Darling – why – what the devil's the matter?*

"In with you," Gareth urged, shepherding her towards the house.

The bathwater came up in buckets. It passed me on the panelled staircase, metallic at the nose, wafting far too little steam. Gareth carried one bucket in each hand – then hurried past, boots eerily quiet on the green carpet, for a second round. He must have been boiling the kettle for it. I'd be lucky if the stagnant assemblage was lukewarm.

You mustn't think me spoiled, Divisioners. I've done the job of every servant I can't afford – also known as every servant – for the last five years. I gave up most of my gaslights in '92, and I only light the fire if I've a letter of Mamma's to burn. But baths are the exception. To sink into scented water, let it warm me through, tip my head back and close my eyes and sprawl into solitary amphibious oblivion – gracious, it's one of my greatest delights!

This bath was tin, a sit-up catastrophe, in a chilly room with no lock to the door. The walls and floor were somehow clammy and dusty at once, tiled about a tiny window and mirror. I twitched on the threshold, shivering – I didn't even want to touch the room in bare feet, let alone strip for that metal monstrosity.

"Stop this," I hissed, my voice sliding down the tiled corners. "You have to. You're filthy, damn it – "

The thought tugged me to the mirror. *You haven't seen yourself.* Rosamond was right: I hadn't had chance to look since before the escape – before the Sweetings –

I gasped.

The thing in the mirror was a pitiful wraith. It wasn't just the wreck of my evening suit, the bloodied ruin of my white tie and shirt, the broken seam at my shoulder. The face – a face that flinched when I flinched, that stared open-mouthed with trembling breaths –

No wonder the face hadn't protected me. Hadn't charmed or menaced Gareth into swifter acquiescence. Hadn't done *any* of its jobs. Whether it was the light, or the unaccountable sea-sickness – my skin had simply gone off, from its usual olive to the queasy brown of badly-done steak. My hair was slimy as the walls, shaken out of shape with pomade clinging to the fringe, slick dark tendrils drooping down my forehead. And under my eye – the scar Maggie Sweeting had left me. A jagged vertical slash on my cheekbone, thick with new-scabbed scarlet, cut with all the finesse of a child carving initials into a school-bench. It had bled, everywhere, smudged and crusting on my face and neck and shirt.

And you let this happen.

I stared, the bath's waning temperature forgotten. The mirror-eyes were darting now, trying to pinch the features as they used to be, as they should have been. I was handsome – before – brilliantly and usefully so – I'd never doubted my face as a perfect composition, all sharp jawline and strong eyebrows, what Whistler might call a symphony in brown. People stared, and it wasn't purely because of my odd colouring, nor the wearisome impulse to guess me a girl or a boy. I had, as I knew too well, a face that had swayed the very Sweetings from robbery to collaboration – that had maddened Septimus into months of clumsy surveillance – that Rosamond had deemed *magnificent* within seconds of discovering it.

No wonder I'd had trouble being worthy of Pip Property. I barely resembled them.

I stumbled away from the mirror's petrified scrutiny. Crashed into the tin-bath. Wrenched at my clothes with taut-fingered fists – no point being careful, the suit was past salvaging – until they were a bedraggle on the tiles, and I was all bones and gooseflesh, shuddering against the murky room and the murky water. The bath crumpled me, knees jarring my collarbone, cold metal jabbing my back, a gesture's-worth of chilly water slicing me at ankles and thighs and waist. I couldn't just shiver – I had to scrape the dirt from my nails, the pomade from my hair, the dried blood from my skin, all in silence broken only by the mocking rattle of my teeth.

I wouldn't have it. This was not me. Rosamond deserved better, and I needed better. The alternative – the idea that this vile metamorphosis was permanent, that I'd never again smirk in a suit or plait an elegant quip or stride forth in silken defiance of a hempen world –

Maledizione. It was too appalling even to contemplate.

CHAPTER TWO

I AM REMINISCING,
AND YOU SHAN'T STOP ME

The Notebook of Doom, Continued

Concerning the first months of 1890

Now, Henry, let us settle your infuriating doubts. I want it firmly established that I would never do a thing to wilfully endanger Rosamond. I grant my entanglement with your sister was a shock to you – I'm aware we kept our secret well – but, gracious, sweet youth, *you* can surely see why! Rosamond is an heiress, exquisite in face and fortune, a Cambrian nymph whose marital prospects are of interest to the Surrey noblesse. I am – I nearly wrote *a mess*, confound me, but I won't belabour *that* point – I am not a marital prospect. I am a solitary tradesperson of no discernible gender – which, for Miss Edwina Nettleblack and her ilk, rather supersedes the fact that my father was a professor and my mother's side claim dubious descent from doges. The only capacity in which I have been invited into the Nettleblacks' Dallyangle residence is as a supplement to the family tailor. Of course Rosamond and I had to be subtle.

Well. *Our* definition of subtle.

"Sir? Ah – miss? Ah – sir? Ah – "

"Property," I snapped, and instantly regretted it. I was

twenty-three, every thought stiff as my mourning crape, and I hadn't yet discerned how oddly Father's uncontextualised surname could sit in a stranger's ears. "Pip Property. Your mistress summoned me for some sartorial purpose."

I'd been staring at the house for some time before I rang, undecided on whether my scrutiny was genteel scorn or grudging respect. The building had preened at me all the way up the street, even amidst Catfish Crescent and its miniature mansions. It was so gaudily new money it made me wince, but I had to admire the commitment to theme. The green-curtained windows were gleaming, the green paint was gleaming, the nettle-patterned knocker was gleaming, and the nettle motif worked into the Corinthian pillars on the porch was – well, one could hardly say *out of place*.

The butler, more boringly English than I'd been expecting, actually bit his lip at me. "Miss Nettleblack requested that you use the servants' entrance."

(I'd seethed for it since her note had reached my shop – and then, in a fit of incredulity, changed out of full mourning. Petty logic, perhaps, but I'd already worn it longer than expected, and I wanted to thrust vibrant sartorial very-much-not-your-servant colours into Miss Edwina Nettleblack's impertinent face. I was half-tempted to confound her with my old credentials too: *you know I've been presented to the Queen?* would have done the trick. But the consequences of *that* were still too raw.)

"Miss Nettleblack was mistaken." I pinioned the butler with a smile, then hoisted him out of my way with it, and strolled into the hallway before he could protest. "She certainly was if she wants my expertise. I'll wait in the drawing-room, shall I?"

As with the façade, the family name could not have been absorbed more thoroughly into the hallway's decoration, short of staining *Nettleblack* onto the walls in metre-high calligraphy – but it was eerier inside, and inclined to murk. The wallpaper had been stewed green, the wood painted black, the window above the staircase split into stained-glass nettles. I strode through, smirking for every table-rap of my boots, and the butler scurried after me – "Miss – sir – miss – sir – "

But I'd grown spectacularly adept at dampening the sound of those titles.

I flicked one of the interchangeable doors open. Beyond was little more than darkness, shadows, drawn curtains, the acrid smell of a badly lit fire. My glimpses of Edwina Nettleblack in the street, bone-pale inside stiff-necked tweed, had always left me with a vampiric impression, but – gracious, it was the middle of the day! –

Something struck my knee. I stumbled, gasping, and the obstacle gasped too. A shadow sprang up in front of me, streaked through the gloom and shoved the curtains wide.

I froze.

Slung between the curtains, one hand curled round each velvet drape, was the most disarmingly unusual young woman I'd never thought to imagine.

She was younger than me, clambering towards her twentieth year, with flecks of roundness not yet flinted off her pallid face. She styled young, too, or perhaps just eccentrically: her long hair was unpinned, spiralling black curls that could have been drawn with ink. Her green dress was clearly expensive, but she wore it with the offhand crumple of a chemise, sleeves rolled to her elbows, collar loose, skirts high above thick woollen socks. Her throat and wrists were very bare, and very slender, the latter corded with wiry muscles. (As she told me later, she climbed a lot of cliffs in her adolescence.)

I wanted to stand and gape. But I hadn't survived this long without poise – and I wouldn't disappoint her – so I snapped my mouth shut and gave her a bow even the youthful Disraeli would have envied.

"Miss Rosamond," the butler gabbled at my ear. "Terribly sorry – your sister's appointment – I would have told her – him – ah – "

"*Them.*"

It crackled on my nerves. I don't think I'd ever declaimed

it with such confidence. But with her startled gaze at my lips, how could I not?

"I – ah – excuse me?" the butler faltered, inevitably.

I kept my eyes on hers, watched them widen. They were the most staggering shade of green – everything the decoration aspired to – all the complicated brightness of a new fern-frond with the sun behind it. "Neither *she* nor *he* is appropriate, so please don't topple from one to the other. What is it you mean to tell me?"

His face probably did something. It wasn't her face, so I didn't bother checking. "Only – ah – Miss Nettleblack is out, and I cannot say when – "

"Dim problem!" Her. Miss Rosamond. A voice that sparked and skittered like a swift. "Dw i'n gallu aros gyda nhw – "

"Miss Rosamond!" the butler cried. I had to glance at him then: the man was stricken, hands floundering through the words I'd been attempting to chase. "You know your sister's ruling on the matter of the – the Welsh!"

She flinched. But her brilliant eyes dashed across my face – presumably found nothing of whatever she feared therein – until she brisked to a wonderful sidelong smirk. "I said, I'll stay with them. Our visitor. Until Eddie remembers she's got one."

Did the butler protest? Did the butler leave? Did the butler decorously combust and sweep away his own scorched remains? I can't recall, and I didn't care. She had called me *them*, in two languages, and made a song of a single syllable. And now we were alone, and she was gesturing me over, to set us side by side in the window's light.

Much as I didn't want to break our stare, I had to give the room a cursory glance. The chaise would be the best bet, if she asked; the last time I pleasured a lady against curtains she brought them down on my head. By then, I had my suspicions about why privileged women might contrive to be alone with me.

"You can't be Edwina's friend," Miss Rosamond Nettleblack declared, dropping it between us as a pebble-solid fact. "Eddie's friends are awful."

I didn't doubt it; I'd heard Edwina ran with the Miltonwaters set. "Miss Nettleblack wishes to enlist my services. If her sister were a scrap less charming, I'd be inclined to withhold them."

I watched her chin tilt, as her voice sidled into a murmur. "What services?"

"For her, apparently, the sourcing of obscure accessories. For you, miss – " – and I lifted her bare hand with its surprisingly strong wrist, framed a knuckle in my lips – " – whatever you might decide."

She grinned. After her opening gambit, I hadn't expected shyness, but this unabashed excitement twisted my chest like a spirit-lamp. "You know what you look like?"

"I am aware."

"Then you know you're – " – she flinted her fingers for a word, lips twitching through several, not all of them English – " – magnificent. I didn't think Surrey could do magnificent."

Her look could have made a mouse conceited. And in these circumstances, alone with a lady and dancing about the point, I was used to taking scraps: *you'd be very handsome, if you were a man*, or *your colouring is so delightfully exotic*, or even *what an intriguing thing you are!* But *magnificent* – alone, undiminished – gracious, I'd cherish it.

"Well, you must give Surrey time. I've not even been here two years – perhaps I'm too recent an arrival."

"So am I," she blurted, with a strange urgency that clenched her fingers around mine. She wasn't teasing now – she was too heavy at the words, as if she meant to stamp them indelibly onto the house. "Rwy'n dod o Gŵyr."

"I beg your pardon?"

She plucked a sigh in her throat. "Damn. Siarad Saesneg. Cymraeg – Welsh – it's my – I mean – the one I prefer."

I frowned. Perhaps I should have set my lips to her collar-bone and distracted her – but, miniature rake that I supposedly was, I could never keep a proper rakish distance. The ladies usually raised their barriers high enough for both of us.

"And now your sister won't let you speak it?"

She flushed.

"Forgive me, miss, I didn't mean – "

"Not your fault." A bitter smile. "You're not even wrong. Eddie gives the orders in this house, and I just – let her."

"That's hardly true. If you followed Miss Nettleblack's orders so zealously, I wouldn't be enjoying your company – I'd be loitering at the servants' entrance."

She stared at me for a moment that slipped the clock. The bitterness dropped like bad silk, some sharper green light striking behind her extraordinary eyes.

Then her hand tugged, back against her chest, pinning my palm to her gown. For half a breath, we were close enough for her features to blur – for me to register what I ought to do –

But before I could move, she grabbed my cravat, and yanked me into a kiss so fervent it bruised my mouth open.

I always had to kiss. I'd never *been kissed*. And this beautiful slip of an heiress was kissing with everything at her disposal: her tongue, her teeth – Dio mio, her *teeth*. She bit my lip, and to my infinite consternation I heard myself rise to it, the sound half-stifled against her. Damn the curtains – if she did that again I'd smash the very window – !

She broke the kiss as suddenly as she'd started it, grinning through parted teeth. I dived for her again, with (regrettably) all the panache of a schoolboy, but she held me back – "That's the front door, bach!"

We sprang apart. I dashed to the mantelpiece, hoping for a mirror to straighten my cravat – but there was only a sloshy family portrait, three pallid siblings with not a scrap of human feeling in their likenesses. My mouth was throbbing – *I* was throbbing – I didn't dare look at her, I could hardly think –

"Please forgive my delay, Miss Property."

Miss? The *deuce*?

Edwina Nettleblack strode through the door, sailing on her terrible tweed skirts, upright and rigid as an ill-fitted corset. Her eyes – I hate the eerie resemblance to Rosamond's – darted between us, never quite settling on a face. She frowned down my suit, and the feeble remains of my common-sense tacked a meaning together: she'd only chosen *miss* because the butler would never have left a man alone with her sister. What she made of me – the flower of androgynous masculinity, lips red and cravat askew, gasping for breath against her mantelpiece – I hardly dared imagine.

But, once again, a Nettleblack surprised me. Edwina looked disapproving, but there was nothing of real understanding in her too-pale features. She seemed more annoyed to have mistaken the prefix. Had she simply not noticed the state of us?

"Just Property," I managed, stammering a little. *Me*, stammering! "Pip Property. And it's no trouble at all, Miss Nettleblack. I – I was just – "

"Good." Edwina nodded crisply – then pierced Rosamond with a glare. "Rosamond Pleasant Myfanwy Earlyfate, go to your room and tidy yourself this instant. You do not want visitors to this house thinking you some unmannerly slattern."

Rosamond scowled back. Lifted her chin, with the slightest glance at me. "Rwy'n gwneud yr hyn dw i ishe, chwaer fawr, a ni fyddwch chi'n gwneud i mi aros."

Edwina went whiter, somehow, jaw taut as the gathering in her sleeves. "You will not like it if I have to ask again."

Rosamond answered the threat with a valiant scoff – but she stalked out all the same, cheeks flushed, socks shushing against the polished floor. I couldn't gaze after her with half the fervour I wanted, wasn't sure if she'd be able to contrive a glance back at me –

But she did. Quick and furtive in the doorway. Those wonderful eyes rolled, lashes dipping in a wink. She might as well have drenched me in beeswax and touched me to a match.

"Please excuse her," Edwina declared, in a tone that hadn't much of *please* about it, slamming the door as decorously as possible. "My sister is young and silly, and enjoyed – ah – great freedom in her upbringing. Nothing she won't grow out of in England."

I cannot recall how I managed to scramble through that conversation. Edwina discoursed on nettle-patterned trim with the cold precision of a military commander; I made noises and notes and ran my tongue over the dent in my lip – which, given how pointedly she refused to look me in the face, I had a lot of licence to do. In a moment of genius – or desperation – I persuaded her to take my cravat catalogue, just so there was *something* in that house to remind Rosamond of my name. That – and to furnish her with my home address, hastily scribbled on my photograph.

Not that I left with anything like hope. The Nettleblacks were celebrities, especially in the tiny town that was Dallyangle, Surrey – of course Edwina would guard their reputations with the utmost rigour.

At least, I thought as much, until the winter evening rolled in, and Rosamond turned up on my doorstep.

I crept to the door with a rapier in hand. My darling youthful sword, snatched off the wall, otherwise untouched since the last fencing practice with Father. It was past ten-thirty – I knew no one in Dallyangle well enough for an ordinary call, never mind a late-night raid. My imagination was in mutiny: it could have been Mamma's lackeys, back to try again – *don't struggle, Miss Property, we only want to help you –*

I flinched off the thought, yanked the door open, feet already in porta di ferro – and everything jolted out of place. Burnished by the streetlamps, bulky in an overlarge greatcoat, inky ringlets still defiantly loose, Rosamond Nettleblack grinned at me.

"Nice window-boxes, Pip Property." Her grin widened. "I do love a fern."

As sneakily as I could, I shoved the rapier into the coat-stand.

"Gwell a gwell!" She sauntered past, shrugged off her great-coat without hanging it up, fingertips stretching to trace the corridor's walls. "You're an artist!"

I'd fledged the hall with my sketches. Some designs I'd turned into cravats, others were wilder ideas I hadn't yet risked. Rosamond studied them, with eyes and hands alike, fingers slipping through the overlapping pages. As I stared, wondering whether *good evening* was far too pedestrian, she touched a fingertip to a charcoal sketch, smirked at the grey dusting on her skin.

"Why so many paisleys?"

I cleared my throat.

"Homage to my grandfather. Terribly stylish man. And that pattern you've a thumb on – " (she didn't move her thumb, and it thrilled me to a maddeningly disproportionate extent) " – was filched from the floor of San Marco. I'm Venetian on my mother's side."

"Of course you are. What about these trees, then?" Her smirk softened to a startlingly fond smile. "They look like Ilston Woods."

"If you like." I remembered, at last, to shut the door on the cold, leant against it in an attempt to match her languor. "That's the selva oscura, where Dante Alighieri tumbles about before Virgil leads him into Hell. My father is – " (maledizione) " – was – quite the Dante scholar."

She arched her neck to peruse the higher patterns. Her dress was the same as earlier, her throat tremendously open. I complemented her dishevelment now: it was late enough for me to have discarded my waistcoat and unpinned my collar, the rest of me little more than trousers and braces with a dressing-gown for warmth.

"You don't sound Italian," she mused. "You talk like a right sais."

"I beg your pardon?"

"English. Edwina hates it when I say *toff*, so – " – and her face sharpened, a tiny victory smile – " – like a right sais toff."

"I had a choice of accents. I cultivated my father's. He – "

He was the one who used my name? He defended me against all I wasn't? He's the reason I can defend myself now?

I shrugged awkwardly, grateful her eyes were still on the patterns. It was rather too much, and too much past tense.

But then she turned, thumb forming a little crease in the San Marco design. "Chwarae teg. And good for you, that you can choose – from a whole Continent of a family, too! But it's just you here in Dallyangle? Alone?"

I stiffened. I was perfectly capable of saying it without shaking. "Father died in '88. Mamma went back to Venice. What she does there, I neither know nor care, as long as it doesn't gesture anywhere near me."

"I see." She wasn't smirking now. "I'm sorry."

I kept my voice deadly polite. "I don't want your pity, Miss Nettleblack."

"I'm not giving you it," she retorted, visibly surprised. "I assume you know what happened to *my* parents."

Actually, I did. Even in my youth, they were the sort of people to claim inches in Father's newspapers. The husband-and-wife heads of the Nettleblack's Tincture empire, killed in a carriage accident in 1880, the fortune dropped on their eldest daughter. Rosamond was much younger than Edwina; she couldn't have been more than ten when it happened.

"It was a practical question, anyway." A flash in her eyes scorched off the solemnity. "If you're alone, we've no need to fret about being overheard."

Well. The sneaky sorceress pulled the very air taut with that. I let my voice fall light and teasing – acutely aware, all the while, of the way it plied at my pulse. "And what, precisely, might be *overheard*?"

She dropped the sketch. Walked towards me. Swaggering, purposeful, as if *she* was the one with the mind to seduce *me*. In full seven years of diverting ladies, I'd never seen the like.

"I think you know. I think you've been pondering it ever since I bit your lip."

She closed the distance before I could react, leant against me with that disarming strength, pinned me flat to my own front door. Her charcoal-dusted finger trailed up my throat – lingered a moment, to feel me swallow – then slid under my chin. "Admit it."

The gesture lit a candle in my gullet. It wasn't panic – or perhaps it was – a kind of hot choking involuntary cowardice. I was just so accustomed to playing her role, paraphrasing those words, prising others' poise open and leaving my own intact. "Miss Nettleblack, I – "

Her hand twisted out of its gentle touch, clamped over my mouth. "*Rosamond*. Os gwelwch yn dda. And whatever you think you know about proper young misses from respectable families, I want you to forget it. Wyt ti'n deall?"

She didn't let go. I've no idea how the state of me hadn't scalded her palm. If it had been anyone else – I would have fought, twisted, bitten, anything rather than be held like this – but I couldn't move. She simply didn't give me leave to be afraid. She must have felt what her impertinence had done to my heartbeat, traitorously feral under my shirt, sprinting ahead of my shattered thoughts.

I *liked* it. And it was obvious.

"Well?"

Heaven knows how, but I nodded.

She dragged me to her lips. I grabbed for her, her waist and dress in fistfuls. The kiss was, quite frankly, murderous – ricocheting down the corridor, smashing sketches off the walls. A sharp diagonal kicked us into the drawing-room, hurtling round the chaise; of course she ignored its velvet cushions and shoved me onto the hearthrug. Under different circumstances, I would have feared for my clothes – but then she was on top of me, kissing the thought from my mind –

"Gracious, you're practiced!"

"No sheltered little heiress, me. The maidens of Gower were devastated when I left." Her lips brushed along my cheekbone, light with a whisper: "I had them in the ruins of Pennard Castle."

She bit my ear. I yelped. "I am not a *maiden*!"

"Well, that's obvious." She shifted back to study my face. "You're practiced too, I think. Let me guess – blushing debutantes, furtive corners, kissing hands, playing the rake?"

"Actually, yes." I managed a breathless smirk. "Nothing so Gothic as a ruined castle."

"And nothing like this from the debs, I bet?"

She snatched my wrists, pinned them together on the rug above my head. I didn't struggle; my stillness was as much admission of my baffled delight as I meant to give. "Oddly enough, nothing at all."

"But you enjoy it?"

Damn you, Rosamond Nettleblack! "Perhaps."

"Perhaps?" She kissed my neck – bit my neck – didn't stop until I squirmed – "Only perhaps? Then *perhaps* I ought to let you go – "

"Don't you dare!"

It was a spasm of a cry, wrenching open some complicated lock inside my chest. *Nothing like this from the debs* – well, there hadn't been! The *debs* never touched me! They'd only sigh against my cheek, settle themselves as they wanted and not care how I had to contort my wrists, straighten their skirts with half-affronted huffs when they'd had enough! *It hardly counts*, they'd whisper, *now please don't talk to me again.*

Not this. Nothing like this. *This* was like tumbling into a Swinburne poem.

"Bendigedig. Mind if I tie your hands?"

"I – I beg your – ?"

"Trust me. You won't keep still." She affected a pout, which was truly more of a preen. "I'm very good, and I always get thwacked in the head for it."

I let her. Against all the scorching incredulity of my mind, I wanted her to. She used my cravat, looped it round the chaise, told me to tense my wrists against her while she adjusted the knot – a trick, she said, to loosen the bindings out of too-taut risk. Hovered over my face for one last moment, her hair tangling around us, her brilliant eyes alight.

"You're a pallid and poisonous queen," I gasped.

She beamed. "Diolch yn fawr!"

Then she slipped down my chest, mercury-fast. Flicked

open the buttons of my trousers – hissed when she realised there were braces too (it was, as she told me later, the first time she'd dealt with masculine attire). At the risk of sounding far more of an ingénue than I was, I admit she urged me to a scream with the first press of her tongue. But – gracious, I'd never been touched by anyone who wasn't me – and *very good* was a spectacular understatement – I can't be blamed for an exultant shriek! –

Wait.

The Division are meant to read this. Rosamond's *sibling* is meant to read this.

Oh, to the devil with bowdlerisation! You locked me in the morgue – now you can take the consequences! And if *this* doesn't convince you all I cherish her, I've no idea what will!

CHAPTER THREE

I AM THE TERROR OF
THE GOWER PENINSULA

The Notebook of Doom, continued

Concerning Sunday 5th November 1893, and the fortnight that followed

The early days of 1890 were a delight. Regrettably, Divisioners, I'm now obliged to drag you out of them, lest I fill the notebook with too much excitement for your sleuthing to tolerate. If you'll recall the miserable wretch in Gareth's cold bath – well, let's not abandon *that* Pip entirely to bloodstains and despair, shall we?

The rain shook the flame in the nettle-patterned spirit-lamp. I hadn't seen rain like this since Venice – powerful, muscular, slanting sideways to strike at unexpected angles. The window-panes writhed in their mock-Tudor lattices. I'd squinted through them, when it was finally time to put doors between me and that ghastly bathtub, and it seemed I had Nettleblack House to myself: Rosamond was dashing round the grounds with Gareth, apparently rescuing his gardening tools. Unless there were more servants here. I hadn't yet seen them. I didn't altogether like not being sure.

But if other limbs twitched in the house's shadows, they

left me alone. I sat in Rosamond's bedroom, her father's dressing-gown heavy on my shoulders, the damp from my hair congealing in its collar. Her room had every vivacious twist of her soul – the four-post's bedposts were fantastical carvings, of lizards and snails and clumpfuls of nettles, whilst her walls were painted with fruit, flame-winged moths, and the splay-tailed streak of a red kite – and inky scribbles, too, unauthorised at child's height, *Rosa* and *Henry* labelling two stick-figures atop a mountain of figs. If I'd not been so damnably morbid, I would have smiled for it.

I wasn't yet close to smiling. I was glaring into the mirror on Rosamond's dresser, studying the non-existent progress of my face. I'd underestimated how much the Sweetings relished the theatrical – killing me immediately was insufficiently exciting, not when they could scar my future and steal my savings. For all I knew – for all I didn't want to think – they'd smashed my study window again, gutted every room in my house, copied my cut onto chaises and cushions until the upholstery was little more than spilt entrails –

"And yet you've called *me* Narcissus!"

Rosamond leant on the doorframe, sparkling with storm. Vigorous and element-beaten suited her in a way it never would me. "Beth sy'n bod, cariad?"

I sighed. "Da iawn, diolch."

She perched beside me on the bed's end, dragged an armchair over to serve as a table. She'd assembled a tray: damp cloths, a mug branded with Nettleblack's Tincture. Of course it made me flush.

"I don't need – "

"I want to fuss you. Indulge me."

Her smile glinted, with raindrops and lamplight and her usual slyness. None of it flickered, not even when I squinted – so I rolled my eyes and let her cup my chin. She was deft tidying the scar, fingers quick as sparrow-feet on the edge of my eyeline: darting, settling, darting away again to pinch for her next cloth. We alternated the mug like a wassail-bowl, sipping nettle tincture in nettle tea, until my very throat could have sprouted weeds. When she was done, she swept my hair back and kissed my forehead, then folded me into her arms, both our faces tilted to the lamp.

The window was still a pin-box of rain. Her lips were soft behind my ear, heedless of my wet hair. I could feel the words scraping my teeth, for all that her hold was so comfortable, so bafflingly voluntary –

"I'm sorry you're obliged to endure this."

She stiffened behind me. "Endure what?"

"This. Me. A mess."

"I'm not enduring anything." She bit my ear with a huff of exasperation, disproportionately loud. "You know I love you when your cravat's askew."

She had to, to proffer that kind of unwarranted benevolence.

I'd no answer – understandably! – so I tipped back over her collarbone and stared out our shadows on the wall: we looked and sounded like a rustle in the undergrowth. Ominous, slightly manic, furtive and conspiratorial. But she wasn't scrambling away.

"I think," she murmured, arranging kisses in my hair between every few words, "that might be enough self-hatred for one evening, don't you?"

I lost my hold on time and rain both for a while after that. I believe I fell asleep in her arms – woke, when the lamp was a little starker in its divisions of light and shade, to her nudges and a plate of scrambled eggs – then slept again, with the curtains drawn round her four-post, and the sharp heavy warmth of her an admirable defence against cold thoughts. Then there were more curtains, some slashed at the gathering, some still clattering with rings – for she'd dashed round the house while I dozed, torn down hangings from other bedrooms, splayed her floor in the nettle-addled patterns so I might cut new cravats with her mother's sewing-kit. Then we took a trip to her father's wardrobe, hand in hand down the gloomy corridor, to pick and tailor a tincture-tinted suit.

Then my arms were tight round her waist, my face eyebrow-deep in her hair, as the two of us simply held each other atop the pile of verdant fabrics.

Then, restored to attire and equilibrium (more or less), I suggested we repair to her bedroom. I slid onto the bed, flexed my fingers from their scissor-welted stiffness; she leapt astride with force enough to knock out my breath. I should have interrupted – something to the gist of *tell me you locked the door!* – but I forgot that, along with everything else, when she found her rhythm. And what a delight it was – *is*, perpetually is – to be wrenched out of my head by her! What a mercy, when her grip and her gasps stop me thinking, when we sketch between us a world in which I don't have to hold any pose, and she can chase every pose she chooses!

"Better," she gasped, after finishing in a fashion I'm not sure you'd appreciate me quoting (I do not swear, not even at the crucial moment; she does, in two languages), and crumpling on my chest like another of her felled curtains. Her curls were spangled with dust, jolted down from the four-post's canopy. "I won't have you despising yourself in every mirror. We're here to escape – and to rest – and we'll reprise this every day until you start doing both!"

I grinned. She was looking at me – *me*, in my state, with my appalling face and wayward hair and borrowed clothes, without a hint of revulsion in her glittering stare.

But I see now, with all the horrible overthought of hindsight, how that zeal might have been our first mistake.

I can't pick the moment at which Gareth noticed. Perhaps the startled silhouette at the corridor's end had been nothing more than a prudish ghost, the day we kissed along the pattern of the Morris wallpaper. Perhaps he didn't know why we had him prepare such a lavish picnic – and picnic-blanket – for a ramble to Pennard Castle when the grass dried. Perhaps it really did take until he walked in on us atop the breakfast table.

It served him right – or so I thought at first, giddy with Rosamond's leftover recklessness. If he wanted to know why the scrambled eggs had been dashed to the floor, he was positively asking to be scandalised. He didn't even know the whole of it – the additional dalliances with others she occasionally indulged alongside our romance. (In the matter of dalliances, I might add, she was by far the more prolific. She'd even managed to seduce a Divisioner – whilst my solitary attempt with Septimus was... let us say, unsuccessful, albeit predominantly because I was trying to rob her on the same night. Regardless.)

I almost thought, as Rosamond certainly did, that Gareth ought to be pleased with his little discovery. After all, he desired nothing but his protégée's happiness, did he not? *My* happiness was another matter – but it mattered to Rosamond, and *I* hardly planned to abstain from my own reassembling to soothe a servant's sensibilities. Every caress, every cry, even and especially the bites on my neck that upstaged Maggie's scar – it was proof, all of it, an unexpected and glorious defence against the wraith in the tin tub. *She still loves me*, I wanted to snarl at Gareth, with my cravat very much askew, *and if my own hideous incompetence can't stop her, what the devil makes you think* you *can?*

But then I caught his eyes over the *next* morning's breakfast, whilst engaged in the mildly gloating act of massaging my wrists. I knew his look: fear, fury, taut-clenched disapproval – and the first tentative twitches of a scheme. If I'd taken a razor to his beard, and cut sharp the softness of his features, I could have been staring out my mother.

It was, consequently, both the best and worst of times for Rosamond to gift me her father's swordstick.

We were splitting the day in the garden. The sky was disarmingly wide, the clouds stretched silvery-thin; below them, Nettleblack House jutted from the clifftop with the brightness of a false tooth. Rosamond had sprinted from the table halfway through my laverbread, promising a new present – the laverbread, I suspect, was meant as a demotion from the morning's scrambled eggs, for Gareth hadn't realised how much his least favourite Venetian would relish a seaweed dish. I tested the same thought I'd been trying all morning, light on the bruised remnants of my strategic mind: *if I was an overprotective servant dissatisfied with my mistress's choice of lover, how would I get rid of said lover? And how might I be stopped?*

"Pip! I found it!"

Rosamond careered across the grass, a tangle of loose curls and bare feet, clutching a walking stick. Its silver top had (of course) been carved in the likeness of a nettle-leaf, plant-veins and all – as I'd plenty of liberty to notice when she prodded me in the chest with it.

"You," she declared, "are panicking again. I can tell."

I arched an eyebrow. "I do not *panic.*"

"Well, you definitely won't be when you have this! I was looking for cravat pins – I remember Tad having some – but I found better. It'll be just like Henry – calming *her* nerves was a task and a half until we worked out she was a trick shot. I used to make her targets on the headland when no one was around. Edwina nearly throttled me for it! *Rosamond Pleasant Myfanwy Earlyfate, what do you mean our sibling can't sew or play or minuet her way through life? Pistols are not an accomplishment, you vagabond! –* "

Her grin faltered. Something glanced across her eyes, bunched her fists around the stick, her knuckles suddenly fingernail-sharp. It all vanished the moment she saw me notice, into a smile so firm it could have sanded wood.

"But pistols aren't particularly Pip. So I brought you Earlyfate!"

I had, by this point, abandoned all hope of following her darting thoughts – indeed, I was rather more concerned with that troubling tweak in her expression – and her expectant pause caught me off-guard. "Sorry, darling, that was a lot of words – "

"Says you," she smirked. Then, with another flourish of the

nettle-topped stick – "This is Earlyfate. My father had it made – I think after Uncle Rhys tried to steal the business? Or maybe just because Uncle Rhys was taller than him? Anyway, it was my namesake! Tad chose all our middle names. Edwina got a Welsh queen, which she hates, which is great – Henry got a sweet little plant – and I got the best of the three, obviously!"

"Your father named you... after his walking stick?"

Her grin blazed, Caffeinated Beatrice in reprise. "Better."

She twisted the nettle, yanked the stick like a scabbard – and proffered me a *sword*.

I gaped. Then I studied. The late Morgan Nettleblack's swordstick was no flimsy foil. Here was a thumb-wide blade with true and false edges, tall as my seven-year-old self, the sort of thing that – with a little sharpening – could cut rapier-deep. It didn't have quillons, and the grip wasn't what I'd learned with, but in every other respect –

Rosamond beamed at me over the blade. "Would Professor Property have approved?"

I took it, and slid from my chair. Rosamond leapt back, still grinning – I grinned too when I followed her gaze, and found myself already arranged in a fair approximation of porta di ferro stretta. "Dearest, you know you would have been *adored*."

For my father, fencing like an out-of-time Renaissance man was – as far as anyone asked – purely for the good cause of academic research. He and his club of medievalists rented a hall in Bloomsbury; he was their undisputed leader, being the only one who (by marriage) could master the Italian accent their old manuals demanded. He'd been unflatteringly astonished when I'd asked to join him – I was still young enough not to have dented my future as the family debutante. But I had joined, and shaken his fellows' hands, and borrowed a new favourite word to introduce myself: as his *progeny*, no *son* or *daughter* required. He'd raised his eyebrows, but he hadn't questioned it – then, or since, in all the years I snatched with him.

Come now, Pip. (It pains me to confess I can't recall the sound of his voice, but I modelled my own upon it, and the phrasing one doesn't forget.) *Step the guards properly for dear dall'Agocchie. You don't* start *in porta di ferro stretta.*

I adjusted. Upright, heels together, sword in an imaginary scabbard. Rosamond curled into my chair, filched a bite of my laverbread, and licked the seaweed off her thumb: "Now stop fretting and enjoy yourself!"

Then I went for it.

Falso – riverso sgualimbro – into coda lunga stretta –

Now I ought to explain. I know that gushing about my youthful pastime of rapier practice is hardly conducive to settling certain Divisionary minds on certain disastrous matters. When I say *went for it*, I only mean stepping in the guards, which is *not* an attack, simply a delightful exercise in which one strikes elegant poses with an elegant weapon, if one wishes to show off a nettle-tipped swordstick to the beloved who borrowed its name –

So Gareth's decision to sprint into my path with arms akimbo was entirely uncalled for.

I caught myself mid-falso, whirled Earlyfate away from him. He beat me to incredulity – "What on earth are you *doing?*"

I could have snapped, *reminding myself that I am my father's progeny and my darling's cariad, not a helpless convalescent with a stranger's face* – but trusting him was rather a pre-requisite for that answer. "My dear man, what does it look like I'm doing?"

"Endangering Miss Rosamond!" (Damn.) "You shouldn't be swinging that so close to – God rest him, is that Mr. Morgan's swordstick – ?"

"Paid poeni, Ga," Rosamond drawled, still tangled on her chair. "Surely Edwina can't stop me gifting it to Pip?"

He blinked far too much. "Well – of course not – but you must be careful – that silly thing was always so troublesome – and it might be sharp – "

"Gracious, it's not sharp enough." I pinched the blade, watched him frown along the false edge. "It should break fabric and skin with the lightest touch."

"Beg pardon," he retorted, against all sense of the phrase,

with a glare at my scar, "but I didn't think you'd want much more to do with breaking skin."

I flushed.

Of course I didn't—*maledizione*, that was the *point!* But I had criminals with designs on my life. I had a houseful of belongings in the town I simply wouldn't *leave behind*. I had him, scowling at me with my mother's look, quietly numbering our days here. I had Rosamond's baffling kindness to repay with decent protection, and Rosamond's anxious looks to smooth away with decent scheming. I had, in short, more than enough reasons for wanting something to parry with, the next time someone took a fancy to stab at my face!

It's alright, Pip. That mismatch voice again, Father's words transposed to my key. *I promise. Come out, now—you can put the sword down.*

I can't, though, can I?

"Mr. Evans." I made myself smile, insufferable with innocence. "I want to sharpen Earlyfate's blade. I trust you can furnish me with the necessary equipment?"

CHAPTER FOUR

I AM PERTURBED BY AN
UNPLEASANT DISCOVERY

The Notebook of Doom, continued

Concerning that stressful yet halcyon fortnight, until Sunday 19th November 1893

Va bene. Between the swordstick and the Swinburne, I'd finally broken him.

Gareth had never done more than tolerate me, with slap-heavy politeness and suspicious looks. An unwelcome guest, devoid of gender and marital claim, flaunting meddlesome grammar and a strange complexion – oh, but he'd endure it, for Miss Rosamond's sake! And you know, already, how the truth of my carnal relations with his favourite heiress knocked him sideways. But the fact that I now had a weapon – thanks to his beloved charge, no less! – *that* snapped the last of his deference.

And, even flimsily repaired as I was, I simply would not be undone by toast in human form.

He made it his bustling mission to get Rosamond alone, after Earlyfate appeared. Given that Rosamond had made it *her* mission to tie me to something at least once a day in an effort to reignite my character (noble darling!), it wasn't diffi-cult to thwart him. I suspect he was unprepared for how much

I noticed – this time, at least – a household conspiring against me. And I wouldn't let it happen again. I wouldn't let him poison the only mortal soul who cared for me – the only soul ever likely to care for me now.

He was the threat. Undiluted. I searched the house again, just to be sure, when he was too busy with his eggs to scurry after Rosamond: there were no other servants. It transpired she was responsible for it – she'd ordered him to dispatch both cook and skivvy on indefinite holiday while I was grappling with the first bath. *Ga can do everything brilliantly,* she'd explained, with a pointy shrug, *and that's two fewer people to go gossiping to Edwina.*

Ah.

I'd guessed his next move then, strongly suspected he was more than halfway to guessing it himself – especially when he'd burst in with tea not four seconds later. *Warn Rosamond* was the imperative, as soon as I could banish him beyond eavesdropping – but what good was a warning without a plan to accompany it? A plan I could actually accomplish, to illustrate past all doubt that she'd be safe with me henceforth, that there truly was nothing in any mirror for me to despise?

I had to wait for the ember-lit privacy of her bedroom – even then I did three turns of the corridor to make sure Gareth wasn't listening outside. Rosamond was cosy in a fireside chair, basking in the lazy half-hour whilst the bricks warmed the bed, staring out the fire over a mug of Nettleblack's. So peaceful and unruffled, it stung to speak. But I had to puncture the idyll, if purely to patch it with a solution.

"Narcissus." Her old nickname. I leant back in my chair, affected a calm not even the crackling hearth could make me feel. "Might I ask a serious question?"

The sleepy scaffolding of a smirk. "Oh?"

"What did you mean, when you said you wanted to *leave Dallyangle behind?*"

She started. I sipped my tea, fingers shaking, but she didn't answer.

I thought myself prepared for such evasion. I'd seen it on the boat, in the expressions that flashed through her too-defiant glee. I'd hoped she would shed the reticence of her own accord – certainly that I wouldn't have been obliged to chivvy her. And – very well, I admit it – her determination to prioritise the brightening of my world hadn't been unwelcome –

But it had been distracting. It had left me thoroughly *un*prepared for everything that crowded into her face now: not just evasion, but fear, stiffening her in the chair, feet still tucked up in a ghastly parody of comfort. She was utterly terrified, and I –

Had I not noticed? Had I simply let her veer me off the subject?

And if I hesitated much longer – she might set down the mug, and grab Earlyfate from the corner, and demand another dall'Agocchie demonstration. She might slink onto my lap and twist her hand in my hair. She'd do something, again, to stop looking stricken, and I'd stop fretting about it, stop thinking altogether –

And how, exactly, will that protect her?

"I can quite understand why you're reluctant to return. But you don't seem inclined to settle here either. We never leave the house but for solitary walks – no calls, no invitations for old acquaintances, not even a glimpse of the Gower maidens who must be missing you terribly. And I understand the logic – as you say, if the rest of Gower don't know we're here, and Miss Rosamond Nettleblack's sensational return with her lover stays out of rumours and papers alike, Edwina shan't suspect our whereabouts."

She nodded warily. Her hands were shaking too, the surface of her tea puckering like bad satin.

"But that – " – it was like lowering myself into a horrible crevasse – " – was never the plan. You asked, if I recall, not to hide from Edwina, but to visibly disdain her. This was to be our Disraeli tour – a string of holiday escapades and a return to Dallyangle in triumph and infamy – the last blow against your sister's endeavours to make you look marriageable. I believe your words were *I need her to give up on me?"*

She winced. "Well – yes – but for that we needed the Continent. And we can't get off this island now your savings are gone, so – that's that."

I sipped my tea again. Eyes shut, fingers taut against the mug's warmth, for as long as it took to drown the voice in my skull. *Whose fault is it that the savings were stolen? Who complicated the plan past all hope of success? Who compromised Rosamond's safety* and *Rosamond's future?*

"I concede our position has become rather more – precarious. But we can't hide here anymore. Gareth – "

"Ga only wants what's best for me – "

"Precisely." I sighed, mostly to soften my voice. "What *he* deems best for you."

"But – "

"You're his long-lost protégée, and I'm – " – it only required a gesture, to myself in her father's dressing-gown, to the cravat I'd cut from the spare room's curtains, to the sharpened swordstick leant on the fruit-dappled wall. "And you're indulging me. You've done nothing else all fortnight. You couldn't pass for a blushing debutante if you tried – this isn't merely a question of gently extricating you from your youthful folly, or my corrupting influence. This is, as it were, above his wages. He knows you won't get rid of me."

"Then that's fine! Isn't it?"

Oh, dearest. "But he also knows who could. You told him not to write to her. I suspect he's broken that promise."

She jolted. Tea splattered the floorboards, sharp as dropped nails. *"Edwina?"*

"So it's rather not the time to leave Dallyangle behind. Whatever I can salvage from my house – *that* is our only chance at safety. *We* are our only chance at safety. You wanted to blaze out of Edwina's grip on your own notoriety, and you can't do that if she prises you from this house like a naughty child – "

"Pip," she gasped.

As her interruptions went, it was barely even vigorous – but there was something choked and splintering in it that shattered my words. She buckled in her chair, eyes wide, one hand plucking at her throat. Spasmed, teeth bared, through several scraping breaths.

I sprang to my knees at her side, snatched her mug before she drenched herself, fumbled the blankets off her back in the petrified assumption that she was choking –

But there was no cough. No change to her skin. Just those awful desperate gasps. Then she cried out, a ragged snarl, eyes crumpling with frustration.

"No! No, it's the Henry thing – *just* the Henry thing – "

I cupped her face and pulled our foreheads together. Calling Gareth was impossible; the man would only blame me. "What do you – ?"

She grabbed my wrists, far tighter than usual. "Breathe – breathe at me slowly – "

Much as my every thought was shrieking, I had the sense to obey her without question. I closed my eyes when she did, and hissed steady breath after steady breath through distinctly unsteady teeth, until my wrists screamed and the room melted around us like a spoiled photograph. Slowly, too slowly, she patterned her gasps to mine.

Her hold on my wrists slackened, her thumbs circling my veins by way of apology. My fingers throbbed in insolent involuntary complaint.

She groaned. "Oh, chwaerlet. No wonder you're always so stressed."

I tipped back, enough to stare at her. "What – ?"

"That's what happens to Henry." She opened her eyes, startlingly large in her taut face. "Started after we moved to Dallyangle. She'd have these – like that – get so scared she couldn't breathe. But I – *I've* never – "

She gulped. She was very careful with her breaths, stretching them between her teeth.

"I'm not like Henry. I'm not scared of things. But – maybe

47

she is braver than me. Brave in her youthful obliviousness. She ran first, after all – suppose it's easy to run away when you don't know what'll happen if you're found."

I could feel her heartbeat under my hands, still far too swift for my liking. "Forced betrothal to an aristocrat, you mean?"

A chipped little laugh. "That's just if Edwina likes you."

Maledizione.

"What has Edwina said?" Of course it was a growl. "Darling?"

Her green gaze was bruisingly solemn. "You're not to sprint headlong into fixing it, alright? I don't want you smashed on the wreck of another scheme."

I've no idea how I kept my face still. She might as well have flung the tincture in it.

Of course it hurt! To have lost the trust and awe she'd harboured for my abilities – to have my every future chance throttled by one misstep – to be chaperoned, damn it, by my newfound incompetence! And this was no entanglement on the bed, no gloating whispered orders in the only context that let me tolerate helplessness. This was her, wretched with her miserable secrets, *pitying* me.

"What happened?" I managed weakly. I was practically proving her right.

She shivered, a sudden violent twisting thing. Plaited our fingers and clung with a pale-knuckled grip. "You remember our last chess-match in Dallyangle?"

Under any other circumstances, I would have sighed. I do so hate that silly little euphemism she picked up from the Divisioners. "In your attic?"

It had been a peculiar night, two days before our escape, a furtive medley of embraces interrupted by Edwina's demands for a family row. I'd snuck out of the house whilst Rosamond kept her sister distracted, and nearly walked into a sodden young Divisioner in the street – the skittish one about whom I'd speculated (but I don't wish to presume, so I'll keep the speculations to myself). We'd repaired to my house, I'd fixed her haircut and adopted her ferret – *not* a silly little euphemism – and all had been scented baths and pleasant conversation. It only took two more days before anyone saw fit to tell me that Divisioner was Henry Nettleblack, the youngest sibling, Rosamond's favourite relation in a prodigal disguise.

"Remember Eddie wanted to talk to me?"

I frowned. *That* conversation, I'd missed. "Go on."

"It was about Henry first. Where she was hiding, how to find her, me suggesting we just let her escape. Then I started poking holes in Edwina's marriage plots, so she told me to get out. But I didn't. I pushed it. I pushed her. And she – she – "

"What?"

She blinked. With reason. Gracious, she was crying.

"She said she would never give up on me. She said her dear friend Lady Miltonwaters – you know, the awful one – had told her she should put me in an asylum, see if that fixed my defects. She said heaven knew any asylum would take me, with the spectacle I'd made of myself – the tricks I'd played to get rid of suitors, the mad things I'd spent her money on, the way I dressed, my hair, my Welsh – you can add my preferences too, not that I think she *understands* them. She said that, for my own good, I really shouldn't push her anymore – not now I knew what the consequence would be."

You will not like it if I have to ask again.

I couldn't move. Rather more to my horror, I couldn't speak either.

"Of course I didn't want to tell you. And then – cariad, you nearly died. You'd schemed our escape on your own, and I'd been stupid and complacent and terrified enough to let you, and you *nearly died*. If I'd said anything while you were facing the Sweetings – whispered *by the way, Eddie's sending me to an asylum* while Maggie was breaking your face – you would have been straight over to Catfish Crescent to defend my honour next, never mind how fragile you are! And Edwina would have trapped you too! And you barely escaped an asylum the first time!"

With all the disproportionate effort of throwing off a nightmare, I closed my eyes. Opened them again. Pinned myself, careful and thorough as a pattern-piece, to everything in the room. Dying fire, naturalist wallpaper, spider-seamed four-poster, sibling sketches on the wall, warmth and silk and the green-set monochrome of Rosamond's face.

"I'm sorry," I stammered. "I had no idea."

She sighed. "That was the point, cariad."

My thoughts spluttered, the first flares of a fresh-lit candle. *Find her a defence.*

"And I'm sorry I kept it from you. I just – I knew what you'd do. What you'd think. You know what you're like – I have to tie you down to get you out of your head – "

What had Henry said about Edwina, before the Sweetings turned on me, tangled in all the other revelations? *She's engaged – to a lyric tenor – and our family tailor – same person –*

Rosamond grabbed my chin. "Are you doing it *again?*"

"The family tailor," I blurted. "Edwina's secret engagement. She has her own illicit liaison to protect – no wonder she's reaching for such an extreme. And – we could – yes, the secret could ruin her, but it wouldn't *endanger* her – "

"No!"

"Darling?"

Her jaw tightened. "I won't blackmail her. I can't – not – just – no."

"Va bene." I kissed her, very gently, against the bitterness in her voice – buoyed, I admit, by a sudden weird relief. "I didn't much want to either."

Quiet curled up around us, a thing of fidgety windowpanes and crumbling logs.

"Are you alright?" she whispered, as if I'd not leeched the question from her far too many times. Never mind *Narcissus*; I'd have to find her a new nickname. "You – asylums – I didn't want to – "

"Quite alright." I would be, if she needed it. "As you say, they never got me into one."

"How did you stop it?"

Her voice cracked, as if she'd meant not to ask and felt the words scramble out regardless. Then her eyes widened – "You don't have to tell me – not if you don't want – and, for the love of your every limb, please do not start turning it into a scheme – "

"No, I can tell you."

And I can tell you too, if you keep the secret with me.

You may well scoff, or scold Rosamond for her lurid fascination, or (if you've sympathy left for me) cry *the poor dandy's splintering enough as it is!* But my darling was proffering me a lifeline in this nervous request – the very one I needed. *Talk, cariad! Turn yourself into elegant spiel, and transform your every frightening memory into a hard gem-like anecdote! Preen atop your creation, far too much its designer to be its victim, Pip Property to excelsis!*

I scooped her from the chair and settled us in bed. Tucked her head, with all due gratitude, into my shoulder, held her too close to shiver, stared out the dusty sag of the canopy. She slid a hand under my dressing-gown, splayed her fingers over my heartbeat.

"I was younger than you, sweet. The worst debutante of the season. I made it the *debut* for my white tie and cropped hair, though Mamma dragged me out of the palace before the Queen saw me. I thought I'd proved my point with the risk – if she didn't believe I knew myself before, surely I was unavoidable now!"

The palace corridor stank. It had been a devil of a job to slip away, after three stagnant hours queuing with neither sustenance nor seat. I remember ducking into an alcove, tearing from the gown until I tore it in earnest, picking free the pieces of suit I'd tacked inside the skirts and train. I remember the gasps, all the way back up the corridor, like the steady inevitability of a murmuration taking flight – wide eyes, trembling ostrich feathers, the scuffle to clear my path.

And I remember Mamma, next in the presentation queue, frozen in horror as every scandalised stare slid from me to her.

"But a few weeks later, when Father was out teaching undergraduates the secrets of terza rima, two gentlemen and a lady paid us a visit. Confound Mamma, she was clever – she trapped me at the first infernal pronoun. Between that, and my name, and my attire, and my antipathy for compromise, and the visitors' smiling fascination with everything I said – I talked myself into trouble, just as she knew I would."

The strangers beamed at me. It was a difficult angle; we were in their carriage, rattling out of Bedford Square, and they hemmed me on either side – the bulkier gentleman ended up sat outside with the driver. Mamma disappeared from the square of window, shoulders trembling, gloved hand at her mouth.

"An ideal candidate," the lady effused, squeezing my hand. The man clapped my shoulder, and didn't let go. "A tremendous opportunity!"

I smirked. Thinking of Father, of fencing, of showing off, of another posed picture for his medievalism journal. "Much obliged to you! Might I ask what the opportunity is?"

Their grip tightened as one. "Why, you, my dear."

"The lackeys gave the game away. I thought myself about to grace some elegant research project – but *I* was the project. For someone to research, and ideally cure. As the interview had shown, I was unarguably insane, and Signora Property's suggestion of time in a genteel asylum for wayward ladies was apt indeed."

One arm clenched around my neck. Another slammed across my knees. The lady's hands bit into mine, pressing them together. Alone, they weren't strong – but there were two of them, and they'd readied their grip.

"Don't struggle, Miss Property, we only want to help you! Think how ashamed you'd be – five, ten, twenty years from now – if no one checked you in your disturbed fancies! You can't play the principal boy in your life, dear – and in front of the Queen, too!"

Then, when I didn't stop screaming – "Get the chloral."

"I hadn't proved a damned thing. I hadn't changed Mamma's mind. And I lost, there and then, the delight of having a foe as sharp and theatrical as I, a nemesis content to keep our battles familial. Believe me, darling, I know how *that* feels."

I froze. Somehow.

"Wait! Don't – I'm calm. I'm sorry. I don't need chloral. Look."

They looked – close, peering, hot breath in my eyes, faces flushed from the struggle. The man nodded curtly. "Signora Property didn't mention anything about – fits."

"Of course not!" *the woman gushed.* "Docile, *I think, was her description. And whyever wouldn't you be, a pretty little debutante like you?"*

Docile?

The rest terrified me. The lie made me furious.

I hardly breathed until their arms withdrew – until their hands slackened – until they'd both sat back and settled in their corners. The woman's eyes were still shining.

"I don't know what's confused you, but I promise we can get rid of it. No need for tears and torment. We won't let you hurt yourself anymore, and you'll be the lovely young lady you are before you know it!"

Va bene. Tell them I'm docile. *Don't tell them I've had a decade of rapier lessons.*

"As to how I stopped it – well! I simply waited my moment, then threw myself out of the carriage. I was faster than them both, you see, and defter too with the bolt on the door. I could find my way to King's College from anywhere in London – I knew Father's word would be credited where I'd scuppered all trust in mine."

I tumbled into the lecture hall. Dusty, filthy, shedding street and horses' hoof-pickings. Grabbed the benches to drag myself the last of the way. The undergraduates cringed in their ill-fitting suits; it was Canto Fifteen week, and I must have resembled one of Dante's sprinting sodomites –

"Father was outraged, of course. Changed his very will by way of retort, crafted an inheritance for me that no one could touch, no matter what might be claimed about my soundness of mind."

"Pip! They won't come out. Gracious, Ditta, what were you thinking?"

"I was thinking of our family," Mamma snapped, shaky-voiced beyond my bedroom door. I curled my fingers tighter around my rapier; it was clumsy and I knew it, but I couldn't stop choking the hilt. "Our families. You do not realise what she has done, Ralph. The danger she is in – has put us all in! If it continues – if it becomes known that the business at court was not a single, curable moment of madness – if it is said that we indulge such perversion – "

"Then we'll go back to Venice! Wait with the Participazios until everyone forgets!"

"My family will not countenance it either. She was meant to marry wealth!"

Father's voice was cold. "To send yet more wealth to restore the Participazio ca', in a glorified tomb of a city?"

"Do not speak to me as if this is my fault. Our only child – our only daughter, for all she wishes to deny it – unsexed herself in front of your queen. I have been cut in society for a week. Do not tell me there have not been questions raised at the university about your position."

"Nothing I can't address." He scoffed, sharp and determined. "Nothing another monograph won't fix."

"You cannot simply write a monograph every time she humiliates us! What if it does not stop? What if she does worse? It is your livelihood at stake too, caro! We have to be seen to be doing something – "

"Like throwing Pip to the wolves?"

"The place was respectable." Mamma's voice crumpled. "In the countryside. There was a fishpond. It is not what you think – the owners were kind. I told them not to use force. Perhaps, you know, they would have fixed her."

"There's nothing to fix," he snarled. "If saving our reputation means destroying Pip, then let's be pariahs all!"

"Maledizione, Ralph, these are our lives you wish to – "

"Go, Ditta. You've done enough for today."

And then, soft through the keyhole, after her footsteps had

stumbled away: "It's alright, Pip. I promise. Come out, now – you can put the sword down."

I cracked the door a notch, let him ease the rapier from me, wept into his shoulder –

I cleared my throat.

"So you see, darling? Here I am, ten years later, unscathed. And Mamma never dared try again, not after I thwarted her. I think she told the Participazios I'd become a nun."

Rosamond snorted, half-asleep, a drowsy twitch of derision – and I smiled, at last. Anything to quicken her smirks, and her broken confidence, and her belief in my capabilities. She'd sleep tonight, too tangled up in me for a nightmare to touch her –

And she'd have all the liberty I could give her, all her faith in my *schemes* restored, when tomorrow rushed to meet us.

CHAPTER FIVE

I AM A MONSTROUS HYPOCRITE

The Notebook of Doom, intensified

Concerning Monday 20th November 1893

N. B. The first part of this segment is strictly confidential, and only to be shared (within a trusted circle) with the express permission of Mr. Matthew Adelstein. I trust he will understand the reason for the request – and that you, Divisioners, will know to respect it.

I was awake long before the sky. Rosamond slept late, while I crept about her room with a taper, and the kites on the walls watched me curiously from the shadows. I had nothing to pack beyond Earlyfate – much as it wrenched my soul, my white tie was past rescuing – but I could still curate a suitcase for Rosamond. Given what I had to work with in her adolescent wardrobe, it would be composed primarily of fisherman's jumpers, but that was no less bizarre than her Morris drapery; I'm rather the sartorial component of our relationship, even in a borrowed suit and curtain cravat. And if I took last night's revelations as my compass, Rosamond would hardly want to visit her Dallyangle house for a change of clothes.

Her house! Faugh, as the novelettes would say. That preening mausoleum had only ever been Edwina's.

I set my teeth, folding knitwear by feeble candlelight, kneading jumpers flat until my knuckles itched. Of course I'd always known, in a peripheral sort of way, that the eldest Nettleblack was a tyrant. I'd seen her butler nip at Rosamond's heels for speaking Welsh, and my darling never left the house without a tiptoe sneak. And in four years of dealing with Edwina and lying to Edwina and growing bolder as Edwina failed to notice her sister's teeth on my neck – gracious, I'd never met a colder fish! Those monstrous tweed gowns, the pale colours of her face and hair, that frozen-puddle expression, the finicky voice half-strangled by its desperation not to show a Welsh accent. A *fussy* despot, I'd thought, a little queen in a kingdom of polite society. Someone to be gleefully thwarted, not seriously afraid of.

Idiocy. Inexcusable idiocy, from me. Polite society and asylum threats were two colours in the same wretched pattern.

I was sketching paisleys – a swarm, crashing across the nettle-headed scrap paper like elegant Valkyries, the only anxious habit I could indulge in perfect silence – when sleep relinquished Rosamond. She groaned, shedding blankets as she twisted towards the light; we had it from the window now, a freezing slant of sun and a sea-breeze that rattled the panes. "Cariad, what –?"

"Morning, darling!" I waved my pencil at her from the armchair. I'd made a bower of the seat, draped it with her suitcase and my swordstick, and the jacket I meant to whirl into as she dressed. "Scrambled eggs – if I'm permitted them?"

She rolled her eyes, spitting tendrils of hair. "I wanted to have you before scrambled eggs."

"Flattering as that preference is, we've rather a lot to do this morning. For a start, we need to get to Swansea."

It cracked her bleary smile. "Why?"

"There'll be transport there. Never fear, we're packed already. We'll be back in Dallyangle by nightfall."

"What?" She recoiled, sharp and frightened, back against the pillows. "I can't – "

"You can." I smiled – a smile perfectly curated to embolden, to reassure, to meet her every need and match them tenfold – or so I hoped. "Don't worry, it's the politest scheme I've ever invented."

Now she looked unabashedly horrified. "Pip, for God's sake –!"

"Edwina won't know you're back. You'll hide in my house – I'll say you're already on the Continent. The funds can be settled – if the Division have caught the Sweetings, they can give me back my savings – if not, I'll devise an alternative. A respectable alternative. I'll sell the chaise – I'll rent out my house – and I'll give up the rent on the Sweetings' attic – on the cravat shop, if I have to. Whatever you need. And then, my sweet, we've our escape assured!"

This would be gallantry worthy of admiration, would it not? To sacrifice a cravat shop and an expensive bath, to consign myself to another banishment, all to rescue my beloved from the same familial machinations to which I hadn't succumbed? Gracious, the poetry of it! The elegance! A plan, at last, worthy of Pip Property!

"The Division won't help us."

Until one sorry sentence snagged the whole wretched weave of it.

"Well – I – they'll have to! They wouldn't withhold my savings. Most of them don't even know I worked with the Sweetings. Septimus let me go, told them I wasn't a threat – "

"Not her. Your neighbour. Matthew Adelstein."

What? "That prim detective's never credited a word of slander about me – "

"Detective! Exactly!" Her voice was shrill, her hands twisted tight in the bedsheets. "He lives on your street – you don't think he'll notice me hiding in your house? And I can't do it – I don't *want* to do it – it only worked for Henry's sake – "

"Do what?"

I was sharper, perhaps, than I ought to have been. But I had just offered to uproot my life, far more thoroughly than the original plan had ever demanded – why was she snicking at the gesture with yet more mysterious qualms?

"Nothing," she blurted. I arched an eyebrow. "Or – no, not nothing – but I – "

"What?" It was a supreme effort to keep my tone measured.

58

"Gracious, not another secret?"

She coloured, as well she might.

"If you'd told me Henry was hiding in the Division, I might have devised a better escape plan. If you'd told me about Edwina's threats, I might have devised an answer to them *before* your manservant's correspondence forced us out of this house. Rosamond, I need you to stop doubting my capacities – I need you to confide in me!"

"And I need you to promise you won't despise me!"

I froze. The wind didn't; in the sudden silence, it was clattering the panes worse than ever.

"I did it for Henry," she stammered, half terrified half defiant. "Before we left. I didn't want to! But Edwina had Matthew Adelstein looking for her, and he found her, and – by then I knew what Edwina was capable of – so I made him leave her alone. The only way I could."

"What – ?"

"Fine!" she cried, flinging up her hands. "Ready to stare into my terrible depths? I blackmailed him, Pip. He's in love with his lodger – the rat-breeding chap – and very bad at hiding it. I told him I'd call gross indecency on them both unless he stopped chasing Henry."

A bitter little smile. "Still promise you don't hate me?"

I stared at her. I had been strained already, but this broke all my threads at once, yanked me straight out of pattern until my thoughts hadn't shapes. She curled up on the bed, raw and messy as an underdrawing – a miserable composition altogether, a countenance that should have spurred me across the room with embraces and reassurance –

But the *Blackmailer's Charter* –

Rosamond, my darling, what have you done?

If I'd just kept her safe –

"You have to apologise." Every word shook; even now, I can't discern whether it was terror or anger, nor for whom it was meant. "To Adelstein. To his lover. You have to tell them that it was monstrous hypocrisy – that you've no intention of carrying out the threat."

She winced, knees to her chin, voice a sullen tremulous mutter. "But it's never monstrous hypocrisy when it's you, is it?"

I choked. "I – I beg your pardon?"

"You." Her head jerked up; she was biting the words out of the air. "You can abandon your morals when your safety's at stake. But the moment *I* dare to do it – "

"I would never put someone at risk of *prison* – "

"You don't know what you'd do. You don't have siblings."

"Saving Henry should not mean stooping to Edwina's level!"

She sprang off the bed just as I slammed back the chair, as stark and sudden as if I had slapped her. Hair spiralling from its knot, nightgown creased and shoulders bare, face blotched with terrifying fury, a green-eyed glare that made blackthorns of my veins. I saw it on her – self-loathing straight out of my mirror, pulled taut and defensive as a bowstring –

"Shall we look at what you *have* done, Pip? Scheming, blameless, never-stooping Pip? The paragon of charm who couldn't stand to lose face to burglars – who invented a criminal enterprise just to stop the Sweetings stealing their fine home furnishings! The gallant who tricked their admirers into the Sweetings' traps, and stole the hair off every pretty girl in Dallyangle, and broke Division Sergeant Septimus's heart *and* career in the doing! The chivalrous lover who kidnapped my little sister – and gave her to the Sweetings too! The sartorial saint who apologised to – let me think – precisely *no one* at any point in these proceedings! Who owes half these wronged Divisionary souls their life, after they had to be rescued from their own ridiculous plan – and still didn't bother to say sorry!"

It veered into my face like a wasp. "I – "

"And at what point, pray tell, did I start ordering you to do penance? At what point did I stop believing you had your reasons? I forgave you every time! I calmed you down, I kept you sane – "

"Kept me *what?*"

Her eyes widened. She stumbled the last of the distance, fingers stiff and convulsing in my shirtfront. Beneath her grip, my heartbeat was far too fast; it was shaking her, shaking both of us.

"Please, Pip. I didn't mean – I only – but we're as bad as each other, aren't we? Just as ruthless when threatened – just as poisonous. Please. It isn't only me. Don't act as if it's only me. And don't you *dare* throw my guilt at me like you haven't got any!"

She gasped for breath – once, twice, her colour draining – hissed *not again* – and buried her face in her hands.

I clenched my fists. It was all I had to stop me from doing the same.

The very room was trembling – the chimney groaning, gutted by the breeze, the sound of the windowpanes like fingernails on glass. The bedsheets curdled over the floor. Earlyfate had skidded off its slant on the chair, without either of us noticing. The paisley sketch sprawled beside it, my pencil-lines inelegantly smudged.

You are not poisonous, I wanted to whisper to her – or me – or both. If I – if I even deserved – if I could be sure in my case that it was true –

"I'm going outside. We can finish this discussion in a calmer state."

She nodded, smothered in her hands, snatching thin panic-breaths through her fingers.

Villain that I am, I left her there.

The gorse-bushes clustered to upbraid me, bare and skinny in the wintry sun, writhing in tandem with the sea below. The wind clawed back my hair as I staggered out of the gates – I'd let it get stupidly overlong – and scratched at my eyelashes until they were thick with tears. Not *true* tears, of course, simply the weather's pale imitation. Sobbing is beneath my dignity now; I haven't crumpled beneath the impulse for four years straight.

I'd left my jacket behind. The breeze dragged me forward, unfazed by my shivering shirtsleeves, dropped me between two thuggish heaps of gorse by the cliff-edge. Panic twisted in my throat: the sea, my lost native element, had already betrayed me once this month, and now there was far too much of it below me, white-tipped and churning.

"There's surely a limit to this wretched Byronism," – and I'm amazed I managed to splutter it through my chattering teeth. "She's – not wrong – but that hardly means I can't put it right. And I *did* apologise to Septimus! More or less!"

Despite all tempestuous interferences, talking was settling me. Even if my only audience was a thrashing mob of shrubbery. If it worked – and it *had* to work –

"Rosamond shan't despise herself. I won't let her. Confound these Nettleblacks and their wretched self-deprecation! And confound how infectious it is!"

Gracious, was it too much to commence unabashedly yelling at the sea?

"Va bene! Is it not enough to save Rosamond from her terrible sister? Must I clear my debt to the Division too – find them the Sweetings, clasp the hands of every Divisioner I've wronged, burn through my charm until they forgive me? You don't think I can manage it? Ha! Don't you know who I *am?*"

Then, of all the demented impulses, I had to laugh. High, giddy, scorching in the throat. I truly was the Italianate fiend of Gareth's nightmares – arrogant and oddly dressed, bellowing Pobbles Beach into submission!

Wait.

Gareth.

Idiot, Property!

I whirled round, sprinted into a wall of wind. Grabbed the gate so wildly the nettles sliced my palms, smashed the shells underfoot, wrestled the front door from its swollen frame. Scrambled for the stairs – dashed against my last scrap of sense – and stopped, bedraggled and breathless, one flight from Rosamond's floor.

Murmurs from above. He had her alone. If he resorted to full Cymraeg, I was finished.

Absolutely not, I thought, with roughly the same vehemence with which I'd shrieked off the clifftop, and crept up the stairs.

"Dw i'n iawn, yn wir." Rosamond's voice was small, even with a door between us. I closed my eyes, clawed through a translation: *she's placating him*. "I'm not upset."

"You can tell me, Miss Rosamond," Gareth urged. "If that Property chap – " (must he?) " – has been causing you grief – "

"It's not Pip's fault. And they're not a chap." She sniffed. "I'm the problem, Ga. As usual."

I bit my knuckles. It was that or start snarling exasperated dissent.

"Beg pardon, miss, for the indelicate question, but – it's not the money, is it? You haven't – ah – lost it? *Pip* hasn't stolen it from you – or made you spend it, or – ?"

What?

"Money?"

"You mustn't think I'd judge you." I flattened myself to the door; his voice was softening into a murmur. "Nor that I'd be shocked. Miss Edwina told me, you know, about the other times – the ferret incident – and I only want to help – "

"I don't have any money."

He yelped like a dog underfoot.

"Ga? That's not new, I've never had money – "

"But your inheritance?" he wailed. "Miss Edwina only kept it until you turned twenty-one! What about that money?"

Maledizione – what about it indeed!

To capture the lot in a suitably stunned description: it was as if the very ceiling had cracked above me, and the sky above the ceiling, until a spiralling ladder of a Jacobean persuasion came tumbling down, inches from my nettle-scratched hands, every rung emblazoned with a Wonderland incentive. *Eat me! Drink me! Investigate me! Climb me, immediately, out of your mutual helplessness!*

"I thought you'd lost everything," Gareth spluttered,

obliviously, "When you dismissed the servants – when you and that *Pip* started living off my wages – and I didn't want to pry, but I can't just keep you forever, and I don't know what else to – "

At which vital moment, I kicked the door down.

They jumped as one. Gareth clasped his hands about Rosamond's shoulders, face scalded to the most scandalised frown yet. She just gaped at me, eyes raw and hair unravelled, swathed in the dressing-gown I'd been borrowing, fingers gouging into its collar.

"You have an independent inheritance?" I demanded, for want of anything else in my head. I doubt I could have looked more like a fortune-hunter.

Gareth, of course, promptly snapped. "Now see here, Property – !"

"How do you know what Rosamond should have? What is she owed?"

"If you think I'd give that out to a barefaced stranger – "

"*I* don't know!" Rosamond cried, twisting out of his grip. "I thought Tad left everything to Edwina!"

His jaw dropped. "But that's not true – I witnessed his will, God rest him – Mr. Morgan gave all three of you Nettleblacks a third of the fortune, and – and – "

I tried – I truly did – not to glitter too blindingly with sheer vindication. "And Edwina should have given Rosamond her share when she came of age. Two years ago. Yes?"

"Two years?" Rosamond echoed, with fearless fury so reassuring it was all I could do not to fling myself at her feet. "Eddie's been stealing my money for *two years?* Two years I could have been out of that house – free of her threats – nowhere even *near* an asylum?"

Gareth, having been neck-deep in the proverbial fire ever since I interrupted him, was now consummately burnt. His knees buckled, and down he went, crumpling into a chair with the look of a man who could be reached by neither scrambled eggs nor Nettleblack's Tincture.

Rosamond met my eyes, and I hers. For a moment, there was nothing but the quiet combustion of Gareth's gasps.

I swallowed. "About what I said earlier, I – I didn't mean – "

"Neither did I," she interrupted, with a strained little smile. "I've been a fool. So have you. Shall we – not be, for five minutes?"

If it kept us in smiles, in bright defiant stares, above the fear and the panic and the horrible self-loathing – gracious, it was hardly a question. I nodded dazedly. "Go on."

"We need to pay back Ga's wages."

"Most assuredly."

"I need to apologise to Adelstein."

"I need to be even more thorough!"

"We need to tell Henry she's safe – she's twenty-one, she can be as safe as me. And then we – we can do whatever we want – Edwina can't stop us – "

Then she blanched. "Bugger everything, but she can!"

"What? Why?"

"She has Tad's will. The original. Keeps it locked in her desk. I nearly goaded her into thwacking me with it once, but that's the closest I've ever been. And it's our proof this is true!"

"Surely there must be a copy?"

"I can make enquiries," Gareth faltered, staring up from his torment. "In Swansea. The solicitors. And I can testify what I witnessed, for what that's worth. It's the least I – after I – Miss Rosamond, I am so sorry – "

I sighed. "When did you write to Edwina, Mr. Evans?"

He shrank in the chair, as panic jolted across Rosamond's face. "I posted it this morning. But I was only trying to keep you safe – I didn't know – "

"Let me guess. You told our dear sororial despot that Rosamond had fallen under the sway of a sword-wielding androgyne with a silly name, a scar, and no satisfying explanation for their existence, evidently intent on ruining the young miss's prospects unless her elder sister swept in? Intent on stealing her stolen inheritance too, no doubt?"

He flushed. "Miss Rosamond, I – "

"No!" she snarled. "No more decisions over my head! If you've warned her – *and* told her where I am – I won't give her time to plan a counter-attack! You make your enquiries and hold the fort here – I'll get out of her way – we're going back to Dallyangle to get that will – and don't you dare give me that victorious smirk, Pip Property, or you'll be flat to the floor before you can quip!"

I grinned. It was among my last moments of unbridled elation – let me have it, why don't you? "With pleasure."

She twitched an eyebrow. I slackened my cravat.

Gareth simply staggered from the room.

CHAPTER SIX

I AM AT DALLYANGLE'S MERCY

The Notebook of Doom, commencing doom in earnest

Still concerning the same damnable date

It was at this point, Divisioners, that everything got worse.

It's also when *you* hurl yourselves into my business. If that's a coincidence, I'm – well, not locked in your morgue with a notebook, I suppose. You seem to have forgotten that fact, given I've written this much without even an interruption. Perhaps you've gone to sleep. My watch stopped at ten-thirty, and I've no reference to wind it – no windows either, not that the Dallyanglian rainstorm would tell me anything.

But the time, whatever it is, is *perilously inconvenient.*

Why? I'll tell you! And you shan't interrupt!

To sweep back to this morning – when I was in Wales, and Rosamond had just blossomed into an heiress in earnest, and for the first time in fifteen days a scurrilous secret had *helped.* In the secret's immediate wake, I was on the bedroom floor, with Rosamond on top of me, gasping for every twitch of my fingers. She bent over me when she'd finished, grabbed my jaw as her hair curtained our faces, bit my lip until she had me pleading – then sprang to her feet, the Cambrian minx, one hand out to drag me after her. *We've a busy schedule, didn't you say?*

When the desire settled, and we were inhaling the fastest scrambled eggs known to guilty Welshman (eggs, for me; gracious, Gareth was in apologetic mood!) – *then*, our every touch was tentative, our words sand-edged and nervously polite. We didn't mention our quarrel; an onlooker wouldn't have guessed we'd had one. But we both peered for permission before clasping hands, and clasped all the tighter for permission received.

Later, obviously, I'd restore amends. I'd escort her to Matthew Adelstein's house, and watch him slump as she hauled her blackmail off his shoulders. I'd swallow my pride – in a gallant and elegant way – and let her escort me to Septimus, to Henry, to anyone and everyone who required *my* apologies. I'd hold her close, in my bed, in my hard-won house, and whisper away the self-hatred seething under her skin: *you are not an appalling person, simply a person contending with an appalling position. And I shan't be a monstrous hypocrite anymore, I promise –*

Later. When we had the will, and she was as liberated as Father's will had made me.

Not that the will would take credit for salvaging us! The whirligigs of fortune and an unexpected inheritance was a boon beyond imagining – but the repair of our sorry selves was our prerogative. And what a luxury it was, that'd we'd have space and security in which to do it!

So we left the clifftop. Gareth took us out in an open-topped gig, drove slowly enough that I hardly noticed the house receding until he leapt down to lock the nettle gates on it. I hadn't a hat, so I touched my forehead in salute to the gorse-bushes on the track, writhing in the wind like the weird spiky dryads they were. Rosamond strained for one last red-chim-neyed glimpse, then bit her lip and squeezed my hand hard. I, meanwhile, was obliged to slacken my grip on Earlyfate, when Gareth called our destination from the driver's bench: "Swansea station, of course! There's a train under the Severn now, don't you know – goodness gracious, Miss Rosamond, whyever did you come here by boat?"

He paid for our tickets, with another mumbled apology. He nearly lost his footing when Rosamond embraced him – gracious, I could have told him of her astounding capacity for forgiveness! Under the rickety metal Gothic of the platform canopy, he actually offered me his hand, the sort of frank-palmed grip that suggested he hadn't abandoned the *Property chap* idea.

"You look after her, alright? If I'd known her sister was doing her wrong, I would never have – "

"Of course." I gave the poor man a smile; I was feeling benevolent too. "Rosamond does rather compel one to desperate things. Diolch for the meals, they were superlative."

He nodded gravely. "Pob lwc, bach."

Then Rosamond was urging me towards the quietest carriage, hair frizzing in the steam, and Gareth was a loaf-coloured smudge behind a grubby window, and the train's wheels were shuddering under our feet. Rosamond craned, again, and I followed her gaze. It made me scoff: I'd lived on the Grand Canal, named the San Marco horses, cut my suits in marble-fronted London shops – yet there I was, truly sorry to part from my darling's fey little peninsula.

"We'll come back?" she murmured.

Well, I was hardly Edwina. "I believe your phrasing would be *wrth gwrs?*"

She curled my fingers from the swordstick, kissed my palm until I gasped.

Even we didn't risk more on a train (yet), so the journey was spent in delightful daydream. The frayed edges of Dallyangle lay before me, ready to be trimmed into a sensible shape. My house, all hot water and Florentine soap. The Division, a bastion of harmless gratitude, graciously accepting my gracious apologies, with the Sweetings graciously retired from their ungracious burgling. Edwina Nettleblack, stripped of stolen power and threats, banished from Rosamond's life. Matthew Adelstein and his rat-breeding lover, beaming for our new-sworn silence. And then – *finally* – the Continent and the

Disraeli tour, everywhere that wasn't Venice, anywhere with good food and better fabrics and sun to polish Rosamond's hair!

I smiled. Not the prospects of a *mess*, I think you'll agree.

But then you Divisioners have always had such a mania for ruining my life.

Much as Rosamond wishes it otherwise, it's a troublesome journey from Swansea to Dallyangle. Four trains, if you count the London Underground; Rosamond, sweet sea-breezed innocent, spent that part coughing like a consumptive, to the sullen alarm of everybody in the carriage. We both breathed easier when the Waterloo train slung London behind us. By now, the sky was navy as my best greatcoat, the carriage thin and sparsely occupied – for who would leave the capital on a Saturday night for the joys of bad provincial theatre? Suburbs flattened into fields, until the darkness flattened everything. Rosamond dozed with her head on my shoulder, and I sat with my pocketwatch, hoping every station ours and sighing when they weren't. How late was too late for a house-call, when one's scheme was something shaky and half-formed between squabble and theft? Did we risk waiting another day – by which time Edwina might well have outmanoeuvred us? Could I risk stealing Morgan Nettleblack's will, *and* still manage a charming apology for Henry and Septimus?

I have to confess, though you won't like it: not once did I consider enlisting the Division. Sweet vigilantes, do recall that Edwina commissioned you to hunt a missing sibling barely two weeks ago – can you blame me?

Dallyangle!

We staggered from the train, Rosamond still yawning, and nearly blew off the platform. The wind was almost as bad as the cliffs, damp with the threat of impending rain, yanking the station gaslamps so frantically they could hardly fix on my watch-face. It was eight o'clock, bitterly cold, and quiet beneath the shrieks and rattles of the wind. The square about the station hadn't a human soul to it – only spirit-photograph silhouettes behind curtained windows, and a few ancient Halloween turnips blown across the street in rotting dregs. Every lamp palsied at the breeze's behest, and their epileptic shadows made things jump: doorways blinked, cobblestones rippled, and turnip-innards crept greasily closer.

The taxi-rank was empty, beyond the carriage I'd had to abandon there – but the latter had been pilfered of a horse. Not that we had any money.

Rosamond shuddered. "We have to walk?"

I flushed. Gracious, Pip, don't you spoil your beloved?

"It'll be fine. It's hardly the witching hour – over at the theatre, Frederic will only be on his second tantrum about the nursemaid's age – "

"I meant the weather! We'll be drenched! And you don't have a coat!"

"You do. I'll manage. Straight up the town to my house, and then I'll see about a rustic meal – my credit should still be good at the pie-shop. If you want to try for the will tonight – "

Then I caught myself. *No more decisions over my head.* "Unless you've a preferred alternative?"

She beamed at me. "Let's get to yours first. And – diolch, cariad."

For eight o'clock, it was desolate. We passed the odd carriage, drivers bundled against the thickening rain, and occasionally glimpsed figures crossing the end of a street – but nothing like the usual evening bustle. If the town was still packing out the theatre for *The Pirates of Penzance*, we truly were in the dregs of the fin de siècle – though the weather was perhaps the more obvious culprit. Bareheaded to the freezing wind, hair soaked to my scalp, clutching Rosamond's hand until my knuckles were almost as pale as hers, *I* would have tolerated more than Mr. Gilbert's irritating lyrics for the sake of a roof.

I'd forgotten how loud the cobblestones were. By unspoken accord, we were striding forth with the smugness of dragoons

– or certainly aiming for it – and our progress outclattered the storm: our boot-heels, scraped free of mud, and the asymmetrical rap of the swordstick. We kept to a straight line, to streets wide enough for carriages, to places with enough lamps for us to guess the colours of the houses' front doors. Gangly tenements gave way to red-brick cottages, though even they were hard-pressed to look cheerful in this twitching puck-light. Eventually – with a sodden yelp of delight from Rosamond – we reached Angle Drag, the broadest thoroughfare, currently a blur of puddles and carriages. A quick dash across, leaping the glittering gaps in the cobbles – ducking between two drivers, both oblivious to the possibility of pedestrians – past the neoclassical toad of the town hall, up into Pole Place –

My street. Four houses to pass before we struck mine. I couldn't see it yet – everything in Dallyangle curves like a fish-hook, and these streetlamps were as wind-harried as the others – but the closeness still urged us to a run.

Or, at least, it would have, had we not collided immediately with two sprinting silhouettes. Everyone toppled. I scrambled up first, offered a hand, pure chivalrous reflex –

Rosamond didn't take it. But Maggie Sweeting did.

"Bloody hell!" she cried, springing off the cobbles like a shattered puddle. "Norman, it's our treacherous toff!"

I don't fully know how to explain that particular terror: when something that would happen in a nightmare, that *has* happened in your nightmares, that conforms only to the unhinged logic of unpleasant sleep – when that something starts happening in waking earnest, to far more of your senses than mere imagination. As I shied back and yanked my hand free, I *felt* the scratch of her gloves, and the gap where she'd lost a finger to the Nettleblack ferret. In rain this relentless, the wax on her coat stank. Everything in my chest buckled inwards, fear so sharp it was practically insurrection –

But I had wit enough to draw the swordstick. And that I resoundingly did.

Behind me, Rosamond splashed to her feet. Behind Maggie, the flickers of light were assembling Norman. He followed his sister's gaze with a loose-hinged jaw (as is his wont), then grabbed her arm – biceps jostling in the raincoat, just as strong as hers, the pair of them a towering advertisement for Muscular Criminality –

"Not now, Maggie!" he gasped. "Bigger problems!"

Maggie glowered at him, a quick silent squabble. I jumped – jumped again – the whirling lamps kept tugging movements from their stillness, light snagging and shifting on the creases in their gloves.

Far too swiftly, a sprawling groan: "Oh, brother, you're no fun!"

Then they both flinched. Between their shoulders – clattering, snorting, bulging towards us – a carriage was hurtling round the Catfish Crescent corner.

"Maggie!" Norman yelped – and bolted past me.

Two sharp looks from him to the approaching carriage – a rain-mottled roll of her eyes – and then Maggie kicked off the cobbles after him –

But she stopped. Grabbed Earlyfate at the blade, dragged me close to her. Of course she'd snatch the sharpened edges; I'd seen her climb a broken window without wincing.

"Sorry, Pip," she growled, breathlessness tearing her words like half-cut pages. "Not tonight. You were right though – there's nothing worth stealing in your house!"

I couldn't slacken my hold on the sword. I could barely move. "My – what – ?"

"Check your property, I would." She grinned, with the face of a woman who truly thinks herself the first to make the joke. "Welcome home, traitor!"

She seized my shoulder – I couldn't dodge, terror cramping my every limb – and flung me up the street. The speeding carriage was far too close, its lanterns scorching holes in my vision. The cobbles blurred, blazed – the horse snorted half the storm into my face –

Not for the first – or last – time that evening, my existence tumbled into Rosamond's hands. Her elbow round my waist snagged us off the road, out of the carriage's path; I saw it bucking, trying to halt, the driver having noticed movement beyond the rain on their hat-brim. Then the carriage vanished: Rosamond had cupped my face, squinting at me through sodden curls and dripping lashes.

"Beth sy'n bod? Was that – it wasn't – ?"

I shivered, far more violently than I meant to, convulsive between her fingers.

Gracious, you think that's it?

I should have spoken. Never mind *spoken* – and never mind my damnable fear – I should have plaited Rosamond at least three sentences' worth of adventurous pluck, or unfazed wit, or incisive analysis. I should have flicked the Sweetings from our minds, taken her arm, and sprinted us to my door. *Well, darling, whatever strange interlude those two wished to stage for us, they clearly can't stay to see it through!*

I had almost the semblance of it on my tongue – when a total stranger, with arms which can only be described as *contextually unfair*, wrenched me from Rosamond's hold by my lapels and dragged me back into the middle of the street.

"Pip Property?"

What?

"No?" I spluttered.

The lantern on the brougham jolted, sharpening the corners of this new perturbation. An unknown woman, scowling into my face, hatted and gowned like a godly governess, her breath sooty and her teeth alarmingly clean. A valetish man on her heels, and the carriage at his: he jumped down from the driver's bench and scurried over, lit from behind in bristling silhouette. Rosamond, frozen where we'd been, gaping quite as much as the scene deserved. Earlyfate, tugged apart to sword and stick, scattered on the cobblestones.

I was still neck-deep in the Sweetings nightmare. My fear, leftover and lingering, clenched a little tighter round my throat.

"Of course you are," the strange man spat, perfect virtuous vowels. "Or does this town possess more than one wrong-headed dandified androgyne?"

The woman twisted my jacket. "Enabling the Sweetings' escape, were you?"

Rosamond dived through the wind, snatched the woman's shoulder, prised until her fingers paled – with no success. "If you want the Sweetings, we're not *with* them – "

"Enough," the man snapped, grabbing her arms and tugging her away. "I'm afraid that lie won't work on us."

Do something!

But the woman beat me to it. "By the authority of – "

"Not yet," the man muttered.

" – of – of a Concerned Citizen – "

(I can't explain how she capitalised the words, but my eyebrows felt it.)

"I charge you with disturbance of the peace! You control the Sweetings – you dictate their thefts and plan their schemes – you thieve and terrorise with reckless abandon – you have unpicked the civic authority of this town – and you shan't get away with it any longer!"

For one sprawling moment, it shocked the very colour from my mind.

But – that makes no sense – Septimus never told anyone about you and the Sweetings –

"What do you think?" the man hissed. "Will this be enough?"

The woman nodded curtly. "We'll take them both."

"Wait!" – maledizione, words, at last, shrill and painful as a corkscrew in my gullet – "If it's me you want, then let her go!"

Rosamond stared at me. Scalding-eyed, not quite furious and not quite terrified.

"Pip, you utter – right, how's *this* for a preferred alternative?"

She gouged her elbow into the man's stomach, ducked his flailing hands as he tried to snatch her again. Her knees buckled – I gasped, thinking she'd fallen – but she bounced off the cobblestones, sword in one hand and stick in the other, brandishing both at our assailants like a demoted musketeer. She was utterly majestic, gale-twisted and tempest-lit, a goddess to confound every decadent metrical peculiarity, with her sodden hair slicked all to snakes.

"Gwrandewch!" she shrieked. *Listen.* "I am going to *impale* you, in a *creative location*, unless you let go of my cariad *nawr ar unwaith!*"

The woman's fists spasmed on my lapels, but the man blurted before they could slacken – "She doesn't know how to use it."

I absconded responsibility. "That won't stop her."

And thus my glorious, impatient, vengeful Rosamond lunged forward, with an unrepentant snarl and no discernible fencing strategy, and stabbed the woman clean through the hand.

"*Now* we run, you chivalrous dolt!"

The woman dropped me, screeching. We didn't wait. Having missed spontaneous impalement by mere inches of bone and calibration, I prised the swordstick pieces from Rosamond as soon as I was close enough. Their damned carriage was blocking the way to my house, but we baulked as one and skidded round – back towards Angle Drag –

The man swung into our path, shaped from the very rain, fists sickled to grab –

Rosamond's hand slammed between my shoulder-blades. Without exaggeration, I ran for my life.

Maledizione! You think *that's* it?

Pure luck got us across Angle Drag. Without the force of Rosamond's shove, another churn of horse-and-cart would have cracked me on the cobblestones. My world had shrunk, to splintering lungs and skull-rattling breaths, to terror I could neither span nor control, to the leaping shadows of the street ahead. The shopfronts clustered close at Market Square's uppermost corner – too close for the strangers' bulky brougham to jostle through. Beyond them, a slanting diagonal in the slanting rain, there were lights on in the Division.

Then their headquarters flew out of my sight. The whole square did. I'd snagged my boot on a broken-toothed cobble, and the fall threw me forward, helpless with my own momentum. I hadn't even the sense to drop the swordstick, crashed down hard on my elbows and knees, gasping for the cold shock of pain – too painful, in the first sickening seconds, to let me move, my untrimmed hair stinging in my eyes.

Just a moment. Just let me have a moment. It's too much – too fast – a nightmare, with all the demented logic of one –

Breathe. Again. *You wake up from nightmares. You can wake up from this.*

"Forgive the bewilderment, darling." My voice wasn't airy enough – too choked with sprinting and spit. "It's nothing that can't be fixed!"

Rosamond didn't reply.

I struggled up. Twisted to squint past the darkened fishing-shop, where the street widened and zigzagged towards Angle Drag. But for carts and rain and trembling shadows, there was nothing.

She'd been with me – she'd followed me across the thoroughfare –

Hadn't she?

Someone seized my arm. Someone else seized the other. They hauled, terrible tandem, until they'd spun the street around me. I flipped the sword in a tramazzone, got a startled yelp as the blade wheeled round – but a blow to my elbow burst the hilt out of my fist, and another did the same to the stick. Then a *third* intruder (third! Dio mio, call it seventh now!) mushroomed from the empty market in front of me, with Earlyfate's dismembered pieces bundled bloodily to her chest.

I squinted at her. Vaguely familiar, not enough for a name: a sturdy creature with ruddy cheeks and damp-wheat hair, the ends of her knitted scarf squirming like maggots in the wind. But I knew her clothes. Brown jacket. Burgundy cuffs, collar, belt. Buttoned-up split skirts to match, glinting with lamp-struck buttons. And, either side of me, one to each arm like sodden plumage: two more variations on that fussy little uniform. Most unnervingly of all, the three Divisioners – for Divisioners they were, sartorially at least – shared far too much resemblance, family facial features split between them like Dallyangle's answer to the Graeae.

"Oh, for the love of Dante's tombs!" I cried, slapping the trio verbatim with my sole coherent thought. "You took your hapless time!"

If Divisioners were getting involved, they could damn well make themselves useful. I'd go back across Angle Drag with a triolet of detectives – they'd outnumber the Concerned Citizens –

"Dante's what?" offered one of them dazedly, the gangly boy on my left arm.

Va bene, less encouraging – but not impossible to work with –

"Hapless, are we, Property?"

Their wheat-headed leader curdled me on a look of unbridled rage – *excuse me?* – then jerked her head to the others. They twisted my arms behind me, pinned them to my spine in clumsy folds – clumsy, but effective, pain sparking in every joint when I strained against them. Too sparking, too painful, to dispute. Benevolent assistance this was decidedly not.

"What – stop it! – what do you think you're doing?"

The wheat girl scowled up from a squint at the sword. "You're *stabbing* people too?"

I concede it wasn't the most outlandish conclusion to draw from ample bloodstains, but – "Never mind that! There's – gracious, I don't know, an abduction – a man and a woman – she was strong, but she's wounded, and the four of us could –"

"Cass?" blurted the girl at my shoulder.

Wheat nodded. "Cass."

And they started dragging me across the square.

Incredulity struck me in the chest, out of plans and sense and everything else I still possessed. My wretched hair was in my eyes again. I shoved my heels into the cobble-seams – into their legs – it didn't stop them – and the distance from Angle Drag was stretching, brittle with the strain, about to snap –

The scream sprang from my tongue.

"Take your hands off me! Rosamond Nettleblack needs my help! We have to save her! I swear I'll have you shut down tonight on every complaint you deserve if you don't – !"

They didn't stop. Neither did the nightmare. The girl beside me yanked the unpinned cravat out of my collar, and shoved it into my mouth.

CHAPTER SEVEN

I AM NOT THE DIVISION'S
FAVOURITE INDIVIDUAL

The Notebook of Doom, doomed

Still concerning a dastardly evening which simply will not end

I would dearly love to declare an interval. I'd love to declare that the Divisioners saw sense! Surely this treatment was excessive, even for a bloodstained swordstick. By the time they got me to their double doors, we were as drenched in freezing sweat as infernal rainstorm, them gasping for breath and me wishing I could. It was both beneath my dignity and above my abilities to chew through my cravat, but that's hardly to say I didn't try it.

If this retrospective speculation, dear ruffians, gives an impression of sneering indifference to my own situation, let me assure you that I'm nothing of the sort. It might be a strange comfort now, to peer down from the gods with my notebook and wince for poor Pip Property's plight – for, more to the point, *Rosamond Nettleblack's disappearance!* – but there's really no escaping how much it's happening to both of us, nor how much I've lost all control of it. And I promise it stings like a cravat pin to the gullet.

The trio hauled me past the log-shed. Something was snapping overhead – gracious, was that a telephone wire, glossy against the storm-clouds?

But I couldn't stare; the wheatsheaf leader kicked the doors in.

I mean this with all possible snideness: the Division looked *clean*. The dust and dirt and ashes had been scrubbed from the reception's floorboards, the front desk and waiting-bench and dormitory door gleamed with varnish, and the plastered walls were astonishingly devoid of scratches and stains. The wood-burner glowed like a spoiled infant; when the wheat girl twisted the gaslamps, not one of them even hazarded a splutter. I hadn't been wrong about the wire: the corner beside the window had a gleaming telephone fixed to the wall. They even had *pigeonholes*, for heaven's sake, sleek little boxes with reams of post for *Cassandra*.

But Cassandra, whoever the devil she was, wasn't there. Neither was my neighbour Matthew Adelstein. Gaping at us from behind the desk were Division Sergeant Septimus and Henry Nettleblack, and I couldn't even pinpoint which one looked closer to combustion.

Septimus was, of course, incongruously ravishing, a late-Rossetti stunner with a slightly sideways nose, its break (va bene, my fault) healing with the crooked charm of a prize-fighter. Her chestnut chignon was still an exquisite goldmine, her uniform was ridiculously neat for her, and – before she realised what she was looking at – her lovely churlish face was more cheerful than I'd seen it in months. The reason for her cheer stood trembling at her shoulder, skinny as her sister with mousy hair carefully cropped, Rosamond's eyes huge in her pallid face. The Nettleblack resemblance nearly tripped me; I've really no excuse for not noticing it sooner.

But what sad piece of decadent wreckage were the new sweethearts gawping at – throat bare, jacket half-shed, soaking hair entirely in want of a parting? I couldn't even speak, much less declaim a grand apology.

And what sort of apology was *I lost your sister*, anyway?

"The hell?" Septimus stammered, so sharp and cockney and unavoidably *herself* that my nails shot into my palms.

Wheat blinked at her. "Where's Cass?"

"Alberstowe Hall. With the Director. It's Monday."

My bucolic captor promptly gave herself up to several stanzas'-worth of swearing so comprehensive I'd shudder to repeat it – honestly, I wouldn't have deemed her capable. Henry practically recoiled; Septimus cut it off five seconds in – "Gertie! Explain!"

And thence unfolded the next merciless humiliation in the worst night of my twenty-seventh year. Gertie, of the arable hair, was not choking on a cravat, and had determined to take full advantage of the fact, with an account so unhinged I snarled for every sentence. In her gauche telling, I charged her band with a *bloody sword* – "Plus, y'know," she added hotly, "a bloody sword!" – and attempted to cut down the same Divisionary associates who stood, quite obviously unharmed, holding me back from cleaving their colleague into steaks. I then supposedly endeavoured to lure all three into a trap – she seemed to think the Concerned Citizens were my bloodthirsty lackeys, or possibly that the Concerned Citizens were the Sweetings – and threatened doom on the whole Division when my scheme was thwarted. It is supremely difficult to scoff incredulously with a cravat in your mouth, but I gave it a zealous go.

"And they tried one more thing," Gertie gabbled. "They – sorry, Hyssop, but – they said we had to let them go if we wanted to save Rosamond Nettleblack."

Henry froze. For one terrible tottering moment, I thought she would faint. She lingered at the top of it, a sapling with its trunk sawn and no clue which way to fall – I hadn't even my hands, I'd no way to catch her –

But she had Septimus. A steadying squeeze of her arm, a blazing exchange of looks, a tweaked eyebrow and a curt nod.

"Bolt the doors," Septimus snapped to the insufferable trio. "And barricade the dorm one. 'Case the Sweetings follow 'em here."

"You reckon they would?"

"I ain't taking the chance tonight." She jerked her head to the telephone. "Can you make that thing work? Get a message to the Director?"

Gertie flung the machine a look of murderous disapproval. "I'm not Cass, am I? You won't catch me larking about with that necromantic shit – "

"Fine! Just do the doors. We'll see to this."

Septimus strode up to me, as grim-jawed and cool-faced as if she'd never saved my life. For a horrible moment, she simply held our stare, until she was certain I'd seen every inch of myself in the inksplot navy of her eyes; she was the taller by two crushing inches. Then she seized my collar and marched me away, into a corridor so gloomy I lost all sense of space. I shied like an idiot when something elbowed past – it was Henry, with a bristle of keys, unlocking a door at the corridor's end and striking every taper inside –

I stumbled into the windowless room, clung to its marble – faux-marble – table to keep my feet, wrestled the cravat out of my teeth. Septimus elbowed the door shut, and Henry stalked towards me, with far more boldness than the guileless apprentice of two weeks ago would ever have dared. I confess it jolted me back a step.

"Figs," she hissed, by way of settling herself – and then, with unaccountable ferocity – "Where – is – my – *sister?*"

But my fear was surely superfluous. This was a welcome development – the most welcome development anything at the Division could give me! Yes, I looked a wreck – but they *knew* me, these two, and they'd never been much good at concealing their admiration, and Gertie wasn't even in the room anymore. Henry owed her haircut to my hands; Septimus used to dote on me! They'd seen me in the Sweetings' grip – they'd wrested me out of it – if anyone would listen to my explanation of Rosamond's predicament –

So I swallowed, ragged at the throat, and resurrected a cadaverous approximation of my winning smirk. "Good evening to you too, Henry – "

"Answer the question," Septimus growled. "You've got mine next, and they ain't half as genteel."

Terrified exasperation plucked at my nerves. *You were my saviour – why can't you act like it?* "Not that I wouldn't enjoy an interrogation under different circumstances, but – "

"What have you done with Rosamond?" Henry demanded, finicky voice cracking. "Why are you threatening her? You were quite supposed to protect her!"

My mouth fell open. "You can't seriously believe – "

"The Sweetings tried to kill you!" Septimus cried. "Why the hell would you come *back?*"

"My dears, there really isn't time for this – "

"Was it the money? Did they give you back your savings?"

"Why in persimmons' name are you not on the Continent?"

"Might I finish!"

They exchanged an infuriated glance. I flung myself at it.

"This can wait. Everything can wait. We have to return to Pole Place and rescue Rosamond. She – I think she's been abducted, by two strangers, in a carriage – not the Sweetings – but the Sweetings were there – briefly – "

My voice simply decomposed on my tongue. I hadn't lost it without provocation – the two of them had been gaping at me throughout, disbelief unabashedly evident, disgust so withering it killed the sentence.

I coloured. "I'm not lying!"

Henry glanced up at Septimus – how drastically she had to soften that glare! "I could check – "

"Wait!" Septimus caught her elbow, halfway to the door. "I walked into their trap before. I ain't watching you do the same."

I had, at least, a retort for that – but Henry's pale hands curled round Septimus's face before I was even close to it, the sweethearts' heads dipping together. "I'll take Gertie – and the others – I can't leave Rosamond – "

"Alright. Be careful."

Maledizione, they were *kissing* – and doing a very sweet

pretty job of it – but in this hushed little room, my pocket-watch was audible!

"I don't mean to chivvy you, but we should – "

Henry tipped out of the kiss, still twined in Septimus's arms, a sharp pivot solely at the neck. "*You* are quite entirely staying where you are."

"I beg your – ?"

"*I* am going to fix whatever you've done to my family."

She stalked for the door. Incredulity throttled me to a yell – "The only one threatening your family is Edwina!"

Henry jolted on the spot, all short hair and narrow shoulder-blades.

"Ask her about your father's will. And don't let her anywhere near Rosamond!"

She turned, very slowly. Too slowly. Rosamond flickered in her eyebrows, in the sharp point of her chin.

"Edwina never meant to hurt either of us," she snapped. "Rosamond didn't wait to see her change, but – but she's finished with the threats! She knows who I am – I told her first – she accepts it – accepts *me!* And you – you've quite done enough – you nearly unhinged the Division – you're not unhinging my family too!"

Then she was gone, with a squeeze of Septimus's hands, and not so much as a parting glance for me. I darted after her, but Septimus stepped neatly into my path, kicked the door shut behind her. She was glaring too, arms folded, keys jutting from her fist. I could only mirror the glare, a feeble answer; I knew full well how strong she was, and even my fencing speed wouldn't dodge a grapple with her.

And why the devil was I having to think about *grappling* with her?

I blinked. Henry's face scorched the back of my eyes.

What was their problem, then – the last betrayal? I had apologised to Septimus – though in retrospect I fear it might have been sardonical. I don't recall even getting a chance with Henry. That was it: they were still offended.

But – and the thought squirmed, tiny and ravenous – *but it's not just them* – *none of the Division will indulge you* – *and you're not in a particularly elegant suit, but surely you don't need the suit this much* –

No. Calm. Henry was looking for Rosamond. I could fix the rest.

"I never meant to hurt Henry. Or you. If you're perturbed by what I did, I – "

"You know Henry's still got your cravat?"

I startled. Septimus lifted a brow for my sudden silence.

"Your little bribe. Gift. Whatever it was. And – look, it ain't my place – it just – it weren't only a cravat, and you know it."

I wouldn't let my jaw drop again, but – *did* I know it? Did I know anything, at that moment?

She was still staring at me, scrutiny more than conducive to bristling my skin. What she hoped to find in my face, I'd no idea – I'd half a mind to snap *stop squinting, sweet sergeant*, but the intensity of her look wouldn't allow it. It was a stare like a thumb under the chin, holding me still without touching me, searching and studying. Waiting – and even this I could only guess – for me to lose some kind of nerve.

Eventually, she sighed. "You're a bloody liability, Property, but you ain't heartless. I thought you'd care."

"I do care! I – "

But *that* was the nerve. Nearly lost already. And I wouldn't have her dragging things out of me with soulful looks, or cryptic hints about Henry (as if I hadn't boxed up those speculations!). I wouldn't crumple in the face of something that made no sense. I would *not* let her push me to the stupid indulgence of tears.

I swallowed hard. Then I smiled.

"Septimus. Sweet sergeant. Let me out. I need a delectable reprise of your tactics from last time – Gertie and her insufferables listened to you then – "

"And I'm damned lucky I didn't get dismissed for it!"

"But you didn't tell them about the Sweetings! So why do people know? Did you change your mind about leaving me be?"

"No! You could've gone. You and Rosamond both. I made sure of it. But – God's sake, you never know when to stop!" Her voice splintered, hoarse with weary resignation. "And now I can't help you. Can't trust you. Not even if I want to."

"But – Septimus, I – "

For one heady second – I can't explain why, other than that I needed to – I let myself imagine her expression softening, her hand squeezing my shoulder –

"I – "

But charm hadn't worked. And what was the alternative? Let her lock me up in this glorified stable, waive all ability to ensure Rosamond's safety, shrug off everything that was confusing and illogical and *wrong* about the evening – ?

She was still waiting.

You shan't cry. I won't let you.

"What's happening?" I heard myself stammer, infuriatingly pitiful.

Her eyes widened. I thought – gracious, I hoped – but then she just cleared her throat, turned away, keys glittering on her palm.

"The Director and Cassandra'll be back later. I'll tell 'em Pip Property's in the morgue."

"What?"

A panicky grimace. "Wait. No. Not like that."

"Morgue?"

She fled without another word, wincing right round the door. I staggered after her, fumbled to snatch the handle and call her back –

But she'd already locked me in.

The morgue. This stuffy cell was their morgue. Why did the Dallyangle Division have a *morgue?*

It was barely even furnished. Not that I'm acquainted with morgues in earnest, but – surely cadaver storage is a basic requirement. Surely cupboards and counters are things more substantial than lines marked on whitewashed floorboards.

The only prop in the place was the not-marble table, which might just have been large enough for a lithe corpse. I sprang away from it – how many Dallyanglian murders had been dissected thereupon? – but it looked far too immaculate to have served its intended purpose. An ingénue of a morgue slab. As I fervently hoped.

I shivered. The air was too still, the gale muffled. The door-handle gave me only scalded palms when I tried to twist it. The tapers on the walls flickered for my movement, stubby candles half-smothered in their wax, barely an hour's light left in any of them.

Pallid walls, impending darkness, stifled isolation. All it needed was a fishpond.

Some ghastly soblike sound kicked the back of my throat. *Absolutely not.*

I wouldn't wait. I'd – gracious, what could I do? – I'd take an inventory of myself, and fix whatever was scuppering my charisma. The answer to the latter mystery was apparently a prolific one. My damp suit was scored through at the elbows and knees, my cravat so sodden on my neck I had to wrench it off. I'd not even noticed the extent of the bloodstains – stiff on my lapels and waistcoat, horrible puce across my shirt-front – gracious, I looked like a sentient penny dreadful. Again. Fencing with Father had always been so neat, footwork and wristwork and stepping in the guards – but playing at swords-manship in the Dallyangle streets –

Not that I begrudged Rosamond her sharp self-defence. *I* should have been more effective at defending *her*. I should have been defending her at that very instant.

I bit down on the thought like a clove. Slumped against the wall, slid to the floor, as if polishing my boots with one bedraggled sleeve could constitute even an approximation of useful contribution. Above me, the tapers started to drown.

My watch had twitched through almost an hour before the door rattled again.

I started upright. Septimus was already darting round the door, bizarrely furtive, squinting for me in the last gasp of the candles. I'd failed to salvage the suit, but there was certainly enough strength in me for an elegant bow: "Back so soon, sweet – ?"

She flung a blanket at my head. Hard.

"Catch," she added – belated, dour, as I struggled up from the floor again.

She was piling a motley stack on the morgue slab, feet carefully angled between me and the open door. A second blanket, then a third. A pillow, slimmer than the First Folio. A chamber pot with a Dallyanglian market-day painted on its lid. A scruffy novel – *Life and Limbs: A Comic Romance of the Medical School!* – which I presumed (perhaps unfairly) to be some kind of sly joke. Another book, marble-edged and impressively bound, a bundle of pencils new-sharpened beside it. A twined fist of tapers, with lucifers to match. A chipped plate, upon which she'd arranged a mug of noxious tea, a scorched stack of toast, and a sliced wheel of cheese the size of my head.

She met my astonished stare – nodded brusquely – and marched for the door.

"Wait! Did you – Rosamond – ?"

"They went to Pole Place." She bit her lip. "Nothing there."

Scrutiny be damned, I snatched the slab before my legs could buckle.

"Septimus!"

The yell was Gertie's, becoming louder and more corporeal with every thundering footstep. "If you dare give that thief my family cheese – "

Septimus was back behind the locked door before I could scrape a word, spurring Gertie's protests away until I lost even the sound of them. But the tottering horde on the slab – there had to be something in it – *nothing there* was not the end, her end, not if I could –

The marbled book. Every page was blank. Blank – but for some spiky words on the inside cover, smudged with rain-drops, scribbled in haste.

Tell us everything – leave nothing out – and quite no more lies!
Underneath, as if it needed a signature: *HN*.
She wasn't in earnest, surely –
Dio mio, when was Henry Nettleblack ever *not* in earnest?
"As you wish," I snarled, and seized the nearest pencil.

You wanted everything, my dears? Va bene! Here it is – and haven't I been thorough? You must understand: with Rosamond's whereabouts uncertain, and Rosamond's liberty under threat, there is *nothing* I won't do to save her.

And there's certainly nothing I won't write!

CHAPTER EIGHT

THE ERRONEOUS MUSINGS
OF SOMEONE ELSE

Cassandra Ballestas's Secret Phonograph

(so secret that, for the entire duration of this chaos, I had no idea she had one)

Recording: Fri Nov 10th 1893

Is it working? Am I doing it? Does the long-awaited machine do the long-awaited thing?

I need a better test –
She is the very model of the most disgraced Divisioner,
For handing out that cranium her mother's not forgiven her –
She's bought herself a phonograph, but hasn't an idea of what
She's got as future options now – I reckon that it's not a lot!
She's very good at novelising, if you'd take a second look –
But as of now, she can't decide if she should write a second book.
And Mother wants her not to, wants her never to be recognised –
Though editors are pleading for a sequel to be publicised! etc.
She solved the latest case, but now her prospects have been addled, see,
Because of tricks and plots devised by Adelaide Danadlenddu –
So what's her job? And will she write? Does anyone believe in her?
All sharp and pressing questions for the most disgraced

It works. It *works!* And do you know what? *I* may not have a brother in *The Pirates of Penzance*, but my singing doesn't sound half bad when you play the recording back!

(Oh, yes, I've worked out how to do that too. Phonograph recording, phonograph replaying – just call me the denizen of technology.)

But there won't be any tricks and plots by Adelaide Danadlenddu, not this time. No more unprotected paper and pen for Cass Ballestas! You, my magnificent modern innovation, are as impenetrable a receptacle for thoughts as anything in Dallyangle's ever like to be – I'll be *amazed* if anyone else in town knows how to work a phonograph. Adelaide could steal my papers, but she can't do anything with a wax cylinder. If you'd only arrived a few weeks earlier! I could have kept all the secrets I needed – could have stayed in the Division like a productive protégée –

But – look. Never mind that. You're here now. Book sales well spent. On you, and on the room I'm renting to keep you in, because not a shiny speck of your existence can get back to Mother. As far as Director Keturah St. Clare Ballestas ever need know, her disappointment daughter doesn't keep any more secrets. Doesn't write any more anonymous novels. Doesn't make any more mistakes. Doesn't – oh, I don't know – exist, in summation.

I've still not decided about that second novel. My publishers want an answer before December – will there be a sequel to *Life and Limbs?* Honestly, when I sent off for the phonograph, it wasn't a question. But then I corrected Mother's spelling in the Director's Record, which for your tinny technological clarification is a ledger, in which she bemoans the moral failings of my secretly writing novels at all. Let's just say it wasn't conducive to firing my literary imagination.

And I don't want my mother to disown me. No – she wouldn't, she'd despise me. She hates fuss, to a peculiar degree for the woman who turned on the Metropolitan Police and got her family chased out of London. Though even that was weirdly well-mannered, for the most part: she was already working on the constabulary periodical – because you're allowed to write stuff if it's *worthy* stuff – and it took the editors three issues to notice how much reform she was pushing for.

But – sod it, where was I? – if I don't write another novel, what am I meant to *do?*

As far as the other Divisioners know – or should I just say *the Divisioners* now? – I'm taking a leave of absence after a stressful case. But I *caused* the stress; of course Mother doesn't want me to come back, never mind how much I miss it. No Division, then – probably no sequel at this rate – so nothing! Or scraps of not-quite-nothing, to make it sting a bit more. Helping Dad in the apothecary and pretending it's a purpose. Looking after Johannes, because no one's found my brother a new governess since Adelaide turned spy and traitor and hider of heads. Talking into a phonograph in a dingy attic off Angle Drag, hiding my voice in a cylinder so nobody can use my words against me again.

But I have to say something. Have to hear myself say it. Even if it's just to a machine. If I don't rant, I'll run mad. If I don't talk it out of me, I'll shout. At Mother – again – and this time she won't scrub it off. I – I'll –

Sorry. Lesson learned: you can't scream into a phonograph.

*

Recording: Mon Nov 13th 1893

Working? Good? Good.

I need to rant again. I hope you're recording comfortably – how do you fancy a bit of Story Time for Disastrous Divisioners?

So! Last night –

"*Action was wanting in all members, attached and unattached to Laura. She fled along the corridor, as a ghastly wind shrieked through the medical school—'My God,' cried she; 'Benedict—and in their clutches!'*"

Wide eyes over the quilt, curly black hair in disarray. All ten years of Johannes Ballestas bundle up against the pillows, his bedside taper flickering, my voice the only thing veering through the murk of his bedroom. I pause, and little dark fingers scuttle out of the coverlet, motion frantically for the next bit.

"*Dr Stoker and his accomplices gloated over the helpless body of Benedict, their victim, fastened to the operating table, soon to be deprived of both LIFE and LIMBS—*"

"The title," my brother blurts, half-delirious. "Cass, it's the title!"

"The author's very clever. *As she perceived the loathsome sight, a fiery hatred of the surgeons' guild flared within Laura's breast, cauterising the last of her gentle terror. 'Unhand him!' bellowed she; 'Your quarrel is not with Benedict! You must deal with me now, Dr Stoker—I, the begetter of all this folly; I, the remover of your detested limb; I, your saviour, despisèd the more for the service I rendered unto you! Couldst thou tolerate it so little, that thy life be preserved by a woman? Faugh! 'Twas not in your hand the gangrene lay—'tis in your soul, and I shall cut it out once more!'—and thus she smote the skulduggerous medic with HIS OWN MISSING HAND—*"

"Cassandra, are you up there?"

Sweet Lord.

I drop the book, kick it under Jo's bed, grab *News from Nowhere* from his side-table and carry on without stopping. "*It is said that in the early days of our epoch there were a good many people who were hereditarily affected with a disease called Idleness, because they were the direct descendants of those who in the bad times used to force other people to work for them –* "

Mother looms round the door. It's brighter downstairs, gaslight spilling over her feet. "Why is Johannes still awake? It's nearly eleven!"

(Which is early for *her* bedtime, but I don't dare say that.)

"He's been gripped," I offer, tight-smiled. Just not by William Morris. "Call it my fault."

Well. She'll do that regardless.

"He has school tomorrow. Let him sleep, Cassandra."

I flick Jo a wink in the sneaky half-light. Mother holds the door open for me, very pointedly, so I can't retrieve *Life and Limbs* from under the bed. Morris, stern and sensible and Keturah-approved, I can abandon with – well, with abandon – on Jo's bedside table.

Mother picks our direction, and the staircase isn't large, so I'm chivvied down into the kitchen with her. The air's still thick with Dad's stew, the last remnants of steam misting on the gaslamp-glass. Someone's drawn the curtains. I'm trapped in a cheery-coloured cell: orange tablecloth, saffron cushions, the brown-and-burgundy folds of Mother's Division jacket over a chair. She's piled it with her Director's badge facing upwards, gold as her eyes, surface simmering like a second stew.

I head for a different chair, swat past a low-hanging bunch of herbs. Mother's spread her ledger on the dinner-table; now she's frowning and squinting and pinching under her spectacles. She hates writing, not that she wants the Div to know it.

But she can hide her spelling mistakes with another proofreader this time. *Especially* given I know that ledger. Joy of joys, she's brought home the Director's Record.

"How's everything with the Div?" – and that's me, prodding the knife at my throat, anything to distract her from blotching another ten pages of *why, dear ledger, is my daughter such a waste of space?* (I could quote her Record-versions of that sentiment, but I'm not going to.) "Gertie says you talked the council into restoring the funding?"

She frowns. Oh, don't say I've got Gertie in trouble.

"The council, in the absence of Lady Miltonwaters, have been sensible enough to reconsider their former strictures. They have prepared a year's worth of funding for us, plus half a year's bonus for our success unmasking the Head-Hider. I am due to receive the money in cash tomorrow. It will take some handling – they might have done better to arrange the matter with promissory notes – but the quarterly instalments were always cash, so perhaps they simply wish to continue in the spirit of the original arrangement. They certainly mean to continue in the spirit of that original faith in us."

A wary smile across the table to me. Across the Record. "The speech you helped draft certainly proved persuasive in that respect."

So persuasive that you took my words and threw me out, yes. "I'm delighted."

"And I trust your leave is proving restful?"

I dig my nails into the tablecloth. Where it hangs off the table, mind, so she doesn't see. "Mother, I was wondering – "

"Your father is most appreciative of your assistance in the apothecary. Particularly when that escaped ferret got inside! Clearing up the smashed remains of a Nettleblack's Tincture display is no small service."

Sweet Lord, does she hear herself?

"Well, if you need any help *catching* that runaway ferret – I hear it's causing a bit of chaos across town, and I – "

She sighs sharply, picks up her pen. "You cannot return to the Division yet."

I open my mouth, but her sudden glare's a padlock, so I shut it again. There's not been a raised-voices quarrel between us since the night of the Head-Hider, and I don't think I can bear another one so quick on its heels. I don't know what I might say, what I might not be able to take back. And her Record's said more than enough.

So we just sit, in silence so tetchy my fingertips smart. This bit of the house is behind the shop, so we don't even get market-sounds to soften the quiet – not that there'll be much alive in Dallyangle's market at this hour. I scowl at the range and pretend I'm deep in thought, whilst trying very hard not to be; she strains and scribbles at her ledger. A phonograph of her own would save her a world of trouble. Not that she'd accept one, not bought with *Life and Limbs* money. And I don't want her learning how to play back the cylinders.

We sit – until there's a hammering on the front door that jerks us out of our chairs. Dad crashes down the stairs – Mother glances at me, shifts closer to the door – I'm not having that stupid heroism, so I twist round the dinner-table to even the odds –

Two sets of footsteps clatter along the corridor. Dad bursts through in his dressing-gown. Behind him, ruddy with sweat and out of breath –

Gertie?

She grins when she sees me, though it's a weirdly mirthless smile. I return it, even so. "Alright, Cass?"

"What has happened, Gertrude?" Mother demands, before I can reply. She's right: bursting in on us at home never happens without grim and dastardly reason. "The Sweetings – they haven't – "

"Beg pardon, Director, but the Sweetings have." Gertie plants her hands on her split-skirted knees and gasps until her throat's clear. "The Sweetings and – I don't right know – Adelstein can't get any sense out of her – "

"Out of whom?"

Gertie swallows hard. "Miss Chandler. At the town hall. The bloody Sweetings – pardon again – they've robbed the town hall."

Mother doesn't even retort. Just nods to Gertie – nods to Dad – doesn't nod to me – and dives into her jacket, Director-ready in three heartbeats. Gertie meets my gaze, grimaces a question, and I wink in answer: as far as I'm concerned, my so-called *leave*'s no match for a Division calamity of this scale. My uniform's at the Div headquarters, confiscated in all but name, but my boots and scarf are in the hall –

A hand on my shoulder. Firm as a reprimand. I want to protest, but Mother's too quick, tilting my chin like a sodding child: "Stay here, Cassandra."

Gertie's face crumples – probably worse than mine, I've got rather good at controlling my face. Not that either of us have time to quibble. Dad jumps aside, and Mother propels Gertie out of the kitchen, tugging the door shut behind them. I can still hear them, all the way out of the house, Gertie's panicky half-sentences cut up with *Cassandra's leave* and *too much stress for her* and *you said Matthew is there?* and *tell me everything we know!*

Dad peers at me, all bolstering smiles. "I'm sure she knows best, Cass."

Dad. No. I love you, but you're not helping.

I wait until he's back in bed. I can be very quiet when I'm not yelling at a phonograph, and I'm very quiet now: gas off, down the corridor, key in my pocket, poured into shoes and scarf and out into the night. The temperature's dropped again – I'm desperately glad of my jumper, hand-knitted by the wondrous Gertie herself. At least it's stopped raining. And from the market square to the town hall is pretty well-lit.

I'm not *disobeying* Mother. So I tell myself, fists clenched against the cold, muttering into my scarf. I don't even have to go in. I can just – just a sneaky reconnaissance – just in case there's anything the Div's missed, any scrap of information I can offer, anything that'd have her nod and smile and say *actually, Cassandra, maybe you can return to the Division yet –*

Angle Drag. Quiet as the hour makes it, and not a pedestrian beyond me in the shifting shadows. If the Sweetings are still around, they're even sneakier than I am. And this *is* sneaky, for those two housebreakers – they're normally such fanatics for the smashed window and the lumbering getaway. Staring out the town hall as I hurry closer, you'd barely notice a disturbance. The lamps have painted the flamboyant façade an undignified yellow, but the glossy windows are still perfect, and there's nary a scrap of mud on the front steps. The massive door's ajar – and, when I curl my fingers round it, stuck in place, swollen from the day's rain.

I glance over my shoulder. Silence out there, a faint flurry of voices inside. Oh, we *are* feeling reckless tonight.

This door's too fancy to be quiet. I twist sideways, so it's not in my shadow, test the handle, try a shove and cajole to see how easily it moves. Not at all, is the answer – but someone clearly has moved it, and upset it in the process. The sleek metal lock is glinting with scratches, long and skinny as a cat's claw-marks.

Scratches? When did Maggie and Norman Sweeting – all six foot plus and a pistol of them – ever deign to *scratch* a door?

It shifts. Only an inch, screeching like a baby. Something clatters on the marble as the door bashes into it – small, lizard-sharp, gold without the help of the streetlamps.

It's also not disobeying Mother to pick it up –

I tip it to the nearest light. One end's pointed as an earring, and the other's a neat fingernail of gold, engraved with a paisley.

A cravat pin. And I *know* it.

"Oh, Javert," I breathe. Stagger back, pin in hand, to sit on the steps.

So I have a colleague. And her real name is Septimus – but let's put *that* aside for a moment. I've been calling her Javert for the past two months anyway, because in those months she's had her own little Javertish obsession – she's been blaming every single Dallyangle crime on one person. And that one person, a slinky Valjean by the name of Pip Property, has been repeatedly thwarting her accusations with very long speeches and dandyish alibis.

I thought, much like the rest of the Div, that Septimus had just gone mad – that she'd crashed her stupendously dangerous bicycle one too many times for rational thinking. And Gertie, who cares about these things, told me *she* thought the whole pursuit was some kind of insane flirtation – that, and I'm quoting, *sooner or later a bit of carnal indelicacy between them'll set all to rights!* If Septimus wanted to stake her job on *carnal indelicacy* – well, rather her than me. And *then* Gertie told me Septimus had given that plan up and pledged herself to Henry-Hyssop-who's-actually-Henry-Nettleblack instead, which at this point I'm not even going to question.

But this cravat pin – yes, Cass, back to the sodding cravat pin! – it belongs to the same Pip Property of Septimus's carnally indelicate nightmares.

And if you squint at the door, the scratches match. Property's used their pin on the lock.

Which is just *perfect*. Because despite the obsession and the Javertishness, Mother still thinks Septimus is the best recruit to happen to the Division. And this stupid gold pin in my hand means that, once again, Septimus and her surefooted suspicions will look a thousand times more brilliant than the disappointing daughter.

But I'm the one who found the pin. The only one who didn't miss it.

So I dive through the gap in the door.

There are only patches of light inside, but it's easy enough to find the Div by sound. Someone's wailing, high and shrill, and the murmur underneath is Mother's most furious reassurance. I dart down the corridor, past shadowy lumps that are probably vases and polished doors opening to empty rooms, and the sounds crumple into words. Mother's are her usual decorous Divisionary platitudes, but the shrill voice doesn't seem to be heeding them: "No! I cannot speak to a *man* of such things!"

I shoulder the last door in, stumble into blazing light and blazing chaos. It's some kind of office – the walls crowded with Dallyangle in picture-frames, a stuffed pheasant cowering on the mantelpiece – but there's not a surface unrifled. The rug's a mess of open strongboxes, scattered like metal teeth. All of the desk is on the floor, ink pooling round the broken well, pencils snapped and drawers yanked out.

A shudder of movement drags my gaze to the desk-chair. There's a girl crumpled up in it, with Mother and Gertie and

Detective Matthew Adelstein stood around in a frustrated henge, trying to uncrumple her by impatient stares alone.

I stare too. I know this crumpled girl. She's small and pale and wretched under her dark chignon, but you hardly need to remember her face — she always wears the yellowest clothes I've seen in twenty-five years of life. Every time we've collided — literally collided, on Angle Drag or in Market Square or at the town hall's uncooperative door — she's been exuberant and eye-smarting as an *Iolanthe* fairy, clutching files and papers, asking after Mother and the Div and everything she's funding.

She, you see, is the secretary of the Dallyangle Town Council, name of Miss Chandler. And right now, she looks far too unhappy for my nerves to stand.

Miss Chandler meets my gaze. The henge follows suit — and my throat goes dry. Above the secretary, Mother's look is scorched earth: flashing spectacles, clenched jaw, stiff seething silence.

I try to speak. Can't. Hold up the pin.

"The very thing!" Miss Chandler cries, voice vaulting a sob. "Miss Ballestas — a *lady* detective!"

Lady detective?

It doesn't *not* make sense. Matthew never wears his uniform, and I'm obviously not in mine. I suppose I do look like his counterpart — or would, if he wasn't puncturing me on an indignant stare. I ought to correct her — he's the only one at the Div who styles himself as Detective, and I'm not even a Divisioner at the moment —

But Gertie's started to grin. For her, at least, Cass at the crime scene is the world to rights. It gives me a giddy glimpse of the room through her eyes, of me in the doorway: crucial evidence cricked in finger and thumb, fear neatly tucked behind keen-eyed cleverness. And *that*, if nothing else, fledges a bit of audacity back onto my bones.

"Nice to see you again, Miss Chandler. Sorry it's not under better circumstances." I dip my head to her, by way of dodging Mother's expression. "Did any of you see this?"

Miss Chandler gasps fit to wring out a lung – honestly, every time I've seen her she's done most things fit to wring out a lung – and leaps off the chair, wobbles through the wreckage and snatches my hands. I do try not to flinch, but the angle's jabbed the pin through the skin of my palm.

"I can be assured of your discretion? Your indulgence, your gentle sympathies, your feminine tact?"

My mouth falls open. "...Yes?"

"Do you mind, Mrs. Ballestas?" – and she swings round, tugging me with her, blue eyes big enough to sell a bar of soap to my disapproving progenitor. "Forgive me, I – I just feel so ashamed! But dear Miss Ballestas will not scorn me for my folly, surely?"

"*I* would not scorn your folly, Miss Chandler," Matthew snaps. "If you would simply explain – "

"You are very kind, Mr. Adelstein, but I – I cannot be alone with an unmarried man. I cannot speak as I must with an unmarried man. And Miss Ballestas – " – with a squeeze of my hands, that sets me wincing for how deep it jabs the pin – " – has begun to fathom it already. The details of tonight, they – they are not delicate. I must have a lady detective."

I risk a quick glance at Mother. "I can listen to Miss Chandler, if it helps. And then I can leave. I just want to be useful. Please."

Mother plaits her fingers at her waist. Defiant decorum. "Very well."

Matthew gapes. "But – "

"Find yourselves a room nearby. We will continue assessing the damage." Her eyes narrow. "Be careful, Cassandra."

I gulp. If she means my welfare, I'm that stuffed pheasant.

Miss Chandler – *call me Marigold*, she urges, as she tugs me through the murky corridor – is a force of daffodil-skirted nature, even in her Sweeting-addled state. She prattles us all the way into the next room, only lets go of me to turn the gas on, scoops me through a slightly smaller office to the two chairs beneath the mantelpiece partridge (what's the bet there's a taxidermied game bird for every room?). The door she shuts behind me – the chairs she fusses until they're chafing at the legs, so close I can smell her perfume when I drop into one. I flatten my tongue on a cough – it's a *lot* of perfume for a casual evening.

"Gosh, I must seem so silly to you," Marigold blurts, halfway through a completely different sentence. The fireplace draught catches us at the shoulders, and she shivers with it, brittle in her candleflame shirt. "All this talk of discretion and secrecy. But I'm not of your Division, my dear Miss Ballestas – I have my reputation to think of, and no noble excuse for compromising it. Pray don't think I mean to offend!"

I shrug, with what I can only hope is feminine tact. "It's fine."

(Compromising my reputation, am I? What reputation? I'm the progeny of Dallyangle's most notorious innovator, eldest and very unmarried child of one of the only Black families in the town; *bucolic infamy*'s a bit more like it. *That's Keturah Ballestas's daughter!*, they'd cry in the streets, if Dallyanglians were all secondary characters in my novel. *Does she share her mother's fervour? Is she as clever, as capable, as meddlesome, as dangerous? Will she invent us* another *crime-solving contingent – or something worse? What will she do for the Ballestas legacy?*

Why isn't she doing anything? Can she not *do anything? Oh, what a disappointment! What a relief! What a terrible, wonderful let-down! Just as the Director's Record says! –*)

Sorry. Cass-in-the-room is still intent on Marigold.

"Gertie – my assistant –" (well, she used to be) " – said that the Sweetings have been here tonight. Did you see them?"

She shudders again. Her clattering voice is very small now, like a single dropped teaspoon. "They threatened me with a pistol."

That'll be them, goes my mind, with about as much feminine tact as a spade. "Oh. Terribly sorry for your ordeal –"

"But it is I who should be sorry," she blurts, shrinking about her wide eyes, mouth taut with – not just fear – wait, is that *shame?* "And I am, I assure you. I am so, so sorry. I could not prevent them – "

"Of course! No one was expecting – "

"Miss Ballestas, they took all of it."

And now my heart's an immensely beleaguered pincushion.

"Sorry, what?"

"All the cash we had ready for you. Your Division's funding. A yearly instalment. And the prize we wished to grant you for your work confounding the Head-Hider." She swallows. "It's all – they took – and, as we are, I – the treasurer would know for sure, but I fear we are not presently able to replace it."

Sweet Lord.

And Mother doesn't know. Does she suspect? Do *I* have to tell her – is that my penance?

But, beneath that swirling panic, another thought –

No.

No one has the right to wreck Mother's efforts. No one has the right to yank the teeth out of the Div – out of Gertie's livelihood – out of all *their livelihoods, very much including the remnants of mine. Not last time, and not this time. Not if I can stop them.*

I uncurl my hand. It's been too much a fist, and there are beads of blood around the golden pin on my palm. Marigold leans over it, and I lean too, as if we're trying to read my future from the metal line.

"I found this by the front door. I think it had been used on the lock." I glance up, and she's blushing furiously, enough to snag my voice. "I – I know who it belongs to."

She bites her lip. "Do you see why the matter needs privacy and tact? Why I need *you?*" *I need you.* Because of the *lady detective* thing – but it can't be just that. She knows I wrote the council-swaying speech. She knows what part I took in stopping the Head-Hider – the good bits, at least. She looks at me, just like Gertie, and she sees someone to believe in.

I smile. "In your own time, Marigold."

And she tells me.

And I really don't know how I keep hold of my eyebrows.

Now I must be off. Mother's trying to salvage our funded fate at the town hall – and, as long as there still is one, I have to go to the Division. If Septimus is in – I want a word.

*

Recording: Same day, but later, and worse

Let's start with my office. With me, valiantly pretending it's still my office. I'm not in uniform, not officially anything, clinging to all the filched authority Gertie's smile can give me. I've my old files and ledgers on the shelves at my back, my old notebook on the desk before me, my old scratchy inkstains in the desk's surface. Mother's still with the council, pleading for something to stitch up last night's rent in the Div's prospects – the floor, for as long as she's gone, is mine!

I've only got one spare chair. I want Gertie to take it, but Gertie – bless her – gestures to Septimus, who then of course gestures to Henry, as if the little pantomime needs any more chivalry. It's the first I've seen of the sweethearts since my leave, and the sight's enough to jolt me: the Div's funding might be gone, but – sweet Lord! – this pair are coping far better than they used to cope with life in general. Septimus is a defiantly steady creature of loose limbs and tea-sips, even more staggering given how broken her nose is, and Henry – what is this, *composure?* From the Nettleblacks' nerviest heir?

I squint at her. "Are you wearing a cravat? With your uniform?"

She flushes. "Well – erm – if scarves are permitted – "

"You ain't even wearing uniform," Septimus points out, all bitten lips over the top of her mug. "D'you want something, Cassandra? We're back on patrol in twenty minutes."

Well. I've managed worse in less than twenty minutes.

"Actually, Javert, I do. And don't roll your eyes – it's about Valjean."

Septimus blinks. "What?"

I flip my notebook open. I won't trust many deductions to paper now, but the gesture's oddly reassuring. "You used to insist Pip Property was an all-knowing scoundrel. Might you all-know if there's a chance they'd ever work with the Sweetings?"

I'm expecting a scoff. I'm *not* expecting the whole bloody room to turn into an icehouse. Henry has to stammer in – and you know something's superlatively wrong when *Henry's* the one trying to save it with words.

"Figs – what – what makes you say that?"

Above Nettleblack's curly head, Gertie is giving Septimus the sort of expression I'd have my printer typeset in capitals.

"It's not a difficult question, Hyssop. And while we're at it – do you suspect that same Pip Property might be predisposed to employ – " (oh, why?) " – carnal indelicacy as a means of luring in their victims?"

Tea slops over Septimus's fingers. She doesn't seem to notice.

I sigh, by way of apology to Marigold's dignity. "If there was a sizeable financial incentive, would Property seduce a hapless maiden to get the Sweetings access to the money?"

The sweethearts lock eyes, stiff-stared with horror.

"*Sarge*," Gertie growls.

I drop the cravat pin on the desk, get a nervous tweak in my throat for how violently Henry and Septimus jump. "There's this. And there's a witness. To the robbery last night. Well?"

"Well!" – bloody hell, Gertie's exploding – "Sarge! I *knew* you shouldn't've let Property go!"

That rocks me back in my chair. "Sorry, what?"

And thus do I receive a tale fit to rival anything I ever drafted for *Life and Limbs*. It's a duet, tremulous and jarring by turns, conducted relentlessly by Gertie. Septimus falters through the story of how she earned her own *unpaid leave*: of Pip Property, smirking fit to strike a match, luring her off-duty and into the Sweetings' clutches with promises of – I don't make her spell it and I don't care to know, but Gertie's meaningful look is a fair gloss. Henry darts about this melody, flicking over imaginary pages with her fingers, embellishing details about a villainous pact between Property and the Sweetings – otherwise such unlikely collaborators. The grand finale, at Gertie's prompting, is enough to make me drop my pen. Septimus finally faced down her dandy menace after what sounds like a deeply overcomplicated kidnap of her whole entire sweetheart – escorted said kidnapper past two slathering Sweetings – and *let Property vanish into the night.*

"'Cause they were in danger! They said they were trying to double-cross the Sweetings – to trap 'em for us! And I – I – "

Her voice cracks. Fair enough – I've never heard either Septimus or Henry speak for this long. "I believed Pip. Property. I trusted 'em."

She darts me a glare, helpless and furious, as if she's daring me to sneer. Henry hops off the seat, presses her lips to her sweetheart's calloused knuckles.

A month ago – I've no illusions – I probably would have sneered. But there's too much of Adelaide lurking behind Septimus's glare, or rather too much of me: bamboozled Division Sergeants, charming liars, just-about justifications for dastardly deeds, and now here we all are.

So I shrug. "It's easily done."

Septimus stares at me – wide eyes, rumpled eyebrows, a sliver of teeth in her parted lips. It scorches in my face, how unabashedly shocked she is. I'm not normally *that* merciless, am I?

"So you thought Property'd leave. No more robberies. No need to chase the matter any further. Most of the Div don't even know they're a suspect, and the ones that do know don't have reason to keep suspecting." I sigh. "Sweet Lord, that's well played."

"And casual seductions are all well and good," Henry mutters miserably – to a roomful of stupefaction. "I – erm – greengages – I mean – it isn't just – "

She shudders. "I – I don't know. I quite don't know what to

believe. But I – oh, pomegranates – I know who it might hurt."

There's grim silence. Septimus is leant on the wall – slumped against, more like – with the look of someone who's been repeatedly slapped by a very heavy quarto. Henry unpicks the cravat from her collar, rolls it tight between shaking fingers, shoves it wrist-deep in her pocket.

I clear my throat to steady my voice. "We have to tell Mother. About Property's – history. If there's any chance we can use it to get the funding back – "

"I already told her," Septimus blurts. "Most of it. On the night of the Head-Hider. The night Property left. But – with Adelaide and Lady Miltonwaters breaking in – it weren't the steadiest of conversations."

I'm feebly grateful to her. If it *weren't the steadiest of conversations* – well, I can take *that* as the reason why Mother didn't leap through the roof at my cravat pin revelation, why she didn't clasp my shoulders and cry *Cassandra, you detectival genius, you must be reinstated at once!* when I trimmed Marigold's testimony into euphemisms on the walk home. But I can remind her. *Behold, Mother, from your crime-scene and your recollections: the suspect, and their suspicious past! And then behold even more: your child, who pieced the puzzle together!*

So I scribble some notes. Every letter's naked on the page, far too easy to read. Then I start up from the chair, shove pin and notebook into my pockets and teeter round the desk's rickety legs. Everyone stares at me, so I give the room my calmest explanation, also known as a lie so flagrant it scorches my tongue: Mother wants me to meet her when her business at the town hall's concluded – and isn't there *so* much more for us to discuss, after this little chat?

The morning's fretty sun's been choked by clouds, and throttled the temperature – again – as if it needed to get colder! I've attempted, after last night's uniformless scramble, to dress a bit more like a *lady detective*, which essentially translates to an inch off my waist, a cape swishing in tandem with my scarf, and a walking-skirt cut so high I could march up a mountain in it. At least my walk brushes the worst of the cold off. I'm brisk and sharp-elbowed through the market, dodging stalls thick with the smell of cabbage and eels, ignoring the murmuration of stares in my wake.

The only gaze I meet's that of a distracted young man at the secondhand book-stall, raw-tipped fingers clutching his place in a copy of *Life and Limbs*. He gets a smirk, though he won't know why.

Mother's already on the front steps by the time I dash across Angle Drag, the town hall looming incongruously splendid at her back. Marigold Chandler's wrestling the swollen door shut with all the brawn of a bright autumn leaf. I stamp out the yells from a swerving farm-cart, hurl myself into Mother's path –

"I've got it!"

She stares at me. I don't like the dull sheen the clouds make of her spectacles. "Is something wrong, Cassandra?"

"Not that I can't fix!" She tries to step around me; I dart to stop her. "I've been gathering information about the robbery. I spoke to Septimus and Henry, and I – "

"You were at the Division?"

Thank everything Marigold's so absorbed by that disobedient door. Thank everything Mother's dropped her voice, given me licence to inch closer and drop mine too. "I had to be, to ask the questions I needed. And it turns out there's precedent for this – for everything I told you last night! Pip Property and the Sweetings have been conspiring for months – "

"Cassandra." It's a threadbare warning by comparison with her usual fare, too tired for the full menace. Even so, it stings. "It was good of you to help last night, but you must stop this."

What? "But the funding – "

"I cannot rely upon recovering the funding. Nor can the council replace the missing money at present." She pinches her fingers under her spectacles, like she's trying to snuff a candle – or a conversation. "The Division have permission to continue operating, but – on our own resources, for the fore-seeable future. *That* problem must be my priority. Pip Property and the Sweetings cannot be stopped if I do not have the funds to pay my Divisioners – "

"I'll stop them!" The words topple over my teeth. I'm dangerously close to a shout, have to clench my fists to keep a grip on the very public street. "I'll do it without pay, if that's what has to be done!"

"I would never ask you to – "

"Why not?" *Don't make it a quarrel – don't make her drag her condemnations back out of the Record* – "Because I made one mistake, and apparently I'm the only Divisioner who doesn't get a second chance?"

She grabs my shoulder. "Enough. I already told you, I want you to rest. You were placed under too much strain with the Head-Hider. Your judgment was severely impaired. You compromised the whole Division – and I cannot risk that again!"

And there they are. Brambles right over my head. Happy now, Cass?

"But – " – and I can only flail through her words, every sentence its own thorn-bush, my voice cut almost to pieces – " – but I swear I wouldn't – this is different! Adelaide's gone – and you need all the help you can get! You need me – please! Give me at least a chance to *prove* – "

She opens her mouth, but she's not the one to interrupt. Her eyes skid off my face, her hand slips from my shoulder, and a startled little pivot gets her past me, just as a voice like human copperplate traces through the air –

"Director Keturah Ballestas, of the Dallyangle Division?"

I spin. Stumbling, scalding-faced, fervently hoping this interloper's not been too thoroughly entertained by *Cassandra Crushed Again (Reprise)*. There's a sudden strange uneven-ness to the bustle around us – the street's still busy, but the horse-traffic's slowing down, and Marigold's given up on yanking the door.

The reason? A massive brougham, painted glossier than every set-piece in the Dallyangle Theatre, waiting in the street as if someone's scrapbooked it into place from the pages of a carriage anthology. Everyone's staring; everyone's dodging it. Ramrod on the driver's bench, there's an elbow-laden man with hair the colour of a pencil, and he's staring at Mother. He's not even the one who spoke – that's a woman, descending from an interior that's plush even at five paces, trim and neat and papery of face.

I can only stare, too scratched for politeness – but of course, even now, Mother recovers with bewildering speed. "The same. Are you in need of the Division's assistance, madam?"

The woman beams at her. That papery face is naturally stern, so the effect's a bit bizarre, but the sentiment seems alarmingly real.

"Well – before we get to that – might I just say, Director Ballestas, what an honour it is to meet you? I have heard such things of your Division's innovations, and I am delighted to have chance to profess my admiration in person." She ducks a curtsy, deft and practiced as a servant. With that drab dress and those rough-palmed hands, she probably is a servant. "Dorothea Thorne, ma'am, and a most *ardent* observer of your work. May I be so bold as to hope, one day, to be of my own modest use to your great endeavour? I promise I'd prove myself worthy of it!"

"One day," the driver interjects, with a quirk of the eyebrows. "But today, we've business of a different sort, don't we?"

Dorothea Thorne draws herself up. "Of course. My apologies. You're to come with us, Director, and I'm afraid it can't wait."

Sorry, what?

"To what end?" Mother asks, crisp with dignity. "Is there some perplexity with which you require the Division's aid?"

A twist in my throat. It's the second time she's asked it. The second time these strangers haven't answered.

"All in good time." Dorothea steps back, flourishes the carriage door. "This way, ma'am, if you please."

They're both watching Mother. I risk a look: up and down the street, trying to grab someone's eyes. Only Marigold returns it, frozen by the door with a nervous little smile.

"I can dispatch my Divisioners to your problem at once." Mother's very measured, forcibly calm. Just like she was with the Head-Hider. It crawls under my skin, watching that defiant composure slide over her face again. "Division Sergeant Septimus and Division Apprentice Nettleblack will make the best time, on their bicycles – "

"It must be you." Dorothea moves closer, dips to a murmur. "My employer wishes to speak with you at home. I trust you will have heard of him: Lord Clement Miltonwaters, heir to the marquessate of Alberstowe?"

Miltonwaters.

My stomach jolts.

The slightest quiver in Mother's voice. "My compliments to Lord Miltonwaters, but I –that is, his invitation – in light of recent events – "

One of his relations tried to disband the Div with a severed head, and threatened to have our family hounded out of Dallyangle. It's easy enough to think the words, even if my jaw's far too stuck to stammer them. *So give us one very good reason why she should be indulging another Miltonwaters!*

"Gosh, I do hate to eavesdrop," – and that's Marigold's silverware voice clattering down the steps – " – but surely you two must see why a little persuasion might be necessary in this case?"

Yes. *Yes!* Tell them, Chandler!

Dorothea glowers. "And you are?"

"Marigold Chandler, late of Somerville College, Oxford, now secretary to the Dallyangle Town Council." She's at Mother's side, tiny and haughty. "I have had the – ah – *dis*pleasure of working with Lady Elvira Miltonwaters, and I'm afraid she did nothing but thwart Mrs. Ballestas's every Divisionary effort. I presume, therefore, that – that this marquess-to-be is a different matter entirely?"

"*Lord* Miltonwaters is nothing like his unfortunate relation!" Dorothea snaps, bristling – as much as anyone with hair that neat can. "He only wishes to discuss the Division, and to make the acquaintance of its renowned founder!"

I think Marigold's emboldened me. That, or I just don't trust anyone who gives *renowned* three syllables in their everyday speech. "Then I'm coming too."

Mother stares at me. For one alarming moment, fear flashes across her eyes.

"Who might you be?" Dorothea demands. I dig my teeth into a snarl of *who do you bloody well think?*

"Cassandra Ballestas. I'm her daughter. And she's not going anywhere near a Miltonwaters without me at her side."

"Hear, hear!" Marigold cries. I jump, but I'll take the sentiment.

Mother struggles with a warning scowl, panic flinting through her expression. "Cassandra, please – "

"As you wish." Dorothea brandishes the carriage door at us again. "I am sure Lord Miltonwaters would not object. Please be reassured, ladies – he truly is *most* interested in the Division."

That's really not the reassurance she thinks it is, but what choice do I have? Mother's not being carried off alone to aristocratic doom. I don't care if she'd prefer it, it's simply not happening.

So I dip to Marigold's ear – "Let the Div know about this?"

– and when she nods, I'm plunging into the plush, too ensconced for any Directorial disdain to haul me out.

We drive for – actually, I'm not sure – we've lost the churchbell's chimes, and without them knocker-upping my life I've no idea of the time. Mother's stiff-backed on the bench beside me, gaze pinned to the window; when she finally got in, she gave me a look so disapproving it could have written a tract, but she hasn't spoken since. I've not been in a carriage for ages, and now I remember why. Every jerk of the wheels shoots up your spine to rattle your skull, as if the road's bypassed skin and gone straight to war with its travellers' bones. My poor corset tries to steady me, but against the potholes in this track it's thoroughly unmatched.

No more Dallyangle cobblestones – we've left the town. Fear jumps in my chest, too much out of tandem for me to blame it on the potholes.

"It can't be much further," I whisper.

Mother's eyebrows furrow. "You should not have come. I am perfectly capable – "

"I wasn't leaving you on your own!"

She sighs. Raises a hand, convulsive as everything else in the carriage, cups it round my cheek for one startling moment. "Oh, Cassandra – "

Then the hand drops. "Don't do it again. I can handle myself, but that becomes rather more difficult when I'm worrying about you."

"I shan't promise that," I mutter – but I let the wheels' clattering disguise the words. My face is prickling on one side, colder for the sudden absence of her hand.

She gestures shakily to my window. It's immaculately clear, for a brougham: the pointy hedges and bare fields beyond would be distinct as a landscape-glass, if we weren't rattling about so much. "We must be headed to Alberstowe Hall. Lord Clement Miltonwaters, unlike the lady of our mutual acquaintance, clearly feels no need for a Dallyangle town-house."

"How do you know?"

"Miss Thorne said *at home*. And the carriage is following the telephone wire."

The flat muddy fields are skewered with tall poles, a skinny line trailing between them, like a singleminded spider set one course for itself and refused to complicate it. Or – in the spirit of Dallyangle and its fish-hook streets – it's like the squinting silken stuff Dad uses for his summer fishing-rod, cast over the water's surface, barely visible and all the more menacing for it.

I'd seen the wire poking out of the town hall. I'd no idea where it went. To tug the line this far out of town –

"It runs between the town hall and the Miltonwaters estate," Mother supplies grimly, for the incredulity churning up my face. "A monstrous expense, and doubtless not the most reliable connection. But what was anyone to do, when the farmers rent their fields from the Marquess?"

I'd grit my teeth, if I didn't fear the road would crack them. Are privately-couriered letters not fast enough for this family?

We creak to a halt, then shudder as the driver vaults down, grey-brown hair dashing past the window like an owl in flight. He passes again without glancing in – I flatten to the pane to follow him – and he's headed for a gate, taller than the Div, complicated wrought-iron with spikes raking the sky. The telephone wire soars over it, disappears behind stone walls so smooth I don't think even Septimus would try to climb them.

"We might be here," I hiss.

But the driver scrambles back on. The carriage jerks to life, thwacks my forehead on the glass. We pause for him to lock the gate behind us – of course the sight grabs a fistful of my nerves and twists – and then there's a ridiculously long driveway, a blur of trees and lampposts on either side. The trees are thick-pressed, a private forest; the lampposts are the spoilt twins of the Dallyangle street-lights, carved fish-hooks curling round their bases. Slumped at the foot of a fat oak – I only see it a moment, before I gasp and the window fogs – there's a fallow deer, bloodied at the antlers, slender legs buckled and head sprawled low.

Mother steadies me, voice firm as her grip on my shoulders. "The family are hunters, but they won't have shot it. Probably. The deer rut will be finishing now – it must be spent with exhaustion."

She arches an eyebrow for my bafflement – "I may disapprove of the concept, but I am not so ignorant of the aristocracy and its customs as Lady Miltonwaters thought."

The carriage bucks, snapping my teeth – and we stop.

Dorothea Thorne hands us down, in the oddest combination of matronly housekeeper and brawny footman you've never thought to make. I bunch my skirt in my fist, fumble for footholds on the folding steps. No dirt track anymore, only pallid pea-gravel crunching under my feet. The park around us muffles the cold, but the treetops bristle like kindling, and I'd be shivering regardless of the temperature.

Alberstowe Hall is a house like a stately beehive. The stones are honeycomb, and the glittering windows swarm up four floors in curtain-tinted colours: blue, brown, purple, red. The roof's lined with a parade of statues, stark against the pale sky – pointy-tongued dragons, frightened women bursting into trees, two antler-locked stags that look significantly less dead than the one in the park.

The effect's more modern than I expected – I expected an Otranto castle, or Laura's ever-stormy medical school – but, if anything, the modernity's intimidating. These stone furbelows and endless windows aren't spiderwebbed heirlooms from some Norman battlefield. Someone paid for them in the last century, while wearing a waistcoat only a few inches longer than the ones you'd get today.

Dorothea claps her hands. "This way!"

The entrance hall's open at the middle all the way up, with a square-edged spiral of a staircase, like a ringlet drawn with a ruler. It's a relief when we don't venture too far up: some of the landings just *hang* there, stretched across like bridges, the drop steep and stark on either side. The wall-bound stairs are lined with paintings and weapons – sloshy oily faces with too much of Lady Miltonwaters in their loose chins and following eyes, broad boastful houses starting out of landscapes I don't recognise, rifles so heavy-looking it's a wonder they stay on the wall. Dorothea ushers us down a corridor on the second floor – past a narrow door with *Telephone Room* painted in strident capitals, past a few dozen doors unworthy of labels, and into the last of them. A boutonnière of a parlour, walls and ceiling painted with the last century's pastel-tinted flowers, chandelier blooming overhead. I half-expect the air to smell as fragrant as it looks, get a weird shock when I gasp in the sting of carbolic.

Silhouetted at the huge window, there's a man. Or, when he turns around: a boy, younger than me. Not that his youth's a reassurance. He's one of those pale boys with a body like a fancy drainpipe – not skinny, but eerily solid, like his every meal's had more than a fistful of meat in it. His brown hair – and moustache – are squashed with pomade. There's not a fold out of place in his tweed suit. If you squint, you can see the room reflected in the long toes of his shoes: walls, ceilings, chandelier, flowery furniture, all tiny and trapped twice-over.

Dorothea curtsies. She and her lordling stare at us for a long moment – but Mother offers only a curt dip of the head, and I'm not giving them the satisfaction of anything.

The boy arches an eyebrow. "Mrs. Ballestas. I believe I requested that you come alone."

I swallow. I can't force her to excuse me, not when she didn't even want me to come. "I'm her daughter. And a founding member of the Dallyangle Division. Isn't that what you want to discuss, Lord – " – *lord* indeed, because for all Mother's research I don't know a thing about translating titles into sentences – " – Lord Miltonwaters? Lord Marquess?"

To my astonishment, he seems to brighten. "I am flattered, Miss Ballestas, but I am not quite the marquess yet. That title is presently held by my grandfather. Alas, I am afraid he cannot join us today. He is upstairs, but rarely leaves his rooms – he is elderly, you understand, and terribly frail, and wishes me to manage the estate in his stead."

Didn't this elderly frail marquess kill his gardener on a pheasant-shoot a few weeks ago? Wasn't that where Adelaide and Lady Miltonwaters got the head? – but there's bravery, and then there's reckless idiocy, so I don't say it.

"You may go, Thorne," he adds carelessly. "And send up Nettleblack with some tea."

Wait – *what?*

But Dorothea dips out with no further explanation, and then Lord Miltonwaters the not-marquess is gesturing us into pretty chairs with brittle legs.

"Well, then." He stays standing over us – sneaky fiend – and clasps his signet-laden hands. "You are the infamous Mrs. Keturah Ballestas, whom Poor Cousin Ellie so roundly despised."

Mother's jaw tightens. "Indeed."

"You'll forgive the informal address." He sighs, sharp and hissing as a blast of steam. "For poor Ellie – that harridan hardly merits the title of *Lady Miltonwaters*. I am sorry she bedevilled you. It was not conduct befitting a woman of her rank."

Mother lifts an eyebrow, realises she's done it, drops it like a scalding handle. "Your apology is – appreciated, milord – "

"Of course." He strikes up a pace before us, back and forth across the rug. "I was not here to check her then. Only just finished my studies – a man wants to see a little of the world before he comes home to his future. After the pheasant-shoot was cancelled, she told me I need not come at all, that she would handle the family's affairs while I remained in London. I don't know which was the more pathetic – the lie, or the fact that she thought she *could* lie to me. I arrived to find Ellie and her maid in gaol, rumours swirling about my grandfather, and the Miltonwaters name in the mud. A pretty pickle, I trust you'll agree."

Never have I heard *pretty pickle* enunciated with so much murderous rage. I'm very quick to nod when his glare scorches across my face.

"We meant to have Lady – ah – the Head-Hiders removed from Hartgate Gaol," Mother supplies, tone poised in wary neutrality. "To devise some alternative way of proceeding – the Division has no intention of becoming the police. But Hartgate was adamant that – "

"No need to fret. I bailed them out and dealt with the

aftermath. I am the future Marquess of Alberstowe – the mess was mine to tidy. You need not fear that these so-called *Head-Hiders* will trouble you anymore."

Head-Hiders. Plural.

My heart lurches. It thwacks everything in my chest off-kilter, bashes my breathing out of my control.

"I see." Mother swallows. "Where is Lady Miltonwaters now, milord?"

"*Ellie*," he corrects waspishly, "is in seclusion at a different residence. I have stripped her of her allowance, her social calendar, and her responsibilities in Dallyangle. My inheritance is no longer her playground."

I bite my lip. I hate the sensation, but I don't trust myself without it. *What about Adelaide*, I want to blurt – *what have you done with Adelaide?*

"Now." Lord Miltonwaters fixes Mother with a stare like a barbed fish-hook. "You say this Division of yours is not affiliated with the police. Would you care to clarify for me, then, what exactly you *are*?"

She's slow with her answer. Careful. Stacking the words like cards. And – sweet Lord – I do not blame her.

"When my family moved here, I was anxious to involve myself in Dallyangle's civic affairs. Discussions with the town council revealed both an antipathy towards installing a branch of the New Police, and growing need for an alternative. I suggested I might trial an organisation of my own invention, and the council provided financial support following our initial successes. The Division has been running for just over a year."

"Provided?" he echoes, grey eyes glinting. "Are the council no longer funding you?"

My turn. "They would be, milord – only they had the funds stolen last night. I don't know if you've been here long enough to hear of the Sweetings, or Pip Property, but – "

"Cassandra has theories regarding the culprit," Mother interrupts hastily, with a quelling scowl. "But to answer your question, milord: as of last night, the council are not able to provide us with the funding we need."

He smiles. Smug, unabashed, so bizarre even Mother can't keep from gaping at him. "How fortunate I brought you here to offer precisely that."

For a long moment that must strain every nerve in the room, there's just flabbergasted silence.

I end up fumbling for words first. "*You* want to fund the Division?"

"Just so." He squares his shoulders. "Dallyangle is my inheritance, and you are clearly a crucial part of Dallyangle. It only makes sense for you to work for me – "

"No," Mother blurts.

I stare at her. He stares at her, narrow-eyed, with horrible quiet impatience. And – for once in her life – you don't need my practice to read her face. There's terror there, and revulsion so marked it tugs her spectacles down her nose, and something furious in her eyes.

"Forgive me, milord," she spits, jolting to her feet so suddenly I flinch, "but I cannot accept."

"Why on earth not?"

Her voice is shaking. "You are an English nobleman. I know of your family. I have studied the contents of your paintings – the houses – the plantation. I know how your ancestors procured the funds to build Alberstowe Hall. I am sensible of your generosity, but I will not allow the money they made from enslaved labour to pay for my Division."

Oh.

It's as if a crack's sprung in the walls around us. As if one more sudden movement will topple the room. As if the chandelier is about to snap its chain and crash down on my head.

Or, at least, it is – for me.

Lord Miltonwaters blinks at her. His pale forehead is foxed with a frown, his eyes a passable sham of politeness. But the corners of him aren't sharp enough – there's not even horror in the thin set of his lips. He's just quizzical, restless, mildly irritated, so much that I can't keep looking at him. I squint round his well-tailored edges; my tongue's suddenly leaden, my teeth cutting into it at strange angles.

"Well then." For him, speaking seems insanely, maddeningly easy. "What do you say to your funding coming exclusively from the Dallyangle rents? I'll raise them all. Dallyangle itself can pay for the Division. Would that – soothe your conscience?"

Mother's trembling. I lift a hand – I don't know where the nerve comes from, only that I've got to – and twine my fingers with hers, stiffen against a shudder when his eyes dart to our handclasp. "I – I would not want you to raise anyone's rent, milord – "

"Mrs. Ballestas, may I be blunt?"

He clears his throat. By the sound of his voice, he didn't need to.

"I am not one of many funding offers through which you might pick and choose. I am to be the Marquess of Alberstowe – an institution which, as you know, has been around for far longer than *over a year* – and I must do whatever it takes to restore my inheritance to the perfection it has sadly lost. I do not doubt that your Division would be capable of maintaining my peace with the right financial support – but if you refuse me, I will need to bring in someone more sensible of the situation's urgency."

Another steam-sharp sigh. "Believe me, I too find the New Police distasteful, as should any nobleman worth his salt. Why poor Ellie was so besotted with them, I cannot fathom. But if you will not accept my offer – and, really, I do not want it to come to this! – I shall have to have the New Police installed in Dallyangle, to curtail these criminals – whereupon I imagine they will also immediately curtail your Division. And I don't suppose they will take kindly to people like you usurping their role. I do not know how they might treat you, your daughter, your fellow Division members, but I suspect it will not be gently. Do you think the police will remember you,

Mrs. Ballestas, and all your renegade journalism? What do you think they might do when they find out just how *tangible* your defiance has become?"

Mother gasps.

And his question spills, like bad dye, seeping and burning straight through my mind. I think of Hartgate Gaol and its slimy solitary cells, of shouts through the walls as Divisioners fight and lose, of Septimus's snarl and Gertie's whimper. I think of the closest policemen I've seen, *too* close, leering at me over Mother's shoulder, as their chests clogged our London hallway and their helmets scraped our doorframe – *just a warning, Mrs. Ballestas, just while you've still got time enough to stop.* I think of their split-knuckled hands on her arms, holding her in a dock with her glasses cracked, the only Black face in a crowded grey courtroom – I wouldn't be with her, I'd still be alone in that cell. I'd not know her fate. I'd not even know my own until –

There's a skittery knock at the door.

We're all frozen but him, and it opens at his instigation, lets in a timid clatter of cups. It's a maidservant in a lace cap, handing round a tea-tray from him to us –

But I can't grab my cup. I can't move. The maid's eyes sting on mine for one terrifying second: fear, resentment, boiling through a surface of arsenic green.

"Adelaide?" I stammer.

"Miss Ballestas." Measly words, measly politeness. Not even *Cassie.* "I'm glad to see you looking well."

Mother's voice is hardly steadier than mine. "Milord – you took Miss Danadlenddu onto your staff?"

He sips his tea without wincing. Either it's lukewarm or he's got lips of steel. "I could not permit Ellie to retain her household. And neither could I permit this Nettleblack chit to scurry round the town spreading gossip about my family."

Adelaide retreats with a curtsy and a glance, as vicious and helpless as her last. He clicks his fingers before she can escape, and she ends up hovering, a bone-coloured wraith on his immaculate rug. Adelaide, the Head-Hider, the girl who smashed my life on her palm, but – here, in this room, drab and disjointed round his tea-tray – she's just flimsy. Small. I know her pretences now, know that this deference isn't one of them: he's broken her.

Miltonwaters smirks. "I trust she's repenting her head-hiding now – aren't you, Nettleblack?"

She twitches her gaze to her empty tray. "Milord."

"Why do you keep calling her Nettleblack?" I demand. Though *demand* isn't the word – my voice is too faint, too shaky. "She's their cousin, she doesn't use – "

"She does in my house." He scoffs. "That Welsh translation's a terrible mouthful. And it keeps the Nettleblacks in perspective, you see. From what Ellie told me, that family are prone to getting ideas above their station."

I let go of Mother then, to snatch my teacup before my shaking hand rattles it off its saucer. I've no idea what to say. I'm not sure I *can* say more, with my throat twisted tight and damp as laundry in a copper. The room's not cracking now – it can't crack, not when he's so completely indifferent to how it was built – if anything, it's getting sturdier, closer, brighter, as I lose my grip on a defiance I want but can't word, on anything that isn't the thoughts he's just crammed into my head –

I glance back to Mother. She can't even look at me. His threats are visible, there in all the splinters of her composure.

"I will help you, Mrs. Ballestas, and you will help me. Your charming daughter and her colleagues will tidy up my town – and I will enable you to do it to the best of your ability. Dallyangle will be free of these criminal blotches, your Division will be saved from a penniless and premature conclusion, and my family's reputation will be restored to the respect it ought to command, all thanks to your invaluable aid. We are in perfect understanding now. Yes?"

CHAPTER NINE

THE DREGS OF MY DARLING'S WORST DECISION

Casebook of Matthew Adelstein (translated from an otherwise impenetrable code)

DAMN IT

DAMN IT

DAMN IT

I never intended to be –
I should never have obliged him to –
Enough of this. Send the note.
THERE'S NO ONE TO *TAKE* THE WRETCHED NOTE YOU FOOL
Nicholas was right. On every count. Of course he was.
But I can't – I *can't* –

Pertaining to unpleasantness

To the Matthew Adelstein of two months' time: when conducting the annual review of 1893's casebooks, please ignore the above. I am simply not accustomed to – that is, Nicholas and I do not ordinarily fall into such disagreement. Our opinions will differ, as is only to be expected, but not to the extent of raised voices. Raised voices – from *him.*

But I have trapped myself in the house, and there is nothing else to do but think on it.

I thought we were in accord viz. the present precautions. If Miss Rosamond Nettleblack (whereabouts unknown) means to act on her threat, she will need witnesses against us; therefore, obviously, every potential witness must be cauterised. Henry Nettleblack is, ironically, not a danger this time – investigations so far have revealed her continued ignorance of her sister's blackmail attempt, and her relationship with Division Sergeant Septimus would (*must*) indicate a lack of desire to accuse Nicholas and I; that she also has no idea where Miss Rosamond is, suggests siding with her sister to destroy us is unlikely. But everyone else – the butler, the cook, the skivvy, the hypothetical builders for the broken roof – everything else is too much of a risk. Everyone that comes into our house, glimpses our living arrangements –

I must report, regrettably, the extent to which Nicholas disagrees with my measures on the matter of *everyone else.* Refusing to hire builders (I paraphrase him) was troublesome enough of me, with his rat-attic now almost too leak-ridden for rodent habitation, but dismissing our entire household staff was *too far, Matty, and you know I'd not say it lightly! How'm I supposed to breed rats with a hole in the roof and a house to run?* I explained, again, the danger, but – *I'm not doing every servant's work for the rest of our lives* – which was not my intention, Nicholas, beyond recognition of the simple fact that you're better at cooking and you know how to black a range – *but I've just as much of a job as you!* And I never claimed otherwise – *but how many meals have you made us, Matty? How many fires have you lit?* – but Miss Rosamond's threat – *look, I know you're scared of your parents* – and criminal conviction, Nicholas – *and I'm not saying I'm not scared too* – then you understand we can't risk anyone finding out – *but can you at least not forget that I've been found out already! Found out and thrown out! So please stop acting like that's the moment your life's meant to shrivel up!*

And then he had answered the door, in the absence of our butler, his fingers shaking as he opened a scribbly summons from Cassandra Ballestas. From the glimpse I dared, she appeared to be requesting his aid to catch the still-escaped ferret. I would have accompanied him, but it was plain from his demeanour that he wished to fulfil this new task alone, so I held my tongue as he stormed out with a rat-cage in his arms.

I meant, immediately, to address the disparities to which he had referred: to light the range and prepare a pot of chai for his return. I have watched him flick deft-fingered through his family recipe so many times; I thought that I had also committed it to memory.

It might be surmised from the above that I did not succeed in this endeavour.

No. I did, in one exasperating respect. The range is finally, rampantly alight, and now I cannot leave the house for fear of burning it down.

I *should* be following Nicholas to the Division – separately, yes, if he wishes the space – and speaking to the Director about last night. I should be querying that strange business with Miss Marigold Chandler and Cassandra the *lady detective*. I even penned a note to request the Director's presence here; much as I dislike the idea of Director Ballestas witnessing the state of the house, I do – of course! – acknowledge that the Division's circumstances are too troubled to permit me such qualms. I am done with steering my own solitary course – and steering it clean through the side of the Divisionary ship. I must know what Cassandra discovered. I must –

But now I can't. The servants are gone – Nicholas is elsewhere – there is no one even to deliver any Directorial note.

Perhaps I ought not to ignore the above.

Nicholas, my dearest, I am so immensely sorry.

Addendum: further unpleasantness
I was still endeavouring to dampen the flames when a knock

summoned me upstairs – pocketwatch in hand, resigned not to leave the range alone for longer than two minutes. Stepping across the threshold – and, as it were, from my very wishful thinking – was Director Ballestas herself, her hair pulled tighter than usual, enough to sharpen its streaks of grey. I was obliged to escort her immediately down to the kitchen.

She stared at the unwashed crockery, the scorched kettle, the small explosion of cinnamon and ginger root on the counter; her eyes widened when they caught the flare of the fire, until a tilt of her head turned the flames opaque on her spectacles. "Is everything alright, Matthew?"

I informed her, with impeccable composure, that nothing was amiss.

She arched an eyebrow, then skirted the kitchen table to reach my side, and – to my consternation, regrettably too fierce to conceal – ran her thumb across my forehead. She showed me: soot. I doubted immensely that she had scrubbed the worst of it.

"We are very grateful to your lodger for his assistance with the ferret," she offered, so gently I clenched my jaw. "Mr. Fitzdegu suggested you and I ought to have a word, and I agree. Since your return to the Division, your work and your manner – you do not seem yourself – "

"I should hope not. My behaviour at the Division before the – ah – unwise resignation is certainly not something I mean to perpetuate."

She pursed her lips. "I see. Well. Today's developments will ease the pressure on you, even so. Cassandra is returning from her leave, and I am making her a detective. As Miss Chandler has already confided in her, she will lead on the case of the town hall robbery. You can assist her, as much as you are presently able."

Presently able?

"I can do more than *assist!*"

A sudden frown. "Cassandra is perfectly capable."

I had not, as far I had noticed, claimed to the contrary –

"I would urge you," she added, "to dismiss any conclusions drawn from your discovery of her – her – the *novel-writing.* She has made the choice to surmount it, to try again, to do better – and I cannot deny her that chance. She needs your support, not your disdain. Now more than ever. She has endured difficulties you cannot understand, and she endures difficulties still – far more than I would have wished."

I was unnerved. I admit to having formerly harboured – *disdain* is too strong, *sensible scepticism* more appropriate – for the deductive abilities of the Director's scribbling daughter, but those reservations hardly rendered me oblivious to the fact that Cassandra *solved the Head-Hider case*. Yet the Director's eyes were narrow, her fingers very taut in their fold at her waist, and her voice had taken on the sharpness of a tuning-fork.

I hastened, then, to affirm in no uncertain terms my endorsement of the younger Ballestas. "I purely meant that – if the Division's funding has disappeared, you need every detective fully committed to the – "

She sighed – then smiled, a carving of a smile, too neat to chip. "We will not be without funding. The Division is to be supported."

"By whom? The Nettleblacks?"

She blinked. "Not quite. Henry gave me to understand that the Nettleblack fortune operates on principles not dissimilar to a title – everything to the eldest sibling – and I didn't want our newest recruit thinking she was valued at the Division only for her family's wealth. Besides, Miss Edwina Nettleblack did not make the offer – Lord Clement Miltonwaters did."

I do not paraphrase. I do not – *can't* – duck under a single horrible syllable. It froze the kitchen for a queasy moment, briefly chilled even the overstoked fire.

"If I may, I don't think a Miltonwaters – "

"You can't condemn the whole family for Lady Miltonwaters's actions."

"I can condemn the *institution* of the family! As can you! The behaviour it has encouraged – the entitlement! With the town council in disarray, do you really think it wise to ally the Division with the town's aristocratic landlord-to-be? Does it not ring a little too like – well, too feudal, for a start, and us his private militia?"

Her smile stiffened. "I would never let it come to that."

"Then refuse him!" I scrabbled at my mind, plaiting solutions. "Miss Nettleblack paid us handsomely for Henry's safety – we'll manage until we recover the real funding. Cassandra and I can – "

"The arrangement is already made."

My mouth fell open. "Without consulting the Division? But you said – "

"*I know,*" she snapped.

"Then – "

She cut me off with my name. She is one of the few who prefers it to my surname; it rarely lacks the ability to silence me like a schoolboy, and the effect was all the more bludgeoning on my crumpled shirtsleeves and smudged face.

"I think," – she was stiflingly calm, stifling far more than just me – "you need to worry rather more about yourself than our new patron. I want my Divisioners to be cheerful – unperturbed – able to do and enjoy their work to the full. There will be no more *festering*. You will trust me to manage our patron, and you will focus on managing whatever it is that so disorders your affairs. If you require a period of leave in which to do so, you need only ask. Is that understood?"

I ought to have ordered my mind. There was a compelling argument against this proclamation, and if I had shelved away the disarray of the morning I might have found it. But the disarray wasn't even confined to my skull: the scalding heat on my waistcoat-back, the spilt bits of unbrewed chai, the streaks of soot on the flagstones and my knees and my knuckles, the casebook at an angle on the filthy table – everything in my periphery was a horsefly bite, and I could hardly think for wanting to scratch it all.

I was as unsettled as her to hear what I actually said, the words startling and insistent as a doppelgänger: "Is everything alright, Director?"

She inclined her head. "Perfectly fine, thank you."

She left before I could question it, pressing an envelope into my hands as she turned for the stairs, the wart of sealing-wax slimy on my palm. "Perhaps this might help settle you. A commission from Miss Nettleblack – familiar territory, for you. And this time I trust we can be sure Miss Rosamond isn't hiding in the Division."

Then she was gone. I tore it open, tore it up, flung it into the range.

Addendum again (that's what he says, isn't it???)

The Plan and Agreement for Sorting Things Out, Drawn Up (With Permission) By Nick Fitzdegu, While Matty Goes and Does Step One of It

1. Matty will tell Miss Nettleblack (Edwina) he can't look for Miss Rosamond. Obviously he won't say *why*, or anything.
2. Nick will get our butler back. (*Yes* he will!!)
3. Matty will keep an eye on the Div's new patron in case he does anything suspicious, and also on the Director because she's hiding something *again*.
4. Nick will make not a single meal for all of next week! (Not least because Vernon Vibbrit is going to strangle the whole Div for what the ferret did to his guinea pig unless I catch said ferret and calm him down...)

Well then. Look at this. I'm writing in *the casebook!*

Matty said I could, mind. My grovelling darling. I got home and the place was beautiful – looked it, at any rate, until I sat down and *tasted* his try at my chai. But he did try. And now it's all *have my dressing-gown, Nicholas* and *amuse yourself with my casebook, Nicholas* and *I'll bring us back the whole pie-shop, Nicholas* (fine, he said it in sensible words). I told him he'd already apologised, but by then there wasn't any stopping him. And I'm not going to *not* enjoy it when he's on his knees and kissing my hands and gazing up with thrice more adorable soul than any of Vibbrit's cavy carte de visites! –

I won't even start on how tempted I am to keep going and watch him blush when he reads it – assuming I'm doing his code right! But he's paranoia in a suit right now, so I'll be gentle. I thought I was being gentle earlier – not the row, obviously, when I got back – and he still ended up in tears, poor darling.

But I meant what I said, Matty dearest. Miss Rosamond can only ruin our lives if we let her.

So go forth and get rid of some Nettleblacks!

P.S. the discussion about the roof is not over...

Addendum (yes, Nicholas, that is *'what he says')*
One thing at time! The butler, I concede; strangers in the attic is a step too far at present.

It's only left to report the peculiar circumstances under which I completed *step one* of Nicholas's aforementioned list. (I had no idea he'd taught himself so much of my code.)

I crossed the street in a blaze – apt, when my purpose for the night was to burn a bridge. Disappointing Miss Nettleblack naturally equates to expecting no further financial assistance from Miss Nettleblack: recovering the stolen funding is therefore our sole remaining option for ridding the Division of this Miltonwaters fix. But if this compromise ensures Nicholas's safety – so be it. *He's right. I will not let fear destroy me. I will get free of this family's stinging tendrils, and then I will be a detective in earnest again.*

The butler met me at the front door – decommissioned as I meant to be, I saw no need to scrape down to the servants' entrance. "Miss Nettleblack has given orders not to be disturbed. She has a private fitting with the family tailor."

He changed his mind at the mention of Miss Rosamond's name; dangling the hint was perhaps more callous than I would have wished, but the sister in question had left me with no choice.

The butler vanished at a clip – dashed back with the answer I needed. I had expected the drawing-room, but the butler took me higher, up to what I presumed must be Miss Nettleblack's study, for its ebony desk and green-bound bookshelves.

Miss Nettleblack herself was pinned inside a velvet dress the colour and texture of moss, its unhemmed skirts spilling over the floorboards. She had been deep in murmured discussion, but glanced up sharply when I was shown in. Lorrie Tickering, her conversation-partner, crouched at her feet – and followed her gaze to me, whereupon he made at once a great show of chalking out where her hem ought to be cut.

"Mr. Adelstein." Miss Nettleblack glanced between us, swallowed against her high collar, pressed on. "I believe you are acquainted with my – tailor?"

Mr. Tickering beamed at her, at me; it was disconcerting to see his sister Septimus's sharp-toothed grin repurposed to such reassuring benevolence. "Adelstein! Long time no see! How've you been? And how's Nick? Sept said he'd been helping with the ferret?"

I – did *not* blush. (I concede that Septimus's brother is alarmingly handsome, in much the same statuesque way – or so Nicholas assures me – as his sister, but any recognition of that fact was firmly tempered by the severity of my errand.) "Miss Nettleblack. Mr. Tickering. I apologise for my poor timing – "

"No, it's fine!" he cried, with an appendix of radiant smile for Miss Nettleblack's keen scrutiny. "I've just been *tailoring* for Miss Nettleblack. 'Cause, y'know, I'm her *tailor*. So I'll just carry on *tailoring*, if it's all the same to you!"

Miss Nettleblack returned his smile – smaller on her, with a twitch-lipped tentativeness I would almost have designated *shy* – then lifted her chin, stare fixed on the wall. "Anything you wish to share with me, you may share with Mr. Tickering also."

I confess I was surprised. Miss Nettleblack has – *had*, I ought to say – a mania for decorous secrecy when it comes to her renegade sisters; to permit the family tailor to remain present whilst I confided potentially insalubrious details about Miss Rosamond was odd indeed. Perhaps Tickering's relation to Septimus made him, in her eyes, an honorary Divisioner. (I considered it mere self-projection – then, at least – to detect a fragment of *he's my lodger* about *I'm her tailor*.)

I brought us to the principal subject without further comment. At Miss Rosamond's name, Miss Nettleblack flinched, and urged me not to spare her should the news be unpleasant. The Director's strained smile scraped at my mind; necessity aside, it was disconcerting to feel this chance of alleviating it skidding unhindered over my lips.

"I do not know where Miss Rosamond is. Nor am I able to find out."

Her eyes widened, panicked incredulity in sickly green – a look and a shade I knew too well. "Why not?"

"I cannot say. You will allow me my privacy, as I have always protected yours, and take my word: circumstances have made it impossible for me to do anything your sister might consider against her interests."

It was as much I dared. Her voice trembled: "And returning to safety in the family home is – not in Rosamond's interests?"

"You know your sister best."

She exchanged a smarting glance with Tickering, who had been pinning and unpinning the same inch of skirt for some time. "Let me understand. You will not help me ensure Rosamond's protection? You mean to say I must take the matter into my own hands?"

I coloured – until good sense forced my thoughts to Nicholas, to pie-shop dinner, to tobacco-scented fingers folding over mine. "I hope, if you don't consider it impertinent, that you will withdraw your request for the Division's assistance."

"But why? Why will you not help her? You were more than ready to find Henry!"

"A commission which contributed to the near-destruction of the Division. I appreciate your faith in our abilities, Miss Nettleblack, but I will not become your hunting-dog for another missing sister. That is all I will say."

"*Hunting-dog?*" she echoed, fingers convulsing so violently in her skirts that she yanked the hem from Tickering's hands. "Is that truly what you think I am doing?"

"I – "

"Is that how it looks?" she demanded, turning to Tickering, clasping his proffered hand – not scornful, not indignant, far more akin to a genuine question. "To involve the Division? Do I – do the Division disapprove – does everyone disapprove – would Rosamond assume – ?"

He stood up, curled his other hand round her shoulder. "Rosamond always thinks the worst. It's not *you*, Edwina – "

"But it is! I frighten them all away!"

"That ain't true – Henry and Sept ain't frightened now, are they? – and Rosamond's a menace, you know that, you dealt with that – "

"It was never meant to be permanent!" Her voice cracked. "The Division are right. I should not subject Rosamond to a manhunt. I should not have done it to Henry. I should have – known what to – I am the eldest – I am supposed to – I – "

She slumped against him. He met my gaze over her shoulder, flicked a pointed glance to the door, then gave himself up to holding her close. I deemed it sensible to retreat.

I cannot cross Miss Rosamond's wishes. Nor can I live forever in their shadow, and permit them to unhinge Nicholas's life as well as my own. What I provoked in 5 Catfish Crescent was, therefore, unavoidable. Regrettable, but essential. My concern, at present, simply cannot extend to the fraught intricacies of a family whose squabbles have brought Nicholas and I nothing but fear and inconvenience.

But I must admit I winced as I left. Behind the study door, appallingly audible right down the stairs, Miss Edwina Nettleblack was sobbing.

END OF VOLUME ONE

VOLUME TWO

CHAPTER TEN

I AM THE PRINCIPAL SUSPECT, APPARENTLY

The Notebook of Doom

For the attention of Rosamond Nettleblack

Concerning Tuesday 21st November 1893

My darling, this next is for you.

I thought – *hoped* – my days of scribbling despair in an ill-furnished morgue were over. But you need to know the absurdity that's being bandied about this place, for the (imminent; I shan't believe otherwise) moment when you make your triumphant return. If I can spare you from being caught off-guard quite so violently as me –

I shall write. And you shall read it. Soon.

And I need you with me somehow, because – without exaggeration – I am very frightened indeed.

I do not recommend attempting to sleep on a morgue slab. I avoided it as long as I could, curled up with Henry's notebook and Septimus's belligerent gifts, hoping for another knock on the door – then, when enough tapers had melted to make that unlikely, gnawing on the cheese and reading the novel. I tip my long-lost hat to the anonymous author of *Life and Limbs*: the book was almost a distraction, all the more enjoyable when I noticed I was reading Gertie's copy, and speeding past her ridiculous knitted bookmark. If she laid hands on me again, I'd spoil the ending for her.

My second recommendation: do *not* eat an entire wheel of cheese and read a novel about misbehaving surgeons before attempting to sleep on a morgue slab. My nightmares were proliferous – the strangers with the carriage, driving you off the Pobbles cliffs; the Sweetings impaling me with Earlyfate before the Queen; Mamma and Edwina taking tea in the burnt remnants of my house, trilling *check your property* in unison until I woke with a strangled yell. No one came. Once you've been swallowed by the founding member of the Amateur Morgue Society, not a Divisionary soul can hear you scream.

The morning dragged me out of the only dreamless doze I'd managed, to the tune of several dozen thwacks on the door. In the headache-inducing stuffiness of a room without windows, daylight came only through the cracks in the doorframe. Too groggy for recollections, I mumbled something hopeful about laverbread, twisted in my blankets and reached for you –

And promptly fell off the morgue slab.

"Property!"

I groaned.

"Don't you try anything! We're coming in!"

I'd toppled onto my bruises, and the pain had much the same effect as strong black tea. I scrabbled at my clothes, a blindfold appraisal: fit for company? Trousers – sweet bene-diction, yes. Braces – good. Shirt unbuttoned to my sternum – not ideal. Feet and throat bare, waistcoat and jacket and cravat in absentia –

"Wait," I croaked, to utterly no effect.

Then I was spotlit, crumpled on the floorboards, a tangle of limbs and blankets and knotty dishevelment, hissing for the sting of light in my eyes. The open door was a blinding bas-re-lief: two figures, stocky and statuesque, waiting in mocking silence as I struggled to my feet. There were splinters in the floorboards – which did, at least, stop me backing away – and the rush of air was heavy with woodsmoke.

Backlit as my visitors were, they had full five seconds' unscuppered scrutiny of me before I could make them out. My face flared, and my fingers were fists far too swiftly to hide. The shorter figure tensed, burly arms and broad chest jostling her into Gertie; her serene counterpart barely fluttered. I didn't even need light, then, to know who she was.

"Pip Property." Only the unshakeable manners of Director Keturah Ballestas could make my name sound like a polite greeting. "Good morning."

I should have flung a blanket at her. Addled as I was, I nearly did.

If my consternation was obvious, the Director gave no indication of noticing it; the recent Divisionary troubles had apparently done nothing to dent her stoicism. She regarded me coolly from behind her spectacles – her eyes are a marvellous gold, bright against her brown skin, yet she manages to make the colour look freezing – one eyebrow arching as I fumbled for a response. Gertie wasn't helping, glowering ruddy-cheeked at her employer's side: translation, *I will be revenged for my cheese.*

But, rumpled and twitchy as I was, I could still aspire to chivalry.

"Director Ballestas. My compliments to your morgue slab. I presume you're here as the voice of Bedford-educated good sense, to let me go with a bushel of apologies?"

She didn't even blink. "Not exactly."

"See, Director?" Gertie hissed. "Told you they'd be playing the innocent!"

I set my shoulders. "You do realise this is kidnap. Or abduction. Or – gracious, I don't know the difference, but – my point is, it's a crime! And I'll complain every detail of it to the Dallyangle Town Council, unless you release me at once."

"Will you?" she retorted calmly, with – *what?* – nary a crack in that careful façade. At her side, Gertie snorted incredulously.

"Given your treatment of the council, I'll be surprised if they listen to you."

Clammy fear slid down my back. "My what?"

"You are to be interviewed now. It will be best for us – for you – for everyone – if you cooperate. Gertrude, oblige me by searching them – after what you told me of yesterday, I won't have Cassandra put in danger."

I sprang away as Gertie lumbered towards me, splinters latching like ticks in my feet – "Wait, you dairy fiend, I'm not even dressed!"

Gertie cornered me, stomping and unrepentant. Dragged her fingers over my arms, my legs, shoved a whole hand into my trouser pockets, fussing for all the additional swordsticks I had presumably concealed in my braces, for all that I squirmed against her.

She should have been searching inside the pillowcase. I should have led her there and flourished this notebook at her. But – and I know it was stupid cowardice – in that moment, all I could picture were the pages, smudged and torn in her half-knitted hands. Henry and Septimus had commissioned it; they, at least, would respect the contents. And they'd come back for it, surely, assuming this so-called *interview* didn't fix everything first –

Gertie grabbed my shirt, made to finish refastening the buttons, with the no-nonsense grimace of an aunt thrice her age. *Va bene.* "Laura saves Benedict from the surgeons' guild in Chapter Forty by slapping Dr Stoker with his amputated hand – "

"No!" – mercifully, she leapt backwards – "Don't you dare!"

The Director very nearly scowled. "Gertrude, please do your job – "

Then the corridor itself started shrieking. It was a noise to puncture eyeballs, shrill and metallic. Someone bawled over it – Gertie's ghastly relation, by the voice: "Cass! *Cass!* Make it stop!"

A flurry of movement outside – a door flung open, a blur dashing out of sight – and then the shrieking ceased, given over to a lower plait of voices I couldn't catch. The Director met my stare with a sharp look: "That's none of your concern."

"Reckon there's no more weapons," Gertie added shakily. "But I can tie their wrists, if it'll ease your mind for Cass?"

"Dio mio, you absolutely shan't!"

I elbowed past her, dashed for the Director – couldn't even call myself surprised when Gertie seized my shoulders. "This is absurd! Why am I here? What am I supposed to have done? Why do none of you care about Rosamond Nettleblack's disappearance? I won't cooperate – I won't say a word to your wretched *Cass* – unless *someone* in this Division justifies the ways of me to me, *immediately!*"

My legs almost gave when the Director nodded. "Very well."

She took a breath. Behind her, the voices rose and fell, fretful as a storm at the window.

"You are here because you are the inventor of and intelligence behind a series of crimes committed by yourself, and your lackeys Maggie and Norman Sweeting. These crimes include: hair-theft in the street, housebreaking, the selling of stolen goods – "

(Regrettably, accurate.)

" – the abduction of Division Apprentice Henry Nettleblack, the repeated assault of Division Sergeant Septimus – "

(Of course I winced.)

" – the assault of Division Apprentices Gertrude Skull, Oliver Skull, and Millicent Musgrove – "

(Exaggerated, but –)

" – the misleading of Divisionary investigations – "

(Damn it.)

" – the release of an undisciplined and malevolent ferret – "

(Inadvertently!)

" – and the robbery of the Dallyangle Town Hall, during which you and your accomplices stole a year and a half of the Division's funding."

(*What?*)

"And if there is a shred of truth in your claim that Miss Rosamond Nettleblack is in danger, you are the principal suspect for that too."

I was abruptly, dazedly, giddily glad that Gertie was holding me up.

"I – I – *maledizione* – "

"Indeed. Gertrude, would you escort them to Cassandra's office?"

When I was a spoilt child (I pray you, darling, indulge me), I was unaccountably obsessed with the bronze horses of San Marco. The basilica was the Participazio Mass of choice: every floor's a cravat design under that molten ceiling, and the marble walls are the very pattern of my innards, if you'll permit the vivisectionary fancy. The horses on the roof were my daydream-companions – and, Father being practised in bribing his way onto churches, it wasn't long before I got to see them up close. I was seven; it was a reward for surviving my tumble into the Grand Canal.

But up close – close enough to see the veins in their faces, the scratches in the bronze – my swaggering horses looked profoundly upset. I leaned out on the loggia (*prudenza*, Mamma snapped), locked eyes with my favourite, stared aghast at its mottled panic.

"Gracious, Pip, of course they're frightened," Father observed, hastening at once to my horrified look. "They've been stolen often enough!"

Thus, with my hair rumpled under his hand, I discovered my horses anew – as loot from Constantinople, and then as prisoners in Napoleon's Paris, now returned with all due stress to our youthful Kingdom of Italy. Mamma had been alive to see Venice gutted and fired on, but the Participazio clan made sure their children didn't cringe for those horrors. Thus, as a sheltered youth with a glass chandelier in my bedroom, in a Grand Canal ca' that had been meticulously repurchased by parents, aunts, and uncles, the idea that things could be stolen – snatched away from you, terror-eyed and helpless – was a truly unsettling revelation.

And it came full circle in one dingy tack-room-turned-office belonging to the Dallyangle Division – except the loot was mine, and the feelings it engendered were more than worthy of those poor panicky horses.

Check your property, indeed!

The office, with its unswept floorboards, inky desk, and musty stench, had been stacked shoulder-high with *me*. My Sweetings-ravaged elopement suitcase, open atop a cabinet, glinting with all the waistcoats I should have worn on the Continent. The ledgers from my cravat shop, balanced on the leather folio I used for my household accounts. Pattern proto-types from my hallway walls, annotated – *annotated?* – in a scrawl I didn't recognise. One of the ferns from the cases on my windows, yellow-fronded and drooping in the window-less room. Earlyfate, still bloodstained and bisected, propped in the corner like a naughty child.

The office's back wall, meanwhile –

Gertie didn't need to shove me. I'd collapsed into my desig-nated chair.

The back wall was, without exaggeration, a Pip Property collage. No – worse – a Pip Property spiderweb. At its heart was a photograph of me, the one from the cravat catalogue, all pomade and smirk and scornfully perfect suit. It was pinned like a naturalist's specimen, or (more likely) a dartboard, and every pin had a twist of purple knitting-wool knotted about it, zigzagging to other pinned papers. A sketch of the Participazio ca', ripped from a Venice guidebook. Several pages of Father's best monograph, red ink twined about the dedication *to Pip, sparring-partner and progeny extraordinaire.* An engraving of Father and I – which *should* have been in the frame atop the account books – from *Rossetti's Remnants: An Early Italian Quarterly*, in which we grinned identically and brandished our Renaissance rapiers. A scribbly list of our Bloomsbury household, with ticks beside some of the servants' names. More *Dallyangle Standard* inches than I could squint at. A bad drawing of the ferret Henry begged me to adopt. My sketch of you, with your hair feral and your best Lady of Pain expression, and the Swinburne verses scrawled underneath: *O lips full of lust and of laughter, / Curled snakes that are fed from my breast, / Bite hard, lest remembrance come after / And press with new lips where you pressed –*

The insolent vigilantes had *broken into my house!*

Gertie tugged my wrists behind me. If I'd been in reach of the swordstick, she might have lost an arm.

But, horrifying as the horde was, it whetstoned my panic to grim determination. *Convince them or escape, and don't wait for your own dissection.* I was glad, now, that I'd hidden my notebook – that it wouldn't end up dismembered on this anatomist's wall. I would try – for your sake, I would try – to wring some cooperation from this interviewer, but if I couldn't, I'd not stay to be their prisoner.

So I let Gertie bind my hands to the chair – damn her, she'd appropriated my cravat again – with my wrists tense as railings. I banished her from the room with a clench-jawed recitation of *Life and Limbs*'s five-chapter finale.

Then I slackened my wrists (grazie, darling!) and picked myself free.

The door creaked.

I snatched the cravat, looped it round my cuffs in an impersonation of restraint. The swing of the door behind me covered the movement, and by the time it stopped I was still; I flatly refused to afford the author of that wall the honour of a glance over my shoulder. I waited, glaring out my immaculate photograph, until my inquisitor dodged the desk, and stood unresplendent before her knitted web.

Cassandra – I presumed – was older than her acolytes, closer in age to Septimus and I (though, given her elbow was barely level with your likeness, I'd have a good three inches of height on her, even barefoot). She was also one of the most wilfully ramshackle individuals I'd ever seen. Her Division uniform exploded at the throat and wrists into far too much knitwear, all of which had clearly been dyed purple in someone's shed, none of which matched any of its accompanying shades. Straggly curls spiralled from her bun, twisting an outline for her freckle-splattered face, her skin a sulky sienna which clashed outrageously with the pencil behind her ear. Her features were the youthful spit of Director Ballestas, but as if the Director had also been yanked into the aforementioned shed for a chaotic metamorphosis.

"Ballestas's daughter? What the – you don't – we've barely met!"

She glared, pure incredulous reflex, before she drew herself up, and abandoned the frown for a mirthless smirk. "That's Detective Ballestas to you."

"Give me back my things and I'll call you anything you wish." Hers wasn't a smirk to smile at, but I tried all the same. "Now – "

She cut me off. "Where are the Sweetings, where's our funding, and is this your ferret?"

She hauled something rattling and skinny-limbed round the desk: a cage, in which was dozing a blood-streaked heap of white, body knotted in slumber, barely twitching for the movement of its prison. It explained the smell, and absolutely nothing else.

"Strictly speaking," I hazarded, "That ferret belongs to Henry Nettleblack."

"Who says she gave it to you." She glowered at the cage, not that the ferret deigned to wake up and notice. "And then you set it on Dallyangle."

If there had been a fraction less of my life watching pityingly from the wall, I might have conceded to exasperated laughter. "You can't seriously think I lost a ferret as part of some criminal scheme – "

Then it struck me. "What else has Henry told you?"

She dithered, very deliberately, before she answered – plucking an inkstained notebook from her shelves, then swinging up to sit on her desk, cross-legged with the book on one knee. "What I needed. Septimus too. That pair of saps were soppy as Act Two *Pirates* when it came to you. They didn't *want* to tell anyone what you'd done, until you – oh, I don't know – slunk back to the Sweetings and stole our funding."

It took every fingernail in my fist to keep my jaw on its hinges.

But I defy a mortal soul *not* to have panicked. Detective Ballestas was close enough for me to discern freckle from inksplot, and her eyes were sharp as broken terracotta, a keenness so fierce it could split skin. *Whatever this nonsense is, she believes it. She believes every word. Or, for some bizarre forsaken reason, she desperately wants to.*

And what the devil does she know?

I held her gaze, spiky as it was. "I haven't the slightest idea what you mean."

"Alright, then!" She scoffed. Flipped a page in her notebook. "I know you love lying to everyone, but don't try it with me. I've been wading through your lies all week. You're a wealthy toff with no need to steal money – lie. You don't know anything about Dallyanglian crime – lie. You're nothing more sinister than a sane small-town cravat designer by the name of Pip Property – lies, lies, lies aplenty!"

I froze.

"I've been corresponding with your lady's maid." A smug little grin. "You were a menace to your mother, weren't you, *Properzia?*"

For want of a better word, this was tremendously – inconvenient.

As you may recall, a very specific disaster occurs when someone jostles me unexpectedly against the name my christening inflicted on me. My mind scorches blank, and every edge of the room crashes into me, until I'm so thoroughly pulverised that speaking falls out of the question. And all the while, the individual or the letter or – *whatever* it is, that's reduced me thus – simply goes on blinking at me, as if my tongue could grow back as easily as a salamander's tail.

"Neat of you to change your name. Even neater to bring *pronouns* into it – give us something grammatical and distracting to fuss about, 'til we're all so busy wrangling what you are, we've no time to even think about what you've been! And no wonder you got rid of *Properzia Participazio Property* – sweet Lord, who saw that on a birth certificate and thought they'd done their job?"

I was in utterly no state to reply.

"So you lie. You mislead. You sever your past with a nickname and a bit of quaint eccentricity. And no one ever finds out Properzia was – what did your maid say? – a demented debutante two inches shy of being shut in a madhouse. Your whole life's a jaunty misdirection, and you didn't even have to drop anyone down a well! Oh, the sensation novel you'd make!"

Her grin widened, taut with triumph. The wall sprawled behind her. Dallyangle – my sanctuary, the first place that had let me blaze and dazzle and exist precisely because it had never seen anything else from me – hit the floor in shards.

She must have told the Division. She'd turned my history into decoration; of course she'd told the Division. She'd scrawled her handwriting over mine and beaten my notebook to it. The whole prying legion had already picked over my past – pitied it – vilified it – sliced up everything I was and stitched it back together in the wrong shape –

It stung. Then it burned.

"Let's try again, shall we? Without the lies, this time. Where are the Sweetings, and where's our funding, Properzi– "

"*Enough!*"

I don't know what I looked like. I dread to think. But she'd trapped herself, surrounded by me, and whatever happened on my face struck the glow clean out of hers.

"You will not *dare* call me that again, is that understood?"

"What? I – "

"There is nothing amiss with my mind. There never has been. I know full well who I am, and I don't need you to deduce it for me. Va bene – you want the truth? Then start writing, *Detective*."

I closed my eyes. Forced a painful breath.

"As I truly hope someone in this place has told you, Rosamond Nettleblack and I were attacked last night, and the perpetrators finished the nightmare by making off with her. They were a man and a woman, they had a carriage, and the latter will now be sporting a stigmata courtesy of that sword-stick. I would have given chase, had your subordinates not interfered. At no point in any of this – underline, Ballestas! – did I commit or commission any more robberies. I don't know where the Sweetings are or what they've done. I've simply been the unlucky plaything of every fate under the sky, yourself and your requisitioning very much included. But I'll over-look it all – even you – provided you let me go, listen to me, and help me rescue Rosamond!"

To my (one hopes, well-concealed) surprise, she was making notes. I only noticed when I'd finished – when the words ran out and I had to seep back into myself, barefoot and hungry on her wooden chair, clenched fists throbbing like bruises.

"What's Rosamond Nettleblack to you?" she demanded suddenly.

I swallowed. Septimus and Henry were about as subtle as jewels. Adelstein was in love with his lodger, apparently. You'd seduced at least one Divisioner over Checkley's pints. *And if you don't say it, she'll find it, and twist it, and –*

"The chaotic lodestar of my existence."

Ballestas blinked. "The – ?"

"I love her, you mauveine innocent! I would never harm her. Before you inconvenienced me, I was protecting her from her dreadful sister."

Her pen went clean through the page.

"Oh, yes! Estimable Edwina Nettleblack has been depriving her younger siblings of their inheritances – and she threat-ened to incarcerate Rosamond in an asylum! Surely, if you must have someone to harass, it ought to be her!"

She was still scribbling, mouth tight in an unreadable grimace. I fidgeted the bargain in my thoughts: if she believed me, I'd – just about – forgive her the blunder into my past. If she stopped snarling about the town hall, I'd let her keep my photograph for her bedside table. If she chivvied the Division into saving you, I wouldn't entirely resent the appropriation of my gallant rescue. If she –

Was she *laughing?*

"Now, *that's* a jaunty misdirection! Let's just check I've got it all down!"

She propped the notebook along her forearm, peered at its contents with absurd theatricality, and – started *singing.*

"If you're anxious for to shine, and a fortune you can find,
To replace your empty purse –
But your scheme gets interrupted, and your heiress gets abducted –
Oh, it goes from bad to worse!
You must tell the good detective that you meant to be protective
And her sister's all to blame,
Hoping if you thus importune, we can confiscate the fortune,
And present you with the same!"

It cracked my very thoughts.

"Are you – singing – *Gilbert and Sullivan* at me?"

She snapped the notebook shut with a scornful flick of her wrist. "Now do you hear how you sound?"

"It's the truth! What else do you expect me to say?"

"Well, I'd love it if you actually answered my questions."

"And I'd be obliged if you'd believe my answers!"

She snagged the notebook's spine under my chin, tweaked my face to hers. I was staggered enough to let her, pulse rattling in my wrists, the book's edge scraping the hollow beneath my jaw. The chaffery was flaking off her like bad stucco – and beneath it, she was desperate, eyes fierce and fingers shaking.

"You're not answering. You're doing what you always do – and you're not even the first to try it on me. The twisting tales, the *come now, Cassie* speeches, the justifications that make sense if you squint. But this time, I'm not so trusting. So here's your last chance, Property: where are the Sweetings, and where's our funding?"

"Damn you, I don't know!"

"Fine." Her voice dropped, rushlight-thin. "I don't want to do this, but I've had my orders. Maybe Hartgate Gaol will jog your memory."

My pitch shot an octave. "You wouldn't."

"I have to. If you don't talk. Or talk to the point."

"You can't! It isn't – you don't understand – "

"Then tell me, for God's sake! For *your* sake! Pretend, just for half a second, that anything I've done has been even slightly intimidating, and be honest for once in your life!"

If I'd had anything to give her, I would have. Terrified as I was, I half-considered inventing something. But it was an idea only in the abstract – I couldn't think *what* I might invent – I could hardly think at all, beyond the fact that I was ten years younger and back in that carriage, and I needed to throw myself out of it again, and – and I shouldn't have had to – the Division were quaint and bumbling and clumsily well-meaning – they would never truly –

"Fine," she spat. "This is already your own damn fault."

She dropped me, kicked off the desk, and stalked for the door.

I sprang up, flung myself past her –

The door slammed into me, whacked me across the room. I missed the desk, tripped on the ferret-cage, snatched fistfuls of that horrible wall to keep my feet, purple skeins twisting round my fingers. Gertie and the Director crammed onto the threshold, struggling to fit the poky office – "Cass! How did they – are you hurt?"

Ballestas said something – I think. I couldn't untangle the words. The office was pinching, shrinking, its floorboards keening under my feet. I'd smudged the engraving in my fall, dragged the ink off-kilter over Father's shoulder. He grinned at me – helpless, oblivious, dead, beyond intervention, beyond the trouble I'd caused him, all the assistance for his *progeny* squandered and spent –

"Look at me, you fools! Look at what I am!"

The voice was mine, though I don't know how I recognised it.

"If you send me to Hartgate Gaol, it will not be my mistakes that I end up being punished for! I'm half a foreigner – I'm a deviant – I'm not a man and I'm not a woman – I'm everything mad and perverse and unnatural your histrionic press ever warned you about, and now I'm shackled in the dock awaiting my last judgment! Do *not* insult me by pretending you don't know where that ends!"

"They're right."

The room shuddered, heads twisting and elbows jostling, until the doorway was clear. Clear about a solitary figure in a suit almost worthy of me.

"Hartgate Gaol is not an option. And if Lord Clement Miltonwaters says otherwise, I will counter him myself."

CHAPTER ELEVEN

I AM INADVERTENTLY VILLAINOUS

The Notebook of Doom, continued

Concerning the same

Detective Matthew Adelstein punctured the room with a neat little bow. His russet hair was damp, hastily slicked into shape, and his tie pin asymmetrical; he must have rushed his toilette. Not that it would have been noticeable to anyone who'd never worn a suit, which at a guess probably included everyone else in the office. His fellow detective was certainly in no state to notice: she was staring out the floor, throttling her notebook with a look of unabashed horror.

I wondered what you noticed in him – how you slipped under his respectable veneer. The man's composure was iron-clad as his Director's –

Until, that is, his gaze snagged mine, and the screaming panic between his lashes nearly knocked me from my feet.

He knew, darling. He knew you'd told me. He knew what I could say – what he seemed convinced I *would* say. My every breath only nudged the knife closer to his throat. I couldn't even reassure him – without a shoulder to the wall, I don't think I would have stayed upright.

He swallowed. Turned to the Director. "Henry and Septimus appraised me of last night's developments. Frankly, I am surprised no one saw fit to inform me sooner."

"Leave her alone," Detective Ballestas snapped, her stricken thoughts having apparently spat her out. "It's not her job to send you reports. If you want to know what I'm doing, you can stagger out of your house and ask me."

"With respect," Adelstein retorted, impossibly measured, "*What you're doing* doesn't seem to be getting us anywhere."

Ballestas scorched. "With even more respect, it's very easy to eavesdrop and a right side harder to interrogate – "

"An interrogation which, if I heard correctly, seems to have descended into you threatening to hand a vulnerable suspect over to certain ruination?"

"It wasn't my idea! Lord Miltonwaters gave the order. This morning. On the sodding *telephone*. Get the whereabouts of the Sweetings and the money from the ringleader, and send them to Hartgate if they won't tell me anything."

"The telephone line is precarious. Perhaps he – "

"So now I'm not even competent enough to *hear* his orders?"

"You shouldn't be taking his orders!" he hissed, exasperation snapping a stitch in his scowl. "Lord Miltonwaters is our patron – not our new Director!"

Ballestas and the Director collided at the eyes, something writhing like static between them. For a moment, the pair were lost entirely to their silent communication – lost far beyond Adelstein, who was glancing from one to the other in baffled frustration. He even tried glowering at Gertie; she offered him little more than an uneasy shrug.

"We cannot risk offending Lord Miltonwaters," the Director managed eventually, gathering the tension in Adelstein's shoulders. "I am sorry, Matthew, but I can't allow it."

Ballestas shivered. "*Especially* not for the person who stole our funding."

Some pauperish dependant of hope keeled over in my throat.

But Adelstein, grit-teethed, simply straightened his tie-pin.

"Lord Miltonwaters is, of course, right to take the matter seriously. I presume he means the gaol threat to frighten

Property with a glimpse beyond our lenience, so that they might be menaced into giving up their accomplices? Well. Without wishing to cast aspersions on the esteemed nobleman, that plan is inherently flawed. You, Director, you have seen the injustices of so-called justice – you invented an entire Division to create some pocket of escape from them. If Property is given over to that, the case will escalate – for the very reasons they stated – and we will not get them back. We will lose any chance of obtaining the knowledge we seek. You know what happened with Lady Miltonwaters and Adelaide Danadlenddu – we were unable even to see them once Hartgate took over. Surely our *patron* would understand that incarcerating Property would be, in effect, cutting off our nose to spite our case?"

The Director frowned. Quick, darting, furtive, with a hasty glance down the corridor. "Lord Miltonwaters will not contact us again until tomorrow morning, at least. We could simply – in light of your – of our – of what we are meant to – "

"And then what?" Ballestas demanded. She grabbed for her mother's hands – or, at least, she nearly did, until the jolt of nerve suddenly failed her, and she settled for a panicky glare, arms folded tight across her scarf. "When he *does* contact us, and I'm the only one who knows how to answer the telephone? And what about Property, waiting in our morgue for the Sweetings to rescue them? Either we're shot in our sleep, or Clement comes down from Alberstowe Hall and – "

"Enough," the Director hissed. One hand dropped onto Ballestas's shoulder – and not since my youth have I seen offspring flinch like that; the detective withered like an overwatered fern. "These are not conversations to be conducting in front of the suspect, Cassandra. Matthew – perhaps we should adjourn – "

But Adelstein ignored her. He strode round the desk, held out his hand to me. His fingers were steady, but his nails had gone alarmingly white – and his face, now the rest of them were behind it, was a thing of pure terrible terror.

"You have my word that there will be no further talk of Hartgate Gaol. In return, I would like yours that – " – and he flinched, skittering back from the precipice – " – that you will bring no harm to the people keeping you from that fate."

How to say it, dizzy with hunger and fear, in a roomful of witnesses with no right to the secret? How to undo what you'd done to him?

"Mr. Adelstein, I – "

"You can't promise that," Ballestas cried – gracious, of course she did. "You can't cross Lord Miltonwaters. I don't like it any more than you do, but we have to – "

"*No!*"

It was so furious and unkempt a shout that the whole room gasped.

"Damn Lord Miltonwaters! This is *not* what we do! I will not let him reduce the Division to shattering lives on the grounds of supposed deviance – you might as well shatter me along with them!"

Then it was his turn to gasp, eyes widening as his thoughts sprinted past his anger and caught up with his words, the colour draining from his sallow cheekbones. Everyone was gaping at him. The tapers were too bright to lend any lingering shadows. Ballestas and Gertie were already exchanging a bewildered glance. The Director's shocked face ticked towards a question – the inevitable question – and it was more apparent than anything just how much he didn't want her to ask it –

With my last shred of sense, I threw myself at rational thoughts.

"Well, he's right, isn't he?" I blurted. "About all of you! You've essentially usurped the police – well might they shatter you, if they notice the privileges you've poached!"

Adelstein's mouth fell open. Much like his poor unravelling self, all those assembled were now gawping at me. Even Ballestas had lost her retorts; her and her mother had both gone decidedly, unpleasantly grey. And *you*, my darling – without doubting a shred of my forgiveness, mind you – had better set down this notebook at once to applaud the barefoot remnants of my wits.

The Director adjourned everything. Hence why I've had such incongruous leisure to scrawl this account to you: they simply sent me back to the morgue. I did manage to snatch my suitcase from Ballestas's horde; Gertie seemed too dazed to stop me, and the detective herself didn't even notice, scurrying away with the Director and Adelstein.

Of course the suitcase stung. I'd packed it in such bright anticipation, and every garment sang with recollections, discordant as a broken music-box. The double-breasted green herringbone had been meant for the boat – the *real* boat, not the flimsy Bristol Channel thing. I would have worn the selva oscura cravat in Ravenna, tapped it as I followed Father's pilgrimage and bowed at one of Dante's tombs. My greatcoat, bundled into creases, would have seen me through the Continental winter, alongside you in your amphibious overcoat. The empty wallet, sagging out of shape in my hands, should have financed the lot –

I flipped it over, gouged its every crevice. It wasn't just my money – everything I'd packed in it was gone: cufflinks, collarstuds, cravat pins. *Don't you remember what happens to all those fine heirlooms of yours if you cross us?*

"Damn you both," I hissed.

Then, by way of retort, I snatched up my notebook again.

Darling – bolster me – they're unlocking the morgue door –

CHAPTER TWELVE

A GLIMMER OF GOOD SENSE

Casebook of Matthew Adelstein

Pertaining to Step Three of Nicholas's List

A justification (or several) to warrant further investigation into the present circumstances:

1. There is something amiss with the Ballestases, and our so-called *patron* is squarely at the heart of it.
2. The Keturah Ballestas I know would never have baulked at Pip Property's appeal. She has, historically, indulged a certain caution whilst under public scrutiny, aristocratic or otherwise – but never to the detriment of her own ideals.
3. The Director is also prone to keeping secrets from the Division, particularly regarding our funding (see appendix: pertaining to the council's former ultimatum).
4. To judge from the accounts of Henry and Septimus, and the results of Cassandra's research, Pip Property will invariably lie, and lie eloquently, when faced with danger (viz. allying with the Sweetings, discrediting Septimus's suspicions, concealing a four-year affair with Rosamond Nettleblack, etc.). If Cassandra's ill-advised threat did not provoke a coherent misdirection to mitigate the risk of Hartgate Gaol, it seems reasonable to hypothesise that

Property's blank bewilderment was – not entirely feigned. Or at least worth examining.

5. Said examination is also another necessary precaution. Henry's garbled confession this morning (must the Nettleblacks always insist on bursting into my house?) indicated that Miss Rosamond would share *certain information* with her lover; those suspicions have only been confirmed by Property's precise deflection. I should have kept my temper – Nicholas's antipathy to my paranoia must not push me too far into recklessness – had they not intervened, I – regardless. They know about Nicholas and I. They made sure I noticed. Therefore, they must want something from me, and I will not simply wait for their next move.

To summarise: if the Ballestases will not explain, I must speak with Pip Property.

Pertaining to the result

I chose my moment. The Ballestases had long since turned our meeting into a familial conversation; I left them drinking cups of tea in the Director's office. I persuaded the keys from Gertie, then dispatched her on an improvised errand to thwart any potential eavesdropping. Early evening lurked on the windowsills. I didn't have long – Nicholas was expecting me.

I regret to report I startled when Pip Property leapt off the morgue slab, slamming a notebook shut on a cadaverous pencil, staring as I locked the door behind me. They looked far more the dandyish neighbour I remembered, having exchanged their bloodstained shirt for a suit from their belongings – though their hair had grown longer than its style permitted, falling into furtive curls without pomade. There was a scar on their cheek, a sharp pale line through their olive skin.

"Mr. Adelstein – I must thank you – if I may?"

Their eyes darted to the door. I could hear no shifting floorboards beyond the keyhole, so I nodded.

"I know why you thought you had to save me."

Being well appraised of Property's habitual verbosity, I hadn't anticipated such a swift descent on the point. "I – "

"There was no obligation. There never would have been. Gracious, of course I'll keep your secret!"

Shock silenced my mind. If a lie, it was extremely convincing.

"I can't apologise for Rosamond. But she is sorry." They sank back against the morgue slab, twisting the notebook in their hands. "She's – more ashamed than I've ever seen her."

It sharpened my teeth, my tone, the very air between us. "I dismissed my servants. I can't even get my roof fixed for fear of the workmen's scrutiny. I sacrificed a case – and a funding solution – because of her threats. You will forgive, therefore, my profound indifference to whatever *shame* she professes to feel."

Property winced. I waited, but apparently no further justification was forthcoming. The wary silence was mine to break, with a question so crucial it scalded my mouth: "Is she ending the blackmail? Or will she revive it to ensure your release?"

Their eyes widened. "She would never – "

"Never?"

Another flinch. "Va bene, never *again*. Nor would I ask her to. And – haven't the others told you? She can't – I don't even know where she is! You've nothing more to fear from her, or me, and I'm sorry you ever did!"

It was the voice from Cassandra's office again, the splintered pitch and frantic words. Identical to the tone of their final plea – the one thing they couldn't lie about. *It will not be my mistakes that I end up being punished for.*

If I proceeded, then, on that tentative hypothesis –

"I would have defended you regardless," I admitted carefully. "Or, at least, your right not to be torn asunder in Hartgate Gaol. And I was grateful for your – misdirection."

They stared at me, eyes widening – more incredulous than I would have expected. I pushed on, something traitorously anxious plucking at my throat. "I will not threaten you. None of us will. But – can you truly tell us nothing of where our real funding is?"

"I wish I could!" They groaned, shoulders shuddering with exhaustion, tugging dark hair back from their forehead where the movement threatened to disorder it. "Ballestas and her wall can go to the devil, but – if I knew, I'd say! Do you imagine I want to scupper Henry and Septimus any more than I already have? – "

Then they glanced down – eyebrows rising as their gaze fell – and burst to a startled grin, a sudden spark across their features. "*Idiot*, Property! This is what a diet of cheese does to your wits!"

I was halfway into a query when they yanked the pencil from their notebook, flipped to the opening page, and thrust it towards me. The writing was clear and swooping, calligraphy with the wrong nib, dodging agitated paisley sketches in the margins – and trembling, clutched too tight in their hands. Above it, their expression was a double exposure: the ghost of their audacious charm, beside something feral and desperate, a heady-eyed scrutiny which – foolishly, perhaps – left me feeling rather beyond refusal.

"I can tell you this instead. It's all I know – all I've known for the last fortnight. Gracious, you're in it – of course you ought to check it first! One moment – "

They tore out several quires of empty pages, then clamped my fingers round the remnants. My bafflement provoked only a wry look: "With apologies to Henry's parchmentier, but I still need something to write on. For – for Rosamond's sake, you understand."

I wasn't altogether sure I did, but I took it all the same.

Now, I have the broken-backed book sprawled over the dining-table, and Nicholas's hands performing an impromptu – not unwelcome – caress of my shoulders. He will force me to bed after the butler clears our plates – but I must make a start.

It's all I know. And it could all be another lie. But anything

– *anything* – that might lead me to the funding – that might give the Ballestases new ground – that might slacken the hold gripping us far more tightly than I feared –

Well then, Pip Property. What do you know?

CHAPTER THIRTEEN

ANOTHER SARTORIALLY-
CHALLENGED INTERLUDE

Cassandra Ballestas's Secret Phonograph

Recording: Tues Nov 21st 1893

I can't sleep. After that, I'm not sure I will sleep.

Maybe, given everything that just happened, it's neither calm nor wise to sneak across town at three in the morning to hiss into my favourite machine. But I tried to go home, and it didn't work. So I'll talk – of calmer things, though not by much – until my heart stops twisting out of my corset. And then I'll walk back, and this time I'll rest.

In theory.

Mother and Matthew and I finish our – let's call it *meeting*, rather than *flinty remnants of squabble* – far later than anyone's expecting; reception clock's brittling out quarter to ten by the time Matthew staggers away. We'd been interrupted by lunch, by dinner, but the time's still a shock. I'd not noticed the chimes, and darkness at the window doesn't mean a thing in late November. No wonder Gertie looked so fret-eyed when she brought our third round of tea.

Watching Matthew leave, chin high as his morals, I – whisper it, now – I'm envious. Why, in the name of my every nerve, did I want to give up that obliviousness? *Confide in me, Mother – show me you trust me again, and I'll show you how much you can* – bloody hell! No, Cass! Do you – *you* – not recall what it's like in Mother's need-to-know circle?

I can sneer at myself, and I will, but I didn't recall. Not until this happened. And the worst of it happened in *my* office: when Matthew slapped me with eminently fair points about why it'd be the least Divisionary thing in the world to send Pip Property to Hartgate, and I – couldn't even tell him how right he was.

Matthew doesn't know. None of them know. Mother and I are the only ones who've been to Alberstowe Hall – the only ones who spoke to Lord Clement Miltonwaters in his poisonous parlour – the only ones with *perfect understanding* of what he'll do to a disobedient Div. Mother insisted we keep it secret, as we shivered together in the carriage back – and, idiot that I am, I'd promised.

God, of course I did! To calm her down – to calm *me* down – to make my thoughts mine again! She rebuilt herself on her reasoning, in that carriage, and I was far too terrified to question it: why not have the threat stop with us? Why scare the Div with everything that man made me imagine? Why ignite anyone into trying to defy him, and endangering all of us? Why puncture the delight of a Division restored with the full truth behind that restoration?

Because – and the thought's heavy with Property's scornful vowels – *now you know where that ends.*

Matthew leaves us, eventually, me and my Directorial mother. We're too exhausted to keep talking, so we just lean on her desk and sip tea in miserable silence. She's halfway down the mug before she gets words, and even then it's with a hoarse throat –

"I should have got you out of it."

I wince. She's *forced* to rely on me, and yet she has to keep reminding me how disappointing the prospect is. Not that I can point it out, mind – not when admitting it would sting just as sharp as any sentence in the Director's Record.

"I should have told him you were on leave. You should not have come with me – "

"Well, I did," I snap, again, panic-sharp and terror-sharp, a full stop in three words. "You're not facing this alone – you tried enough of that with the council's ultimatum. I'll keep working on Property, and I'll take those wretched telephone calls, and we – "

"And what, Cassandra?" She closes her eyes, sets the mug down. "We wait, until Lord Miltonwaters makes another terrible demand? Until he acts on his threats? Until he destroys us – one way or the other?"

Don't imagine it. Don't think. Don't. "We – "

"It won't stop," she whispers. "I don't know how to make it stop."

And *that's* not something I can dodge.

It's not just her fear. I wonder if this is worse. It's her despair, the thing that crouches at the end of her late-night Record entries, the bits that used to make me weep after I'd fixed her spelling. It's that moment in the evenings she always insists on working to – the moment where everything turns to peat, and she sinks into it.

I'm not enough to drag her out. But maybe she will be.

"Enough." I clear my throat, then paper it with her voice, her words, all I can paraphrase from her Record. "You are no longer making any sense. I'll sort the last of this here – you go home and get some sleep – and then tomorrow a clear arrangement of resources will manifest itself. It always does, eh?"

Never mind papering – it's like stiffening bile into syllables.

But she perks – not much – just what she needs to straighten off the desk, pinch the sleep at her eyes, glance me over with a weary appraising nod. What a sodding party trick it is, quoting her to her – and what a reaction it gets, every time.

"Very well. And you must rest too." An awkward heartbeat, her hand glancing across my shoulder. "As you say – we must try to rise to this occasion."

When she's gone, I down the rest of my tea, and then the

rest of hers, press my knuckles to my mouth and bite through the fingerless gloves Gertie knitted me. It's the only thing I can think of to stop me screaming, overturning the desk, smashing her certificate, tearing up every ledger in the room. Everything, anything, until Mother lets herself *stop,* until she's allowed to believe there's more to her existence than *rising to this occasion.*

I sit on her desk – I don't dare sit *at* her desk – until ten o'clock chimes. She needs to be properly abed before I go home. I've not quoted the Record just for her to wake up again with *what happened in my absence, Cassandra?* I've still got jobs to finish. Matthew wrote a deferential paraphrase of his argument against Hartgate, which I want to pin to the telephone. Lord Miltonwaters's voice can knock all sense from my head, even when that voice is just tinny in my palm: might as well give myself a prompt against the terror, for when *why is Property not in Hartgate?* comes snarling out of the telephone while I'm the one holding it.

Then I could go to the morgue. Or not go to the morgue. Or – oh, sweet Lord –

I don't know what to make of Pip Property. Is it fair, to resent them, for forcing Miltonwaters's threats into my teeth? For their – I don't know – how much they don't make *sense?* Oh, they fit my research – even if their mother never answered my letter, the rest gave me more than enough of their character, and the *character's* what I thought it'd be. That's the disdainful stare and claret-rich accent of someone raised to a gilded cage, and those are definitely the volatile moods of someone who'd throw a gilded cage out the window to have their own way. That's the quick eloquence I was warned about, the patter-song prettiness, the very voice for deceit on a whim. But then –

But then we hit problems. They won't talk about our funding. They won't admit a shred of what they've done –

What they *have* done.

Haven't they?

I wish I'd more tea to sip. The windows are glossy with dark, and everything's too quiet. My thoughts slide into Adelaide's voice now – her old voice, her confident voice: *wasn't I just as convincing as them, Cassie? Wasn't it a stupid mistake to believe you could trust me? And do you really think this little funding-finding quest of yours can tolerate any more stupid mistakes?*

I sigh.

Right then, Cass. Pin the script to the telephone. Go home. Pull out your brain like a phonograph cylinder, and stick it back in in the morning.

I'm very practiced at walking round the Div with the swagger of a person significantly less harrowed – let's not forget, the Divisioners never guessed I gave Adelaide the head 'til I admitted it, and they've still not guessed even a sketch of Miltonwaters's threats. I fall into those steps now: out into reception with some leftover pins, straight to the telephone, skimming Matthew's neat handwriting as I flatten the paper to the polished wood. *Milord, if you would permit me to explain our rationale –*

"Cassandra?"

Of course I drop paper, pins, all. Septimus glares at me from behind the desk, navy eyes shadowed black in the dimmed gaslights – oh, delightful, and Henry's with her too, just as solemn-faced. The wood-burner gives them both a ruddy outline, these saints of the Div in their lovely ignorance.

"It ain't true – you didn't try to send Property to Hartgate?"

Oh, for heaven's *sake!* You love blundering onto a wound, don't you?

"I didn't know," I snap, stooping for the paper, "about the problem with the gaol. I was just doing what our patron asked."

"But I told you nothing good'd come of prison!"

I stab the note into the telephone. One pin. Another. "Yes, yes, you're always right – "

"Tell me you won't do it."

I've made the colossal mistake of glancing back, and now

I'm trapped in a stare fervent enough to strip my breath. I shove my nails into my palms, wait out the threadbare seconds as Septimus watches me and thinks me ghastly, and marshal every nerve I've got left to stop me believing her.

"I ain't saying they didn't drag me through hell," she blurts. "Henry too. I hated 'em for it! But they were scared – more scared'n they'd ever admit – and I only made it worse. I left 'em alone. Vulnerable. Thinking they'd get no help from me or the Div, even if they weren't too proud to ask. Thinking I was out to destroy 'em. Thinking I – *me* – would ever force 'em into a prison, for all I know about *institutions*. If I'd handled it different – if I'd been honest – if I'd just asked *why* they threw themselves at Maggie and Norman – "

She swallows hard. Henry dashes a kiss to her shoulder.

She won't leave me speechless, I won't let her. "Your point?"

"We can't have 'em thinking we're a worse option than the Sweetings. And if you keep threatening 'em – God's sake, Cassandra! – what else're they going to think?"

Then her eyes widen. I know why; it's the same reason her face is starting to blur. "What – ?"

"I don't want to threaten them." Whether it's my sobs scaffolding my words, or my words fuelling my sobs – I'm too drained to tell. "I don't want to threaten anyone. I don't want to do this – I don't want to *be* this – "

In the shuddering second before I press my hands to my face – the gloves are scratchy, but it's a closer escape than sprinting out – I spot their smeary silhouettes exchanging a glance. There's a scuffle on the floorboards, creaks getting closer. Then – of course I jump – there's an extremely awkward arm about my shoulders, a skinnier (but no less awkward) arm cupped round my elbows, sudden warmth and solidity and breathing far closer than I'm used to.

I'm so stunned I sink into it. The world's strangest, gangliest hug. The fact that Septimus smells more of woodsmoke than the fire, that Henry's chin is ridiculously sharp. The sentiment, tentative but genuine, in the clock-ticking silence. I need that hug more than I'd ever put in words, and they don't need words to notice how much. And the feel of it's like – like nothing I can say, because if I say it it'll sound sardonic, and everything under my skin's full worlds beyond sardonicism now.

That's where Gertie finds us. That's where Gertie *joins* us – of course she does! – squeezing everyone together into a squashed slapdash heap. That's where we stay, until the clock chimes half past, and resolve plaits together from the curls and chignons and knitwear.

We'll sort this out, I promise them silently, amidst the disentanglement and the shy weary smiles. *Our funding. The Div. We'll fix it all.*

And now – before I turn this off – I think I know how we can do it.

CHAPTER FOURTEEN

I AM RECKLESS IN THE EXTREME

The Dismembered Remnants of the Notebook of Doom

Concerning the evening of Tuesday 21st November 1893

Forgive the ramshackle receptacle, dearest. Not my most elegant solution – but what has been, of late? Matthew Adelstein has the rest of the notebook; don't flinch, I have the most audacious conviction that he's on our side. And – gracious, I can only hope – certain baffling facets of my first account might resonate with his detective mind.

But there's more to tell. Fervent apologies, darling, but it's not conducive to ameliorating either of our constitutions.

Mr. Adelstein (even now, it feels too informal to lapse uninvited into the first name of someone with shoes that tidy) took his leave, and – for all that he locked the door behind him – in his wake I was almost cheerful. I felt the momentum quickening around me: at last, at *last*, I could *do* something for you. I hadn't trapped your plight under the glass of the Division's scepticism. I actually considered the possibility of summoning my best recollections – of gloriously sordid self-pleasure by way of nerve-bolstering – recalling everything we'd done on Gower would have been enough –

Maledizione, but not in the *morgue!*

(You would have done it. But I, as you know, am nothing if

not refined in my tastes.)

So – smarting for lack of you, and a sumptuous room, and teeth at my throat – I ended up drawing some illustrations for Gertie's *Life and Limbs*. Each one was placed several chapters too early in the book, of course.

Three burly-fisted raps crashed into the door. Honestly.

"Gertie, they can't – "

"Oh! 'Course not! Bloody hell, it's our bedtime after this!"

I had, by this point, sketched on the novel so thoroughly that the pages sat on their spine like curl-papers; now I simply threw the book at the door, and knocked Gertie back one spluttering half-step. Detective Ballestas caught it, skimmed its contents, her eyebrows soaring – gracious, her eyelashes were spiky. What unimaginable pluck, to wear undaunted the evidence of recent tearful despair!

Then, regrettably, Ballestas looked at me. *Oh, not again.*

"One last question," she snapped. (That sentiment, I gathered, had not been it.)

I glared at her; Mr. Adelstein had made me bold. "Or what?"

She swallowed.

Then she plucked something skinny from her jacket pocket, tilted it towards my face, the taper-light betraying the tremble of her hand. Her gesture closed the distance between us – as much as anyone in this morgue could keep a distance – but I would have known what she held at far more paces and in far poorer light.

"Is this yours?" she asked, appallingly timed, at the very second when –

"You've scratched it!"

A startled glance between her and her minion. "What?"

I snatched my cravat pin before she could close her fingers. "At the end, you see? What the devil have you been doing to it? Do you have any idea how much gold plating costs to replace?"

"Hang on!" She grabbed for my wrist – Gertie did the same – but this time I was ready, and far too swift with the fencing disengages to permit any more of *that*. "You can't just take it back – you'll pick the lock!"

The pin was now safely wrist-deep in my pocket. "I don't know how to pick a lock."

Gertie scoffed. "You were a right little escapologist in Cass's office."

"With a *cravat!* That – it's not – the skills are profoundly separate!"

Ballestas's eyes widened, too quick to conceal, unhinging her frustrated scowl –

But her floundering scrutiny was interrupted. I can take neither credit nor blame, because the interruption was a gunshot.

And then the whole Division went dark.

Ballestas yelped, flung herself into the morgue. I leapt back and struck the slab fit to bruise. Gertie whirled around, blew out the tapers, quick enough to match the sudden murk of the corridor.

I froze, squinting uselessly into the darkness. There were my shallow breaths – no, *calm* – and, below them, the faintest careful creak of movement by the door. I carved my every thought to the shape of Gertie's name, as the only prevention against screaming I had left: *she's just backing away, backing inside, there's no human way it can be anyone else –*

I still hissed when her skirts brushed my ankles. Ballestas squeaked, and the shadowy mess beside me promptly folded into a scuffle: Gertie caught her arm, murmuring reassurance, so fiercely even I could catch its edges.

Out in the gloom, something cracked. Another door, slamming open, struck against the plastered walls.

"Evening, Divisioners! Anyone home?"

As if the shot hadn't been indication enough!

The Sweetings hadn't owned a pistol when they broke into my house. Maggie smashed my study window, oblivious to the broken glass in her gloves. A pretence of menace and a plait of my adolescent hair had saved me then – I'd snared the situation, pulled it taut to my terms like a cat's cradle, and Maggie had beamed at me. *why not? Never had anyone answer us back!*

But my adolescent plait, and every stolen plait since, must have paid for the weapon they were presently wielding.

I bit my knuckles, before the thought could make me retch.

The floorboards shifted. They were pacing the Division's reception. Maggie's singsong snarl sailed over the steps: "Don't say you've gone to bed!"

A whisper at my shoulder. "I sent Mother home – "

"We've never even seen this place from inside!" Closer already, far too close to the corridor's end. "Fancy lighting it up for us?"

"No way out on this side," Gertie muttered back.

"Come on!" A sudden violent trilling made us flinch – a thwack of the bell on the front desk. "We know *someone's* here to receive us!"

Gertie gulped. "Who's on the – ?"

"Sweet Lord, the sweethearts – "

Something splintered in my chest.

"There we are!"

A cry – a shove – the horrible scrape of heels on floorboards. "Very clever, dousing your lights – but even you can't snuff a wood-burner, can you?"

Septimus's yell ploughed through the taunts. "Let her *go* – "

Another shot. Norman, snapping – "You stay where you are!"

The corridor shook – the closest impact yet – and Henry shrieked, too shrill for anything better than pain.

"Well then, sham-sarge! Where's this flush new funding of yours? We hear a certain lordling's been very generous!"

"Please." I hadn't heard Septimus's voice crumple like that for weeks. "Don't hurt Henry – I'm the threat – "

"So you'd think," Maggie retorted dryly. "But if my reckoning's right, we've never had half as much trouble from you. *This* one, though – shot down a lamp on us! And set her ferret to eat my finger! If you think we're still fooled by the timid cherub look – "

"You've made the bloody point," Norman growled. "We've not got all night. Tell us where you're keeping the aristo's cash."

Silence. Sickly shadowy silence, but for Henry's gasps.

"You know what, Norman? I don't think I *have* made the bloody point. Leastwise, I can always make it bloodier. How about this, Septimus? One finger off your ferret-thrower for every minute you hesitate. Don't squirm – we'll be matching!"

I was halfway down the corridor before my mind caught up. Gertie hadn't locked the morgue door – hadn't even shut it – and if either scrabbled to stop me, I didn't notice. The wood-burner lit my way, dragged me onwards, a thing of shards and delirium beneath my suit – into reception, into the scuffle, into four sets of fire-scalded eyes –

"Stop."

And I cannot explain how my voice came out so bewilderingly calm.

Embers and shadows stiffened into shapes. Norman, pistol aloft in an unsteady hand. Septimus, its target, trapped behind the desk. Henry, pinned to the corridor-side wall, wrist clamped in a leather-gloved vice, twisting against the bulk of shoulder and elbow that kept her still. Maggie, holding her there, my stolen scissors in hand, startled out of sawing through the knuckle of one pallid finger.

Maggie grinned at me. She hadn't broken Henry's skin, hadn't drawn blood. Yet.

"Don't be fidgeting with our plan, Pip!" Her tone was incredible – all the fond exasperation of a patronising relation. "We've orders not to hurt you."

I didn't move. Neither did she. "Whose orders?"

"Why, yours, of course!" She winked, tapped her cheek with the blunt edge of my scissors, traced a wry pantomime of my scar. "Very insistent, you were, that we shouldn't repeat the attic tonight!"

"*I* gave you orders not to harm me?"

"And aren't you lucky we answer to you!" She chuckled, scorn flashing across her eyes. "What d'you reckon now? You could run away again!"

The Division couldn't stop me. I was closest to the doors – closest to the draught, the anonymity of the night, the walk to my house, the swiftest pursuit of you –

Henry closed her eyes, crumpled to the wall under Maggie's grip.

The thought gouged my mind like a stitch from a Singer: *maledizione, don't you* want *to see Rosamond again?*

But given the circumstances, dearest, I hope you can forgive me for how profoundly I ignored it.

"I revoke my orders."

Maggie blinked. "You what?"

I crossed the room to perfect silence. Flattened my hand over Henry's. Knuckle to knuckle, veins stark in my wrist as my cuff slipped down.

"You said I told you not to hurt me. Well, I've changed my mind. New orders for you, sweet Sweetings: do your worst."

Maggie flung a glance at Norman. He shook his head, the pistol quivering.

"Now, come on." Maggie tried for a shaky smile, though her voice had curdled into a growl. "You were that upset about your scar! You don't want to – "

"Gracious, why such hesitation? Reprise the attic, my dears!"

Septimus snarled in the dark behind me. "Pip, what are you *doing?*"

"Anything? Maggie? No?" My voice was rising, shrill and giddy, higher than I would have liked, far higher than I could control. "Whyever not? I'm your leader, you said! The compass-point of your loyalty! Why the devil aren't you following my orders now?"

A breath – another – until the pause was far too blatant for the Sweetings to hide. Until they forgot Henry and Septimus, and everything else in the room.

"But then I won't be much of a leader – or much of a scape-goat – if you kill me, will I?"

Maggie gaped at me. Her brother was horrified, unabashed and simple, but her stare was marbled with something else. It nearly broke my audacity, as the moment lengthened, and the grubby contours of her face began to make sense – gracious, was that *admiration?*

"Well done," she breathed.

Norman jolted like a flame. "Maggie – "

"That said," – and she was starting to smile again, split to her incisors with sudden excitement – "Maybe a dead scape-goat's better'n a clever one. And you did ask so nicely."

"Maggie, we swore – "

"Have it your way, you glorious maniac!"

She grabbed my hair – yanked my head back – pressed the scissors to my throat –

Then – to make up, I could only assume, for my absurd inability to protest my own impending death – everyone started shrieking at once.

"*Pip!*"

"Don't you dare – !"

And something very, very wordless.

Maggie threw me across the room. I hit the desk, set the bell jittering into the cacophony, staggered round in a hapless bid to make the clamour make sense –

Half of reception was a tangle of shadows, limbs, skirts, weapons, and – twined like a laurel-wreath across Maggie's brow – a shuddering streak of white. There was Gertie, swinging Earlyfate like a cricket bat, until Norman bellowed and dropped the pistol. There was Henry, skidding on her knees to grab and unload it, scattering bullets across the floorboards. There was – *Ballestas?* – clutching an empty cage, doors jangling for every heave of her shoulders. And there was Maggie, howling sentiments I'd lost all ability to decipher, scrabbling in vain at the tiny bloodstained wyvern currently attached to her face.

"Mordred?" Henry cried.

"She doesn't like people throwing ferrets!" Ballestas yelled, between chattering teeth – "Not one sodding word to my mother!"

Gertie lunged for Norman, but he dived aside, seized Maggie at the collar and hauled her backwards. She hit wall, floor, coat-stand, and Ballestas on the way, still smothered by the snarling ferret – but fear and desperation had given her brother terrible plumage, and he crashed through the doors before a soul could catch him. Gertie kicked off the wall – Septimus vaulted the desk – but by the time they'd grabbed the doors there was only the skeleton of the market, cobblestones and awning-bones. Of the Sweetings and their mustelid reckoning, I couldn't glimpse even a blood trail; the ground was too slippery with rain.

Then Septimus had me by both shoulders, shaky and shadowed against the lamps outside, teeth drawn back in a snarl.

"What were you *thinking?* You don't *ask* them to kill you!"

I could only blink at her.

"Never do that again, you hear me? Never! Not your *life!* You ain't clever and you ain't sensible, you – you – "

I was staring, abruptly, over her shoulder. She had me in a vice-hold, jaw gouging into my shoulder, arms locked tight enough to pin mine to my sides. She was terribly strong, and the position distinctly unconducive to letting me breathe.

"Are you – attempting to embrace me?" I managed, rather choked.

She let go immediately, of course, bristling as she flinched back –

And both my legs gave way at once.

CHAPTER FIFTEEN

I AM REPEATEDLY FLABBERGASTED

The Dismembered Remnants of the Notebook of Doom, continued

Concerning Tuesday evening and Wednesday morning

First she held me, then she carried me. *Septimus.*

And I didn't even gloat about it.

Her grip bruised, all wiry muscle, and she did admittedly misjudge a doorway to the thwacking of my head ("Figs! Careful!") – but I was hardly assisting with my transportation. I'd found myself with a slim sash-window between the world and my capacities: clinging to her was impossible – staying upright was inconceivable – coherent thoughts were gone – it was all I could do not to melt through her arms –

Then I was on a real bed, no morgue slab in sight, with candles above my head and silhouettes massing in the shadows. Septimus scrabbled under my neck, fussing with pillows, until pallid hands tugged her into a furious embrace. I closed my eyes, by way of giving them privacy –

"Millie says try this!"

A gasp, as I blinked, and Henry and Septimus jerked apart. A ram-shouldered silhouette barged through them, mug in hand.

"Persimmons – Gertie – we can't give them *whiskey!*"

"Ain't we got smelling-salts?"

"Nah, it's fine! I put a whole bottle of Nettleblack's in it!"

"Let me," Septimus snapped, by way of retort to Gertie's sloshing gestures, snatching the mug before she seemed fully aware she'd done it. "Or – I – hang on – "

Henry squeezed her shoulder. "What do you need?"

The two of them folded close again – I lost the conversation, not involuntarily – then Henry had Gertie's arm, ushering her into the shadows beyond the bed. "Why don't we check on Cassandra – ?"

A door swung in the darkness, snipped off their voices. Septimus stayed sickled at the bedside, stooping to cup my hands around the mug, to crick an arm about my shoulders and lever me up. The scents were thick enough to bite: the woodsmoke on her clothes, the weedy chaos of the drink.

"You didn't let me collapse," Septimus muttered stiffly. "My turn."

I was far too stricken to dissect her words, or squint out her features, or demand to know whether she'd taken leave of her senses along with her resentment. I was just about sensible of what her attentiveness *meant*, in its most practical sense – that she was alive, unharmed, possessed of a sweetheart in an equal state of safety. She was safe.

I drank.

She took the mug before I could drain it, set it down on a spindly side-table. Her next movement was disarmingly tentative: fingertips light along my jaw, tipping my head up, eyes narrowing as she peered at my neck. She didn't wince, though I did, for the ache that dragged through my limbs with my every movement; apparently, Maggie and the scissors had failed to leave another scar.

"Reckon you ain't wanting to sleep in your suit?"

When I shook my head, she propped me on the headboard and hurried away, dashed back with my suitcase half-open in her arms. We fumbled through it together, a strange silent plan, until I found my nightshirt and she my dressing-gown, into which we managed to pour me, albeit with much painful trial and error around buttons and shoelaces. She tugged at the bedcovers, whacked the pillow to her satisfaction – and then, to my half-conscious amazement, applied herself to the most deft and extraordinary folding of my suit, after the fashion of one used to cramming clothes into very tight spaces.

Horizontal, almost warm, I watched her through my eyelashes until she was done. I remember her brief glance, something between a scowl and a smile – certainly remember my mind's weary insistence that the look wasn't a dream – then I lost myself to a sleep so heavy it flattened my very nightmares out of shape.

Having banished natural light for far too many hours, the Division was now determined to spoil me. I surfaced from blank relief to sun on my eyelids – the sort of thing one only gets in November by way of a benevolent window. I meandered through my self-appraisal, far too weary to clutch and fuss: sprawled, quiet-thoughted, with vague recollections of Septimus not despising me. My teeth tasted vile, but – gracious, the rest was luxury!

I sighed. If it be thus to dream, I saw absolutely no harm in filching five more minutes.

"Pip?"

But that voice plucked the down from my daze; it had a lilt I'd heard rather a lot in the past fortnight. I blinked – struck a wall of sun, hissed, tried again – and the slanting light gave me Henry, perched on the bed, peering at me warily.

Do take note, dearest: your sibling braved my first name.

Now it was teetering between us, flimsy amidst the dust-motes. After the beautiful sleep, and the benign beginning, and Septimus's benevolence, I'd no idea how to answer. Henry wasn't precisely helping with that panicky stare – of all the Nettleblack eyes, hers are by far the most intense, to the point where I wonder how the green doesn't simmer like boiling water.

"Delightful morning," I managed eventually.

"Quite – erm – how are you feeling?"

I swallowed, which given the present flavour of my mouth was a colossal mistake. "Never mind that. Are you alright?"

She nodded shakily, dashed a hand over her hair. It was still in my crop; she'd clearly been careful not to let it grow out. "I – you – I meant to – figs – "

I'd conversed with her enough to guess the utterance wasn't finished, so I didn't interrupt, shunted upright against the headboard. The room wasn't familiar – a drab dormitory with unhemmed fabric for curtains, empty beyond rows of identical beds, spidery at the ceilings and striped with bare floorboards. The beds nearest the door had been cheered into bright idiosyncrasy: there were rag-rugs, gaudy blankets, ablutions bowls and clothes-boxes and battered books. The rest were bare, one bedframe yanked across another grubby door.

"It was my writing hand," Henry blurted, though her voice faltered again for my baffled expression. "Last night – when you – and I swear, it – it was quite never my intention to – erm – to deprive Maggie Sweeting of her finger – I didn't *throw* my ferret at her – the mauling was his idea – cranberries, I hope he's still alive – "

I squeezed the fabric at her sleeve, in what I very much hoped was the fetch of a reassuring gesture. "I'm sure the ferret can handle himself. He survived my involuntary abandonment, did he not? I'm only sorry I failed so consummately at protecting the felicitous mustelid."

Then, of course, I heard myself. "I – forgive me, that's not true. I'm not *only* sorry for that. I'm sorry for – everything. I hardly know where to begin with the apologies I need – the apologies you deserve."

She coloured. "Well – I – let's not forget that you just – erm – risked your life – defending my capacity to hold a pen – "

"Gracious, I should have done more!"

"Oh – no – risking your life was already too much – "

"I should never have dragged you into danger in the first place! I've been a fiend to you – I'm still a fiend to you! I – "

She held up a trembling hand to stop me. It was as much

encouragement as I deserved.

"I think I should have a say in deciding what you were – erm – are – to me. And – *fiend* quite isn't the word. I – I don't entirely think I have the word – "

She glanced round, quick and nervous, though it was only us in the room.

"We're – alike. Well – erm – we aren't – in that you're the most eloquent person I've ever met, and I – am not – but – "

A tiny smile. For *me*. I could do little more than gape.

"But we do share a – the – something. The – erm – the reason I told Edwina I – I can't be a married woman. I – I mean – obviously I'm not a married – quite – but the rest – also – "

She groaned. "Pomegranates, I don't know how to explain without quoting you!"

Every nerve in me pulled very, very taut. Septimus was muttering in my head, some brusque enigmatic speech about keeping cravats.

"But – well – even so – I – I thought it wasn't the sort of confession to – I didn't think I could trust you with it – not when it looked like you'd betrayed me and Septimus – and stolen from the Division – but – but now – erm – yes. Quite. That's clearly not true. And you must believe me, I – I never wanted to think the worst of you – I'd be even more lost for words if it wasn't for you – I – please say something!"

For a long moment, I truly wasn't up to it.

When I salvaged the Sweetings-cropped chaos of Henry's hair – when I'd no idea she was any kind of Nettleblack – I'd caught her eyes in the bathroom mirror, in the seconds after she'd glimpsed the transformation. I'd half-expected the glass to crack, far too flimsy to carry the scalding triumph of that look. It had always been Mamma's contention that I was far too wrong in the head to ever meet my living like, for all that I could gesture to a bookpile's worth of posthumous inspirations. Not that it had kept me from wondering, thoughts gauzy and brief and forcibly nonchalant, several times over for strangers and acquaintances – but nothing even close to my

Henry speculations –

Still, I hesitated. There's a world of difference, you see, between pencil-sketch suspicions about a person, and daring to believe they might have shaded them in. Between wishing for resonance, and hearing it aloud in someone else's voice.

"Are you saying," – and I had to clear my throat – "that the arbitrary notion of two sexes, and all that those figments are meant to shape and see and feel, is at best a hopeless mismatch for everything you are?"

Henry blinked.

(Take it back! Just say – gracious, I don't know – *perhaps you're simply another cravat devotee* –)

Then she smiled again – a giddy grin this time – shivering so much that her teeth began to chatter.

"Figs –*yes!* Quite *there* are the words!"

I stared. The sun sharpened at the windows, carved streaks of gilt into the bedframes, glinted in the tarnished silver of Henry's curls.

"But I won't impose on *they* – erm – that was your idea – "

Sweet youthful neophyte, I don't have any monopoly on a pronoun!

I should have said so. I fully meant to – opened my mouth – then realised, with dazed and terrible certainty, that I was about ten breaths away from shattering four years of tearless self-control.

Absolutely not, I thought, very flimsily indeed.

"I know I must not seem very – obvious – to you – articulating anything of myself aloud is already troublesome – Edwina got my Christian name wrong for four years and I never corrected her – but I – even so! I used to be terrified of everything – of myself – of how much a failure I seemed by the only standards I knew – but you're quite entirely right – they're the hopeless mismatch – not me!"

I twined our fingers. I needed words. Elegant encouragement, graceful reassurance, advice from a seasoned predecessor, everything no one had said to me. *Don't* mention how it sharpens the world, for worse and better – or do? What to do? How should *I* know what to do?

"Thank you for telling me. And if there's more you require – not that you're obliged – only that you're emphatically not alone – "

Maledizione, I was gone.

Self-chastisement, self-consciousness, self-command – all useless. I slumped over our hands, until the sun was a scalding penny-collar on the back of my neck, and I sobbed for the first time in nearly half a decade, with a ferocity that turned the room to molten candlewax. Precisely why, I'm not sure even I can articulate.

Henry, as the poor youth is ever wont to do, indulged my theatrics – even the involuntary ones. One hand patted the juddering wreck of my shoulders, didn't flinch when some muffled clock trilled a time I couldn't count. I'd forgotten how appallingly ungraceful it was to cry, ghastly at sounds and sensations, involuntary as a fall and almost as painful. I'm only grateful I noticed when Henry started easing me upright.

"I'm sorry," I managed, with the assistance of several tremendously purposeful swallows. "To borrow your sister's assessment: I am a mess."

A terrifyingly solemn nod. "I – I'm quite familiar with the state."

"And *they* is not exclusively mine. After all, I'm clearly far less singular – " (I should have laughed, but it fractured into another infuriating sob) " – than I imagined. If you want – please don't feel it's a presumption – "

"You're quite sure?"

"Of course! But if you'd rather be surreptitious – "

"Not with you." Another grin, like the sideways flick of a very bright candle. "Or Septimus. I – I can – clementines, thank you!"

The blazing gratitude was surely misplaced, but I'd not the heart to snuff it. We just sat there, for another strange slackening of time: Henry squeezing my hand, myself hoarse against the headboard, until I met her eyes – gracious, *their* eyes! – to find them sharp and intent.

"I – I want Rosamond to know. I – you swear – you've not the faintest where she is – "

I gulped, diving for words, grabbing my best weary fistfuls. "I'm sorry – I don't – "

No – not the crying again – devil take it, finish the thought –

"It's not at all my intention to rile your sisters into battle. But as far as Rosamond is concerned, they're already in one. For her sake – and for yours – ghastly as it is, you must speak to Edwina. I know you've more faith in her than I, but – take Septimus with you? Just in case?"

Something glinted in their eyes, some quiet satisfaction I couldn't decipher. "That – erm – shouldn't be a problem."

They hopped off the bed without further elaboration, brushed the blanket's moult off their culottes. "Right! The Division's in reception – I think they'll want to hear the specifics of last night from you – and also be reassured that you're quite entirely still functioning – at least, I'd be obliged if you'd reassure Septimus – so if you want to – erm – get dressed – your suit's here – or if you have any – more suits – "

I managed (at last!) a wry look. "Hylas, you don't imagine I exhausted my inheritance with only a single three-piece to show for it?"

Henry pinked – whether it was the old nickname, or the uncomplicated good-humour, or the fact that I had finally patterned a sentence that sounded like Pip Property, I couldn't discern. "Well – quite – but first – I do hope you don't think I mean to insult you – "

They fumbled under the bed beside us, proffered me a green porcelain jumble. "But you really are in terrible need of a bath!"

It was a jug and ablutions bowl, stinging with painted nettles, a bar of Pears' gleaming at the bowl's heart. And their words – they were a thing apart from Henry's usual cadences –

Of course. Their words had been mine. When I turned on my taps, and left them to frolic with every lavish thing in my bathroom.

Superbly choreographed, young Nettleblack, if I do say so myself.

Crying at Henry had been unavoidable, but I'd no intention of letting the other Divisioners notice my sodden-eyed lapse. I scrubbed my face so violently my scar blazed, shaped my hair with watery fingertips, ran through the whole jug before I was satisfied: if it was obvious I had washed, it would surely seem natural that my eyelashes were sharp. I chose my olive-green herringbone, restored my poor cravat pin to its proper use – so-called evidence be damned, cravats simply do not stay still when the waistcoat is double-breasted. I profoundly hoped my appearance rendered me untouchable, in a glossy, oil-on-canvas sort of way. If anyone *had* touched me, mind you, I would have smudged horrendously.

I flung wide the dormitory door. The doors to the street burst apart.

"Chai for all!" someone bellowed.

Gone was the pristine perfection of the cleaned-up reception, pale walls and polished pigeonholes and sterility worthier than the morgue slab. In the wake of last night's calamities, the Division had *Divisioned* it. The room was a jumble of chairs – the bench from the wall; the stools that lived behind the desk; the two rickety miseries from Ballestas's office, attended by one more rickety cousin, all clustered round pillows and a picnic blanket only Gertie Skull could have patronised. The desk had been given over to crumb-pocked plates, buttery knives, three jars of hedgerow-flavoured jams, another wheel of cheese, water-jugs, the market's best fruit, and a stack of toast with fork-holes punched through every slice. The wood-burner was blazing, the sun splayed surplus rugs over the floorboards, and even the chill from the open doors couldn't shunt off the cosiness. Perched about their fairy grove, the Divisioners skidded round – Gertie on the bench, her two minions on the blanket, Henry and Septimus hand in hand on the chairs, Ballestas nearly toppling off a stool –

"God's sake, Nick!" Septimus spluttered. "Don't sneak up on us today!"

Upstaged as I was, I followed her glare to the new arrivals. Matthew Adelstein was back, solemn with a ruler-sharp satchel; at his side was a ramshackle fellow in a mustard coat and striped trousers, grin bright and hair bedraggled, wielding a teapot and several mismatched cups in his basket. I frowned – this stripy Puck was familiar, if whistling outside my window counted as a degree of acquaintance –

"You poor things!" he cried. "Matty and I were *shocked* when he got the Director's note! Sweetings in the Div! Gunshots in the air! What *is* this town coming to? I said to him – Matty, we must bring them comfort, the Div'll be reeling!"

Matthew sighed. "As you say, Nicholas. Don't damage our cups, if you please."

All oblivious to Matthew's winces, Nicholas dashed into the Divisionary nest, furnished every hand with a cup, until the air was gaudy with spices and I was eagerly awaiting my turn. He prattled all the while, juggling cups and basket and teapot, clearly accustomed to complicated dexterity –

"Try this, now – ancestral recipe – great for your nerves – the very thing after a break-in! Got any Nettleblack's? It takes Nettleblack's like a dream! Oh, Divisioners – Henry, my field-mouse, there's for you – and the ferret saw them off, Matty said? About time that little killer did something useful! Even if we've got to catch it again. And I can't deny it wasn't *something* when it ate Vibbrit's guinea pig! Go on, Cassandra, chai won't kill you – and not to speak ill of the dead, but that guinea pig got a lucky escape. Why you'd debase a rodent's dignity by dressing it up for a carte de visite – *The Cavy of Shalott*, honestly! And people *buy* these pictures! And – halloa, it's Pip Property!"

I barely noticed my name. There was a cup in my hand, and he was halfway through pouring chai into it – but I was gaping at his beaming brown face in absolute bemusement – *He's in love with his lodger – the rat-breeding chap – and very bad at hiding it.*

Gracious – *this man* was Matthew's lover?

I glanced down at the cup. Mine was the daintiest of the basket's offerings, delicately patterned with an inscription round the rim: *for Matthew on his bar mitzvah – 1 May 1877 – all our love, Ma & Ta.* This man was *definitely* Matthew's lover.

"Nicholas, I believe? Very possibly my neighbour?"

"That's the one!" He grinned at me, by way of a handshake, righting the teapot just in time. "You can call me Nick. Nick Fitzdegu. And it is a *calamity* that you've been only a few doors down and I've not had chance to ask: d'you like rats, Pip Property?"

I arched an eyebrow. (Dearest, however did you have the stomach to threaten him?) "I sense you're about to make sure of it."

"Nicholas!" Matthew hissed, incredulity struggling up from its prostration. "Not now!"

Nick swirled round on a mock-indignant sigh. "I thought Property was fair game, now they're not commanding Dallyangle's criminal underworld!"

It was my turn to interrupt. "Whilst we're glancing against that ghastly chestnut – Divisioners, may I speak?"

Nick scrambled obligingly out of my way, and I crashed into Ballestas's scrutiny again. But what a change for the aniline detective this morning! Wary gaze, pinched grimace, eyebrows hunkering down against my inevitable gloat. I waited until she broke our stare, let her flick an inkstained hand in my direction.

"Much obliged, Detective Ballestas. Now."

(A fortifying gulp of chai first. Dio mio, it was exquisite.)

"I'm profoundly hoping that, in the wake of last night, you might finally feel inclined to trust my word. I have no control over the Sweetings, and no idea they meant to target you here. It would be my amateur suspicion that they framed me for robbing the town hall – to what end, I wouldn't presume to speculate."

I swallowed. Henry watched me, fingers pattering on Septimus's knuckles; stiff and scowling at their side, the latter was barely blinking.

"But I'm not such an arrogant fool – " (of course Ballestas rolled her eyes) " – to presume myself unjustly wronged by anyone in this room. I haven't made it easy for you to trust me. Septimus was right – I used to work with the Sweetings, and I've made some recent choices I deeply regret. Maggie and Norman are only so damnably able to set me up because I drew them the proverbial pattern, if you'll permit me the whimsy. So, for all that I *have* done, I – I want to – I'm sorry."

And I couldn't even call it insulting, how utterly flabbergasted the Division looked.

"If I can help you stop the Sweetings, I will. And if you can help me find Rosamond Nettleblack – if my asking anything of you isn't impertinence beyond measure – I'll be more grateful than even this delightful chai permits me to articulate."

There wasn't a hinged jaw in the room. It was so abruptly silent that the very market crept in, a chattering tumult beyond the doors. The Divisioners were exchanging glances in baffled groupings: Henry and Gertie, Ballestas and Matthew, Nick and the Skull collective. I did try to untangle their expressions, but the twisting panic in my chest made it infinitely harder.

The scrape of a chair set us all flinching. Septimus was up, scowling to find everyone's eyes on her, her lower lip bitten to blood.

"Right. Well. Ain't my case, but – "

She glanced to Ballestas, who groaned into her chai. "You'll just explode if you don't."

The remark provoked only a wry scoff, until Septimus turned back to me, shoulders set, face terrifyingly solemn. Gracious, of course I trembled.

"Reckon that's an apology." Her eyes narrowed. "'Long as you don't go back on it."

I hardly wanted to stammer in front of the Division, but – so be it. "I – I wouldn't – sweet sergeant, you have my word – "

She nodded brusquely. "And don't worry about Rosamond. We'll do everything we can."

"You – ?"

"All of us!" – gracious, neither Septimus nor I were expecting a contribution from Gertie, but she waved her chai at us all the same. "'Course we'll find her! She's a bit of a fiend, but she's your fiend – and I did *not* want to marry her anyway!"

We blinked. She beamed. Henry caught my eye, mouthed something that looked bizarrely like *I'll show you my journal later* –

"Right. There you go." Septimus cleared her throat – and then there it was: her sudden sharp-toothed smile. "There's help if you want it. We're the Div. 'S what we do."

Behind her, Henry broke into a grin. Ballestas had lost her eyebrows to her hairline – but even she couldn't manage a scowl. Gertie raised her cup in cheery acquiescence; her entourage watched her do it, then hastily did the same. Matthew and Nick snuck each other a glance, a furtive squeeze of the fingertips.

Held aloft on Septimus's stare, lifting my hand to shake the one she offered, I'd lost my chance of sneaking anything. Not that I wanted to hide – gracious, far from it! Well might she notice that I cared for her good opinion! Let her see how much it sang in me, to finally have it back!

"What the blazes are you all doing?"

CHAPTER SIXTEEN

I AM RAKISH AND CONFUSED

The Dismembered Remnants of the Notebook of Doom, continued

Concerning Wednesday 22nd November 1893

Everything of the Division turned to scramble. Septimus whirled round before our hands met, thwacked her chair over, dived to retrieve it. Hers wasn't the only felled furniture – all those sat down were hurling themselves upright with little care for the consequences, churning the picnic blanket and flinging the pillows and tumbling sideways in unlaced boots. Matthew sprang in front of Nicholas – you're right, darling, they're not subtle. Gertie yelped a curse when half her chai slung down her front, then clapped a jam-stained hand to her mouth. Out in the corridor, a door smacked against a wall, and the Director hurtled into reception, gold-rimmed panic flaring on her spectacles.

Stiff and incandescent between the swinging doors, the interloper glowered them all down, apparently in full antici-pation of a coherent answer.

He was no Divisioner I'd ever met, nor common-or-garden Dallyanglian; if anything, he had cultivated his appearance with a view to securing an ensemble role in the Peers Chorus of *Iolanthe*. He was young – with a face that shiny, he couldn't have been older than Henry – not that it softened the sharp-ness of his sneer. He had willed himself a moustache, and apparently pomaded it too, unless the natural state of his hair was as rich and unmoving as a rosewood armoire – and his suit held a menace all its own, a glossy dappled-tweed thing that spoke both of financial resources and disinclination to use them imaginatively.

"This is not," he chastised, with adagio fury that curled my nails into my palms, "conduct appropriately reflective of our circumstances."

The silence twisted. The doors swung shut. Not even the hushed clamouring of the market could settle the moment – and the tumultuous geese outside certainly gave it a go.

"We – ah – we'd no idea you'd be here, milord," Ballestas stammered, edging between the stranger and the rest of the Division. "I – I thought I told you – on the telephone – that there was no need to come?"

"I disagreed with your assessment, Miss Ballestas." *Milord*'s caustic baritone was a ridiculous mismatch with his youthful features. "This insolent manoeuvre from Property and the Sweetings requires a retort."

Maledizione.

"It weren't Property's doing," Septimus blurted. "Last night – the town hall – none of it."

A finicky frown. "*Wasn't* Property's doing?"

She flushed. "'S what I said."

"Nonsense. Miss Ballestas is adamant that this unsexed tradesperson played you all for fools – not that I intend to permit further leniency on – "

Profound unease had me by the throat, but I hadn't given myself bare-wristed to the Sweetings only to be scorned in the abstract by the Understudy of Mountararat. "If the unsexed tradesperson might interrupt – I've really no idea who the devil you are."

Every limb of the room jolted, galvanised from rigid fear to writhing panic. I'd summoned enough drawling disdain to sink the Participazio ca', and the newcomer startled, a vein creasing in his linen-pale forehead. Fidgeting at the edge of my eye, Ballestas darted me something which, had it been from anyone else, I might almost have called a look of concern.

"Let me correct that," he spat. "Lord Clement Miltonwaters, future Marquess of Alberstowe, acting manager of the Miltonwaters estate, and patron of the Dallyangle Division."

He lifted his chin instead of his hand, stared me down with a smug little glitter to his scowl. I could barely keep a grip on my answering stare, not with my head given over to shrieking recollections –

Damn Lord Miltonwaters! This is not *what we do!*

My incarceration in Hargate Gaol. It had been this man's idea.

"Well, then," he snapped. "Have you given the detectives what they need, or must we take harsher measures?"

I opened my mouth – but my mind was flickering like a rushlight –

"It wasn't them."

The wire-thin voice made me start. Ballestas, dreadfully still and grey under the eyes, one fingernail skewered through her scarf.

"Last night, the Sweetings admitted they'd been using Property as a scapegoat – and then Maggie tried to kill them. I witnessed it – half the Division witnessed it. As the lead detective on this case, I'm officially absolving Property of suspicion. Milord."

I wasn't the only one gaping at her. My look was, at least, sheer astonishment – a sentiment made significantly less benign by Lord Clement Miltonwaters. He blinked, settled himself, incredulity sharpening into something ghastly between pity and resolve.

"I'm sorry to hear that, Miss Ballestas. How very misguided your efforts have been."

"I know," she blurted, quick and deliberate as a parry, for all that her voice crumpled beneath her. "But I have a new lead now – "

He raised a hand to cut her off. "You seem under the

impression that I mean to indulge another of your little experiments. That this Division, after yet *more* failure, can afford to tolerate anything less than perfection."

The Director frowned, fingers folding in a painfully taut clasp. "Lord Miltonwaters – "

"Come, Mrs. Ballestas, we'll have no family favouritism here. You wouldn't want one bad apple to sour everything about your surname – believe you me, I speak from experience."

"Hang on!" Gertie cried. "It was one mistake – and we all made it! You leave Cass alone!"

Ballestas flinched. "Gertie, don't – "

"I would recommend a suspension," Lord Miltonwaters continued, pinioning the Director in his glare, without even curling a lip for Gertie's outburst. "Unless you simply wish to get rid of her and be done with it."

Gertie went puce. "For *what?* Realising it wasn't the obvious suspect? Following every order you give, even the stupid ones?"

"If I may," Matthew interjected, "Perfect results on the first attempt are unusual in our line of work – "

"There! So you can't punish her for it!"

Septimus nodded. At her side, even Henry was glowering. "Reckon Gertie ain't wrong."

"Figs – quite!"

"Tell him, Director!"

Lord Miltonwaters was very pale – but his voice was steady, without a glint of alarm in the plummy vowels. "Is this the sort of impertinence you permit within your ranks, Mrs. Ballestas?"

The Director caught her breath, fingers slipping loose.

"I'm sure," he added softly, "that *other* organisations would know their place a little better."

I had never, until that moment, seen Keturah Ballestas lose all control of her features. I'd regrettably tried to provoke it, in my wayward younger youth, thought myself vindicated when I could spiel her into a snappish retort – but this was infinitely worse, worse than I ever thought she'd permit with the whole

Division watching. The spectacles slipped an inch, and the mask slipped entirely, and she stared at the lord with a face of pure helpless terror.

"Wait!" Ballestas – the younger – flinging up her hands in surrender. "There's no need for that, milord. I – I'll – what do you want, for me to resign? I'll resign. Right now. And – " She skidded round, stumbling a little, until she had her back to him. With her corkscrew curls to shield her from his scrutiny, she snuck every assembled Divisioner a crumpled warning look. "Lord Miltonwaters is right. You must remember that. He's your patron, and you owe him gratitude and respect. Especially if you mean for the Division to be productive to its fullest potential."

Miltonwaters inclined his head, peevishly mollified. "Sensible girl. The rest of you – clean this place up at once."

Gracious, he couldn't surely be shocked when no one moved?

But the Director straightened her glasses, and her face with them, jerked her head to the broken picnic. Ballestas rushed to her rickety chairs, tucked one under each arm, hurried into the corridor – and only then did the rest start twitching into similar obedience. Chairs, blankets, pillows, plates – all scattered into chaos as the Divisioners descended, crashing and clattering in defiant clamour. Nick darted about collecting cups, prised my chai from my hands with a wince of apology. Lord Miltonwaters didn't spare anyone another look, simply snagged the Director in whispered conversation, lost beneath the slamming of chairs and crockery.

I just stood there. Hardly swashbuckling, dearest, but I'd long since lost any sense of what a helpful response might be. The Division tumbled around me, their hard-won composure scraped bare as the plates –

Then Ballestas seized my arm. I hadn't noticed her return – no one had. She had me in one hand, and Earlyfate in the other; she dragged the pair of us outside before I could think to protest, escaping the building at a hectic scuttling sprint.

I meant, as soon as we were out in the freezing sun with the Division ten paces behind us, to tear myself free and demand an explanation. Ballestas didn't give me the chance. She flung me away the moment the doors slammed; thus disencumbered, she gave herself up to a hearty kick of the scarlet-painted gig beside the log-shed, punctuating the gesture with a nervous glance through the Divisionary window. Apparently reassured, she stormed through the market, discombobulated several crates, ignored my pursuit until she'd set every single stall between us and her former place of employment, then –

"Sweet Lord! That man!"

The nearest stall-owner – jellied eels – was regarding us both warily. It went against every instinct I possessed to refrain from mouthing *I'm not with her*. "He's your patron? You can't be that desperate!"

She fumbled in her pocket, hurled a fistful of coins at the stall, snatched a tub of eels. "Don't you start."

"But – what the – did you just *resign?*"

"The situation needed fixing. Needs fixing. And nothing was getting fixed in there." She tugged at her scarf – presumably to straighten it, but she grabbed the wrong side – and strode off through discarded cabbage-leaves. "Come on."

I dashed after her. Out of the nest of eels and vegetables, past the roaming hordes of geese, up on a relentless diagonal, until the awnings were behind us and the wind had bare street enough to bite. "But why the devil is *he* funding the Division? Surely the Nettleblacks could replace the stolen money?"

She flicked the words over her shoulder. "He made an offer. Very zealously."

"And the Director just – "

"The Director didn't have a choice."

She whirled round, sharply enough to require a veritable fencing dodge. Her voice was brittle, a skein stretched too taut between us.

"Didn't you see? Or do you think you're the only one stuck between the police and a hard place? If we don't take his money and do his bidding, he'll have us disbanded. Arrested. And you know who'll get it worst, if he follows through on that threat?"

Of course. "Your mother."

She ducked towards her eels, by way of hiding her face – but the spasm of frightened exhaustion was far too obvious. For one startling moment, I found myself flinching with a stab of sympathy for her, sharp and involuntary as a knife to the gut.

"So you – quit?"

"If it calms him down." A morose look between bites. "But I'm not giving up on the funding. You don't need to tell me it's a feeble chance – even if we do find it, I don't know if he'd – still. It's not nothing. Right now, it's as far as I've got."

"And you need my help?"

A curt sigh. "For my sins."

"Gracious, you brought me! And my swordstick!"

"Can you blame me, with the Sweetings still lurking? I – " – her voice snagged – "I don't know when I'll get back to my office."

There it was again: sympathy, and concern, and pity so unexpected it felt positively treacherous. She was, after all, the same sardonical young woman who had filched *evidence* from my house – who had skewered a pinhole in my favourite engraving of myself and Father – who had plucked at my regrettable history and flung down my discarded name like a gauntlet.

But she had defended me. And she'd known it would cost her.

I eased the swordstick from her hand. "What can I do?"

She blinked. Glanced me up and down, incredulous, terracotta eyes sharpening again. But this time – whatever wariness she felt obliged to surmount – her pondering was swift.

"This way."

The road was rattling with carts, traffic stamping the cobblestones flat. Angle Drag, the town's busiest artery, difficult to cross at the best and worst of times, infinitely harder when the wind is up and your guide is a rogue detective in too much knitwear. Hope nearly knocked me into a Shire horse – was she taking me home? Would I – a meagre request in the circumstances, but even so – be permitted at last a glimpse of my house, my ferns, my Surrey sanctuary?

But she tugged me away from the turn into Pole Place, hustled us instead past a sprawl of stone steps. I glanced up, and the façade of the Dallyangle Town Hall glowered back, a bulbous medievalist thing of oak doors and bloated arches. It had been recently restored, and poorly, the red-brick mismatching the colour of the surrounding shopfronts. One of which, further down the road, happened to be mine. Was that our destination – my lovely shop with its glossy cabinets, and *closed until further notice, sweet customers* emblazoned on the doors?

Gracious, we were pinwheeling *again!*

She finally stopped in an alley beside the town hall. A finicky gesture warned me to wait as she crept further in, flattened herself to the clashing brick wall, until she was past a bulge of rooms and forming an impromptu shutter for a sash-window. Very slowly, too tense for self-consciousness, she unpeeled her head from the bricks, squinted through the glass, nodded, resumed her furtive stance.

I stared at her. "What are you doing?"

By way of elliptical answer, she beckoned me over – then snatched my arm and flattened me to the wall beside her.

"What the – ?"

"Surreptitiously," she hissed. "If you can."

I didn't entirely appreciate her dubious expression. "Yesterday, you thought me capable of criminal genius."

"Until you ordered the Sweetings to murder you, yes."

"I – it wasn't – !"

She shot me an absurdly dry look.

"I simply had to prove a point!"

"With your life?"

I had to scoff. "What is my life if not a point to be proven?"

"I'd hope, a lot of other things," she retorted, with an irksomely uneasy shrug. "But it's your life."

I elbowed past her, dropped to one knee, peered through a window-box of perturbingly healthy flowers, all flinching with stifled bits of breeze. The sun had blanched everything, and it took several taut seconds before I could glimpse the room inside.

"What am I looking at?"

Her voice was grim with determination. "You tell me."

Springing to the sunlight was an appallingly decorated office. The walls were pockmarked with bad chromolithographs of Dallyangle – the mantelpiece had been commandeered by a taxidermied pheasant – and the leather-topped desk boasted what I can only describe as a daffodil in human form. It was a young woman with her back to us, dark hair flouncing in a chignon, blouse and skirt so yellow they confounded the senses. She sat at the desk, zesty skirts drowning the chair, elbow jerking as she scribbled.

I tipped back to my heels. Ballestas was staring at me with a look far too lean and hungry for such recent eel-consumption.

"Between your scarf and her skirts, this century's colours have much to answer for."

She smiled thinly. "Not even slightly inclined to carnal indelicacy?"

"I – I beg your pardon?"

"Well, I don't know! She seemed like the sort of girl you'd get spoony over! Pale and dark-haired and fancy and badly dressed – "

I was on my feet and back at the wall in two sharp breaths. "Ballestas, my lover is missing. My life is in shards. I do not need to be diverted by a Pandarus in ridiculous knitwear!"

I glowered out every second of her ticking brain, until her eyes widened and her face flamed. "What? No! Sweet Lord, I didn't – "

"Then what?"

She looked positively charred. "*She* says you did!"

"Did – ?"

"Saucy things."

Dio mio. *"Saucy things."*

"Not my area of interest!" she spluttered, clinging to a furious whisper. "Not the sort of stuff you spell out in a family-friendly medical school melodrama!"

I gaped at her.

"Never mind. Look. When the town hall was robbed, that woman was the only witness. Her name's Marigold Chandler – she's the council secretary. And she told me in confidence on the night of the robbery that you'd – well – seduced her."

"I did *what?*"

"Apparently you'd been flirting for months. She said you persuaded her to sneak you into the town hall on Sunday twelfth, after hours, because – and I'm quoting – you wanted to have her on the desk. That desk."

She jabbed a finger towards the window, by way of tremendously uncomfortable illustration – and the gesture broke me. The gesture, the testimony, the revelations, the morning – gracious, all of it! Before I'd any hope or inclination to stop myself, I simply burst out laughing, shoulders to the wall and sliding downwards.

"It's not funny!" Ballestas snapped. "She said you broke the lock with your cravat pin, so the Sweetings could follow you in, and they threatened her, and you took our funding – "

A thought struck, stupid and giddy as the whole predicament. *"Did* I have her on that desk? Was I good?"

"Property! Will you take this seriously!"

I made a valiant effort at clearing my throat.

"I've never met her, Ballestas. I certainly never seduced her. I spent Sunday the twelfth – and, indeed, the last two weeks – eating scrambled eggs, stepping in the guards, and filling Rosamond's Gower abode with – well, I believe your phrase was *carnal* – "

"Point taken," she muttered. "But then why would Marigold mention you? Why not just blame the Sweetings?"

"You heard them last night. *Someone* didn't want them hurting me – "

The thought was a needle under the fingernail.

"She had my cravat pin for the door! Those ferret-addled fiends must have given it to her!"

Ballestas opened her mouth – but the sash-window outsprinted her. Or, to be more precise, outshook her, trembling in its frame with a sudden slam from inside: a door, too close, and a snare of stabbing footsteps on the floorboards.

There wasn't time to sprint – flabbergasted as we were, I doubt even fencing reflexes could have saved us – but the window didn't open, and the stamping strode past, and –

"Have you taken leave of your senses, Marigold?"

"Darling, what – you can't be seen – "

"Your so-called solution is falling to shreds! Why the deuce do you think I gave you that damned telephone? You should have alerted me at once!"

I twitched closer to the glass, but Ballestas pinched my sleeve, her whisper sharp as an eardrop: "Don't risk it, I know it's him."

"Clemmie, dear – " – Miss Marigold Chandler's voice was astonishing, shrill and lavish as the clatter of silvery cutlery – "I have no chaperone, and we have not been officially introduced here. If anyone were to – we'd have to say that you were collecting Lady Miltonwaters's effects, or – "

"Pip Property's name has been cleared!"

(*That* jolted me against the wall like a shove.)

"I – what? – but they're not even in Dallyangle – "

The lordling's every word had splinters. "Then tell me, pray, why I have just been obliged to converse with them at the Dallyangle Division, a mere day after I recommended their removal to Hartgate Gaol, surrounded by a militia of insurrectionaries passionately convinced of their innocence."

"A mere day?" Miss Chandler echoed dazedly. "Property has been back for a day?"

"And you should have noticed. You certainly should have

kept your lackeys in check.

The Sweetings attempted to murder Property in front of the Division yesterday evening – convincing deference indeed to their deviant mastermind."

"The Sweetings did *what?*"

"I would have had those burglars hanged weeks ago. *You* promised they would secure me the Division. You promised you could control them until we could give the Division all three!"

"Do you want rid of the Sweetings? Of course! Gosh, it's easy! Practically done already! Just tell the Division they live in – "

"I don't want to know," he snapped. "No details, no sordidness – just results. Results which you are stubbornly refusing to give me."

"I – "

"I shan't be doing my Division's work forever. I thought I'd done more than enough of it to ensure their service. Your elaborations have been nothing but – but – *overcomplication.*"

"I only – I needed – you needed – I've watched Keturah Ballestas for months, and her hand needed forcing – and the Sweetings needed to – the funding theft needed to be a neat conclusion, not a new criminal – "

"Marigold." Clement Miltonwaters sighed, racking the sound out of its every joint. "This is shoddy form, and you know it."

"Clemmie, no, I – Clemmie, wait! Please! I can fix it, I can, I swear! I'll finish the Sweetings – and Property's an infamous liar, it won't be hard to twist that story back – just let me try! I'll settle it all, my sweet – whatever you need!"

Her last cry was frayed as unhemmed fabric, into silence far too scorched to leave in speculation. I jerked away from Ballestas, crouched behind the purpling flowers: he had her in his arms like a ghastly Millais canvas, ruddy hand splayed round the bunch of her chignon, as if her head were a boutonnière he meant to pin to his lapel. Knotted behind his waist, her fingers were all bone, by far the tighter grip.

"Property could ruin me." He kissed her forehead, or rather prodded his lips against it. "What they could say, Marigold – the whole plan would crack."

Her chin darted up – he permitted as much, still cupping her chignon like a hairnet – and her smile was wide enough to make me wince. "We shan't be ruined, darling. Not for anyone."

Then – gracious, that surely wasn't a sensible angle for kissing – her neck must have been all nerve and shriek – *absolutely not*, their faces were already too close, there was no need whatsoever for her to stuff him against her mouth like a tragedian's fist –

No. There was. If she'd let go, the bind would have broken. He wasn't returning her kiss, he was – waiting it out, open-eyed, with all the scornful patience of a debutante.

I scrambled back. Ballestas had me at once. "What is it? What are they doing? Why do you look so outraged?"

There was but a single refrain: "Carnal indelicacy."

"Lovely morning for skulduggery, is it, Cassie?"

It transformed my companion in a veritable blink. One moment she was keen-edged with deductions and desperation, tugging questions from her sleeves like so many half-strangled doves – but that chilly voice knocked her clean off the wall. I jumped as well; the intruder had snuck up on us too effectively for my liking, and now commandeered the alley in eerie sentinel, watching us watch the window with a horribly pallid grimace.

She was as ghostly as her voice, this newcomer. Pale as an eel's belly in a parlour maid's uniform and muddy boots, colourless hair slipping loose from its knot, the bones of her neck stark beneath an overlarge collar.

The stranger glanced at me. I promptly froze, as well I might.

Dearest – without exaggeration – she had your eyes.

CHAPTER SEVENTEEN

THE PERSONAL PURGATORY OF CASSANDRA BALLESTAS

Cassandra Ballestas's Secret Phonograph

Recording: Wed Nov 22nd 1893

She's there. Fresh from her latest crypt, blocking our way out of the alley. Last I saw her, she was a ghost of her usual ghostly self, with the tray and teacups and broken pleasantries in Lord Miltonwaters's parlour. And she's not lost that skittery fear – there are shadows catching like watermarks under her eyes, and they're nothing to do with the sun.

But she's calling me *Cassie*.

It's a nickname embroidered with the sentences it accompanied – and, much like every bit of needlepoint I've ever done, it draws blood. *Cassie* is patterned with the stem-stitched stings of *come now, Cassie,* and *Cassie, unless you wish things to become very unpleasant, very quickly, I would sit back down with your fictions,* and *if someone – and yes, Cassie, I mean you – is so thoroughly pathetic that they have to stage their own triumphs just to look good, they're hardly someone to respect!* And, before she made that of me, all the lovely lies – *Cassie, this is the best draft yet! Shall I settle Johannes, so you can finish the scene? You could hide your proofs inside the mattress?*

When she tricked me. Before Marigold sodding Chandler

took over that role. Because, apparently, I'm the most deceivable Divisioner in this wretched tumultuous town, and no amount of staging triumphs is ever, *ever* going to change that.

"Property," I manage to snarl. "Sword. Now."

"What? Should we not be careful of – ?"

I grab their arm, march us away from the hellebore windowboxes – enough of a safe distance to make Adelaide stumble back. Good. "There! And you said they're carnally distracted. But she's an ambush, and you've a sword, so – thwart!"

Adelaide scoffs. "Cassie, really – "

"Don't you *Cassie* me! She's Clement's servant now! That plan – their plan – she's part of it!"

There's a cobblestone scuffle behind the jutting red-brick wall – I whirl, just in case, but it's not the window – and then a herringboned figure stalks up the alley, closing off Adelaide's retreat. He's only got a satchel, but he's doing everything he can to look menacing with it.

"Consider this a counter-ambush, Miss Danadlenddu."

Yes, Matthew!

Adelaide's audibly ticking with exasperation, like a pocketwatch wound too tight. "Must you all be so very – *Divisionary?* There is no ambush. Lord Miltonwaters doesn't know I'm here. I'm – " – and she folds an ironical starchy curtsy – " – at your service."

I clench my fists, pull everything of me taut, too taut to tremble. "Don't you dare."

Her lip curls. "Oh, I thought you'd be difficult."

"*Me?*"

("Ballestas," Property hisses, "The window – ")

"You told me I was stupid to trust you! I'm not trusting you now!"

"There isn't time for your tantrum." Her voice is always cold, but the ice in this is enough to split my thoughts; she's coming closer, silent-footed, and her green eyes are arsenic. "I'm risking my future on this chance."

("We should return to the Division, Cassandra – Lord

207

Miltonwaters is gone – ")

"Do you know whose future you *really* risked, Adelaide? Whose future you nearly ruined? Whose future clearly can't do anything better than loop the past, thanks to you?"

"Ballestas!"

Still no sword, but my name's a stab, sharp and urgent enough to cut through. Property's pointing – then scattering, as we all are, flat to the nearest alleyside wall, as a flash-coated figure stomps across the gap – down Angle Drag without a backward glance. Matthew starts off the wall and sprints after him, but he's back as quick as he went, cheeks flushed and scowl set.

"Well," he snaps, with about half the breath he needs. "Addendum. Lord Miltonwaters isn't gone: he's returning to the Division."

His glare skids to me. Of course I flinch.

"If you had let me finish," he adds pointedly, "I could have told you our time was limited. Miltonwaters left reception just after you, with the promise of a swift return."

Don't look at Adelaide. Don't breathe her in. Focus.

"But you followed me?"

"I have to speak with you." *He* can look at Adelaide, a flick of a glance, such restrained proportionate disdain – and fair enough, she left his life alone. "Absolute discretion."

She's on the edge of my vision, arching a bone-pale eyebrow. "About Lord Miltonwaters, is it, Mr. Adelstein?"

He stiffens.

"Ardderchog. For my sake, then – and the sake of a certain heiress whose prospects, I believe, are a mutual concern – I'll join your little conversation."

"Rosamond?" Property gasps, at about half the volume I'm yelling the same in my head.

A tiny smile. "Very good."

"Rosamond sent you?"

"Wrth gwrs. I'm her cousin, don't you know – and she really is getting desperate."

Property's dark eyes widen out of all reasonable wariness. "Where is she? What can I do? What do you want?"

Now she's grinning. "Excellent question."

I want to wring necks. Too many to schedule. It's a nightmare I'd not thought to fortify myself against, watching Property's sharp supercilious features copying everything my own must have done several times over, their desperation striking off her hints like a bad lucifer.

"Adelaide should stay." Matthew, straight to the top of the neck-wringing list, ignoring my horrified stare. "Property furnished me with more particulars of the abduction: whoever took Rosamond knew you were accusing them – and beyond the Division, only a small number of people have access to that information."

Wait.

It won't be hard to twist that story back –

Carefully, then. You can be careful. You *can.*

"Alright – tell us everything." I set my teeth. "But not here."

Of *course* Adelaide suggests adjourning to the churchyard.

In between the unpunctual screaming that occupies the majority of my brain, I can feel the involuntary thoughts twitching away, fingers on a pen I shouldn't be holding. *The macabre young maid with the pale features and scheming streak, luring our heroine to the cemetery to whisper a secret. The macabre young maid snatched from the tomb by Dr Stoker's unholy experiments – the modern Prometheus's terrible little sister – and Laura must discover what the villainous surgeon means by dabbling in necromancy, before it's too late –* Afterlife and Limbs, *Cass,* there's *your sequel!*

And if you really have to leave the Div –

I catch my foot, nearly tumble through the lych-gate. Smother the thoughts until my mind's shiny with blottings.

The grass is long at the graveyard's edge, the headstones sagging, the ground squelching out its closeness to the river. How they've kept a wooden fence here, with the bog underfoot and the Angle just the other side, I've no idea – why they thought it'd be good for burying bodies even less so. The wind's dropped, but the sun picks out lichen and letters, sharpens every fold of stone drapery, glints on the water's surface like a carpet of dropped pins. The river sounds like pins too, with its quick jaunty currents.

Matthew picks his way with his usual care, but Property barely flinches for the mud at their trouser-hems. Sweet Lord, they're just as bewitched as I thought.

Adelaide darts a glance round the bucolic desolation – stop posing her for book illustrations! – and nods approvingly, then drops to her knees at the nearest headstone. I wince when she tugs several stems from the wreath on the grave, pinches them into a bouquet and bows her head.

"Mourn with me," she hisses. "*Loitering* is worth a second look – but no one will glance twice at a graveside vigil."

I can't but splutter. "There's no one here!"

Matthew's look is a finicky mirror of mine – but Property's already crouching beside her. So we drop, grass to our shoulders, and then we're all hunched over *Gregory Skull, translated February 10th 1892, aged ninety-eight years* like a mismatched coven, ready to resurrect Gertie's grandfather.

"Well," Adelaide mutters, eyes on the flowers. "How much do these two know, Cassie?"

Affronted looks on all sides. Property's crackling: "You said Rosamond – "

"I'm coming to her. Now – Alberstowe Hall – Cassie, how much did you share?" A snort, when she notices Matthew's tight-jawed incredulity. "Ah. You didn't."

She just exists to be inconvenient with my secrets, doesn't she?

"Mother didn't want the Div to worry. Or – revolt. And inevitably lose, given what we're up against."

Adelaide rolls her eyes. "Typical."

"We still *know* something's wrong," Matthew whispers. "We're still worried."

Sorry, Mother. But – actually – maybe I'm not. I'm no use against it on my own, not for anything better than desperate stalling and stupid mistakes. Maybe it's time someone prised it out of me.

"Lord Miltonwaters is threatening us. Of course we didn't take his patronage willingly – he forced our hand. Either the Div works for him, or he brings the police to Dallyangle – and our doorsteps. Hence why I very much did not want you to give him reason earlier today."

Matthew snaps like a ruler. *"What?"*

"It's also alarmingly possible," – Property, clinging to composure with little more than fingernails – "that he ordered the theft of your original funding. And blamed it on me."

"As he would," Adelaide adds dispassionately. "He can't have anything traced back to him. Nothing that might pucker that perfect reputation. Lord Miltonwaters, you see, is currently on a grand campaign to tidy up his family name. He's already tidied Lady Miltonwaters into an asylum."

Property topples. Clean out of their crouch, swordstick spat from their hands, knees in the bog and face oblivious to it.

"He would have done the same to me, had I not sworn my loyalty when he bailed us out of Hartgate – though I doubt even that would have worked if I'd shared his surname. But he can't ensure Rosamond's loyalty that easily, so – "

"He has *Rosamond?*"

They're at a mangled snarl. I'm scowling before I know it – "Adelaide, if this is a trick – "

"So paranoid you are now, Cassie! Why would I trick you, when I could gain a fortune from telling the truth?" Adelaide taps the blooms against her bony chin, closes her eyes and inhales, doesn't wince for the sickly smell. "You clearly never noticed that a Nettleblack cousin working as a maid – and governess – and *at all* – was out of keeping with the family's notorious wealth. Well – "

"Edwina controls the wealth!" – but it's not Property's voice as I'm used to. The last time they hit that pitch, they were urging the Sweetings to *do their worst.* "She stole Rosamond's share!"

"So she said! Edwina stole mine too, but that she can do with impunity – my father tried to filch the tincture business, and our side of the family were cut off. I've pleaded my case before, of course, not that Edwina's ever listened. But then I pleaded it again with Cousin Rosamond, and she seemed *much* more receptive. After all, I'm risking my neck to help her escape – it's only fair she give me some decent compensation when she gets her money."

Property's all teeth. "She's your *cousin*, damn it! She shouldn't have to pay you!"

I want to stick a hand on their shivering shoulder – warn them, as I very much can, that this is what Adelaide's *like* – but they flinch away. Adelaide flicks her gaze from them to me, unfazed, dangling a smug little smile. "Do we believe me now, Cassie?"

They're all watching me. Property's wild-eyed, greyish at the skin, and there's a muscle jumping in Matthew's jaw.

If you're anxious for to shine, and a fortune you can find –

"Fine," I snap.

Adelaide leans over the grave, rearranging the flowers in the wreath. We have to lean too – and I hate it – to catch her words over the rustle of the dying plants. There's a fumble of elbows at my side, as Matthew tugs a raggedy notebook out of his satchel, flips through its calligraphic scribble, sets his pencil over a page already cross-hatched with notes.

I want to squint – but Adelaide's started.

"As you might have surmised, Cassie, Lord Clement Miltonwaters is fond of collecting underlings. You've met two of his favourites: housemaid Dorothea Thorne and coachman Peter Hackitt – he used to be Lady Miltonwaters's butler, before Clement demoted him. Now the two of them run his errands in Dallyangle. They collected you and your mother for that first visit."

She's waiting, so I manage a nod.

"Dorothea admires the Division greatly. She's been petitioning her master to let her join ever since he became your patron. And Peter – well, he likes her, and he doesn't much like his diminished new station. I can only assume that's why he didn't stop her when she – in the middle of an unrelated errand – decided to prove her Divisionary suitability to Clement with a practical example. At least, that was the excuse, when she crashed into Alberstowe Hall two nights ago with Peter and a punctured hand, claiming she'd captured Pip Property's accomplice."

Property's head snaps round, neck taut against their starched collar. They're staring at Matthew, and he's furiously circling something in the notebook – "The Concerned Citizens."

My mind's a queasy magic-lantern. "I was *there* two nights ago!"

"And Dorothea wanted to interrupt your weekly dinner. But she had a hole in her palm, and it was bleeding all over the kitchen – she swooned before she even got up the stairs."

Another vigorous note at my elbow.

"She went eventually, and then came the order for strong tea in the study." (She'd brewed it, I assume, as bitter as her voice.) "They'd tied Rosamond to the desk-chair – heaven knows how Dorothea helped, she was giddy on the smelling-salts – and Clement was spitting fire. Threatening, when I came in, to send Rosamond to the same asylum as his unfortunate second cousin unless she gave up Property's whereabouts."

Tangled in the long grass of the grave, Property's fingers have gone white from nail to knuckle.

"I recognised Rosamond from Edwina's family portrait. I told Clement – I thought he'd release her when he realised his mistake. Now *that* would have been advantageous, to have the gratitude of both families, for unfastening such a terrible misunderstanding – "

Adelaide places the final flower, flicks the dirt from her fingers. "But he wouldn't play along. Wouldn't risk letting her go. I suppose he couldn't have a famous heiress telling everyone she'd been kidnapped and threatened by Dallyangle's upstanding future lord. What if she involved the New Police, and lost him his Divisionary militia? And as for the Miltonwaters name – well, what are we on now? The Marquess shot his gardener, Ellie became the Head-Hider and insisted I join her, and Clement's abducting the local nouveau riche. The aristocracy get away with more than murder, but – how long before it's *his* competence under question? How long before someone comes to tidy *him* up?"

Property snaps a whole fistful of grass.

"Of course Rosamond tried to escape. I tried to help her. Surreptitiously – if she failed, which she did, I didn't want to go up in flames alongside her. But I can't get her alone anymore – Clement has Dorothea and Peter watching her day and night. I don't even know where in the Hall she *is* now, nor how much longer it'll take for him to make his arrangements with the asylum. But when he rushed out this morning, I took my opportunity. And now I need to get back. It would be ill-advised to leave my cousin alone in that house. Even more ill-advised to let Clement notice my absence."

She shivers, just once, sharp and convulsive and terrifyingly wrong on her. Then her gaze snaps to mine, fastens tight about my neck.

"You stopped his family before – you stopped *me* – so do it again. This is, after all, a disaster of your own making."

"My – ?"

"Whose deductions ruined Lady Miltonwaters? Whose plan splattered the reputation of the whole dynasty? Who wouldn't give them the capitulation they wanted – who *had* to expose them – who prised their fingers off Dallyangle and made them desperate?"

I glare back at her. "None of that is my fault."

She scrambles to her feet, neatly arranging her apron over the dirt on her dress. "Well, then! Cousin Rosamond sends her love – specifically to you, Pip Property, she was very clear about that. But there's something for Mr. Adelstein too – in her exact words, *tell him I'm sorry – just in case.* I presume we're all happy with our whispers? Lovely. Best of luck, Cassie!"

She drops a curtsy, then twists her heel in the mud, and stalks towards the church. Above her spectral bun, the tower's quaking with chimes – sweet Lord, it's later than I thought –

Even so. I can stand up, but I can't run. I'm only thinking in pointy fragments. *Again* – it's happening again – I kept too many secrets and I listened to the wrong people and now no one's safe –

"It corroborates." Matthew, shaky-voiced, straightening at my side and proffering that notebook page, pencil drawing a constellation over the words. "The Divisionary knowledge. The behaviour. The wounded hand."

"This is your further particulars? *Property* wrote this? – "

Oh, God. Property.

They've not moved from the graveside. Their hands are trembling, in two circles of torn-up grass.

Matthew clears his throat. "Are you quite well?"

They stand, turn, muddy-kneed, blazing at the eyes, cravat pin glinting in the icy sun. "Perfectly. And I have a solution."

At some calmer, earlier juncture, they might have known not to perturb me with a devilish murderous smirk. But the calm's gone, and the care's gone, and now there's just devil and murder in a terrifying rictus.

"I mean to seduce Marigold Chandler."

CHAPTER EIGHTEEN

I AM DESPERATE

The last pages torn from the Notebook of Doom

Concerning despair

"What?" Ballestas spluttered, startling me backwards onto Adelaide Danadlenddu's flower display. "In what deranged world is that a solution?"

I grabbed the headstone behind me to deny the mire underfoot its next victim; it was a miracle none of us had sunk. "This from the woman who staged her own resignation – "

"You said you were on our side now!" she cried, jabbing a finger into my chest, cricking me over the stone with every little shove. "You said you were sane!"

"Do you want to listen, or to turn me upside-down?"

"I want you to listen. To me." She curled her fists, clinging clench-teethed to a maddening approximation of patience. "You have just – *just* – salvaged your good name with the Div. I lost my job for affirming how virtuous you are. The credibility of my next accusation relies on you looking like a vaguely decorous and innocent individual. And do you know what'll *really* help you look decorous and innocent, Pip Property? Only leaping into bed – onto desk – I don't know, and I don't want to think about it – with the secretary who stole our funding!"

"I am not genuinely proposing to offer her any such delight." I think I was smirking, though it felt rather more like a gouge in my jaw. "The seduction will be wholly mental – emotional – call it manipulation, if you prefer. But I need her cooperation, and I won't get it without charm."

She glowered at me for a tremendously long moment. The sun burnished her in grim silhouette – she still had me tilted far too sharply. Matthew Adelstein hovered behind her, twisting my notebook in polite consternation.

"I think we'd both appreciate an elaboration on this plan of yours." His eyes narrowed. "With less of the melodrama, if you please."

Less of the – !

"Va bene. Ballestas and I witnessed an intriguing exchange before the descent of Miss Danadlenddu – it seems Miss Chandler is conspiring with your lordly patron. Conspiring, specifically, to steal your funding with the Sweetings and blame me for her part. But, to judge from what we saw, her interest in Miltonwaters is rather more – ardent, than professional. Now, I know her type, and I know his. She'll relish his every lacklustre caress, and crush all the cravat designers in Surrey for a crumb of his affection – but he'll drop her as soon as she's served his purpose. She's stolen for him, liaised with the Sweetings for him, framed me and lost me and framed herself in the losing, so what do we imagine our paragon of *reputation* might do with someone like that? A clue for you, Divisioners – he won't just be snubbing her at soirées!"

Ballestas tipped back. I straightened my lapels, very pointedly.

"I think she'd rather appreciate a warning, don't you?"

Matthew swallowed. "You mean to turn Miss Chandler against Clement?"

"You think you *can* do that?" – oh, Ballestas, you innocent.

"I talked the Sweetings out of burgling me. I think I'm more than capable." I swept down for Earlyfate, twirled it on my palm, until the nettle-pointed tip jostled with my fingerbones. "If there are no further questions – "

"Wait!"

Ballestas leapt a grave just as I took a step, squashed the boggy grass with her landing, ankle-deep in my path. I spun, of course, but Matthew had the other retreat tucked behind his herringbone shoulders.

"Why go after Marigold? To what end?"

The sigh peeled off my throat. "Ballestas, time is pressing – "

"We need to know! If you want the Div – "

"Did I say that?"

She blinked. Opened her mouth. Closed it. Seconds, maddening seconds. I could hear my pocketwatch, and Earlyfate blazed in my hand.

"Miss Chandler stole our funding," Matthew offered instead. "The Division is already implicated. And if I might remind you – " – gracious, he was lifting my notebook to me, splayed open on two scribbly pages, paisleys festering idiotically in the margins – " – treating our members as pawns in your scheme does not end well for you, as you yourself have readily acknowledged."

I could have torn my very shadow free, all clawing fingers, flung it across the grass and graves to snatch the book from his hand –

"As you wish." But *quickly,* a lattice of words to lift them out of my way: "If I can persuade Marigold that trusting Clement is not in her interests – which it isn't – from there it's but the tiniest step to full betrayal. Full betrayal which will, of course, involve getting me into Alberstowe Hall and clearing my path to Rosamond's rescue, whilst *milord's* distracted in his Divisionary meeting. We'll be there and back before he's even noticed the treachery – and then that wretched little Danadlenddu girl can stop extorting Rosamond for a rescue she can't manage!"

Then, when they exchanged an incredulous glance – "And don't you fret, I'll find out what Miss Chandler's done with your funding."

"What? That's not – no – hang on!" I'd taken another step, and it twisted Ballestas's voice, all that wiriness taut enough to snap. "Your plan is just to – to – do it all on your own? When you have no idea what else Marigold might be hiding? When your best informant on Rosamond's whereabouts is Adelaide Danadlenddu?"

"Adelaide's motive is sound, if uncharitable. And Miss Chandler shan't be trouble – do remember that I have a sword-stick, and the element of surprise, and a fair point to – "

"No!" she cried. Opposite her, Matthew was flipping the pages of my notebook until they chittered worse than the river. "It's too much of a risk. We'll find something else. We'll get word to the Div – somehow – like Septimus said, this is what we do – "

"There's no time. If you insist on fretting about risk – well, why *risk* alerting Miltonwaters? Why *risk* waiting for him to return home? Why *risk* waiting any longer at all?"

"Why risk yourself? You said you wanted our help! Can't you just take it?"

There was annoyance in her tone, but also reluctant incred-ulous concern, the sort of sentiment that might have proffered arm's-length assistance to a broken-winged wasp. *Pity*. Or was it? She was still staring, an illusionist's stare, trying to crawl inside my skull and prise out – what? Why was it so infernally difficult to tell?

Why was she waiting for an answer? Why was *I* waiting?

I –

I froze. Or, rather, the molten heat hardened, turned my tongue and teeth to set glass. Too sharp. Too easy to shatter. Whatever I said – I knew it, even before I'd words to say – it would cut, and it would sting –

"If I might offer Rosamond Nettleblack's sentiments on the matter," Matthew ventured, eyes skidding over my hand-writing, "She specifically asks you not to *sprint headlong into fixing it* – and she doesn't want you *smashed on the wreck of another scheme.*"

And there, quick and bloody, the shattering.

"She was not asking me to abandon her!"

His eyes widened. "I didn't – "

"Don't *quote* her to me. Don't twist my recollections. Don't pretend that *you*, of all people, care a shred about what happens to her."

"Property, he only – "

"And don't you start, Ballestas! You think you know exactly where I should slot into your plans – onto your wall – but you just got in my way before, and I won't let you do it again! I am Rosamond's only hope. I am the only chance she has. And I am the only one to blame for any of this happening to her. If I hadn't provoked the Sweetings – if I hadn't been such a damnably easy target to frame – if I'd simply fixed it myself, as I should have, as I can, as I always have and will always have to – damn you, you can't help me! And I can't wait on your incompetence! And if you want to stop me, to lock me back in your morgue while you scour my past for a solution – well, I respectfully invite you to *try!*"

I saw the very moment their faces changed. The fear. Earlyfate was taut in my fists, half-drawn.

"The Division can't get involved," I snapped – blurted – couldn't tell which. "Miltonwaters has you in a stranglehold, and I won't risk Rosamond's safety any longer."

There was plenty in that, surely, for either one of them to snatch at – plenty that might merit a lively retort – plenty to provoke more than those terrified *stares*, pupils spreading like bruises as the sun scabbed over –

"But fear not," – gracious, soften it, *soften it* – "Once I've lured Miss Chandler out of Clement's clutches, it should be far easier for you to free yourselves! Do you know, sweet Divisioners, I did once call myself your patron saint!"

It dropped, without acknowledgment, flat into the tendrils of grass.

I took a step. They both flinched back.

Once I'd done it, I could hardly slow down. Time had been – *was* – far too flimsy and far too crucial, was it not? I strode round Ballestas, ducked her stare, let the momentum fling me into a jaunty bow, straightened up to silence and bile in my throat. I had to turn, then, had to lift my chin to the cold and saunter away. My lips were too cracked to whistle, but the rest was familiar: the pinch at my collar as my cravat squirmed against its pin, the absentminded smirk, the blinkers on my gaze, the vice round my jaw –

I couldn't look back. And they didn't call me.

END OF VOLUME TWO

VOLUME THREE

CHAPTER NINETEEN

BALLESTAS CONSIDERS HER OPTIONS

Cassandra Ballestas's Secret Phonograph

Recording: I should definitely be asleep now

Sweet Lord. Back to the start we go.

It's quiet in the graveyard, once Property's gone. Their every step flattened the long grass, and there's not enough breeze to tug it up again; the river's just a tremble on the air. The sun's already too close to the twitching water, drooping towards an early dusk. Too early. There's not been enough of the day. There's been far too much of the day.

I can stare out the glittering river – I can wince for the pinch of my nails in my elbows – I can't get my thoughts in a sensible shape. *What else're they going to think?* – that's Septimus, snapping, probably paraphrased, every resurrected syllable sticky with guilt – *we can't have 'em thinking we're a worse option* – the *worse option?* – *the* worst *option* – ?

The words churn in my skull. I close my eyes, but it just makes them heavier, sloshing against the sides until they're a headache in earnest.

"Is everything alright, Detective?"

I blink, and Matthew's there. Tentative steps, pintucked frown, one supremely awkward pat on my shoulder. I shrug, just about.

"I fear I overstepped. I thought Miss Rosamond's words might – "

"No. I made the threats. It was my fault."

He's waiting. And I – sorry, I'm not – I don't know if I've got the words for this bit. I'm barely even thinking in words that are mine. It's – I just – I breathe words, alright? – and I've no idea how I even stay on my feet when I can't put the thing in sentences. Or lyrics. Or flouncy novel prose. It's like choking, when it just goes into – into feelings I can't phrase, that don't fit inside words like *fiery hatred* or *gentle terror* – or *remorse*.

And I don't even have time for this. If I can't phrase it – well, there you go, Cass, that was your chance, your time for *feelings*, and now it's gone. Now there's just a world of problems tapping their watches at you. And there's you, the grand disappointment, scowling at the end of the Record, when *you are no longer making any sense*, and you can't *arrange your resources* and *rise to the occasion* if you cram words full of misery until they snap –

"But there's nothing I can do."

Matthew's frown sharpens. It's weird – as if the phonograph itself suddenly grew eyes and squinted up from the table at me.

"Property's right," I hiss. "If Clement's at the Div, we can't get involved. We can't help. Of course they won't wait for us – all I've done is terrify them and drive them away."

"Lord Miltonwaters was forcing your – "

"I'm still the one who did it! I'm still the one who let him yank out the whole point of the Div! And what *is* the point of the Div, if we can't even help people? If we keep trying, keep proving ourselves over and again – and it's still not enough – and we're still getting it wrong – and still no one *wants* our help?"

That's when I hear it. There, with my throat still hoarse from saying it, as clear and unnerving as every time I've ever played back my cylinders. *The Div* – oh, what a flimsy synonym. Because it's not *our* help Property doesn't want, is it? It's mine.

And they're not wrong. They're not even the only one.

I crumple into tears. Matthew clearly hasn't a clue what to do about it.

"Don't faint, I'm not expecting another sodding hug."

"I'm sorry," he blurts. "I – Nicholas would know what to – oh, goodness –"

Every few breaths, he pats my shoulder again.

It feels, at the start, like he means it to be chivvying. Like he's marking time. Invigilating my morbs. But it – I don't think it is, not really, not when it goes on for so long. I'm just there, crying every word out of my head, crying because I didn't solve it the last time I cried, because Adelaide's right, I can't stage my own triumphs, I can't even stage my own disasters, much as I'd love to stage an ending to this, or write one, or just *have* one –

But it ends when it ends. My legs are blurry, my scarf sodden, my boots ankle-deep in the mud.

"Would you like to go home?" Matthew tries, very warily.

I sniff. "I'm not a child, Adelstein."

"If I may, you are clearly exhausted –"

"I know." I drag a fistful of mitten across my eyes, until he's back in focus. "This is just my life. Phrasing or crying with not much in between."

He swallows. Fair enough; he didn't ask –

"As you wish. I noticed a discrepancy. With the case."

What?

"Sweet Lord, Matthew, no one cares about our *discrepancies* –"

"I would greatly appreciate your thoughts on the matter. If to ask isn't an imposition."

I squint. Bizarre as it is, he doesn't *not* look like he means it. Even so, I fumble. I can't brush the sarcasm off my voice – I'm trying, though, I promise I'm trying.

"You'll be the first who genuinely needs my thoughts."

"I doubt that." He drops his hand at last, shifts his satchel up his shoulder – he's put that book away. "Do you recall Miss Danadlenddu's suggestion that Lord Miltonwaters kept Rosamond out of fear she'd involve the New Police?"

Recalling's an interesting one, in my present state. Every thought's hefting something, or righting something, tidying the day as if it's a room. "Go on?"

"You said Lord Miltonwaters threatened to involve the police if the Director refused his patronage. So – which is it? Does he want the police in Dallyangle, or doesn't he?"

"I mean, he – "

Wait. Wait, wait, wait.

"He did threaten that. But he also had Marigold steal our funding. Why bother risking *that* if he thought he could just – if he had a valid threat already – if – ?"

"What if," – and Matthew nearly smiles, a spiky ironical thing, " – it's not a real threat? What if it's simply a terrifying prospect?"

"He thought taking the funding'd be enough." Words, *words*, dragging me after them like a chariot. "Marigold said she'd been watching Mother. Said she'd need *forcing*, to accept his patronage. So Marigold took the funding. But Mother still wouldn't say yes, not when – when – well, his family's made of plantation money."

He winces. "Of course."

"So he tried to say he'd raise the Dallyangle rents and give us that instead. But that didn't work on her either. And it was only then he started making threats – he even said that all noblemen should despise the police – sweet Lord! It's a *bluff?*"

"It's desperation," he mutters. "As Miss Danadlenddu said. His grandfather is a murderer, and his cousin desecrated the body. He has kept them both away from the law by what sounds like a combination of bribery, concealment, and luck – and he has only had to employ those desperate measures on unsanctioned detectives and a provincial gaol. No wonder he seized upon this plan, this – this calculated risk. He can blame Miss Chandler for the stolen funding, if the theft is discovered and Property's innocence confirmed. Either way, he still gains the support of a detective organisation whose presence negates the need for a local police, but whose abilities are limited by the funds he controls."

"And he convinced us into it with the same thing that's scaring him!"

I gasp. I want to press a hand to my chest, squash my heartbeat back to normal, but it'd be like sticking my fingers through the spinning wheel of a bicycle.

"But what the hell can we *do?* If we bring the police here, that's just his threat come true. He's covering his tracks as we speak – what if we call them and we get it worse than him? What if the police decide *we're* the case worth taking, and that Dallyangle actually is the sort of place they'd love to set up station in? What if they start doing what you said, and chasing crimes that aren't crimes, and suddenly nobody cares that Clement's whole family keep killing people and incarcerating people and threatening people because heaven forbid there be a cravat designer in a suit without the state's permission – !"

"Cassandra." He grabs my shoulders, properly, yellow-flecked eyes wide. "None of that has happened."

"You got to panic about it yesterday!"

A scoff, so prim and dignified it hardly even sounds like one.

"My so-called *panic* has never merely been confined to *yesterday*. If your life is phrasing and crying, mine is – fear. Fear of everything you describe and more. But Nicholas is quite correct – if I am obliged to breathe fear, I can at least refuse to let it choke me."

He arches an eyebrow. "I believe you have your own history of doing the same."

I know it's not wanted. I know it's not much. I know we're deep in a well, scrabbling at walls we didn't make and can't tear down. But we're both of us there – *all* of us – whether anyone wants me there or not, whether or not wanting me should even matter there. I can still try. I can't *not* try.

"Alright then, Detective Adelstein." I straighten up, blink until his face isn't blurry, gulp against the terror 'til my throat stings. "What the hell *can* we do?"

His eyes flash. There's me on their pupils, just as taut as him. "Excellent question, Detective Ballestas."

When we part on Angle Drag, he spurs straight to a pintucked run. Not so fast he'll lose his breath and scupper the ruse, but still quick – quick enough to slip back into the Div with some explanation for his absence, eloquent and inscrutable as the one still pinned to the telephone. I watch the market swallow him, hover on its threshold – you know you're there when you start finding things slimy or alive underfoot – but I won't risk following any closer. The market's packing up, stripped to cabbage leaves and empty boxes, stripy awnings starting to sag. Dismantling every hiding-place. I don't want Clement thinking he *hasn't* roundly defeated me, and I don't reckon I'll look roundly defeated if he spots me staring out the Div windows.

I'm not bound for the Div. I'm scuttling round the back of my family's apothecary, trampling dread into the cobbles, down and along to the town hall. *I'm not getting in the way –* whisper it, under the bustle and the hooves and the carriage-wheels – *but I can still check the dandy's scheme hasn't imploded – I can still make sure that singleminded singlehanded chaos doesn't prove anyone else's undoing –*

"Cassandra!"

Mother hurtles out of the apothecary's back door. She –

Is she *holding* me?

I'm in her arms, elbows pinned to my jacket, frozen in the street, too stunned even to blink. Her hand curls through my hair, cups my skull and pulls my forehead to her lips. There's her heartbeat, jolting through the bruise-tight hold, twitching my eyelashes – and there's her badge, sharp-edged in my chest. It can't be delirium, then; surely I'd not imagine getting jabbed by my mother's Directorial insignia.

I should do something – I can't do anything – but if I don't, she'll never do it again –

She's already leaning back. Her face is drying wax, that strange tender fury trying to stiffen into her usual calm – trying, and failing, the longer she stares me out.

"I – "

"My office. Now."

The embrace sharpens – it's not even an embrace anymore, just a tight hold on my arm. She marches, tugging me with her, through the skinny street between the apothecary and the Fitzdegu funeral parlour. Towards the Div.

"Wait – !"

"Cassandra." Mother hisses it, right in my ear, like she's slicing a letter open – no, nothing so smooth – like she wants to slice, but the penknife's blunt, and it's tearing the paper to raggedy trim. "Do you have any idea what your disappearance has done to the equilibrium of – of the Division?"

"I – I didn't – stop a moment, we can't – "

"We have been frantic! Did you imagine we would not be, after last night? Did you – did you not *think?*"

I try to twist away. She's not having it. "Clement can't see – "

"Lord Miltonwaters is gone!"

"What?"

"I sent him away!" She drags her free hand through her hair as we walk, wrenching spirals from her perfect bun – the only gesture I've ever seen that makes her look vaguely like me. "That meeting can wait! You resigned. You didn't come back. I had the entire Division drop everything to look for you. Your father said you hadn't gone home. I thought you'd run away – I thought the Sweetings had – I thought Lord Miltonwaters's condemnations and threats had driven you to – "

"No!" It rattles behind my eyes – too much, all at once, to make sense beyond the sting. "I'm fine – I'm sorry – when did Clement leave?"

She slams us through the doors. No scarlet gig beside them. It's dark in reception – there's not a gaslamp lit to fill the space of the slumping sun. The blankets are gone – the picnic's been swept off every surface – no one's tending to the smoking wood-burner. But there's a small swarm on the wrong side of the desk.

Matthew's in the cluster, whirling round as we crash in. Behind him, there's a tremendously green person, stiff and awkward in verdant velvet, with a bearded man beside her, and Henry and Septimus either side like mismatched book-ends – brightening, the both of them, when they spot me, far more than I'd expect them to. One look from Henry to the green lady shows the same eyes, the same pallor, the same sharp bones – but this woman is at least a decade older, hayfield hair streaked with stressed silver-grey.

Mother jolts to a halt. So do I. Everything in my head's toppling over again.

"Director and Detective Ballestas, I believe?" The lady's voice is stiff as her, stepping carefully from word to word. "What fortuitous timing. I am Miss Edwina Nettleblack, and this is Mr. Gareth Wyn Evans. Henry and Septimus give me to understand that our testimonies are required, to settle matters relating to my sister."

Somehow, spiky-lashed and dishevelled as she is, Mother clears her throat. "Miss Nettleblack. Mr. Evans. I do hope you haven't been kept waiting – "

"*No!*"

Everyone stares at me. Matthew's about the only one who doesn't look baffled.

"No! No decorum! No Div etiquette! We are *not* just pretending everything is fine! Septimus – Hyssop – Property trusts you – go with Matthew, he'll explain – go to the town hall, go right now, tell Property Clement's gone home before they get themselves – "

Hunched on the wall, the telephone begins to screech.

CHAPTER TWENTY

I AM ATTEMPTING TO UNLEASH HELL

The Natural Successor to the Notebook of Doom

For the attention of – va bene, myself

As will be apparent, I need it.

Angle Drag was teeming. The dregs of luncheon had been sopped up and stacked away: greasy-fingered youths darted between carriages, having pushed their midday break to its uttermost limit. One nearly slipped under the fishmonger's cart, hauling empty eel-barrels out of town on the strength of a sullen-eared pony. In shopfront windows, proprietors were slumping – shelves starting bare through the gaps in their wares, novels sneaking out from under counters. Of course I knew the feel of the hour, creeping ever earlier with the short winter days – any time after two o'clock was fair game for a Whittard blend in the back room. It used to be oddly reassuring, to feel myself sag in tandem with the street, hastening to dusk and rest.

But not today. If they sagged, I sharpened, a pen-nib in a tray of blunt pencils. Sharp at the sounds – boot-heels, breaths, swordstick on the cobbles – and at the silhouette, a long shadow in a well-cut coat, skewering a path with the sun behind my shoulders. I caught the edges of stares, the blinks behind glass – that tardy tradesman only lost his footing for a glance at me. At Vernon Vibbrit's glossy windows, my own first glimpse stopped me in the street.

"Hallo again, Pip Property!"

The ablutions bowl had done its work. You'd never know I'd cried – you'd never think I'd known reason to. My scar was pale, neat with healing, unobtrusive. The suit (olive herringbone) and cravat (chestnut paisleys, amber snails) were an impeccable pair for the cream-collared shirt. The fabrics had been walked free of creases; gold flashed at the pin and watch-chain. Earlyfate lounged at a jaunty diagonal beside my legs. My smirk was just as jaunty: a smirk that felt not a scrap of turmoil, that kept any squirming pinned too tightly to surface.

The sight should have bolstered me. *How they met themselves, indeed! You promised the Pobbles cliffs you'd get it back, didn't you?*

For what purpose? Burning through Marigold Chandler's thoughts, feelings, attachments, like so many cheap matches?

Shiny on the shopfront, I watched my eye twitch.

For saving Rosamond. Because nobody else will.

Then I doubled my pace, up the bulbous steps to the bulbous façade. Struck Earlyfate's hilt against the fish-hook knocker, to the chorus rhythm of *Cat-Like Tread*. The town hall certainly kept me waiting, long enough to fidget with problems: what if they didn't let me in? What if word of my innocence hadn't spread?

Go back to the Division, whispered something small and traitorous, pressed so close to my forehead I could feel every word.

The door buckled inwards, scraping the floor with its swollen edges. I kicked it, to hasten proceedings – and then it was open, and there she was.

"You," Marigold Chandler blurted.

"Me."

She grabbed for the door-handle, but I was quicker. One twist of a passing-step and I'd slipped inside, slicing through the sliver of threshold, elbows on the door to slam it behind me. The air thickened; they'd no windows in the entrance hall, only carpets and dust-tipped frames, a gaslamp blazing on every metre of rustic red wallpaper.

Miss Chandler was backing down the stuffy corridor, her voice shrill with fear. Too shrill, between all those doors. "There's nothing more for you to steal – !"

"I did no such thing, and you know it."

She swallowed sharply. But, at least, she stopped. "What do you want?"

Smile. "I don't mean you a jot of harm. I'm simply inclined to a conversation. Might we speak in private?"

A prim little nod. "I'll make us tea. But you must be quiet. We – "

"Haven't been formally introduced?" (She blanched.) "And yet, by your testimony, we're such intimate acquaintances!"

There was something so unabashedly uncomfortable in her flinch, so much blunter than any sneer from the debutantes. That she'd no interest in flirtation was obvious; that my tone had unsettled her, even more so. Very carefully, I dropped the smile.

She stalked down the corridor. I followed her, clammy-nerved.

Her office was larger than it had looked from the street, the ceilings fussy with finials, a plump fire beneath the stuffed pheasant on the mantelpiece. She bustled to her hearth, plucked a kettle from its hook on the flames and carried it to her tea-table, picking through caddies and strainers and dainty cups. I left her to it – stretched the space between us, until I stood at the same window I'd just been squinting through. The sunlight was drooping on the flowers outside; the alleyway was empty.

"I want to make something clear." I jumped – the silence had stretched with the space, and I hadn't expected her to break it. Metal and porcelain glinted under her words as she readied the tea. "I have no desire to partake in the – the *impropriety* that I claimed you offered me. No matter what that lady detective told you."

I glanced back at her, sickled over her kettle. "Then why say it?"

"Because that's how you do things." She straightened up, two cups poured. "The Sweetings told me everything about your modus operandi – your victims are the people you can charm. I needed this new crime to match your old ones, and that was the precedent you set."

I froze.

Shall we look at what you have *done, Pip?*

She plucked the strainers from the cups, ferried the tea-tray to her desk, gathered herself a spare chair on its opposite side. "Please, sit."

It was as much as I could do to manage it gracefully. She was already sipping, watching me coolly over the rim of her cup. A heady black tea might have slammed eloquence back into me, but from its delicate colour this stuff looked herbal. It was still my cue: to pluck at her trust, to settle the strangeness, to start the persuasion –

To follow the precedent?

"Did the Division send you?" She flicked a finger towards my cravat pin. "When they returned my evidence?"

"My questions first, I think. If you needed a convincing burglary, why not just blame the Sweetings?"

She sighed. "They were hardly keen to embrace a new leader, after what you did! They wouldn't even take the blame unless I promised it meant revenge on you."

Va bene. "And now they've changed their minds again. You didn't actually let them do the burglary – you haven't given them the Division's funding, have you?"

Her eyes narrowed, the very colour of synthetic ultramarine. "How do you – ?"

"They stole my savings, but that wasn't much. If they had the council's coffers – gracious, they could retire on the proceeds! Yet they were at the Division last night, trying to steal the *new* funding. Why would they risk your scheme like that, unless they felt cheated out of something you'd withheld? *You* have the original funding. You've had it from the start."

She stared at me, so intently I had to force my blinks.

Mercifully, it wasn't revulsion now, more a kind of pettish exasperation, not dissimilar to the way Miltonwaters had looked at Ballestas. "The Sweetings said you were no better than an arrogant scapegoat. But you know exactly what you're about."

This last was, I confess, far more of a barb than I anticipated.

"Go on, then," she snapped. "Have your little gloat. What else do you know?"

I cleared my throat. "About you and Clemmie, do you mean?"

She choked. Blotched at the cheekbones, spluttering against the teacup's rim, swatting my assistance away with a furious flapping hand. I waited for her to emerge – or, rather, regathered my words from where they threatened to shrivel.

"Enough to know the danger you're in."

"The – what?"

"I'm sure you feel indispensable to Clement. After all, you've been fixing his problems so very drastically! Stealing the Division's funding, forcing them to accept his patronage, just so he could poach a militia and not lose it to the New Police! But ask yourself this – what kind of person would rather trap an organisation than trust them to accept him on his merits?"

Her chin jerked up. "When there's history between that organisation and his family, it necessitates a little bolstering – "

"A *little bolstering?* Is that what you call splintering peoples' lives?"

"Don't you blame Clemmie for your poor decisions – "

"Clement is using you! You're simply there to shield him from his own skulduggery! He didn't want the details of your plans – he could hardly even bear to kiss you!"

She winced, in perfect tandem with my thoughts.

"You know what he does to those who smudge his reputation. You know what he did to his cousin – what he's doing to Rosamond Nettleblack – what he'll do to me, if he gets another chance to try it! You're a loose end, Marigold, and the Division have found you out – how long do you think he'll let you last?"

The teacup clattered back into its saucer.

"I take it back," she whispered. "The Sweetings were right."

Her shrill voice began to tremble – no, to convulse – a cutlery drawer shaken in terribly strong hands. "You would come here, infamous double-crosser that you are, honestly believing you could make me do the same to Clemmie? On the grounds of – what? Your own hypothesis? Or just your own interests?"

My chest pulled taut. "I – "

"Clement and I are engaged. We have been since Oxford. Do you think he cares a jot for *reputation* when it comes to me?" She raised a shaking hand, pinned down the fingers one by one. "My family lost everything, and he didn't break our contract. I stole to fund my final year, and he didn't break our contract. I was sent down from Somerville, and he didn't break our contract. He sent me here, trusted me to watch his future for him whilst he finished his studies – and he didn't break our contract. As soon as we're finished fixing the mess his family made of his inheritance, he means to *honour* our contract!"

A vicious little smile. "I've ruined your precedent, haven't I?"

"I – I didn't mean – "

But I did –

"I simply know what it is to do terrible things for the person you love – "

Hallo again, Pip Property!

"I – "

She arched a scornful eyebrow. Every word scraped a little more off my throat.

"I'm sorry. This is wrong. I – I just – you can't do this to Rosamond for the sake of a servant's mistake. Whatever you think of Clement, you have to – "

"I have to, do I? Is it orders now?"

"I just want you to *let her go!*"

It scorched. Too much for immediate reiteration. I grabbed the tea, gulped it down, against the snarls and the stifling air –

Then I gasped.

Marigold giggled, blurring at the edges like a bad exposure. "Dearie me."

She swept round the desk, yellow skirts whirling, yanked out a drawer and tipped its contents over my boots. The empty drawer she dropped in my lap with a smile – "You'll be needing this."

"What –?"

The room bucked like a gondola, and lurched absolutely everything out of my stomach.

I couldn't think. I couldn't move. I could barely breathe for retching. It was thrice what the seasickness had been: vomiting so violent it stung my very ribs. Earlyfate skidded from my hand, one sharp thwack against the floor. Marigold snatched it up as she flitted past me – to the door, then across the room, opening a cabinet and tugging out a telephone receiver. She was doing something with the machine – she was –

I slumped over the drawer. The contents were peat-black.

"Thorne, is it? Is your master home yet? – Yes, you do that."

Get up – but the rug singed my knees after three steps. The nausea crawled into my shoulders, tugging them back every time I retched, again and again until they screamed –

"Pardon the intrusion, Clemmie darling, but about that little problem you – yes. Oh, yes, I've dealt with it. Shall I bring them to Alberstowe Hall, or –? Oh! Well, if you prefer the meeting-point. – No, don't worry, I have the skiff. Shall we say half an hour? – Until then!"

I was wrenching at my cravat when I felt it. A hand in my hair – a hand with a perfumed wrist – grip tightening to drag my head from the drawer, polished voice hissing in my ear.

"Now listen to me, unless you wish to meet the same fate as the Somerville bursar's greyhound. I have the antidote for the – ah – *tea* currently inconveniencing you. You won't find its like, unless you happen to know another Oxonian herbalist who can guess the poison – and the remedy – and the dosages. Oh, and did I mention all three are of my own devising?"

Idiot – *idiot* –

"If you want that remedy, you'll do everything I say. Do you understand?"

I had to nod, as much as I could, gullet tight as twine.

"Wise decision." The grip on my hair slackened; her footsteps plucked the floor under my hands. "I'll gather my things. Stay where you are – do try to retch quietly, would you?"

CHAPTER TWENTY-ONE

LONG OVERDUE

Cassandra Ballestas's Secret Phonograph

Recording: Onwards

The Div telephone's still screaming. It's a very literal translation of my thoughts, actually.

"Someone answer it!" A room full of mooncalf blinks. "Someone who *didn't* just pretend to resign in front of the man on the other end!"

Matthew darts forward, fumbles with the receiver. "Lord Miltonwaters. This is Detective Adelstein speaking – I – hello?"

I rush over then, jostle my ear as close as I can get it without snatching the thing. There's a ghostly skinny voice squirming in the machine, fainter than usual – then it fades, to a long moment of horrible scratching, the sort of scratching you can hear inside your own gullet. Cold fingers slip through my ribs.

Matthew gulps. "Lord Miltonwaters?"

That scratching again, even worse. Then, faint, faltering – *"Absolutely not."*

The wire. Extended from the town hall.

"Marigold has your funding. And – regrettably – myself. I can't – I was wrong – are you still – ?"

The scratching splatters over us both, so loud we lurch away from the telephone. When it dies, and we dive back, there's nothing left but the metal in our hands.

I curl up my fists, until the room stops shimmering.

"Septimus. Hyssop. Town hall. Now."

Miss Edwina Nettleblack snatches Henry's sleeve. "I would prefer that Henry stay – "

"And I'd prefer not to be improvising a rescue mission, but here we are! That was Property – they're at the town hall and they need us – now can we *go?*"

It's like a light in their faces. Quicker than a taper. Quicker even than a gaslamp. One sharp electric spark, and suddenly both the sweethearts are looking decidedly less sweet. I know in theory that this spoony double-act have thwarted the Sweetings together, more than once – but staring at them now, I genuinely believe it.

"I'll get the cycles," Septimus snarls, and bolts through the doors.

"Wait!" Miss Nettleblack's still got Henry. "Can the others not – ?"

But she's clearly not expecting Henry to grab her shoulders, nor for that timid voice to scramble over hers. "Edwina. You'll be quite fine. I know it. And *you* know I forgive you – both of you!"

"But I – "

"I want my family reconciled! Not in danger! Communicating! Quite! And this is very much the first step in that exciting direction! You can do it – figs, I believe in you!"

Henry sort of vibrates a moment – like a hummingbird choosing its angle – then darts up, kisses Miss Nettleblack's forehead, and scrambles away after Septimus. I jerk my head to Matthew – he's already following – through the swinging doors, I can see them readying the –

Mother's hand pinches round my shoulder. Painfully tight. Hooking me like a fish, as the other three leap on bicycles and disappear.

Oh God.

But at least they didn't wait for me, I suppose?

"Explain." Mother turns me round, skidding away from

her genteel voice. "Why the town hall? What has Pip Property done? What have *you* done?"

I try to duck her gaze. "Well – "

"Is this a bad time?" the man – Mr. Evans – hazards, very gently. At his side, Miss Nettleblack looks like a heap of broken glass bewitched into a lady. "Henry and – Division Sergeant something, I think? – did say they'd have to carry on looking for a Miss Cassandra once they'd fetched us – if you still need to – "

"This is Cassandra, Mr. Evans." Mother squeezes my shoulder. "Safe and sound. If you'd like to help yourselves to some tea – all behind the desk – she and I will be with you in but a moment. I just need a very swift word with her in my office."

And thus I'm at Mother's desk. Again. The last time I was on this side of it, I had my novel snipped to kindling, my morals dissected, my career upended and my dignity plucked out. The whole room still looks far too much like it did that day, even though the rest of the Div is flush with Clement's trinkets: the desk is still drab, the window draughty without a curtain, the pale walls hung only with the certificate she wrangled out of Bedford College. Without the choking burner, it's suddenly very cold. And the Director's Record – oh, bloody hell – splays atop the desk's papery tumult –

But then I stop. She's torn it up. The *Record*. The last few entries are strewn like lawn bowls, pages creased into feather-edged fists.

She doesn't sit down. Won't even let herself pace. Just grips the desk-edge in one straining hand and twists the other tight in the chain of her spectacles.

I can hear my heartbeat again. Thinking *steady* doesn't do much to help it.

"I take it," she manages eventually, "that when you resigned you took Pip Property with you."

Steady. Steady? Any steadying at all?

"I don't want to resign! I was just scared of what Clement would – but that doesn't matter. I don't think he'll call the police on us. I don't think he *can* – "

"This time. I talked him out of it. But – I understand you were upset, Cassandra – even so, you cannot simply take the last word and walk out with our former principal suspect! Lord Miltonwaters is already moving to discredit you. He claims you lack sufficient evidence to prove that Property didn't stage last night's combat with the Sweetings – "

"What? Of course they didn't!"

A curt sigh. "That point would have been infinitely easier to argue had the pair of you not vanished from the Division like co-conspirators."

"I had a new lead! I had to check they didn't know Marigold Chandler!"

Her eyes shoot wide. Disbelieving. Disappointed. "So now you are – accusing your key witness?"

"I – " – damn it, my voice is moulting – "I saw Marigold with Clement – she invented the whole robbery for him – and Property couldn't have done it, they were – ah – in Gower eating scrambled eggs, or something – "

One eyebrow arches like a knife. "And you have proof of this... *alibi?*"

"I – sort of – they wrote a testimonial thing, Matthew's got it – "

"Can anyone corroborate it?"

"Well, Rosamond Nettleblack was – "

"Anyone who *isn't* missing?"

"I – "

"Please tell me the two of you have not spent the day confronting Miss Chandler."

"No! We were – I – "

"Tell me," she insists, when I sputter out. And then, when I can't start again – "You promised we would keep no more secrets. I have done my share. I have taken you into confidences I never would have wished, at your insistence, against my better judgment. You must at least *try* for me!"

It's almost pleading, not that the tone suits a word of what she says. *Pleading* doesn't stop every sentence twisting my skin until it breaks, doesn't soften the stinging that sneaks through the cuts. With a start, I realise the stinging's real – I have broken my skin, fingernails deep in my palms.

"I am trying."

She edges closer, her step twitching a floorboard under my feet. "What was that?"

"I'm trying to have no secrets. I'm telling you mine now. You – you – " (and I have to close my eyes) " – you aren't making it easy."

I wait, five shallow terrified breaths in the dark, but there's no reply.

"Marigold is working with Clement. She stole our funding for him, so that he could back us into his patronage. But it's not only that. Matthew came after Property and I, and then Adelaide met us in the street – "

"Adelaide?"

"She told us that Clement's servants abducted Rosamond Nettleblack. They thought she was Property's accomplice – they tried to get both of them. Clement's covering the mistake by sending Rosamond to an asylum."

"And I hope you saw at once how outlandish this – "

I tweak up my voice.

"Adelaide's a Nettleblack. Rosamond's cousin. She wants the siblings to owe her a share of the fortune. Property believed her, so they went to the town hall to talk Marigold into helping them rescue Rosamond – "

"And you let them? An untrained cravat designer?"

"I couldn't exactly lock them up again, could I?"

"You should have reasoned with them! You should not have let them put themselves in danger! You should have brought the information to me at once! You should – "

"Will you let me finish *one single summary* without reminding me I disappointed you?"

I gasp, eyes jolting open.

I'm not used to shouting, and I feel it. My throat's already raw, my limbs trembling past anything I can control. Mother's gaping at me, too shocked for anger, a face I've only seen on her once before – a face Henry's wretched transcript can't even hope to describe.

"You don't have to keep telling me that you don't want my help! That you wish I wasn't here! Of course I made mistakes – *keep* making them – but how can I not, when you ask twice as much of me at every turn, and you don't even keep your demands consistent? I'm never enough as a Divisioner – I'm worse as a silly novelist – I'm a nuisance when I scheme with you, and a renegade when I don't – I'm the reason you can hide how much you hate writing, and yet all you write about is how much you hate me!"

I don't have to stop. I don't think I *can* stop.

"But I'm not giving up! I'm not leaving your Division in the grip of someone who lies to you – who threatens you – who has the gall to scowl at a picnic blanket with an heiress locked in his house! I know I can't do much – but I can still do *something!* And if that disappoints you – if my work disappoints you, if my writing disappoints you, if everything I've ever been is just a staggering disappointment – then you can damn well keep it to yourself!"

My voice gives out. The tension in my fists gives too, my palms cold without the barbs of my fingernails. I'm hollow, a fast-beating thing of very swift cogs. The hurt's burned away. The anger's scraped itself bare. All I can feel's – not even relief, nothing so cosy and certain. I don't know if I can feel anything. If there are feelings, I'm too exhausted to grab them.

There's silence. Solitude. No more interruptions.

"It seems it is I," she falters, still clutching the desk, the back of her wrist lined stark with the pressure, "who has disappointed you."

I stare. I'm shaking, even now, can't believe what I'm repeating. I'm shaking then too, as she slips off her glasses and drags a trembling hand across her brow.

"I could never hate you." She shudders, like the word's a blow. "I – I wanted to protect you. To shelter you from everything I have to manage. To give you space to discover your own abilities, without the dread that I – without the threats – "

She prises herself off the desk. Takes a step – another – until she's close enough for me to see the sheen in her eyes. I can't even move.

"I didn't succeed. Not when the Head-Hiders came, and you were forced to endure their torments at my side. And with Lord Miltonwaters, I – it was not that I thought your help a *nuisance*. But you were the only Divisioner I couldn't shield from his threats. You. My daughter. Bearing the worst of it, again and again, because of me."

What?

"And then I saw you today. Defending us from Lord Miltonwaters. Deflecting, soothing, trampling on everything you felt, on your own career, before that man could hurt us. Not just bearing the worst alongside me – bearing it *instead of* me."

She doesn't mean – she can't mean –

"I didn't know what it had done to you. I tried to work it out with the Record, tried to check what you'd done before to see if there might be a pattern, a logical progression, a – *something* – but the only logic I found was me. I drove you to this. Everything I made you read. And I am so very sorry for every single sentence of it."

I grab my elbows. Pin myself together. The pins keep slipping, so I cling on tighter. There are words, yes, but they're not making sense. They're not – or maybe I'm not – but she's really there, and she's really saying them –

She's waiting. Never mind phrasing, she's *crying*.

So you're trusting Pip Property – a scratchy thought, probably unfair, all I've got – *but you won't trust her?*

"That thing you did before. The – the hug. When you – when – when just my being alive was enough for you." My voice shrivels, recoiling from its own strange sardonic sound. "You don't think you could – you know, do it again, or – ?"

247

Then she's there, holding me close, cupping my head in sudden warm silence. I risk an arm round her waist – risk the other when she doesn't break away. It's an embrace to spread through my chest, like wax melting round a wick, until my heart stops jumping and steadies into a half-decent flame.

I don't know if she'll make a habit of it. I don't know if, without my prompting, she'll ever dare try it again once we're out of this room. But – you know what? I can ask. Not just for embraces, but for conversations. If she means it – she'd better mean it – clearly I've no idea what she truly thinks of me. And if she really doesn't want to despise me – I suppose that's a choice I've got to give her chance to make.

So have it here. On the cylinder. I, Cass Ballestas, will *not* let that moment come to nothing. I, Cass Ballestas, will go downstairs in the morning with the –

But I'm getting ahead of myself.

Mother and I, twined in her office, are still spinning at the heart of a very fast clockface. I'm just a right side steadier there than I've ever yet been.

I tip my head back. She's very close, all lined golden eyes and spiky lashes. There's a question in her face, silent, light on the lift of an eyebrow.

"Let's deal with Miss Nettleblack," I suggest. "Quickly. When Property and the others come back, I suspect our schedule will get very complicated."

She smiles. Too lopsided for decorum.

Hence how I end up at my desk, with far too many people in my office, and Mother taking a taper to my haphazard candles. Gareth Wyn Evans offers to stand, so Edwina Nettleblack's in my spare chair, frowning above my head – up to where I haven't fixed the wall, where Property's photograph still smirks down from my collage, and –

Sweet Lord, and sits right next to the drawing of Miss Nettleblack's missing sister with bare shoulders and tumbling hair and spirals of poetry about lips and lust and –

"Ignore the wall," I blurt. "Just – detecting. You understand."

She drops her gaze. She's clasped her hands on my desk, trembling fingers in kid-gloves almost as pale as her. "Perhaps I – or Mr. Evans – might begin with the matter of Pip Property?"

This, I'm not ready for. "But – you said you were here about Rosamond?"

"Henry suggested I ought to be comprehensive. Gareth – the letter?"

Mr. Evans jostles a battered envelope from his waistcoat pocket, proffers it to me like it's a thing with the capacity to struggle. "Don't you mind about some of the – the sentiments in here, Detective – it's the date you want to be looking at – "

Mother hurries round the table. Dazed as I am, I can just about tip it up to her. *Monday November 20th, Nettleblack House, Gower, Wales* – and lengthy scribbled discussion of *Pip Property, our visitor of the last two weeks* – lots of *deep concern for Miss Rosamond* and *strange grasping ways* and *breakfast indiscretion* and three paragraphs'-worth of rant about sword-fighting –

"I was overhasty," Mr. Evans mumbles. "Miss Nettleblack came to Wales as soon as she got it – Miss Rosamond was gone by then, of course, and Pip Property went with her – they both left the day I sent it. But they'd been with me since Guy Fawkes Night, see. They only left because I sent that letter – I thought there was some plot to take Miss Rosamond's money – "

"I failed her."

Miss Nettleblack's voice cracks, like porcelain. To the room's collective horror, she's shivering inside her sumptuous dress, her chipped little words tumbling onto my desk.

"Property is not to blame, and neither is Gareth. I do not wish to – excuse my conduct, but I can explain it, if it will prove of use to your investigations."

Even given my present state – even after the day I've had – *even* I can just about deduce that *thanks ever so for this crucial corroborative evidence, now would you happen to be stealing your sister's inheritance?* is not the femininely tactful pivot I'm hoping for. "...Please do?"

A shaky nod. "Are you familiar with Rosamond, Detective?"

But the next one's unavoidable. "Gertie had a row with her in Checkley's once. And I think Gertie sold her your ferret before that? I – don't look so worried, Miss Nettleblack, Gertie's far too sturdy-minded to worry what some drunken heiress thinks of her – I mean, what your sister – your eminent sister – yes – "

I tried, alright? I'm very tired, and I'm almost convinced my mother might not actually hate me, and now I think about it shouldn't Matthew and the rest be back already – ?

"She never wanted to move to England," Miss Nettleblack admits; her fingers have twisted free, and now they're twitching on my desk like terrified arpeggios. "She was distraught when we came here. I could not let her go home, though, without breaking our parents' wishes – without ruining her chance at an aristocratic marriage. She despised me for it. And I – I confess I found her conduct extremely embarrassing. She would snarl at me in Welsh, when I tried to remonstrate – I could barely even understand her."

She closes her eyes. "Property's friendship did far more for Rosamond than I – and I felt it keenly. But Rosamond wanted nothing from me. I brought her suitors, then new suitors when she sent the first set fleeing. I gave her unlimited credit with my own inheritance before she came of age, stipulating only that she could not use the money to return to Wales. But what-ever she wanted in Dallyangle – whatever it took for her to want to *be* in Dallyangle – "

Her fingers are still going, faster and faster, spurring her on. "She took my stipulation. She made it her revenge. The bills I received – the amounts she spent – and on such wilfully provoking things! She must have been setting the prices, and setting them as high as possible. Forty pounds a night in Checkley's Tavern. Seventy pounds on cravats for Henry. And when she paid your colleague one hundred and fifty pounds for a ferret – "

"She *what?* That's a *year and a half* of my salary!"

"I withdrew my credit after that. I did not trust her. I did not know what absurdities she might wreak with her own money. If I had given her what she was owed at twenty-one, she might have no inheritance left! I – I know it was not my place, but I could not let her do that to herself. And I – I – I was angry. She was ruining our family's name – our marriage prospects. I assumed then – incorrectly – that marriage prospects were of great importance to Henry – certainly they were of great importance to our parents."

She shudders. "Rosamond was terrifyingly naïve. Her birthday passed, and she seemed to have no idea she was owed anything. I only meant to keep her money until she stopped ruining herself to spite me. But she got worse, and then Henry came of age too – and I knew it was time to settle it, to do what my parents wanted without destroying my siblings – or vice versa – but – there were so many demands – and I could not reconcile them – and Henry ran away – and Rosamond did the same – and I made them do it – "

Then she buckles on a sob. "And I do not know how to ask their forgiveness."

There isn't really a Div protocol for when Edwina Nettleblack of the Nettleblack's Tincture Nettleblacks starts weeping uncontrollably at your desk. Gareth Wyn Evans looks ready to faint. I glance at Mother – panicky force of habit – but she's not glaring at me, not even slightly disapproving. She even sneaks me a smile, a sort of *my turn now*, as she glides forward to squeeze Miss Nettleblack's shoulders.

"Please don't distress yourself," she murmurs. "Cassandra and I are very grateful for your honesty. Might we ask what provoked you to share it with us?"

Mr. Evans is the only one even half-close to an answer. "Beg pardon, ma'am, but we're only just back from Gower. I – well, I – I might have – perhaps – possibly – dragged my employer to the family solicitors' the moment she arrived at Nettleblack House – also need to beg pardon for that – anyway. We're back. Henry and that nice tall cyclist came to find us – said they couldn't stay, but that Pip Property had told them we all needed to talk – "

Hang on.

"Miss Nettleblack. Ever so sorry to keep – well – doing this, but – Property also told me you threatened to put Rosamond in an asylum?"

"*What?*" – bloody hell, she jolts in the seat, voice skidding like a blade on ice – "I never threatened her! There was a threat, but it wasn't mine – I was warning her about it!"

Mother stares at me. Unabashedly incredulous. Sweet Lord, I'm the same. I'll never tell Adelaide what either of our faces do, mind you; that ghoul doesn't deserve any more gloating.

"It was Lady Miltonwaters, wasn't it?"

Miss Nettleblack flinches. "She said it was how her family would handle such an embarrassment. She said her young cousin – your new patron, I believe? – had made connections at Oxford that would have allowed for such a course of action. She said that, when he came here, he would be more than happy to make the introductions for me – "

She breaks off, gasping, at a *slam* through the walls.

The double doors. Footsteps hammering through reception. My office door, crashing open, flinging Mr. Evans into a pile of Property's ledgers.

I leap off my chair. "You took your sweet sodding time – !"

But it's not Matthew. Not Henry, not Septimus, not even Property. It takes a few blinks to place him, without company, without rats, without his usual summery smile.

Nick Fitzdegu? Alone?

I take it back. I can *definitely* still feel. I can feel every grisly inch of it, when this new and terrible panic frays my veins like cheap embroidery thread.

"Henry and Septimus've already gone. Matty's at the town hall. He's found – he thinks – reckon it's probably for the best if you come."

I slump – can't pull anything taut, can't –

But Mother's at my side, hand on my elbow, voice soft at my ear. "I'll gather the other Divisioners. I believe we will need to ready ourselves for a complicated schedule."

Is she – quoting *me?*

I clasp her hand. Then I sprint after Nick.

CHAPTER TWENTY-TWO

I DO NOT KNOW WHERE I AM

The New Notebook of Doom

Concerning concern, for myself and everything else

Apparently, I've a terrible knack for vomiting in picturesque locations.

Not that I could have pinned my whereabouts to any Dallyanglian map. I knew we were on the River Angle, but the town had long since dipped behind hedges and fields – we'd followed the telephone wire, then twisted away from it round a bony elbow of riverbend. The sun was low ahead of us, golden and fraying as a chanterelle, catching the Angle in glints as it slid towards the horizon. Against it, yellow on yellow, Marigold Chandler was all stiff arms and sticky face, straining at the oars of her little skiff, bruises of sweat darkening on her sleeves.

"I could help," I'd offered, ten minutes ago by my watch, "If you'd not poisoned me."

She'd snarled through her dainty teeth, and conversation had lapsed accordingly.

I wasn't purely seeking to needle her. Rowing was, at present, as beyond my capabilities as using Earlyfate for anything more than walking support – Marigold had to concede me *that* much, though she'd snatched the sword-stick straight back the moment I sat down. I'd barely made it out of the town hall – ghastly breadcrumb-trail that it was, I'd been spectacularly sick on the back door – and getting into the boat at all would have been impossible without my youthful practice clambering around traghetti. Now, I was congealing in the stern, knees to my chest, spine like a rusty hinge, my stomach in a state worthy of every clammy clementine under the sky. The only flimsy mercy was that I seemed – as of five kindly minutes ago – to have finally exhausted my capacity to retch.

I glanced up from my watch. "You'll be late."

Marigold's breath came sharp, matched to her rowing, the boat lurching through the Angle's spindliest vein. Head-height on either side, shaky with our forward momentum, there were banks and fields, empty but for the flashes of rabbits' eyes. "Please be quiet."

"You said half an hour on the telephone. And you said you'd furnish me with an antidote – "

"Which you don't yet need."

"*Yet?* What sort of poison is this?"

"Stop fussing," she snapped, glowering at me until another swipe of the oars jolted the frown from her forehead. "If I wanted you dead, you would be."

I permitted myself an extremely painful scoff. "Gracious, of course! I'd almost forgotten you mean to give my death to Clemmie as a courtship gift."

She glanced up; her gaze was a scalpel, albeit one held in shaky hands. "Don't you be vulgar, please. Clement Miltonwaters is *not* his grandfather – he would never stoop to *kill* you! We simply need a little more discretion than you seem able to manage."

"Then what?" I was shaking too, without any hope of concealing it – she'd seen, caused, enough of my fear now to recognise its every twitch. "Hartgate Gaol again? The favourite family asylum?"

"So lurid," she hissed, sweeping at the water until it carded in the reeds. "If the Division adore you as much as he thinks, there's no point making a martyr of you. No, you lucky thing, I suspect Clemmie will be buying your silence – and your passage back to whatever Continental mishmash you come from."

"If he doesn't trust Rosamond not to talk, why the devil would he trust me?"

She sped up. The boat veered towards the reeds, snapped half their spines with one sharp stroke. She was still lagging behind her promised time, but we were far outpacing even a sprint, and the Angle towpath had melted into a mere muddy hem for the water's edge.

Someone had answered that telephone, in the blurry seconds before I'd had to drop it. If we moved too fast – if the sun set in earnest before anybody followed –

If anybody followed –

But that thought was a rapier wound – or, at least, it could be, if I let it, festering until the tiny tip-cut felled me. *Think of something else – anything else.* The slimy stern round my shoulders, my crumpled sock of a stomach, the pale cold picking at my fingers. White-tailed twitches as rabbits fled up the banks. A narrow chevron of geese, black on the bone-coloured sky, escaping the sunset. Ahead, the stoop of a willow on the riverbank, bare-limbed and drooping, like a mourning sampler.

"Well, Chandler? Why would he? He didn't even plan to abduct Rosamond, and he's still too scared to let her go!"

She huffed. I saw it, misting down her front like a lace collar. "Will you please give up this nonsense about Rosamond Nettleblack?"

I stared.

"As if Clemmie has time to bother with those beastly Celtic climbers! It was Poor Cousin Ellie's terrible idea for him to court the new-money chits – it would have been stupidity even if he hadn't a prior engagement! The eldest must be nearly forty, the youngest ran away to be the Division's pet, and Rosamond – well, *she* was infamous! Ellie had to tell Clemmie's grandfather she didn't even exist!"

She managed a vicious smile between gasps. "So you can bally well stop suggesting Clemmie has any interest in carrying off *that* little harlot!"

If I'd had the strength to twist the sword from the stick –

No. Bite down on the anger – *concentrate* –

"He hasn't told you."

She blinked. "Don't be tiresome – "

"He said I could ruin him. I can – but not for the reason you think! Maledizione, I thought you knew!"

"Knew what?"

I braced myself against the stern – her pace was slipping, the boat bucking beneath us as her oars crashed at odd angles. "Indulge your victim, sweet Marigold. Where do *you* suspect Rosamond Nettleblack is?"

"I shan't – "

"And another question: why do you suspect Clemmie is so desperate to get rid of me? The Division know I'm innocent, the detectives know you're the principal suspect, and he knows you're too devoted not to take the blame for him – so why am I still such a threat?"

"I – I won't be – "

I grinned. "Because I know what his servants look like."

"Marigold – *careful!*"

She yelped, gouging the oars deep as the boat veered into the willow-branches, until we shuddered to some shaky approximation of a halt, jolting and plunging while the water churned to silt around us. I crumpled forward, hands and knees, gritted my teeth against the slick of nausea in my throat. Up on the right bank, sprouting from the willow's roots like a tweed-jacketed parasite, Clement Miltonwaters glowered into the boat, a hunting rifle cricked over the bend of his arm.

I could reach under her bench, get my fingers round the sword-stick. Brace my legs against the poison's shivering weakness. Swimming this glorified tributary would be thrice as easy as that youthful plunge into the Grand Canal. If I had to leap off the boat – well, I'd leapt out of the carriage, hadn't I? –

Ten years ago. In full health. Without pressing need of

Marigold's antidote.

I froze, staring out the slippery planks of the hull.

"I can't stay," Clement snapped. "I have already been obliged to wait."

Marigold was all gabble, fast and fussy enough to set the boat quivering. "Jolly sorry, Clemmie, it was a little – but never mind that! Look! The problem's fixed! No more shoddy form, not today, you see!"

A jab of a glare in my shoulder-blades – somehow, horribly, I felt it. When I dragged my chin up to meet his look, the sheer detestation in it nearly poked my eye out; he'd clearly been softening his expressions back at the Division.

Even then, the temptation was thick in my teeth: *well, Clemmie, will you tell her or shall I?* I would have said it, if he'd not brought a gun – if the two of them weren't shuttlecocking my life over my head – if Marigold had exhibited the slightest inclination to consider my questions – if I'd permitted a step of progress to be made on Rosamond's rescue, if I'd not blundered into the path of any progress at all –

He hoisted an eyebrow until my face smarted. "How appalling you look."

Marigold beamed. "Just a little poison, so they'd come quietly –"

"Poison?" His lips twitched, half disdainful half impressed. "I thought you'd given that up after the bursar's greyhound. What's the science of it, then – does it take longer to finish off anything bigger than a dog?"

Her smile slipped at the corner, a pin prised loose. "Well, Clemmie, I assumed – "

"Because I can't prolong this, you know. I've an – errand, shall we say, to settle this evening." He glanced at his rifle, brow furrowing, one hand fidgeting up the barrel. "I'd rather you didn't make me have to, really – but I suppose the principle can't be so very different from pheasants, if Grandfather's anything to judge by – "

I started back. Marigold did too, hands scorching off the oars. "You won't *kill* them?"

He shrugged. "My dear, you're already killing them. I'm just speeding it up."

Too many words. Too ghastly a mismatch, between them and the huffy impatience of his tone, between the gilding sunset and the click of the rifle's back. My mind tipped, spinning like a magic-lantern – slides too fast to catch – *think* –

"You can't." I'd lost all sense of what yanked out the sentence: terror, threat, nausea, pain, they were all interlocking as paisleys now. "You can't shoot me. I'll be found. The Division have a morgue – they'll discover how I died – "

"Ah, but the gun-wielding Sweetings also want you dead – don't they, Marigold?"

"Clemmie – "

"The Division took the Sweetings' gun," I blurted. "Last night. And that was a pistol. Rosamond Nettleblack made Henry a trick shot – I rather think they'd notice the difference!"

He stiffened, rifle tucked in the crook of his shoulder, eyes pinched in a squint –

Then he scoffed, curt and defiant, and snapped the gun open again, reddening across his pale nose. "As you wish. Marigold, take this insolent deviant to the Sweetings, and let those brutes clear up the mess for themselves."

He smirked at me. "I suppose you'd prefer I made it quick now, eh?"

"Clemmie, please!" Marigold cried – and thank heaven she did, for my throat had pulled far too taut for even a squeak of self-preservation. "We don't need to be killers! Just – oh, I don't know – just give them a little something and put them on a ship – "

"I do not need to *pay off* the likes of them," he growled, still pinning my gaze. "And you wouldn't go, would you, Property? You'd rather turn the whole of Dallyangle upside-down in your ridiculous bid to incriminate me."

I swallowed. *Risk it – just one proverbial step in the guards – just the slightest glance to the rower's bench –* "I don't care about you. I'm trying to save Rosamond."

"Oh, for goodness's sake!" Marigold spluttered. "Will you

please tell them, Clemmie?"

Still alive. One more step.

"I will go." I'd no hope of recovering the smirk, the swagger, the shopfront poise. My fear would cover the lie – it had to. "I'll get on this hypothetical ship of yours, and I'll disappear, and I'll keep my mouth shut on the many, *many* dreadful stories I could tell about you and your lackeys and your ignoble secrets – *if* you let Rosamond come with me."

His whole face flared this time. "This is not a negotiation."

"Whyever not? You've plaited so many deceits around the Division – surely you can't risk another one? Especially not one which relies on the Sweetings taking credit for my murder – the Sweetings, who've been oh-so-historically obliging when it comes to playing along with your plans? This way, you wouldn't even have to lie! Everyone can discover, and be heartily unsurprised, that Pip Property's the same double-crossing trickster they've always been – that I seized my chance to run away again, and damn the consequences for anyone but me! If that's what you need me to be, then I'll do it! With Rosamond!"

Marigold gaped at him. "What – ?"

"Do you really imagine it's easy to squirrel missing heiresses into asylums? Wouldn't my proposal save you tremendous hassle?"

"I know how to manage asylums," he spat. "I have done it before. The arrangements are already in place."

I managed a brittle sort of laugh. "*I* escaped en route to an asylum when I was seventeen, you fool. Nothing's *in place* unless she's already incarcerated – and if you've an urgent errand to settle tonight, I rather suspect she's not!"

"Clement, *what are they talking about?*"

Marigold all but screeched it, springing off the bench until the boat roiled, oars skidding away across the sun-glittered water. He jumped – I jumped, and nearly tipped off the skiff – and she didn't wait for our recovery, pale features cracking –

"You don't have Rosamond Nettleblack. You're not – you can't be – you said Cousin Ellie was the regrettable exception

– you said you'd ceased all dealings with that beastly asylum
– !"

He watched her, a little dazedly, as if waiting out a terrier's bark. "I do not have to tell you *everything*, dear – "

"But – no! – Rosamond is not part of our plan! It's too much of a risk – for both of us! She shouldn't even be involved – "

"She got in the way." A patient smile. "Wrong place and time, rather – and certainly wrong associates. And she really is mad, you know: won't dress like a lady, won't pick a language, took a sword to my housemaid, presumably plunges into unmentionable obscenity with *that* prattling thief – "

"How long have you had her? Not at Alberstowe Hall?"

"My dear, needs must – "

"It's not seemly!" she shrieked. "You can't just pluck women and make them vanish – you are a gentleman! A Marquess to be! We're *protecting* your reputation, not making a lie of it! We, Clement Miltonwaters, are supposed to be wed within the year – and you're filling our future home with stolen heiresses!"

"There is no lie, Marigold. My character is impeccable. Once Nettleblack and her criminal consort are gone, there will be no one left to doubt it."

His eyes narrowed, much as they had when he'd cocked the rifle, his voice far colder than the flush on his face. "And I think you presume too much with regards to your *future home*."

She jolted us in the boat again. "What?"

"You got caught. Unless you can cover your tracks – do think sensibly, girl. You are forcing me to a choice I did not wish to make. You or the Division. You or Dallyangle. You or my inheritance. And a Marquess to be, as you say, cannot throw up his hard-won inheritance for the sake of a scheming secretary, no matter how charming the schemer in question."

I know full well that she'd bottled my life into her antidote, but – I would have been a corpse already if I hadn't twinged for her then, broken doll that she was, frozen where she stood in the sharp rays of sunset. The slanting light caught her too-blue eyes, turned her horrified stare bright as stained glass.

"So cover your tracks," he added coldly. "Get Property out of my sight, leave their remains to the Sweetings' revenge, and clean your own reputation before you think about entangling it with mine."

He stalked to the bank's edge, tossed one of the floating oars back into the boat – and turned on his heel. I just stared – even she wasn't up to more – as he marched away through a field, rifle swinging on his arm, towards the glint of the telephone wire in the pinking sky.

CHAPTER TWENTY-THREE

MATTHEW ADELSTEIN, CRIMINAL EXTRAORDINAIRE

Casebook of Matthew Adelstein

Pertaining to a discovery

In justification of what might otherwise appear an irredeemably rash decision –

Nicholas and I had the Division's darkest lantern. We had our purpose and pursuit. Above us, etched sharp onto a sky with no breeze, the telephone wire kept us mapped.

Beyond that, we had very little else.

(I told Nicholas, I should note, that he was not obliged to accompany me, when Cassandra suggested I might follow in Henry and Septimus's cycle-scorched tracks. He had seen Cassandra's expression as she tore through Marigold's tea-things; he knew that our search for Pip Property in the Alberstowe-adjacent fields might not result in pleasant findings. But he still chivvied us out, kissing my knuckles with admirable surreptitiousness: *I'm trained as an undertaker, Matty, you'll be the one needing me.*)

The sun had just set. I'd brought the Divisionary hurricane-lamp, and fumbled to light it while Nicholas held it steady between us. A flurry of moths circled our efforts, writhing in silhouette. Neither the road, the fields, nor the river had yielded us anything yet. I kept myself pinned to the search, of course, peering out the boggy ground and the potholes and the raggedy hedges – but it was still difficult to refrain from recollections: of Property's frantic snarling in the graveyard, of the terror in Cassandra's eyes when she studied that tea-tray. Of the notebook I had scoured, annotated – of the mind I had spent the night inside. I couldn't imagine their face without movement. I didn't want to. I fear I gripped Nicholas's hand far too tightly, as we stumbled on, and the shadows length-ened around us.

The first human thing we found, just where the telephone wire bisected the river, was a boat. Shallow, empty, drifting in and out of the tree-roots to which it had been roughly lashed. We dashed towards it down a sloping field, splattered at every step where the river blotted into the grass, until a fringe of broken reeds warned us to stop. Our lantern caught the boat at the wrong angles, left its innards in shadow, even at the outer-most reach of Nicholas's arm.

"Anyone there?" – he slipped, several jolting inches, until I caught him – "Property? Pip?"

Nothing but the twitching reeds.

"There's something inside," I hissed, squinting, dusk scratching on my eyes. "But I don't think it's a body."

Nicholas gnawed a long breath. "Reckon we can make the jump?"

The Angle is a starveling sort of river in places, and the deserted skiff was stuck in it like a fishbone. My curt nod sent Nicholas whirling over the water in a tangle of scarf and coat-tails, the moths chasing the lantern with papery outrage. I had a harder leap of it – the boat was still trembling for Nicholas's exuberant landing. He grabbed me before I could tip out, kissed my hair as he struggled to revive the guttering lamp –

In its flickers, I got the view I needed. Tucked under the rower's bench, too sharp-edged to be a shadow: a clothes-box, with *M.C.* shimmering in gold paint. I scrambled towards it, grabbed for the insignia, and a cold heavy knot bulged in my palm. *Padlocked?*

I shook it, as furiously as the boat and the country hush permitted. A padlock indeed, and doubtless nowhere near its key. Hence, presumably, why the boat and its cargo had been left unattended.

"Chandler was here," I muttered, as Nicholas twisted to my side, the mustard of his coat starting out of the lamplight. "And she clearly means to come back."

I drummed my fingers on the padlock. We had passed no footprints on our dash down the field; the boat was fastened to the roots on the other bank. If Miss Chandler was up there – if she'd taken Property with her – if the two were on foot, they couldn't outrun a bicycle, especially not one with Septimus at the handlebars –

"D'you think we can pick the lock, Matty?"

I started. Nicholas blinked at me, incomprehensibly serene.

"If she's meant to have taken your funding," he added, apparently by way of reasonable clarification. "Can't be impossible, if you all thought Property did it with that cravat pin."

"Well – in theory – but – "

He plucked the tie from my waistcoat – it was hardly an appropriate moment for me to gasp, but the impulse was unavoidable – and eased the pin out, deft and gentle, until my face was scalding and I'd forgotten my objections. I remembered them, of course, the moment he started jabbing at the padlock –

"Nicholas! We cannot pick locks in other people's boats – !"

A soft *click* unlatched my very voice from my throat. Nicholas swung back on his heels, set the boat quivering in a skitter of ripples, his giddy grin springing from the gloom like the ridiculous Wonderland cat. "Not with that attitude!"

"How – ?"

"Got to be dextrous when you work with rats." He tugged the box out on its conquered padlock, just enough to prop up the lid. "Say it, Matty. Say I'm a genius."

I stopped gaping, with dignity. "You are the love of my life."

"There's the boy! Now get us some answers!"

I lifted the uppermost layer from the box – and dropped it just as quickly, for it was all garish yellow skirts and petticoats, delicate and flammable and wildly ungentlemanly –

But as they fell, they *crackled*.

"Forgive me," I whispered, to decorum in general.

With such sporadic light, it was easy to feel the discrepancy. There were stiff papery folds between the silks, the sharp edges of envelopes under the linens. I pulled off a glove, pinched the garments until I found their hems – lumpy, wisped with left-over thread, cut open in haste and clumsily re-sewn.

I apologised again – and set my teeth to the botched tackings in the uppermost skirt, bit through the weakest thread. The new gap was barely wide enough for two fingers, but I could just about pin something between them, tug until it rustled out, and tip it to the lantern.

A banknote.

Take the clothes she'd hidden it in? – too unwieldy, too time-consuming. Take the whole box? – too difficult to manoeuvre. Take – *something* – we could hardly leave –

Then I flinched. We both did. Up on the far bank, the shadows were shifting, a faint rattle skittering across the boggy ground. The rattle I knew, even at this distance. Bicycles, too far off to hail, their lamps swinging as they scorched into the field.

My mind sliced through the lot, cut it up into sense: *if she sees Divisioners, she'll run. If we leave her the chance, we'll never see any of it again.*

"Nicholas." I cleared my throat. Composure was of the utmost importance. "I do not suggest this lightly. But – we – the risk must be taken."

"...Alright?"

"If Henry and Septimus are handling the rescue," – and I drew myself up, tucked my tie into my waistcoat, abandoned myself to his piratical spirit – "We have to steal this boat."

CHAPTER TWENTY-FOUR

I AM USELESS

The New Notebook of Doom, infinitely more doomed this time

Concerning my foolishness

Are you happy now? Marigold Chandler had snarled.

Then she'd rowed, short vicious strokes with sopping oars, her neat breaths splintering as the water slapped her in the face. The force of it had slung me back into the crook of the stern, hoping that my expression provided sufficient answer to her question. But she'd said no more, and I'd been too stunned to devise even the skeleton of an appropriately conciliatory response, if conciliation was at all appropriate under the present lurching circumstances –

Then she'd stopped, with as much hectic floundering as the first time, drove an oar into the bank six inches deep to shove us sideways across the river. She'd hooked a rope around jutting tree-roots, then made an impromptu ladder of them, hauling herself up to the bank with Earlyfate in her fist, and barely a glance at the muddy streaks on her skirts. She'd skidded round on the boggy field's-edge, squelching at the ankles, lashed out a pale hand – "Come with me."

"What –?"

"*Antidote*," she'd spat, stark enough to fleck my cheek.

Now she was splashing our path up the same boggy field, ruined skirts in shaking fingers, jerking her chin every two steps to check that I followed her. I'd staggered as I climbed, a little more than strictly necessary, and she'd duly given me the swordstick back – but her pace was too murderous, and my limbs still too weak, for me to split the pieces and actually *use* it. The sun was almost gone, the ground pocked with shadows where her button-boots had squeezed it out of shape. There wasn't even a sprinkling of grass to steady the slop underfoot; Earlyfate sank a third of its height with my weight on it. The rake of the hill swung the mud close, and the sky was bruising far too quickly for my liking.

"Marigold, I'm sorry – " I wasn't altogether sure I was, but it seemed a kinder response than *what did I tell you?* "I – "

"Don't." Every word a dropped pin to dodge. "You've done enough."

Her shoulders buckled, and I faltered back a step.

She staggered us uphill until we struck a barn. Red bricks greying in the dusk, huge-beamed doors loosely looped with a chain – its padlock slack-jawed and dangling. Panic gripped my hair in its fist, but she didn't hesitate, knocking scuffs into the doorframe. *Earlyfate. Now. Stepping in the guards – if you have to fight – start in coda lunga stretta –*

But I could barely wrestle the swordstick from the marshy ground, let alone jolt myself into sudden movements –

The barn doors twitched.

"Mr. Sweeting?" Marigold snapped. "I've brought payment."

I'd no time to step in anything before Norman snatched my arm. Marigold tugged the chain clear, and he yanked me through a gap just narrow enough to scrape – and then it was dark, too dark even for dusk, and matted hairy things crouched in the shadows. The skidding momentum had been bad enough, but the stink of straw curdled my stomach again, slumped me limp and spluttering in Norman's grip. The next I knew, I was on my knees, head splintering, Earlyfate slipping from my hand, sharp-ended straw jabbing between my knuckles.

Above me, a gloomy silhouette against roof-high bales of the ghastly stuff, Norman rocked back on his heels. A rustle in the straw, and then there were two silhouettes, Maggie's snarl high and feverish at her brother's side. "Bloody hell, Pip, not even a *good evening*?"

"I poisoned them," Marigold explained cheerily – as cheerily as she could, after a gulp and a sniff. "Slow-acting. Just to get them here, you see. Now – gosh, what *happened* to you?"

The gloom was settling – and Marigold's genteel wince was not at all misplaced. Maggie's hair had slipped its bun, clotting to her forehead above a makeshift bandage, mottled across her left eye amidst a swarm of crusting scratches.

"Nothing," she chuckled.

"Ferret," I groaned.

"And it's your fault!" Norman burst out, stamping his heel on my spare hand by way of retort. I yelped, of course – but he was scowling at Marigold. "I'm done with your games, Miss Chandler. Just give us our money back. Maggie needs a physician, and we won't get that in Dallyangle – "

"Shut it, Norman." Maggie elbowed him, grinning. "Takes more than a Nettleblack ferret to stop me! Now what're you after, missy?"

Norman winced, but Marigold was quicker. "Oh, dear! You can't *still* be sore about those scrappy little savings?"

Savings?

"Those scrappy little savings were ours," Norman growled. "We stole them first. You'd no bloody right to – "

"But I did. I tracked you down and I burgled you – and would you have taken me seriously if I hadn't? I doubt it. So, really, whose fault is it that you had to lose a few spoils?" Marigold dashed her knuckles across her eyes; when her face emerged, it was tight in a painful smile. "Now don't be tiresome, not when I've brought presents."

He blinked. Maggie brightened too, though she was already fairly giddy, beaming down with sweat slick on her lips. Marigold lifted her chin, eyes glittering.

"If you can bear to store your vengeance for later use, I've just procured you the perfect chance to clean out Alberstowe Hall."

It spiked, quick and scorching, like a poker through my brain.

"*No!* Marigold, don't you dare – *don't you dare!*"

I was on my feet – knuckles scraped raw – and the barn was listing, a gale-stricken gull – until a stinking waxed elbow pinched under my chin – and sweaty palms grabbed my wrists –

"Lord Miltonwaters will be preparing for an errand this evening," Marigold added, with a neat step backwards. "He and his – *lackeys*, they'll be utterly preoccupied with it. If you set off now, while they're all distracted with readying their sordid arrangements – my goodness, think what there'll be for your burgling delectation."

"*Marigold!*"

The Sweetings yanked me away – there was nothing distinguishable between them now, just bruising fingers and too many arms, a spreading fungus across my chest. Maggie's voice swung bemusedly overhead – "What've you done to the toff?"

Marigold shrugged airily. "I promised you revenge."

"*Rosamond is still in there!*"

"And doesn't it feel delightful?" she hissed, dipping towards me with a splintered smile. "When all your efforts for your lover come to nothing?"

I flung myself at her – into a net of Sweetings, which hauled me back like a landed fish, straw bristling under my boots, further and further into the barn's festering nest. Maggie was querying, thrice as light as her grip – "Do we know a Rosamond, Norman?"

"Rosamond Nettleblack," Marigold supplied with a sigh. "From the papers. The new missing heiress. She's at Alberstowe too – do with that what you will."

A sharp crack of laughter. "See, Norman, I told you Miss Chandler'd bring us luck!"

"You're not well enough for this," Norman muttered. "The height on that gate – "

"Will you buckle it, I'm fine!"

"Time presses," Marigold trilled, tugging the barn doors wide.

Struggling was like being thrust into kelp, into all the seaweeds tangling round the seams of the ca': submerged, choking, twisted tighter and tighter in the tendrils. I writhed, eyes shut against the nausea – my legs skidded and gave way – a beam struck my back, pushed between my shoulder-blades –

And then the kelp receded, leaving cold slippery spaces everywhere I'd been grappled. The only thing holding me now was a burly fist of rope, knotted round my wrists, anchoring me to the barn's central beam.

As if I didn't know how to slip out of knots – !

But I couldn't reach them. Could barely feel my fingernails to try it. I'd fought, squirmed against the Sweetings with my full fencing strength – it must have tightened the rope.

Maggie stooped to pat my cheek. I'd ended the struggle in the straw, legs elflocked in a stupid parody of a languid seat. "Save you for later, eh?"

"I won't let you hurt her!"

She scoffed. "Sorry, dearie, we're still on your old orders. *Do your worst*, wasn't it?"

Then she tried for a wink – winced, around the bandage – and heaved to her feet. One hand clapped round Norman's shoulder, urging him out of the doors. They tore across the field with a loping sprint, scattering rabbits, down the shadows' gullet until both were lost to the slope and the dark.

Marigold peeled off the straw-scratched wood, clutching her elbows with a shiver. She was still watching them – she'd the longer view. "Best of luck, Clemmie."

I yanked on the rope again, like a fool, gasped for the sting under my nails. "Call them back, damn you! You can't – you said you didn't want to be a killer!"

"Oh, do stop fizzing and think for a moment. Clemmie won't *die*, not armed with that hunting rifle – and neither will you, not if he truly wants to debase himself with murder. The Sweetings shan't be coming back – and, my goodness, what a destructive exit they'll make! *Me or his inheritance*, indeed – well, let's see how much of his *inheritance* those burglars can smash before he shoots them!"

"But Rosamond – "

" – was far beneath him, you must agree. That he would stoop to such a horrible scheme – that he wouldn't ask me to fix it decorously! That he even dares to think he *can* scheme, *can* fix, without my help! He'll be nothing without me – he'll be begging for me back in a week! But I have your savings, and his precious Division's precious funding – I can have everything my family lost, with or without his assistance. So I'll make him wait, and I'll make him see, and I'll make him bally well smart for his silly mistakes."

She glanced back, a little blurrily. "And you have to stay here, I'm afraid. Can't have you summoning the Division to chase me."

Oh, *maledizione!*

"It won't work!" – I was yelling, of course I was – "I tried it, and I promise you it won't! You can't use the Sweetings – you can't use anybody – you can't flatten everyone into cobble-stones to pave your grand escape!"

"Can't I?" A shaky giggle. "Not even if I'm the only one protecting poor little me?"

"That's not true! There – there could be – the Division, for a start! They forgave me, they – "

"I'm not staying as a penitent in Clemmie's town! I won't watch him pretend we've never been introduced!" Her voice shrilled. "If he'd even let me do that!"

"The Division could protect you – "

"I think I've upset them too much, don't you?"

"No – listen to me – "

"I've done nothing else all afternoon! Good *night*, Property!"

"Then just let me go! I'm already poisoned. The Division don't know where I am – they never chased either of us. Just don't give me the antidote. I won't last long enough to – to get back to Dallyangle – to find the Division – to tell them – "

I closed my eyes. Hauled them open.

" – to tell them anything. But I can still stop the Sweetings from hurting Rosamond – "

"You'd delight in that, wouldn't you?" She shook her head, as if tipping water from it. "A nice heroic death in your lover's arms. Gosh, you really are exhausting! *I'll* just take the grand escape and count myself satiated, thank you very much."

She snatched at the doors, strung herself between them, the darkness steeping her to a silhouette. "And you don't need an antidote. You won't die, not from the tiniest bit of hellebore infusion. It was just enough to frighten you. Sorry to disappoint – I'd no idea you were so eager for a tragic fate."

The swing of the doors. The shrilling chains. The padlock.

For far too long, I couldn't move. My capacity for useful thinking, shattered beneath my hair, seemed to be rebuilding itself from scratch. The barn was a blindfold: with the doors shut, and not a window between the beams, I'd little more than sensations to smart for. Viper-tipped straw biting under my trouser-hems. Cold wrinkled wood between my shoulders. *The tiniest bit of hellebore infusion,* still shivery under my skin.

I scrabbled for the knots again. My fingers wouldn't do it. I'd permitted all the mistakes Rosamond and I were so careful to check for – the spiky pain in my hands, the scorch-tight rope on the veins of my wrists – *wretch, why didn't you tense them?*

Stop it. Stop wallowing. Think.

"Division!" The yell burned like bile. "I – I – "

But I couldn't. That raggedy voice in the darkness, the fraying edges, the pathetic pitiful mewling – the thought of the rabbits outside, the only ones to twitch their ears to it – bolting back to their burrows, away from the panic in the sounds and syllables –

No. Something else. There had to be. I couldn't pick out the knots – *va bene,* I'd snap them, or cut them, or –

Earlyfate.

Dropped in the straw, in my last recollections. Marigold

hadn't taken it – the Sweetings hadn't noticed it. It must have been closer to the doors than I was, but the distance wasn't tremendous, not if I could stretch out my height.

I twisted down the beam, flat to the dirt floor – as close as the shriek in my arms would let me get. The straw swarmed my ankles. Slowly – tapping each foot in a careful circle – if I kicked the swordstick away, I'd be lost. My arms began to shake. I scraped my head sideways, tipped it back past the beam. Nothing but straw, jabbing under my trousers, sneaking one sharp sudden stab beneath my jacket, between braces-buttons and waistcoat buckle – and then I was choking out expletives I'd never permitted in my life, eyes streaming, wrists screaming –

My heel caught. I froze, then dragged. Something long and slender eeled across the floor.

I had to sit and gasp when I'd hauled the swordstick to my side. My horizontal endeavours had tightened the ropes again, two cuffs of branding-iron. Most of my thoughts were far too scalding to hold, beyond the nibbling selfish ones: *what if you've broken the nerves?*

What if you can't move your fingers? What if you can never move your fingers again?

One heel on Earlyfate's hilt, the other on the stick. Peel the sword free. My soles slipped, mud-slickened. There wasn't even a glint of light to catch on the blade. Guess it, then – scoop the sword round the beam with one leg, close enough to my throbbing fingers to –

To slice through the lines on my palm.

"Stupid useless fucking pigheaded dilettante!"

I sawed. The blade bashed off the beam, scored through my sleeve. Again. Slippery fingers, grabbing at anything. Again. Gouging my heel into the dirt, snapping straw on its edge, my best distraction. Again. *Again.*

My arms burst out like wings – like wings breaking through skin. The slackening threw me forward, sword clattering beside me, straw bristling on my tongue. The ropes snaked along my forearms, cut in two. I clawed my fingers knuck-le-deep in the dirt – still had *that* – until my toes bit, until I could drag myself upright and hurtle for the doors –

Still chained and padlocked.

Back to my knees, scraping the ground for Earlyfate. Back on my feet, stabbing into the dark. The join of the beams – of the doors – if I could get the sword through that gap –

And cut a solid metal chain. If I had to.

There! Wizened wood, two doors buckling away from each other, even as the chains on their handles pinned them together. Jab the sword through the sliver – *missed* – jab again – just too narrow. I'd make a bigger gap, then. Two steps back, into coda lunga stretta, and thrust –

"*Fuck!*"

The jolt nearly broke my arm. It completely broke my sword.

Still no sight – but I heard the *snap*, the clatter of the hilt on my shoes. I dropped to feel for it: the jagged edge, broken two-thirds down the blade. The other end must have been stuck between the doors. I scrabbled – it was – jammed in the too-narrow gap like a toothpick. The blind stab hadn't missed – I'd struck where the wood was weakest, widest – it should have gone straight through – it should have worked – it should have –

I kicked the doors. I rammed them with my shoulder. I grabbed for anything handle-shaped and yanked. The other piece of Earlyfate snicked to the floor. The dark itched on my eyes. Each gasp was straw and blood.

Rosamond's heirloom. Rosamond's namesake.

And every other thought had fangs.

I was crying, again, and only knew it when I raised a hand to my face. The ghastliness of sobbing, lost amidst all the other smarting sensations. I felt my fingers on my cheek, but not my cheek on my fingers – the oddness of it made me blink, as if the gesture was someone else's, another numb hand cupping my face, far more gently than I would have.

A sob folded me into my palm. My hand was slick – blood, by the taste of it – it must have been where I grabbed the blade, the first time or the fifteenth.

"Chivalrous dolt," I whispered.

I twitched the fingers on my other hand: clumsy, but serviceable. Eased the pin from my cravat, refastened it into my jacket lapel. Slipped the cravat loose from its knot. Steadied my cut palm, then wrapped it in one layer – another – of the silk. Tied off the makeshift dressing with fingers and teeth, too slowly to pinch.

"There." My voice trembled. "I'm sorry. I'm sorry for everything."

Slam.

I leapt back almost to the beam. Then, with considerable difficulty, I cleared my throat.

"Is someone –?"

"Stand away!"

That voice. Those spiky cockney consonants.

"The doors," Septimus added, a snarl, receding with ominous purpose. "Get clear. 'Bout to drive two bicycles through 'em!"

CHAPTER TWENTY-FIVE

I AM NOT TEMPTING FATE AGAIN, CONFOUND IT

The New Notebook of... undesignated possible peril

Concerning resemblances

Almost every beleaguered remnant of me wanted to sprint towards that voice, excepting – crucially – the pieces which recalled my tempestuous history with Septimus's cycling habits. The incorrigible stunner once chased me to the theatre on cycle-back, slammed into the wall when I dodged, with force enough to dent even that grandiose auditorium – and that was only with *one* bicycle. I fled to the beam, then darted behind it.

She struck. Let there be light – and there suddenly was, a cracked and splintery light, glinting on the broken metal in the straw. One more thwack and I could see my filthy boots. The third thwack – I spat dust, for by this point it was dropping onto me with the smothering consistency of sfogliatelle sugar – finally showed me what the feral cyclist was about: charging one of the doors by hurricane-lamp, two bicycles yoked in her grip like plough-horses, until the old wood began to snap from sheer astonishment.

The front wheels receded from the raggedy gap. "That's person-sized, ain't it?"

I was scraping my brain for a reasonable answer when the lamp sprang through the hole, with Henry's pallid face swooping in behind it. "Pip?"

I gaped.

Then, of course, I ran. *Hurtled.* Through the gap, a twisting dive to keep the splinters off my jacket – into lamplight and cold and air of a significantly less necromantic quality, dead straw gratefully exchanged for living grass. I nearly skidded over in the churned-up mud, but Henry caught my elbow, swung me into an embrace so fierce it was a jostle of bones, elbows and ribs and fingers and spines. Above their head, Septimus was engaged in a cursory repair of her battering-ram – but she glanced up when I gasped, lip quirking at the corner.

"I'm a fool," I managed, voice stifled in my sternum; Henry still hadn't released me. Septimus rolled her eyes.

"That ain't news, Pip."

"We quite should have been faster," Henry spluttered, a sort of gnawing on my waistcoat buttons, "But the towpath gave out – we had to improvise another route – figs, I thought we'd lost you – "

"'Til the yelling. Weren't exactly *help me*, but it did the job."

I coloured. "Do forgive my language, sweet sweethearts, I – I was – I didn't think anyone would come."

Henry tipped backwards, taut with incredulity. "Of course we came!"

"I told Ballestas I didn't want the Division involved." Their frown was a slap; of course I dropped my gaze. "I'm sorry, I shouldn't – "

Then I started. Septimus leaned round Henry's shoulder, bicycles balanced in one hand – the other one, to my utmost consternation, was under my chin, compelling me to look at her. "Pip. Yes or no. Do you want help?"

My palm was still throbbing. Even so, my voice was damnably small. "Yes."

Septimus actually grinned at me. "Good."

Then she let me go, and Henry did too, both springing back to squeeze their bicycles' handlebars. "Adelstein and Nick're looking for you too. And Cassandra's leading the rest to Alberstowe Hall. Weren't much time to explain – but apparently you want to go there?"

My first attempt at a coherent confessional was anything of the sort. I had, at least, managed to convey the necessity of locating Alberstowe Hall *now*, before all the threats of and at the place crashed down upon Rosamond and Ballestas both. I'd then been flung onto the pannier-rack of Septimus's bicycle, instructed to cling for my life, and urged to convey everything else I knew in the most laconic sentences I could manage.

Embellishment was impossible in my new circumstances: clutching Septimus desperately enough to scour off my freckles on her shoulder-blade, legs swung into dangerous nothingness beside a perilously fast wheel, jolting through sludgy fields which protested in every way against our terrifying speed. Henry was quick and deft alongside us, though gasping so deeply they'd no breath left for questions; Septimus, admirably athletic as she is, interrupted me as easily as if we'd been talking over tea. She barely slowed down when we re-crossed the Angle – there were two planks braced across its narrowest span, and we rattled over them before either I or Henry had time to yelp. The water rolled under us like a fish, there and gone in one slimy glimpse. As far as I could tell: no boat.

We slammed through a hedge – thankfully, it was brittle and Novemberish enough to snap. The bicycles shied like anxious horses, dodging potholes. I'd exhausted my explanation, and no one spoke again until the road changed, bending like a cheap hairpin, towards metal gates thrice the size of those at Nettleblack House.

The lamps on the handlebars swung when we braked, flung their light at the gates: no ornamental nettles here, just sharp bars and spikes at the top. Septimus vaulted down to shake them – "Locked. Sweetings must've climbed."

Henry scrambled off their bicycle, leaving me in the rather odd position of propping both contraptions upright – not that it wasn't a tiny victory, to realise the hellebore hadn't stripped me of the strength to manage it. "You're quite not climbing alone –!"

"'Course not." Septimus kissed their forehead, caught them close in a one-armed squeeze. "What d'you reckon, then – another battering ram?"

I spotted it before Henry could reply. It was silhouetting them, with light beyond their lanterns, and churning up sound underfoot: pea-gravel, parting under wheels in heavy currents. The sweethearts dashed to my side – grabbed a bicycle apiece – and hauled the assemblage backwards, round the tight corner, painfully close to the blackthorn fangs in the hedge. We clustered in front of the bicycle-lamps, peered through the branches like a hydra: behind the gates, the carriage was halting, someone jumping down to twist a key in the gate lock.

The carriage. *The* carriage. Even haphazardly illuminated by its own lanterns, I knew it. The glossy black brougham of Clement's incorrigible servants, alias the Concerned Citizens, now crawling through the open gates –

Then the brougham lurched.

The driver on the ground – Peter, or Dorothea, it was impossible to discern – was busy tugging the gates shut. The driver on the carriage had two fractious horses to calm. But the *window* of the carriage had smashed, a tiny blizzard of glass that had presumably never been kicked in all its preening life – and then there were boots, heavy, made for country walks – fabric so patterned it writhed on its own, sliced to tentacles by the window's broken teeth –

I simply waited my moment, then threw myself out of the carriage.

"Rosamond," I gasped.

One last whiplash of looks between the three of us. I don't know how to translate them, beyond the certainty – bizarre, unfamiliar, yet utterly indisputable! – that we understood each other, that the very *looks* had plaited into a tangible idea.

Then I was sprinting, and they were scorching on the bicycles, lights blazing, bellowing with every ounce of spare breath –

"Stay where you are!"

"For the Dallyangle Division!"

It was hardly a surprise when no one stopped me. When no one *noticed* me. I was a thing of hurtle and stagger, too shadowy to spot next to the sweethearts' valiant imper-sonation of an exploding gaslamp. I snatched her up where she'd tumbled into the potholes, then flung us away from the carriage, as deep into the hedge as momentum could get us, until everything was mud and spiderwebs and darkness. She twisted against me, bit until I yelled – but Henry and Septimus were yelling too, more than enough to drown everything else.

"We're quite requisitioning you!" Henry shrieked. "Or enlisting you! Or – plums, call it both! Lord Miltonwaters is in danger and the Division needs your help!"

Oh, you genius! You fruit-spluttering genius! Gracious, I couldn't be prouder!

– but I emphatically did *not* shout as much, occupied as I was with hissing my name into my darling's bewildered ear.

"You're Miltonwaters's servants, ain't you?" Septimus, by the sound of it, was playacting her old surly self; Henry seemed intent on flying through the deception on delirium alone. "The Div got a warning. The Sweetings're robbing the Hall tonight. Like as not, they're on your grounds already."

"The *Sweetings?*"

It froze me and Rosamond both. Dorothea – still, presum-ably, hollow at one hand – spluttered to the limits of her perfect elocution.

"They are here?" she cried. "They would dare? What can we do to stop them?"

Peter's voice was closer to panic than outrage; he clearly hadn't flung off all thought of their *errand*. "Dorothea, we can't just – "

"Just what?" Septimus demanded, a magnificent snarl. "What're the two of you up to, exactly, that's more important than preventing a burglary?"

Another genius – geniuses, both!

He faltered into a stammer. "Well – well, we were – there was – ah – Dorothea?"

"It does not matter!" she blurted. "The Division needs our assistance!"

"For the last time, milord won't let you join – "

"He might!" Henry yelped. "If you help stop the Sweetings from wrecking his house! The Division could even petition milord on your behalf! Septimus – don't you think?"

"That I do. Milord'd practically *owe* her a place with us, I reckon."

"Dorothea – "

"No, Peter! The Divisioners are right – no errand can surpass the requirement to be useful! And I know precisely what must be done, to thwart those burglars once and for all!"

"You don't mean – "

"We must. Now turn this carriage at once!"

Given that the man's choice came down to *oblige*, or *admit a failed attempt to incarcerate an heiress*, I wasn't precisely stunned that he fell upon the former. Henry and Septimus stayed with them, chivvying and urging, ringing their bicycle-bells against any pesky remnants of defiance. I couldn't see a thing, with Rosamond tangled on top of me, but I heard the sounds fade, until there was nothing on the road but country quiet and the creak of the hedge.

The press on me shifted. The shadows rolled off, and welled into Rosamond, bare-armed and scratched and far too pale for the murky darkness. Her fingers crawled up my cheek, tracing – for my scar, apparently.

Then the hedge simply slung us together.

She was sobbing. I could feel her – the haphazard dip of her waist, the hair caught in muddy strands at my lips, the pinch of her chin in my shoulder, the hurtling rattle of her heart. All the terror and panic, everything I'd kept locked inside the fern-case of my chest – never mind that the glass was steamed and brittle and ready to crack – now, it all shattered, so violently I shuddered in her arms.

"Cariad – he said he'd got rid of you – he said you were dead already – "

I swallowed, not that it worked; her sobs were infectious. "Darling, he's wrong – you're safe – I'm safe – "

"I nearly didn't," she whispered. "Didn't jump. Didn't try. I – I thought – what's the point, without you? – but I knew you'd still want me to – "

Oh, darling.

I held her. She clung to me. Beyond that, there's no embellishment.

When the rasp in her throat had softened, and her shoulders conceded to shivering more with cold than despair, I eased us out of our thorny nest. Not back onto the road – right through to the other side, where we could curl up together on a mercifully grassy field. I twisted out of my jacket and coaxed her into it. She pressed our foreheads together, closed her eyes.

I thought of Marigold, sneering down from the barn doorway. *You'd delight in that, wouldn't you – a nice heroic death in your lover's arms?* More alarming still: at the time she'd said it, I think – fear – that she wasn't wrong. I would have thought that conclusion fitting. I would have abandoned Rosamond just to see her safe.

Now, I curled my fingers round the cravat on my palm. *Absolutely not.*

"I don't know if it's foolish," Rosamond murmured, lips twitching on mine, "but this doesn't feel like Edwina's fault."

She cleared her throat, nestled closer.

"Lord Miltonwaters said the same as her, about the asylum. Almost the same words. And – I know she stole my money, I'm not ignoring everything she *has* done, it's just – she wouldn't kill you. She wouldn't send anyone to tell me you were dead. I – I can't pretend I've any reason to think it, but – but – I didn't know there'd be a line for her, until someone else crossed it – and – oh, God, Pip, am I being stupid?"

"I don't know. But – " – I was testing the words, warm and furtive on my tongue – "I suspect Henry can help us find out."

It was too dark to see the colour in her eyes, but I could feel her watching me, and just about squint for the surprised snag of her eyebrows. "Surely Henry's given up on me?"

"Darling." At last, strange and painful, I smiled. "Didn't you hear? You'll be drowned in fruit if you dare suggest as much in their presence."

"Their?"

I nodded – I wouldn't choose the words for it, not before Henry had the chance – and she sighed, let it pull her face back until she was grinning wide and white through the darkness. "Ardderchog. I don't know my siblings at all, do I?"

"Well – "

"No, that's *good!*" She beamed at me, both hands cradling my face, hoarse and shivery and solemn. "I don't know either of them. But I want to."

We kissed – faltering, then fierce –

The ground beneath us started shaking. Dazed and fragmented as I was, I would simply have given her the credit and carried on, but she jerked back with terror in her eyes. Her green eyes. I could see the colour.

And she'd seen the lights. Great juddering streaks, slicing through the hedge. Behind them – approaching, too fast – some clattering flurry of movement. She flung herself into the grass, dark hair splayed to cover the pallor of her face; I pressed myself to the branches and squinted. If Peter had slipped away – if he'd brought the carriage back for her –

No. The direction was wrong. Whatever it was, it wasn't clattering out of Alberstowe Hall – it was *approaching* it.

I snatched her shoulder. "Darling – "

A farm-cart. And bicycles. A veritable *fleet.*

In the weird constellation of light – lanterns hooked to belts, lanterns strapped to handlebars, lanterns swinging from panniers – this swarm of vehicles hardly looked like separate entities. They were one creature, a spirit drawing gone terribly wrong, a thing with spokes for fingers and proliferous lamp-eyes. It pelted up the road, through the gates, all limbs, tumbling and whirring, too fast to hail, too fast to stop –

I know – I think – I saw Ballestas, appalling purple scarf torn out behind her, streaked like a wound in the creature's side. There was more than one figure on the farm-cart, jutting like a spine above the lanterns. The rest – it was there and gone so quickly, I couldn't –

Rosamond gasped. She'd crawled up beside me, and she was staring too. For one long, dazed splay of minutes, we could do little more than watch the darkness regather.

Triumph simply crammed my throat. Gracious, was this how it felt, to find oneself enmeshed in a plan that was *working?* Henry and Septimus would have all the bolstering they needed in that many-legged Divisionary beast. Clement's own servants would join them. The Sweetings were unarmed, and wildly outnumbered. Clement couldn't grab the upper hand again, he couldn't, not on his own against all of it –

Crack.

What?

Rosamond dived back through the hedge. I followed, on instinct and fencing reflexes, caught her arm on the other side. "What are you – ?"

"We have to follow them."

To my astonishment, she was pointing at the still-open gates. Shadows were thickening around them, like strange mould: there were fallow deer there, their hooves frothing with pointy-tailed pheasants, hastening to freedom through the gap. Admirable logic, mere seconds after that gunshot had snapped the very night.

"The Hall," she stammered. "Henry's in there. And Edwina's about to be."

"What – ?"

"Eddie was on the cart! With the Division! And someone's *firing* in that house!" Her hands closed over mine, pulled me close. "We can't just run away!"

We couldn't. And, before the ghost of Marigold Chandler twines her fingers through my hair again: it was not in the least any desire for a *nice heroic death*.

I squeezed her hand. Then we sprinted, as fast as the dregs of the hellebore would let me, scattering pheasants as we hurtled through the gates.

CHAPTER TWENTY-SIX

FATE IS TEMPTED REGARDLESS

Cassandra Ballestas's Secret Phonograph

Recording: Still not done

Alberstowe Hall. The driveway's smudged with my breath. The path's mulchier than last time, the trees skinnier, and no one's bothered to light the pretty lampposts. The front gates are already open – there's a spike of panic, to puncture the pain in my legs! – but we don't catch up with anyone on the drive, beyond glitter-eyed pheasants and their creaking shrieks.

I stumble off my bicycle, stagger forward on its momentum. The massive door's intact, but the windowpane beside it is glinting dust: no finicky pin-picking, just stones sprawled on the chequerboard flagstones. I squint through the hole, craning round the window-frame's sharp new teeth. The candle-flames are jumping in their sconces like agitated constellations, and the white stones are crusted with mud.

Then, of course, it jolts into sense. *Smashed window. Muddy soles. Are the* Sweetings *here?*

Wariness jostles round the whole Div, as we splinter into groups. Gertie's with me, squeezing my arm until I manage a shaky smile. Mother has Millicent and Oliver to keep her safe: they'll be following the footprints. Oliver scrambles through the smashed window, unlatches the door for his sister to haul it open.

A murmur in my head, lavish voice knotting round the words: *if I can persuade Marigold that trusting Clement is not in her best interests – from there it's but the tiniest step to full betrayal.*

And if Marigold's giving the Sweetings their orders –

Behind Gertie and I, Edwina Nettleblack clears her throat.

Not that she looks like Edwina Nettleblack, not fresh off a farm-cart. She's torn her velvet skirts, and her grey-blonde hair's a blur of wisps, evaporating from its chignon with her every step. I did tell her, mind you, that she wasn't obliged to join our search for Rosamond and Property – Gareth Wyn Evans reiterated it with far more gnashing of teeth – but she'd not hear it from either of us. *Protecting Rosamond has been my life's work, and I have done it badly. Allow me, please, to do it better.*

Gertie glances between us. "Sure about this, Miss N?"

She swallows sharply. Nods. Well, that makes one of us.

We're in. I yank a taper off the wall, wax snagging under my fingernails. I don't like the way the dark pools between the candles – dark that could have anything in it, at this rate. Clement probably carries a candle when he's home, one man wandering between too many rooms. Maybe he had to choose: gaslamps or the telephone, a dilemma for the modern gentleman.

This is, by the way, exactly what I'm thinking in the moment. Panic's chased me all afternoon, bolting through my head until my thoughts start bolting too; I conjured about ten new novels on the cycle here. Is it better than blank-brained terror? Than playing back Property's telephone plea, scratchy as a phonograph cylinder, until too much repetition crashes the whole machine of me?

Concentrate.

Clement's house is writhing in its sleep. The grand staircase is open all the way to its uppermost banister; one of its landings stretches across the air like a bridge. Creaks echo down from above, where bits of the staircase branch off into corridors – the flinching of floorboards, the sudden stark slam of doors. The thought's a sting at my temple: there's nowhere to hide on that staircase. Every step's open. Every step's loud.

Miss Nettleblack darts past us, gloves pattering along the wall at the staircase's foot. She's tapping it, though – mercifully – the gloves soften the sound. Between the frames – under the candle-fittings – until the wall itself lunges out at her –

I gasp. Gertie grabs my arm, a breath at my ear: "Steady, Cass."

"The servants' stairs," Miss Nettleblack whispers triumphantly. There's a square of darkness in the panelling, stale darkness, so thick the flame of my taper goes flat. "When I visited Lady Miltonwaters, the staff were anxious not to stray into the Marquess's path. Forgive me, I – I thought it might be safest."

Steady, Cass, indeed – and I can be steady, just for a bit longer, I promise. "Not bad, Miss Nettleblack."

She blinks – she seems to be parsing my tone – but then she smiles, smaller and more timid than I'm expecting, and gestures us both inside. Impeccable manners, of course.

The spiral to these stairs is a veritable knot. Splinters and silence as we climb and I ponder – and try not to set fire to the neck-crick of steps above us. It's fine. It's manageable. It's the last bit of the night before everyone's safe. If Rosamond's already tried one escape, it makes sense to start higher – too high for her to climb out. Then down the house, silent, sneaky, searching, until Rosamond is safe and Property is safe and everyone is –

And *that's* when we hear the gunshot.

Louder than that pistol in the Div. So loud I drop the candle – have to stamp, hasty and scrambling, to snuff any flame left on the wick. Then no one breathes. No one moves.

It's in the Hall. Below us, by the sound. But it's not in the staircase.

"The Sweetings?" Gertie hisses, half-strangled, as close to mouthing as the dark lets us.

I try, very hard, for one shaky skein of breath. "We took their gun."

Don't choke on the fear – don't you *dare* choke on the fear –

Because what else can we do, but keep climbing? Keep climbing, and trailing my fingers in search of another hidden door, and telling myself that there wasn't a scream, that there won't be another one, that we just have to find them and then we can leave.

Under my hand, jabbing my palm – a latch, chilly metal in a nest of splinters. I press an eye to the gap. Empty corridor, draughty taper-light. Jumping shadows. None of them alive. But plenty of doors.

We slip the latch. We creep across the fish-hooks on the gloomy rug.

"Detective Ballestas!"

I don't shriek – but, sweet *Lord*, I come close. Dorothea hurtles round the corner, crashes into my hands, wrings them, her face too pale and too bright in the murky corridor. Gertie bristles at my shoulder, fists clenched; Miss Nettleblack scrambles behind us.

"Thank heaven you've brought reinforcements!" Dorothea cries. Too shrill. *Far* too shrill. It's all I can do not to stuff a glove between her teeth.

Wait. "Reinforcements?"

"The Sweetings have presumed to burgle the Hall," she gabbles, only dropping to a whisper when I stab my nails in her palms. "Peter and I have been assisting your colleagues – trying to apprehend them – "

Whisper. It's fine. Everything's fine. "Which colleagues?"

"Henry and Septimus, I believe? They're still searching with Peter, never fear. But they said Division-work was all about showing initiative, so I just thought I'd slip off and bolster our defences while they looked – after all, you Divisioners don't carry weapons, and there's no knowing what those Sweetings might – "

"Then the gunshot was you?" My voice scrapes in my ears, every syllable a jagged edge. "Please tell me you didn't – "

"Oh, no, Detective! That gunshot must have been the Marquess!"

It kicks straight through every thought in my head.

"What?"

"I called upon the Marquess of Alberstowe. Lord Miltonwaters's grandfather, you know. Better that than leave him useless in the attic! He won't suffer criminals in his house. The Sweetings won't thwart you today – I've made sure of it!"

Words are happening, somehow, very faint and far away.

"Well. I see. The grandfather was in the attic. Of course. You'd better find my mother and tell her what you've done."

She beams at me. "You truly think I've done enough?"

I can't even retort. I just snatch the keys from her belt, swing her round by the shoulders on her own flabbergasted momentum, and throw her back the way she came.

Gertie's swaying on the spot. "Is this the Marquess who shot his gardener? The Marquess who gave the Head-Hiders the head? *That* Marquess?"

Don't choke. Don't choke. Don't choke.

"Doors," I manage to stammer.

We fray, one to each door, relaying Dorothea's keys between us. Soft-footed and silent as we can manage. Flatten our ears to the slimy varnish – knock, count the quiet into seconds – twist the key, the handle, feel it give, start back from a room full of dark corners and dust sheets. Repeat. Faster and faster, down the corridor. *Where the hell are you both?*

Until I'm biting down on my breath, cheek to the latest door, just to make sure the ragged gasps beyond it aren't mine.

Gertie and Miss Nettleblack scurry over. My hands are shaking so wildly, it takes two rounds of the ring before a key bites. The gasps inside turn to whimpers when I turn the handle. Miss Nettleblack's straight in: "Rosamond? You mustn't be afraid – we are here to get you out – "

"You?"

The voice – too loud, *again*, everyone in this sodding house is too loud! – yanks me across the threshold. Gertie tugs the door shut behind us, our best attempt at muffling the sound. Before us, shaky on her feet between sheeted furniture,

Adelaide's face starts out of the darkness. There's a solitary candle in the room; it makes her pallor bright and ghostly as a fox's eye – but for the bruise on her cheek, blotching her skin like dropped ink.

Adelaide.

My throat twists like a rag. "You're – "

"Just say it, Cassie," she spits. "Getting careless."

Miss Nettleblack gapes at her. "Where is Rosamond? What – why are *you* – ?"

"Do you approve, Cousin Edwina? Is this what Uncle Morgan asked you to make of me?" A scoff, bitter enough to wrench Adelaide's bony chin up. I'd almost forgotten they were related – but, this close, you can't dodge the resemblance, two scrawny effigies on the same family tomb. "If it's Rosamond you want, you're too late. They've already taken her. For what it's worth, I did try to stop them."

"*No,*" – and Miss Nettleblack buckles over, hand to her mouth, scraping her fingers with gasps. Gertie's the one to hold her – Adelaide just watches, shivering. I suppose I'm little better, but my thoughts won't let me move: *it's not fine, nothing's fine –*

Steady. "Is Property here?"

A damp-lashed scowl from Adelaide. "Not that I've seen."

Something creaks in the corridor.

"Then we need to go. Come on, you revenant."

Adelaide's mouth falls open. She looks, for once in her after-life, as young as she is. I – I mean, if I were calmer, there'd be a goodly swathe of me keeling over with sheer incredulity – but I can't just leave her in this nightmare, can I?

"I'm afraid none of you will be *going* anywhere."

Clement Miltonwaters, rigid with rage in the doorway, more dishevelled than I've ever seen him. He's twisted the collar of his smoking-jacket, thrown it on so violently the fastenings have torn. At first skidding glance, his glare just looks petulant – until I notice how little he's blinking, as if his eyes might scorch his lashes.

Bent over his arm, he's carrying a hunting-rifle.

The candle jolts him. Makes it look, for one horrible moment, like he's coming closer.

You've done this before. You faced down the Head-Hiders. Slow breaths, slow movements. Don't scream. Don't startle him. Don't – don't –

"Your little ploy will tidy everything rather well, I think." He chuckles – or bites down on a chuckle, at any rate, tears it to gristle in his teeth. "My demented grandfather is loose in the house, with his own precious copy of this very rifle. The papers love to speculate on how free he is with it. Any number of people could get hurt, in such terrible circumstances. And then, when I find him, I'll simply be finishing him off in self-defence."

He snaps the rifle together. Raises it, shifts it, frowning down the barrel – from Gertie, to Miss Nettleblack, to Adelaide, to me.

My whole head goes suddenly, queasily silent.

"You can't," – it's all I can stammer.

"Or what?" He grins, his teeth far too white in the gloom. "You'll call the police? I don't think so, Miss Ballestas. We're bound together, the Division and I – we can't hope for anything from *them*. Really, an alliance between us would have been so much neater."

I'm too terrified even to feel my words, but there they are, cracked and half-whispered. Too much to risk my life on – too much not to be said. "The Division is nothing like you."

"And yet the Division are trying to get me killed by my own grandfather!"

"We – ?"

"Unlock the Marquess's chambers, hand him his gun, let him do the job for you, and hide my head in your infamous morgue." He's still smiling, tight and furious. "I never thought you kindly detectives capable of such ruthlessness, but here you are. Not that I intend to let that doddering embarrassment do anything of the sort – he's already ruined this family far too much for any more of my indulgence."

A glint. A chance. Fumble towards it.

"Nobody's trying to kill you. Your own servants got the Marquess involved."

He scoffs. "They wouldn't disobey me – "

"They've improvised before, haven't they? We've just seen them – they said the Sweetings are robbing your house."

It snags, grips, tugs the bones of his face askew.

"We don't want to hurt you. You don't need to make this worse. Just tell us where we can find Pip Property and Rosamond Nettleblack, and nobody has to – "

He strides towards me. Gertie struggles forward – Miss Nettleblack does too – all of them, to block his path –

But he shoves them aside. Grabs my jaw, twists it up. "The Sweetings are *what?*"

I open my mouth – and there's nothing left.

"You're lying," he snarls. "The Sweetings would never come here. Marigold would never let them. Marigold would never dare – "

"Intruders in my Hall!"

Clement jolts like a flame. Drops me, staggers back – then lunges, painfully clumsy, to yank the ring of keys from my hand. He skids for the door, towards the shout – the new voice is unfamiliar, rasping and plummy at once, like a stale twelfth-cake – and he's muttering something too, clipped, nib-sharp, under his quickening breaths: "That interfering deviant, I should have shot them on sight – !"

I crumple the moment he slams the door. Hands taut in my hair, the sheets and the shadows soaring around me. Bile in my throat. More hands – Gertie – bracing, or trying, but the room won't stop whirling –

Miss Nettleblack skids past. Torn velvet skirts scraping my shoulder. Then she blurs, and I gouge my head into Gertie's plait.

My chest throbs, secondhand, with Gertie's voice: "What're you – ?"

"Help me lift this!"

Scuffling. Scrapes, felt right up through my knees on the floorboards. Gertie's face, sallow in the candlelight, warm at the breaths. "Cass? Can you stand?"

I couldn't answer her then. I can now. Maybe it's this certainty – this moment, at the phonograph, phrasing, crying, everything in between – maybe some scrap of it scratches back through the night, back to that shuddering detective in the shadowy room.

I stand. I join Miss Nettleblack, Gertie, even sodding Adelaide. I grab the last empty side of the half-sheeted chaise. Then we run it straight through the door.

CHAPTER TWENTY-SEVEN

I AM VERY NEARLY SPENT

The New Notebook of an Uncertain State

Concerning as much as I can recall

The front door gaped by the time we cleared the driveway. My throat was a box of knives, unpolished and sharp – the grounds were sprawling, and not an ounce of my body wanted to sprint a single additional step. Rosamond had to drag me the last of the way, one arm around my waist, fingers gripping the feeling from mine.

Up and onwards over the marble steps, under the statue-stricken façade with its snarling stags, into a hive of candle-flames. Rosamond hissed through her teeth to see it all again, and I admit I gasped: you could have slotted my house into this entrance-hall, neat between the bends of the grand staircase. The steps twisted upwards across the hall, statues clustering on the stone banisters – the first-floor landing hung between the walls. Ornate, expensive, hideous, and thrice as impractical as Nettleblack House.

"*Intruders in my Hall!*"

The shriek was loud enough to snag us on the threshold. We froze as one. Unwisely.

A quilted blur burst onto the first-floor landing, jolting to a halt halfway across. The movement made the candles jump, flared the apparition into particulars: ruddy skin pinched with red veins, straggles of pencil-lead hair, a plush dressing-gown – no, velvet, costly – clumped with crumbs and old stains. Mottled ankles through the banister's gaps. Slippered feet.

And *another* infernal hunting-rifle, hefted over the banister, trained on us.

"Not another step!" the deadly octogenarian bellowed.

Maledizione – had someone stabbed Clement's portrait?

"Who are you?" he snarled, the rifle quivering in his gnarled fingers. "Where did they go? I got one – now I want the set!"

Rosamond squeezed my hand. I saw them then, blurry and peripheral. Flattened to the wall underneath the landing, just close enough to the gloomy portraits to dodge their assailant's scrutiny. The Director was there, spectacles glinting in the flames – and that pallid smudge of face must have been Henry. But crumpled in their midst – someone was on the floor, spilt and spreading, clutched back from full sprawl by taut fists and straining arms –

I risked a darting glimpse. *Maggie.* Maggie, with her head wilted onto her chest, her coat yanked open, her grimy sleeve sodden and burgundy at the shoulder. Norman held her, fist in his mouth to stifle his sobs. Bunched around them, gripping tight – Gertie's contingent, Henry and Septimus, the Director, even the Concerned Citizens –

What in the name of – ?

Then the recollection clattered like a teacup, bright and irritable in Marigold's voice. *Clement Miltonwaters is* not *his grandfather!*

"You're the Marquess of Alberstowe," I spluttered.

Rosamond gaped. She was still holding me up. "We're – here for the pheasant shoot?"

"Do not chaff with me, girl!" He gave us a puckered scowl, tottery and quick as a mosquito. "Where are the burglars?"

I heard Norman's snag of breath, saw him buckle beneath the blur of my lashes. Gracious, he didn't earnestly think –

"The burglars are gone." I had a valiant go at the bow I'd once offered the Queen, albeit with my darling steadying me against the dizziness. She complemented the gesture with a feeble wave – then, clumsy with afterthought, a feeble curtsy. "We're – ah – "

" – leaving too!" Rosamond finished, stammering a little. Her arms were very tight around my waist. "But, if you can find him, I'm sure your grandson would *love* to explain."

His eyes widened. It was visible, even at this distance: the jerking and slackening of his face, as far too many pieces crowded into his mind –

But I fear I can't fully explain what happened next.

I know that the Marquess whirled round on the landing.

I saw Henry and Septimus springing off the wall towards us.

I heard the shot, though I didn't see it fired – because Rosamond and I had just been tackled to the ground by a blur of green velvet.

I glimpsed Marigold – *Marigold?* – upside-down between the Hall's front doors, staggering in from the night with both hands to her mouth.

Someone gasped, though I've no idea who it was –

And then someone fell.

I struggled to my elbows when the *crack* shook the floor. The first-floor landing was empty. A shadow darted out of a panel in the wall, sharpened into Ballestas, and sprinted over the chequerboard. The Director rushed to meet her there, with the Concerned Citizens close behind, and the lot of them dropped to their knees, beside something crumpled and plush and disarmingly shrunken. A spidery ankle jutted out of a slipper. A face cricked where it shouldn't have been, on a neck that shouldn't have bent like that. *The Marquess.*

Movement – a twitch on the uppermost landing. Clement, so small he could have been one of his statues, sickled over the banister, breaking the back of his rifle.

"The shot was for Property! That's what you all saw, isn't it? I aimed for the thief! Perfectly within my rights to shoot trespassers on my land! Isn't it? Just a gentleman defending his inheritance! Yes? *Yes?*"

The weight on me shifted. A bundle of torn green skirts, rising off my legs – two leg-o'-mutton sleeves flung out until I couldn't even see Clement anymore. Edwina Nettleblack was on her feet, wild-haired, yelling, wholly oblivious to Rosamond and I – and our open-mouthed bewilderment.

"If you fire at my sister or her lover again, you shall answer to me!"

The hellebore must have surged back. Overcome my senses at last. The rest was surely unbridled botanical fantasy. The very hallway had started to shimmer.

I slumped against the freezing stones in Rosamond's arms, and closed my eyes.

CHAPTER TWENTY-EIGHT

RECORDINGS

Cassandra Ballestas's Not-So-Secret Phonograph

Recording: The last bit of the last cylinder

So here's where I've ended up. Back in my room, with my scarf crammed under the crack in the door – only because it's nearly dawn and *definitely* past Johannes's bedtime – and the phonograph's in the house. My house. The trip to get it was tonight's final stagger. We've a few minutes left on the cylinder, I reckon, and then I'll sleep.

Thanks to you, indomitable machine, I might actually manage to sleep!

I can't stop when we get back to the apothecary. I'm rattling from the inside out, like a box of pen-nibs. Pelting round the shop at Dad's instructions. Skidding between far too many people in far too small a room. Clammy Maggie Sweeting splayed on the counter, slimy as a landed fish. Marigold Chandler, tiny and stricken, voice dissolving like a sugar-lump, scribbling in the corner under Gertie's scowls: *finish the list, go on, everything you put in Property's drink!* Heaps of Nettleblacks (persons and tinctures) in every corner, until Rosamond wriggles out and flees to the Div to gut my office of Property's – I'm very tired and thus immensely tempted to say *property*, but in honour of a certain imminent business proposal let's just say *stuff*. And Property – conscious again! – waiting their turn for Dad's ministrations, open-palmed by the ferret-ravaged window display, with Septimus picking a bloodstained cravat out of their hand.

Mother grabs my elbows when she spots me spinning. I've a jar of dried something in one hand, a fistful of Nettleblack's in the other; I think I'm trying to invent Property a post-hellebore restorative from scratch. But she prises it all away and cups my face, and tells me to go to bed like it's the most noble pursuit in the world.

I smile – and I mean it, mind you! – but I still only get as far as the top of the steps. There's light cast up from the kitchen, and the clatter of feet and jars and kettles every time someone sprints in and out, but I'm too shadowy and overhead to spot, folded on the floor with Jo's wall at my back. I'm still shaking.

We couldn't fix everything, you see. I don't mean it in disappointment: we had to choose, so we did. I stuck my fingers to the Marquess of Alberstowe's pulse and felt it stop. Clement shot him in the head, shot him straight over the banister, cracked him on the chequerboard floor. And he'd *explained* it, snarling over his shoulder as Dorothea and Peter hauled him to the attic, the colours pressed taut beneath his skin like cured meat. Sneak onto the uppermost landing, aim over his grandfather's shoulder, hit Property while the Marquess was threatening them with an identical rifle, blame the shot on the Marquess, tidy everything away, claim the title with a flick of the trigger. *Just a gentleman defending his inheritance.*

Well. He knows we can't arrest him. But he also knows we've withdrawn from his patronage with immediate effect. And he must have heard Dorothea – she was twisting his arm off – calling out to us as we left: "Never fear, Divisioners! We shan't let it pass! And you shan't topple with him!"

I tip my head onto my knees.

"Ballestas?"

And then there's Pip Property on the staircase. Not poisoned and bloated in the Angle's reeds, not bleeding out on Alberstowe Hall's threshold, not skewered with their own stupid swordstick – bulky-shouldered in Gertie's blanket, and proffering a mug to me. They've got one, too: Dad's given them the biggest, painted all over with chub and perch and pike, won in a raffle from Dally Anglers' Fishing Tackle. It's thrice the size of Marigold's flimsy tea-set.

I take the mug. They sit beside me, sip their drink. "I – "

"Is there whiskey in this?"

I've blurted it before I even notice them speak: I'm not Mother's teetotal heir, but this drink is *strong*. Property darts me a little scowl, for the interruption, then slumps on the wall with a sigh. "Blame Gertie."

We keep sipping. The fish swim round their mug in the shadows. I stare at them, to stare at something beyond my mind. It is, I have to say, a lot harder to stare at your mind with someone strange beside you, sharp-elbowed and breathing.

"I – gracious, I'm – that is, I didn't – "

They swallow an inch from the mug. I watch the fish tip vertical.

"Thank you," is their final pick. We don't precisely meet each other's eyes, but it's not cold: we're sat close as books on a shelf.

My turn for a bolster-gulp. "And sorry."

"Va bene," they murmur, quicker than I'm expecting. They lift the fish to me in their bandaged hand, and I lift Gertie's zealous concoction in my shaking one, and the clink of the mugs is so loud we both scoff. And – *fine* – smile.

It's them I leave the message with, when the mugs are drained, and my legs stop trembling, and the scuffling downstairs is starting to wane. *If anyone's worried, tell them I'm bringing home my secret phonograph.* Gertie nips out of the shop to help me carry it. Mother spots us through the bottles in the window, lifts a brow, but doesn't stop me.

*

Recording: A new day!
   If you wish in the world to advance,
   Recordings you'll need to enhance
   Your Division's position – philanthropic mission –
   Just trust me and give it a chance!

Alright, I lied, the phonograph's not done!

But this *is* a new cylinder. I'm just starting it off.

So here you are, Mother – a gift from your wayward child. My very first Edison phonograph. And don't you demur when you listen to this – I *know* you hate writing, I *know* your spelling is chaos, and I *know* you're good at spontaneous verbal articulation – it's a perfect match! The Director's Record, Kept in Phonograph!

Don't worry. I've already ordered another one. I'm not sure how well it'll go, yelling my next novel, but I'm curious to see what it does to the creative process. Because there will be a next novel. And I'd like to put my name on the first. And – though, really, ask an editor, you could have phrased it better – I know what you meant, about *Life and Limbs* not being the best of my abilities. Maybe it's not. But the only thing I *can* do better is the next one.

And look, for the Record – I wasn't trying to stamp on your example. I think you've been a brilliant example, in every sense of that weird slippery word. But I also think it's about time we stopped being *examples* to each other, of success or failure or whatever else. I'm coming back to the Div – I'm sure we can find other ways to jostle.

So the rest is yours. There's a bet, on whether I'll manage to stay in the room while you listen to this little sliver. I'd rather Gertie won it than Property – so I very much hope I'm listening now!

CHAPTER TWENTY-NINE

RECKONINGS

Casebook of Matthew Adelstein

Pertaining to recoveries of many varieties

An Inventory of Everything We Did Not Steal.

1. Item: a skiff, two oars, unnamed, currently in a vacant berth behind the town hall, for want of anywhere more sensible to put it. As observed, said skiff does constitute evidence; as also observed, in Nicholas's apt summation, *I love you, Matty, but I'm not dragging a boat across Market Square with you.*

2. Item: a box, its padlock defeated, containing the clothing and personal effects of Miss Marigold Chandler, contents to be returned to Miss Chandler if possible.

3. Item: a year's worth of funding for the Division, in cash, extricated from the linings of Miss Chandler's clothes.

4. Item: half a year's worth of funding for the Division, in cash – the additional money in recognition of the Head-Hider case – also extricated from Miss Chandler's wardrobe.

5. Item: an envelope, Town Council stationery, containing cufflinks, collar-studs, cravat pins, and yet more bank-notes. Abundance of paisleys on the former would suggest these items belong to Pip Property (the 'savings' first stolen by the Sweetings).

The above was written whilst awaiting news. Nicholas and I were in the Division, unpicking hems, counting notes across the reception desk. I had attempted to contact Alberstowe Hall three times on the telephone and received no answer. It seemed foolish to row the boat *back* to the Hall, but the evening was thickening on the windows, and pacing obliviously round the desk was beginning to feel dangerously absurd. I had lit the wood-burner upon arrival – rather expertly, I fancy – but Nicholas assured me it could be comfortably left to its embers, should we be obliged to venture out onto the water again.

Indeed, we would have done so, had the double doors not swung open with force enough to flutter half the banknotes into a swarm –

"No need to keep grovelling, Rosa!"

"Even so – I really am sorry – I honestly didn't remember, bach, idiot that I am – "

"Stop! You're alright. We're alright. Though if you start the drunken yelling again, I'll get you banned from Checkley's, you see if I – bloody hell, Adelstein!"

Nicholas and I froze. The banknotes twittered to the floor. The doors swung shut, shoving Gertie Skull and Rosamond Nettleblack another few feet into reception: both bedraggled, the latter tucked inside Pip Property's jacket. Gertie had one hand to her chest, gasping her surprise. Miss Rosamond twitched, gaze shying towards her muddy walking-boots, as if in the vain hope that she might melt into them.

I interrupted several breathless and silly remarks suggesting our likeness to Divisionary ghosts, and – with all the provocation in the world – demanded an explanation. Gertie certainly attempted it. To tidy her testimony, as much as anyone could: there had been some sort of confrontation at Alberstowe Hall, *the old gent* had shot Maggie Sweeting and then been *shot off the stairs* by Clement Miltonwaters (I confess I startled when she revealed the *old gent's* identity), Pip Property's poisoning had not been fatal, Miss Chandler was across the square in the Ballestas apothecary with the injured Miss Sweeting, her brother, Pip Property, Adelaide Danadlenddu, and the rest of the Division, and Miss Rosamond had been found – "Well, obviously!" she finished, sheepishly, with a flail of her fingers into her companion's vicinity.

Nicholas was gaping. I determined, obviously, to get everything corroborated.

"And what's this?" Gertie scooped up a fistful of banknotes. "Not the – "

"We didn't steal it!" Nicholas blurted, apparently unmoved by my pointed stare. "Just sort of – y'know – got it back!"

I was obliged to intervene. The identity of the funds was confirmed; Gertie whooped – there is regrettably no other word for it – and announced her immediate intention to inform the Director. She turned to Miss Rosamond as she pelted out – "Dorm's just through there, Property's suitcase is on the bed!" – and then, to my sudden alarm, she was gone, and there was nothing between the middle Nettleblack and us but the tick of the clock.

I cleared my throat. This time, at least, the advantage was mine. I had peered through Property's penmanship and seen her in Wales, in despair, in a portrait of regret that surely – *surely* – could no longer be considered a deceitful affectation. *Tell him I'm sorry – just in case.*

"I am glad," – admittedly, my voice was still a little stiff – "to see you safe."

She shivered, like a plant, with a kind of mirthless chuckle. "Pip's still being checked – hellebore and stuff. I'm grabbing their suitcase for them. I – I'd no idea you were both – "

The rest of the sentence visibly shrivelled.

I handed her the council envelope, clinking with accessories. "You might take these too. It seems Miss Chandler ended up in possession of Property's missing savings."

"Diolch!" – and she darted for them at once, awkwardness apparently overcome, grinning down at the jostle in the envelope. "Oh, Pip'll *relax*, for once in their sodding – "

Then she flinched again, glancing up, eyebrows crumpling.

"Sorry. Sorry, just – oh, God. Sorry."

I hadn't forgotten – not even in the depths of my terror and exasperation – her unexpected capacity for sincerity. I saw it again now, even wincing as she was, every one of those repeated words cut from under her ribs (I cannot claim credit for the ghoulish expression; Nicholas suggested it afterwards, and I believe he borrowed it from *Life and Limbs*). Miss Rosamond held our stares, but she didn't scald them: intent, contrite, certainly not cajoling. *This time*, she could have said, *I won't force your hands.*

I looked to Nicholas before I nodded, all the same – and felt my stomach lurch. Miss Rosamond followed my gaze, eyes widening for the stern slim line of Nicholas's mouth, the glare carved neatly across his forehead. It was profoundly unnerving, to see my habitual expression stiffen the cheeriness from my lover's face.

"In light of your apology, Miss Rosamond," – it was his old professional voice, for his old profession, dourness straight out of the funeral parlour, "I must ask you one extremely important question."

She blinked – at him, at me. I flatly refused to shrug. "Alright?"

"D'you like rats?"

Nicholas!

He was already crinkle-eyed, shrugging off the stern look with a mischievous grin, bright as an electric bulb. Of course it struck Rosamond in turn; of course she lit up from eyebrows to porcelain tooth. I would have been obliged to have words if she hadn't.

"You'd need to set the price," she managed, voice shaking in her smile. "I've really no idea of the reasonable sum for a small chaotic animal."

"I'm a reputable tradesman, Miss Rosamond! And you wouldn't just be buying one – you never keep a rat alone – we could start you off with three and see how you go. I've got this lovely trio just about ready to scurry forth – need to sell off some more, you see, got to clear the attic so we can hire some builders for the roof – "

I breathed out.

Miss Rosamond was at the desk, scribbling an impromptu promissory note for her fancy rats. The funding was still, more or less, all over the floor. I would have tidied it – I did tidy it, later – but Nicholas caught my hand when I first moved, twined our fingers one by one, raised the entanglement to his lips. I trembled. Then he curled an arm around my waist, and – indecorous, sneaky, swift and scorching under the scratch of the pen – we kissed in the Dallyangle Division, for the first time since I started these casebooks.

(And I'll do more than kiss him when he's done scribbling!)

Nicholas, if you are going to add to the account, you must at least adhere to my system.

Addendum: pertaining to Matty joining me upstairs! Now!

Better.

CHAPTER THIRTY

I SHALL DECLARE, AT LAST,
WHAT IN FACT I AM

The New Notebook

Concerning Thursday 23rd November 1893, and beyond

I am – passionate applause, if you will! – not in the morgue.

Better yet – I am in the *bath!*

But I haven't lost my impulse to scribble. I've been at it all afternoon, at a delightful little table balanced across my bathtub. I seem to have spent the past few weeks steeped in regrets for my choices, chastising my past self out of all unreasonable shape – but one choice nothing would compel me to regret or chastise is the furnishing of the Pole Place bathroom.

The papers are crinkling; the room's all fragrant steam. Rosamond has the original notebook and its extra quires, and Henry is due for it next, provided they furnish me with their journal (in which, apparently, I appear) in exchange. But the latter made a fiendishly fair point when we parted this morning – why should my scrawling stop in that graveyard, in turmoil and terror, with Rosamond still missing and my fingers bristled with torn-up grass? Why not write in the bath too?

Va bene. I can be thorough.

I slept like a very midsummer night. Jewelled dreams, none of which I can recall, and hours enough to flick the hands off a clock. The next I knew, the sun was poking through Rosamond's dusty skylight, and a crumpled pillow was endeavouring to cup my cheek. (My savings, I remembered, were underneath that pillow, still crackling in their purloined envelope; I'd take no more chances with their location until they were back inside my house.) We'd spent the night in Catfish Crescent – I have the haziest recollection of Gareth Wyn Evans, of all people, making us a bedpan – and she'd woken before me, slid a hand into my hair, her fingers tracing gentle patterns on my scalp.

"I lost Earlyfate," I admitted, bleary and contrite, after we'd kissed. She smirked, humouring me. "Darling, I'm quite serious – I shattered the blade and left it in a barn – "

"*I* didn't lose *you*. That's the point. Why else do you think I even gave you that swordstick?"

"But your father – "

" – wouldn't have wanted my cariad dead." The smirk settled; her fingertips crept to my face, traced my cheekbones, sketched the scar. "No more would yours. And you won't need a sword at the breakfast table, even if Eddie's presiding."

Put the sword down. I would have conjured the rest of his words – all his words, everything I snip out of context and set alight in my mind, a whole basilica's-worth of paternal votives – but her final gambit rather distracted me. "What's happening at breakfast?"

A one-armed shrug above the nettle-patterned quilt. "Ga called up while you were still sleeping. The Nettleblacks are taking breakfast together, and every single sweetheart's invited. I said we'd join if they didn't mind waiting half an hour."

"Do we need half an hour?"

Now she arched an eyebrow. Patient and triumphant all at once. I noticed, quick as a scald, that her grip had tightened under my chin.

Well. *Well.*

In all my recollections of the Catfish Crescent house, its rooms had never felt quite this lively – or quite this airy, with the curtains pushed back and the windows so bright they stained my eyes. The breakfast table was still palpitating: with Rosamond and myself (only mildly dishevelled), and Henry and Septimus, and Edwina sipping nettle tea at its head, flanked by a hempen Apollo whom I recognised as Septimus's elder brother. The scrambled eggs came on a silver salver – it was impossible to discern whether the plate or Gareth were glowing with greater intensity. He beamed to see us; Rosamond beamed back, and I was giddy enough to copy her.

Henry smiled over their teacup, fingers drumming the painted foliage at its rim. "Figs. Right. Edwina – erm – please quite entirely communicate with Rosamond."

"Me quite entirely first," my darling blurted. "Eddie, I – I'm sorry. For many things. Some of them costly. And – it's the silliest thing, but I think I might have missed the nuances of a certain point you were making about me. And asylums. Yes."

The eldest Nettleblack swallowed hard. In all the years I'd spent dodging the woman, colouring her in arsenic-heady tints – gracious, I'd forgotten far too much of what she actually looked like, how brittle she was, how deep the lines of stress on her forehead. "I was not clear. Or you did not listen. Or – "

– after a look from Henry so pointed it nearly cracked the stone in her brooch –

" – no, there is no blame. I do not understand you – but neither do I want to fight you, or deceive you, or frighten you, or tell you what to do, or drive you away, for a moment longer."

Rosamond faltered through the words. "Not even for the Welsh?"

"You know I do not follow the Welsh." Edwina took a neat forkful of scrambled eggs. "But if you can believe that I am not constantly scheming to fetter your life, I can trust that you are not plotting the ruin of our family every time you switch language."

Rosamond snorted in surprise. I snatched up my tea, by way of disguising my bewilderment – of all the oddities, I'd emphatically not expected Edwina Nettleblack to dip an approving nod for her own ironical humour.

"I also mean – in agreement with Henry, and I hope with you – to adjust our family's focus from that fixation on *ruin*. When our parents told me to marry you into the nobility – to keep Miss Danadlenddu away from the money – well, I do not think they fully knew what they asked. They would surely never have wanted us to emulate a family that would police its own – and prune anything it deemed unworthy – and destroy whatever it had to for the sake of – of – of what? Of protecting the same *reputation* that has stymied my life?"

Her voice had risen, tight in her sharp-boned throat. She closed her eyes, clenched her fingers around her fork, parcelled breaths between taut lips. Septimus's brother – Lorrie Tickering, if I remembered the *Pirates of Penzance* playbill – curled a hand round her shoulder.

"I am sorry I deceived you." Edwina blinked, met Rosamond's gaze for one startling green moment. "You and Henry both. I shall bring down Father's will after breakfast and talk you all through its contents. Adelaide will not trouble you either – I have funds enough to provide her with the modest allowance she has so desperately pursued. Your money is your own, Rosamond. If you wish to spend your inheritance on more expensive ferrets, it is not for me to stop you. I – it is quite simply – I just want my family back."

Rosamond gaped at her.

Something – barely perceptible, just there in the twitching of the dust-motes – was flaking off her Morris-draped shoulders. Not every scrap of the taut fear she'd carried back to Wales and winced beneath for the last two weeks, nor all the glints of wariness she'd been sharp with ever since we met in her English purgatorio. But – *something*, some crystallised terror, the sharpest points of her –

And who could blame her? With such prospects unfurling before her, all the apologies and forgiveness and life one could never be guaranteed –

"If it's family you want, Eddie," she declared, twining her fingers with mine, "You ought to know I don't come without Pip."

Then, of course, she burst out laughing. I admit I did too; it was that or crawl under the table. Septimus flushed to her hairline. Henry's head dropped into their hands.

"*Bendigedig,* I'm a wit! The point still stands!"

"It does," Edwina agreed, swiftly enough to startle us both out of impromptu delirium. I froze in my seat – she was talking to me. "You kept her here. In every sense. The – the intimacy you share, the support you have given her – you cannot imagine how grateful I am. Any happiness she has felt in Dallyangle is entirely your doing."

Rosamond squeezed my hand. "Ardderchog. On *that* one, Eddie, you understand me perfectly."

"You're – erm – quite entirely at liberty not to associate with us," Henry added, from between a lattice of fingers, "Given how much we're clearly incapable of sensible conversation – but – figs – *I'd* like us to start again! As a proper – coherent – incoherent – well, just as you all say! As a family!"

"Me too." Septimus grinned. "If you want."

It was all so unabashed. So undemanding. Even if everyone was watching me, waiting for something – elegant words, any words – until my mouth fell open and my face grew hot. But the warmth, it – it wasn't unwelcome, not in the slightest – it was far more akin to the first sip of a new tea, bizarre and delightful, too unfamiliar to explain.

I swallowed.

"Well, I – the concept's a strange one – "

Rosamond kissed my cheek. "Dim problem. So's the family!"

She did so again, by way of wincing commiseration, as we stood hand in hand before – at last – the façade of my house. Not one of my ferns had survived. The plants had been watered, too lovingly, watered some more in a panicking bid to fix the damage; now the pots pooled with boggy puddles and the

313

fronds swooned senseless over the sides. The smell was that of a fairies' graveyard. The doors of the fern-cases had been left open, presumably to counter the greenish smudges mottling the glass.

And, plastered to that same glass, mouldering at the edges, a screech of a note in Henry's handwriting: *FIGS FIGS FIGS I'LL REPLACE THEM I AM SO SORRY* –

I could do little more than arch an eyebrow. "Well, I did lose their ferret."

"And the ferret remains at large!" Rosamond's eyes glinted, voice swooping with melodrama. "What new menace have you brought upon us *now*, Pip Property? Will the mustelid thrive in the Surrey countryside? Will the whole of Dallyangle be overrun by Mordred's offspring this time next year? Is there no end to your dastardly deeds?"

I scoffed. "Shelter your fancy rats while you may."

"About that – I did buy some rats last night – don't gasp, at a sensible price! Shall I keep them in Catfish Crescent, or will you mind if they come here?"

"I was inclined to ask you the same question."

She stared at me – with her porcelain-edged smile, the very smile to quicken my senses and cleave them to hers – "Move in with you?"

"Provided you don't mind a hallway full of patterns, and you don't flood the bath, and the rats respect the cravats, and – "

I cupped her face when she spluttered. "Darling, I tease. I only – I mean – I love you, and I love being with you, and the fragmented glimpses I've had of my world without you only serve to strengthen both convictions. If I've ensured your happiness, you've been the lodestar of mine. So – would you stay? With me? Os gweli di'n dda?"

Her nod drew us together, forehead to forehead. That warmth again, spreading, one taper lighting another. I slid my thumbs along her cheekbones; she tweaked my cravat.

"I love you too, cariad," she whispered. "You make sure to believe it."

Of course we both trampled the post. The post nearly trampled us, a slippery molehill on my doormat, envelopes shoaling around our boots. I sighed – at least the most immediate bills could be dealt with – and that creamy Venetian stationery there, the calligraphy and marbled edges and sealing-wax, *that* could serve as kindling for tonight's fire –

Then I turned it over.

The name. Or, rather, the lack of name, of prefix, of all her usual barbed embellishments. Just *P. Property* and my address.

My fingers twitched on the lovely paper, ready to tear –

But I didn't. I have it here. Permit me a moment, if you would.

Addressing the Prodigal –

I have received correspondence from a so-called Detective Ballestas of the Dallyangle Division, *informing me that you have been spearheading a criminal enterprise, and asking (the nerve!) whether I might provide information to help discover your whereabouts.*

Dio mio. I do not know whether to deem it a comfort or an exasperation that you have not changed! You always possessed the most extraordinary blend of self-preservation and self-destruction. Do you remember when you fell into the canal? The churning water dragged you too far to snatch at, a speck amidst chaos – and it was chaos! Steam-boats, defiant gondoliers – and us, horizontal on the traghetto, struggling to turn, to get you back.

And how serene you looked! You did not even splash – just spread your arms and stared at the sky, never mind that you were about to be dismembered by several steam-boats. You saved yourself from drowning, yes, but in the most dangerous way conceivable, and you did not even seem to care just how dangerous it was.

I had – have – always been wary of you. After that day, wariness be damned, I was afraid of you. For you. Both. And have I not been proved right to fear? You treat your very life like the Grand Canal – you sprawl at its heart, so serene, in defiance of how closely you drift towards all that could tear you apart. I thought you incapable of protecting yourself. I thought someone had to pull you out. But the choices I made in attempting to do so were not my finest, and I have regretted them for ten years.

Va bene. I cannot watch you drift to your doom again. Tell me what the insolent detective requires to curtail this persecution of you, and I shall provide it. Tell me how – if – I might assist in keeping you from danger. I will not dictate the help you receive – but I will furnish you at once with the help you request.

Tua mamma,
Maria Giuditta Participazio Property

I don't know, just yet, whether I can reply. But I shan't burn it.

Now! The bath oils are almost exhausted, and my dressing-gown awaits me. It's long past time I cut my hair.

EPILOGUE

THE DALLYANGLE STANDARD

NO. MMCCCXLIII.   Registered at   MONDAY, DEC. 4th, 1893
                   the G. P. O.   7s. p. a.
                   as a Newspaper.

THE DIVISION TRIUMPHANT!

In long-awaited and welcome news, the Dallyangle Division have brought an end to the housebreaking tyranny of Maggie and Norman Sweeting!

MATTERS SETTLED!

The indomitable Director Ballestas has revealed to this editor that these former rapscallions are now repaying the community, occupied as they are with work on the Skull Family Farm, while Miss Sweeting recovers from an injury inflicted by the late Fifth Marquess of Alberstowe (*please see page four, as below*). Their latest accomplice – in a startling revelation, the former Town Council secretary Miss Marigold Chandler! – is also busy on the farm, though this editor trusts she has not been permitted anywhere near the family accounts. Many of the items stolen by the Sweetings have since been recovered, including a considerable sum of money belonging to local cravat designer Pip Property; the merchant's Angle Drag shop will be reopened to its 'sweet customers' early next week.

THE FUNDING RESTORED!

On the subject of money – this editor can exclusively reveal that the Town Council funding for the Division has been rediscovered and reinstated, after the cessation of an arrangement with Clement Miltonwaters, Sixth Marquess of Alberstowe. (*Readers* are advised that full particulars of the Miltonwaters affair, including an illustration of the murder weapon, the date of the Fifth Marquess's funeral, and Lord Alberstowe's plea to the charges brought against him by his servants Miss Dorothea Thorne and Mr. Peter Hackitt – 'not guilty on grounds of insanity', at last report – can be found on pages four to six.)

THE DIVISION EXPANDS!

If You, Reader, harbour a desire to embrace the Division still further: discard timidity, for they are *recruiting!* Please apply to Director Keturah St. Clare Ballestas at 3 Market Square; for further information, and testimonials concerning the opportunities offered by the work, please seek out Division Sergeant Septimus or Division Apprentice Nettleblack at the same address.

A LITERARY NOTICE

LIFE AND LIMBS

A COMIC ROMANCE OF THE MEDICAL SCHOOL

The beloved companion of readers everywhere!

FOURTH EDITION

AMENDED AND IMPROVED BY THE AUTHOR –

DALLYANGLE'S OWN
MISS CASSANDRA BALLESTAS

WITH ORIGINAL DESIGNS AND FORTY-SEVEN NEW ILLUSTRATIONS

BY PIP PROPERTY

4to. Cloth, 8s. 6d.

SOON TO BE ACCOMPANIED BY ITS SEQUEL – AFTERLIFE AND LIMBS: A NECROMANTIC SCANDAL IN THE MEDICAL SCHOOL!

"Criticism subsides into, 'Read, enjoy, it will more than satisfy you.'"--*The Rodent's Gazette.*

NEILINGTON & SON PUBLISHERS, London.

ACKNOWLEDGEMENTS

Profound and prostrate gratitude to Gwen Davis, doctor of botany and books and increasingly deranged Dallyanglian dilemmas. Without you – without exaggeration – this book would still be in the grip of an Oxonian crime syndicate.

To my other readers – to all who have endured *Earlyfate* in any of its five hundred early and ill-fated first drafts! To Katie Barrowman; Cassandra has been thoroughly enriched by our conversations (though I'm still waiting for your Gertie Skull cosplay). To Emma Hinds, correspondent and novelist-comrade, for thoughtful editorial magnificence – may Mordred's descendants sprint over your doorstep. To Prue Bussey-Chamberlain, whose encouragement and generosity urge on both my writing and general academic existence.

To the Shire of Flintheath and its formidable sword contingent: especial thanks to Brian/Edwin, for introducing me to dall'Agocchie and Pip's favourite rapier-based exercise. I can only apologise for what happens to Earlyfate.

To the two departments which have supported me at varying stages of writing this book: Royal Holloway's English Department, and the English and Creative Writing gang at the University of Exeter. To Christine Lehnen (angel of musical common-sense) and Roxanne Douglas (snapper of impassioned fingers), and to Arun Sood and Lotte Crawford, for permitting me to rant about the process more thoroughly than even the Notebook of Doom; to Edward Mills and the mighty individuals of BG32c, for scooping me off the floor and into the draft; to Sam North, fairy monarch of Dartmoor, for trapping a roomful of benevolent individuals and making them listen to Pip versus Cass with absolutely no context.

To the readers and supporters of *Nettleblack* – in all their guises! Your enthusiasm brings me more joy than I can articulate. To the brilliant independent bookshops – including but not limited to Bookbag, The Common Press, Gay's the Word, Lighthouse Bookshop, and the ones I don't yet know about but keep delightedly discovering. As ever, to Courtney O'Donnell, bright-eyed star of shelves, stacks, and socials.

And, of course, to the publisher who lured the Div and friends out of my brain and then wanted another book of them – Jack, Ellis, Wolf (with apologies for Crabgate). I will always be grateful for your leap of faith in Dallyangle's direction. Fervent thanks also to Laura Jones-Rivera, for once again indulging my desire to arrange words in odd ways.

To my mother, who *did* order *Nettleblack* to far more Gower libraries than either I or Gower were entirely expecting, and offered truly staggering suggestions for editing the showdown in Alberstowe Hall. To my late father, from his strange child. And to Claudia: marvellous, incisive, perpetually adamant that I shan't fall – that's you.